C000125732

The King's Mistress

The First of the Niscerien Chronicles

The King's Mistress

The First of the Niscerien Chronicles

Ray Tyrrell

Copyright © 2010 Ray Tyrrell

The moral right of the author has been asserted.

Apart from any fair dealing for the purposes of research or private study,
or criticism or review, as permitted under the Copyright, Designs and Patents
Act 1988, this publication may only be reproduced, stored or transmitted, in
any form or by any means, with the prior permission in writing of the
publishers, or in the case of reprographic reproduction in accordance with
the terms of licences issued by the Copyright Licensing Agency. Enquiries
concerning reproduction outside those terms should be sent to the publishers.

Matador
5 Weir Road
Kibworth Beauchamp
Leicester LE8 0LQ, UK
Tel: (+44) 116 279 2299
Fax: (+44) 116 279 2277
Email: books@troubador.co.uk
Web: www.troubador.co.uk/matador

ISBN 978-1848763-647

British Library Cataloguing in Publication Data.
A catalogue record for this book is available from the British Library.

Typeset in 12pt Perpetua by Troubador Publishing Ltd, Leicester, UK

Matador is an imprint of Troubador Publishing Ltd

Printed in Great Britain by the MPG Books Group, Bodmin and King's Lynn

To my loved ones, family and friends,
without whose support and encouragement,
this book would never have been written,
and to my father, who never got
to read it.

Prologue

Princess Patrikal stood at the edge of the escarpment, looking across Nisceriel towards the River of Number, which was just visible in the far distance. To the north, far to her right, a plume of thick black smoke rose lazily into the early evening sky, until as if it had reached a glass ceiling, it spread horizontally like a large dark rain cloud.

It was the smoke from the burning village of Gloff. Its defenders still held out behind fortified walls against the retreating army from Whorle, whose surviving soldiers were really just trying to cover their retreat, back across the bridge that had cost so many lives to secure the previous day.

She fingered her silver beech leaf brooch and thought back to the day just over thirteen years before when all this had started. She had only been four, but it was all so fresh in her mind; her journey with the dogs; her first meeting with Ranamo and his brother Ranor, both Elvish Forest Wardens in the service of their King Retalla; and the three seeds she had carried home to Castle Nisceriel. From these seeds had grown the Bumbleberry bushes. They had brought great health and happiness to the people of Nisceriel, but they had also been the root cause of so many deaths and of her sorrow now.

She knew there had been a great battle near Gloff, but there had been no news of her family. Her father King Gudmon would have been there, that was certain, but none of the signs of a victory could be seen; no celebratory beacon fires that should have carried the news across the Kingdom.

Smoke also rose from the Castle Nisceriel, her home, where her mother Queen Bertal and her brothers should be. There was not a lot of smoke, and from where she stood, she could not see if it came from the Royal Quarters in the Keep itself, or from a building of the village within the main walls. Even Retalla's elvish eyes could not tell her.

Moreton had warned her of some great upheaval, of great danger to some of her family, of treachery, deceit and death, but exactly of whom and by whom, he would not say. With him she had brought the Bumbleberry bushes back to the forest, sacred elvish bushes that had proven themselves beyond mankind's ability to respect. Greed, lust and ambition had all played their part, and now her life that had been privileged and sheltered, was uncertain in a way she had never experienced, particularly after Moreton had left so hurriedly the day before.

Retalla took her arm and steered her back into the forest. She looked over her shoulder and thought she could see a smudge of dust rising in the distance, a single horse. Please let it be Moreton she thought, he will know what to do now.

She would find her family, she vowed to herself, and she would avenge any harm that had become them. She quite shocked herself at the intensity of the emotions she felt, the fear, the uncertainty, and her deep set anger, most of which centred on herself for starting all this, for indeed she blamed it all on herself.

Chapter 1

It was one of those days she had adored since her childhood, but none of them had brought her the fear and pain she was to experience that day.

It was not two moons past mid-winter, yet the night had been cloudless with more stars than one could imagine in the clear night sky. As dawn broke the sun rose shining brightly in the crisp cold air, twinkling on the tiny crystals of ice in the heavy frost that covered the fields around the Castle, just like the stars had twinkled above only half a watch before.

Queen Bertal had woken as the cockerels announced the dawn. The blankets over the windows had kept the cold at bay, at least enough for the huge log fire in the bedroom hearth to have kept the room bearably warm. The baby she carried shifted reassuringly inside her and she rose gracefully, pulling one of the fur pelts from the bed and draping it around her bare shoulders. She had never been able to sleep in a nightshirt.

The King still snored lightly in the bed, although occasionally snorting loudly. Perhaps that was what had awakened her. He usually left for his own King's Chamber after his visits to her, but occasionally remained through the night. As her pregnancy had progressed and with just a moon to go now, she had had to become more imaginative in her lovemaking to satisfy her husband's needs, but now she had the distinct feeling he might have come to prefer her new efforts to the norm. The soft sheets were crumpled beneath him and the thin leather and fur hides were scattered over the bed, only partially covering him. He would wake cold she thought, but the fleeting moment of tenderness was gone before she could round the bed to cover him and she moved towards the fire.

1

She would normally have rung for the servants, but instead she walked to the small window and pulled aside the blanket. The cold air hit her body like a blow and she enjoyed the feeling of skin tightening across her chest and goose flesh tingling over her body. The view down to the River of Number was magnificent in the heavy white frost. The tide was out and she thought the mud flats' dirty brown scars rather spoilt the view, but then again, somehow the contrast added to the overall effect. The baby kicked hard, or perhaps a punch. It must be a boy, Patrikal never kicked so hard.

Finally arriving at the fire, she gently pushed Rowl and Rawl from in front of the hearth. They were her devoted wolfhounds, and they wagged their tails and nuzzled at her as she pushed them away. "Don't you go near that bed and wake him," she whispered as commandingly as she could at that volume. "I don't want him bothering me yet, he'll only get all amorous and we should be out enjoying the morning whilst it lasts."

She bent and placed a couple of small logs on the fire so that they would catch quickly. The fire was a bed of red-hot embers, the remains of the stack of logs she had piled on the night before. The top of the open fireplace was almost the same height as her with the cavernous chimney bending away from her up into blackness. The logs began to spit and burn. She tossed on two more and stared into the fire as the flames grew.

She slipped the pelt from her shoulders and placed it at her feet in front of the fire, squatting slowly then sitting cross-legged, still engrossed and fascinated by the flames. Her mother had always dressed her as a child in front of the fire. It had been one of the few moments of the day alone with her mother in their aristocratic home, and somehow sitting naked by the fire always made her feel safe and sheltered.

This was no good on such a wonderful day, and she was determined to give her daughter moments to remember with her. It was all too easy to leave her to Nanny Serculas or dear Moreton. No, she would dress, fetch the Princess and take her for an early walk down by the river. Her daze broken, she rose smoothly and quickly despite her bulge. She enjoyed being pregnant and never thought of it as an illness, as some of the more gentile ladies of the court certainly appeared to. The dogs moved quickly to her sides as she wrapped the fur around her shoulders again.

Opening the door to her antechamber caused a sudden flurry of activity as her two Ladies in Waiting, more hand maidens really, had not expected her to appear so early. Besides which she normally summoned them in with the bell.

They jumped from their pallets, casting off fur covers to show themselves dressed and ready, in case they had been summoned in the night.

"Your Highness we…"

"I know I know, it is of no consequence." Bertal felt a presence to her right and turned to see Greardel seated but rising in a far more measured way.

"Your Majesty." He bowed very correctly but still somehow with an air of impertinence.

"Don't wake His Majesty yet Greardel, he needs to regain his strength." What appeared almost a leering grin flashed across his features. Bertal was angry at herself for putting it the way she had and giving him the opportunity to twist her words with innuendo. Wey, she detested the man. Why Gudmon trusted him as his closest servant she would never know, but she supposed he must have good reason. "Your Majesty," he acknowledged.

She turned back to her Ladies. "My dressing room Allaner. Reassel, wake Serculas and have her dress Patrikal and herself warmly. We are going for a walk before breakfast. Then tell the stables to have a cart ready, and no escort. I want this to be a pleasant outing."

As Allaner helped her to dress, the thoughts of her mother dressing her in the mornings came back to her. She missed her childhood home sometimes and could feel quite alone. The forests of Deswrain were similar to here, but she missed the open moorland, and most of all, the craggy cliffs where the waves crashed ashore.

A castle was much the same anywhere, but here she had no comforting memories of rooms or hallways, and no real friends. Still, it could have been much worse. She had married a decent man and Nisceriel was no bad place to be.

It was a small but rich Kingdom. Three days steady ride on a strong horse would carry you its length from north to south, and at its widest just two from east to west, but it had been at peace for over thirty summers. This was partly due to its greater economic and military strength than its neighbours, but mostly it was because the old King Gudrick had himself married the daughter of the Duke of Merlbray, and as soon as his son Prince Gudmon had reached marriageable age, he had married him to the Princess Berissa, Bertal's eldest sister and daughter of the King of Deswrain, making his two most likely enemies into family.

To the north the border was ill defined along a range of low hills that fell away again to a flat plain where nobody strayed very often, inhabited as it was by unruly tribes that always fought and squabbled amongst themselves. Both the hills and the plain beyond were of patchy woodland with small tribal settlements of houses and farmland. Here the farmers struggled to hold back the advance of the trees and to grow enough crops to survive, whilst all the time defending the little they had from their neighbours. Not a very happy existence.

To the west was the large River of Number. The fortified village of Gloff stood on its bank in the northwest corner of the Realm, having grown up at the first bridge to be built over its narrowing width. Though still marginally tidal there, the river flowed south-westerly, surprisingly strongly, through two wide meandering curves before opening out into a large estuary with enormous tides that drove mounting waves upriver each time it raced in. It formed an impassable natural border with the Kingdom of Whorle, where a different language also added to the cultural gulf between neighbours.

Downstream, the river Ffon joined the estuary, a tributary of notable size. It flowed from the east through a large gorge marking the southern border. The hills beyond the gorge dropped quickly away into impenetrable marshland, beyond which again lay Deswrain.

To the east more hills separated Nisceriel from the neighbouring Dukedom of Merlbray. These hills were densely wooded, a forest to most, and here Elves led their lives independent of men but in tune with the trees and the natural world around them. Few men travelled eastwards as there was no road. Apart from the tracks beside the Ffon, only rough paths entered the trees, and they were quickly reclaimed by the forest if not used often. Many a person had lost their way in trees so tall that they could see neither sun nor stars for guidance. They could then only wander. If they were lucky the Elves would find them and see them to a path home, but for some, if they were not, they could become prey to wolves or bears, or sometimes just roam until their minds were as lost as they.

With hills to the north and east, and rivers west and south, Nisceriel was an undulating fertile plain of scattered farms and villages that sloped gently down to the west. The Castle Nisceriel stood at its heart. Although it favoured the eastern banks of the river, it was far enough inland to avoid even the worst winter floods.

King Gudmon was a strong but kindly man. He was quite tall for the time and more than somewhat portly. Bertal fed him constantly, insisting that the extra weight he carried was the best way of showing the world he was rich enough to afford that much food. It wasn't the food that was the problem to King Gudmon though. Food was plentiful enough at small enough cost. It was everything else that went with being his size that cost the money. His clothes cost so much more than normal. It took the hides of two large cows to make him warm winter leathers, where one would suffice for most people, and then there was the furniture, all strengthened to take his extra weight.

His bed for instance, was of finest oak, with a carved post at each corner supporting an ornate trestle overbed that was draped in fine wools and linen. Soft wool sheets were spread over fur under lays that softened the hard oak boards of the base, itself a work of fine carpentry to combine style with the necessary strength. Her bed was even sturdier!

She however was thin, lithe even. Her narrow hips were too small to be in proportion with the rest of her, as was her bosom too large.

She had married Gudmon five summers before, after the tragic death of his first wife, her eldest sister, in a summer boating accident. He had always noticed her on her regular visits to court, though he had never really appreciated her natural beauty as he had never looked at her face.

He had quite literally bumped into her rounding a corner in a cloistered passage and had been greatly impressed by the soft impact. He asked her to join him for luncheon by way of an apology. Not believing her luck, and though other ladies of the court would never believe it, luck it was, she happily agreed. She had found his power and wealth terribly attractive, and he was totally beguiled by her.

They were married within three moons, only just enough time to properly arrange a royal wedding, but enough to make it a wondrous occasion, with the King going so far as to import fireworks from the Warlocks of the far west. He had had no children with her sister, but she had borne him a daughter within a year of their marriage, and now she carried another child who was due to enter the world within a moon.

She told herself she loved her husband but feared she loved her status more. She kept his weight on really to make him less attractive to other women at court, but in some respects she was finding this display of wealth and power only made him more so to some, whilst actually making him less so to her. Making love to a man of that weight could be unpleasant.

Still, she had a lovely daughter and she was sure, a son on the way. The Princess she had called Patrika, after her half elven grandmother. Unfortunately, the people of Nisceriel all added an L to the end of words ending in a vowel, so the Weypriest had named her Patrikal in the bornbless ceremony, and despite her protests, to Niscerians she was Princess Patrikal.

At four years old she was a sharp young lady, intelligent and advanced for her age, probably as a result of all the stimulation to her young mind that living in a royal castle brought, but also through the subtle tuition of the Weymonk, Moreton, who had been a friend of Gudmon since their childhood together twenty five summers before. He played quiet games with her, which kept her captivated and entertained her for many a watch. This made him very popular with Queen Bertal, but even more so with her Royal Nanny, Serculas. It gave her more time to pursue her clandestine dalliance with Rebgroth, Second Officer of the Royal Guard, who was built for just such a position. Indeed his physique made Serculas think and do the most unnannylike things. Her flushed cheeks and pink neck in the afternoon were rarely anything to do with playing with the Princess.

But the Princess was never short of company; her pretty features, blond curls and infectious giggle endeared her to all around the court except Greardel, King Gudmon's body servant. He was all smiles and graces on the surface, but underneath was an unpleasant and envious soul that begrudged the wealth and position of his betters, and it was slowly turning his mind.

He felt no malevolence towards the Princess, in fact if not for her royal status, he would have quite liked her, but as it was, it was all he could do to tolerate her whilst he lived off the scraps of prestige that fell from the royal table. He earned commission from wealthy merchants when he ensured the King was seen wearing or using their produce, and this he carefully saved towards the day when he could afford to leave the job he despised. He would only do so after he had found some way to avenge himself on Gudmon for his life of servitude, and on Moreton, whose place at court, but for a quirk of fate, might have been his.

The old mare plodded at her steady pace down the rutted track. The royal stables always used her on such occasions, as she was so docile it was almost a problem. Nothing upset her. During her many years of experience in the Castle's employ she had seen almost everything she was ever likely to. She had long forgotten what it was to shy or bolt. Short of being struck by lightning, she was safe as they come.

Although a heavy horse, as used to pulling a plough as a cart, she did not dwarf the simple but weighty vehicle she pulled. It was sturdily built of solid timber with a single rotating axle. Each wheel was cut from a single piece of wood half a man's height in diameter. A single seat, raised a forearm high, ran across its front leaving a load space behind, with wooden sides and back that hinged down for easy access.

On the right sat Serculas, holding the reins and apparently driving, although with the mare, start, stop, left and right was as far as it went. Between her and the Queen sat Patrikal, wide eyed and enjoying the ride after a good night's sleep. She was ready for anything, which was just as well that day.

They had exited the Castle gates, Patrikal gazing up at the iron portcullis as they rode beneath it. The wheels rumbled on the drawbridge planking before they began to bump along the road. It was only slightly rutted here as much time was spent filling them in with loose stones, but in wet weather wheels dug in again, slowly pushing the stones down into the mud. They turned south onto the main road, then within moments, turned right again, taking the dirt road that ran beneath the Southern Battlements and down to the river.

They had just cleared the Castle and started to cross the fields and scrub when the old mare stopped in her tracks, raised her tail, and broke wind loudly just an arm's length from their faces. Unbidden she trudged on. Patrikal screeched with laughter, almost falling backwards from her seat, shaking uncontrollably and waving a hand theatrically in front of her nose. Queen Bertal found herself laughing out loud too, but not so much at the horse. Whilst swept along by her daughter's obvious delight, she was actually convulsed by the fact that Serculas had immediately begged the Queen's pardon on behalf of the horse, and now sat there red faced and bewildered. She quite quickly smiled broadly though and giggled loudly when she realised the Queen's laughter was genuine, and then she glowed inside at sharing such an intimate moment with her.

As the Queen laughed she felt layer upon layer of tension lift from her. She had not laughed so much in the last six moons put together, and had not realised the stress she had been feeling. She had been drifting slowly away from her husband during her pregnancy.

At first, keeping his carnal needs satisfied, when she did not feel the least aroused herself, was a duty she performed willingly, a duty that her mother had impressed on her, a wife and Queen must not shy away from. She had always stressed that a wise Queen never let her husband feel the need to spread his attention. That way led to intrigue and royal family politics. All that was needed was a favoured or ambitious bastard or two around the Castle to lead to real trouble, and a genuine threat to her children.

She was right of course, but as time went on and the King's desires had grown more demanding. She had begun to resent him, begun to hope he would not enter her chamber after she had retired, slipping through the double adjoining doors between their rooms. During the last moon however she had really begun to feel somehow dirty and used even, rising from her bed, rinsing out her mouth and washing herself after he had returned to his room.

She deliberately pushed these thoughts from her mind, determined to enjoy the occasion for her daughter's sake. Her eyes swept over the fields around them, pointing out rabbits, sheep and cattle to Patrikal. The two dogs trotted beside the cart as it bumped towards the river, one on each side as always, Rawl on the left, Rowl on the right. No-one else could tell them apart for certain, which always puzzled Bertal because their faces were quite different and Rowl's tail bent upwards more tightly.

Some fields were ploughed; some grass covered for grazing, but wherever the land around the Castle was uncultivated, however small the plot, thorn bushes of all types grew in abundance. The local people had become masters at producing juices from them and the Kingdom was famed for them.

As they approached the riverbank the bouncing of the cart ceased as they came to a halt beside a stack of cone shaped wicker baskets, each as long as a man is tall. One end was an open ring two forearms wide, and they tapered slowly to almost a point at the other end. Bertal explained to Patrikal that these were salmon traps, although many another fish were caught in them. They were weighed down on the mud flats, often just tied on the back of the carts that brought them, with the open end downstream. As the sea flowed in and covered them, fish coming in on the tide would swim into them, struggling to squeeze through the narrow end. Unable to go forward, and unable to swim backwards the fish were trapped, and as the tide receded the fishermen would return and empty the traps, leaving them for the next tide, or as now, pulling them in to dry and for repair.

Patrikal jumped down eagerly for a closer look, followed more slowly by Serculas.

Looking back at what followed from the cool calm of the King's private study, Serculas found it impossible to be sure about the exact sequence of events, only that she had pleaded with Wey to role back time so she could change them. No matter how she tried she could not rationally justify all her actions logically. She had been working from instinct and immediate reaction in a crisis, and no matter how differently she thought she might have reacted, she could not be certain whether things would have turned out for better or for worse.

The King was just staring at her from his seat by the window, waiting for her to begin. Rebgroth had been recalled from a visit he had been making to his sister in Brocklow, a quarter watch to the north. He stood near the fire beside his superior, the Royal Guard General Gratax. Serculas was sitting on the work chair at the King's desk, one elbow resting on it. In the other hand she clutched a soiled and damp handkerchief, not realising her tears were soaking into the stains of the Queen's blood it carried. Her dress was damp and stained too and she shivered as her body slowly warmed after the cold she had felt outside without her cloak around her.

"Tell the King more slowly what you told me happened," ordered Gratax, "and try to stay calm while you do it."

Moreton entered the room quietly, without knocking, and stood by the door.

She took a deep breath and began.

As she took the first couple of steps away from the cart the Queen grunted and called her back. Her waters had broken. Hardly surprising she thought after that bumpy ride, but Queen Bertal had studiously ignored her when she had hinted this might not be a good idea. She knew well enough not to tell her so.

It shouldn't have been a problem though. She would leave the Queen with the dogs and walk quickly back to the Castle with Patrikal. She could return by horse with guards who could carry the Queen back on a litter. It would be far less bumpy than trying to return on the cart, but as she climbed up beside her she gasped. The Queen's dress was not just wet, it was blood stained. Bertal looked down at herself and screamed.

Serculas begged Wey for guidance, if only they had the escort with them, but the Queen hated having two guards dogging their every movement. They were perfectly safe on Royal land this close to the Castle, but they were supposed to be with them more as servants and runners. They were going to be missed now.

Rowl suddenly growled, joined almost immediately by Rawl. Serculas looked over her shoulder to see three wolves lope out from behind a thorn thicket only four or five cart lengths up stream. The largest seemed to have a bundle of white cloth in its mouth. She thought she heard a baby wail but it was drowned by The Queen's cry of agony as she clutched her stomach, her body shocked by a sudden and violent contraction.

"Wey help me!" Was that her or the Queen? Both probably. The dogs raced towards the wolves. She vaguely heard barking and yelps as she laid the Queen back across the seat. Another contraction. The Queen screamed again and she felt Bertal's nails dig deep into her arm as she clutched her for support. So violent and so close to the last one. Something was terribly wrong.

Should she run for help? Should she stay with the Queen? Could she send Patrikal for help?

Patrikal, Wey where was Patrikal?

She shouted her name as she lifted the Queen's stained skirts and now blood soaked underwear. The Queen screamed again. She gripped her hand and thought she saw Patrikal in front of the cart holding one of the dogs by the fur on his shoulder. The Queen's hips were renowned for their narrowness, although Patrikal's birth had been a relatively straightforward affair. This however looked like death for mother and baby.

Bertal was just screaming now, the baby was coming but it was too soon. She really only knew about childbirth from ladies chatter and odd comments from her mother, or from the idle talk of her father and his friends about difficult births with their animals. Please Wey let me remember all they said. Stop screaming I can't think.

She looked closely at Bertal. She was worried that if she hadn't dilated yet, and she couldn't have in the time, either the baby wouldn't come and would die, probably killing them both, it would come being crushed, or it would come tearing the Queen apart. Oh Wey she didn't know, her thoughts were probably nonsense.

The easy thing to do would be to run for help. Make the responsibility someone else's. She wouldn't hear the screams if she ran.

The Queen was slipping in and out of consciousness. She looked around for Pratikal and called her name. The Queen's body arched in a contraction. Dear Wey. At least there were no screams now. That baby's wail again. Where was Patrikal now?

She sat in a trance for a few moments. It was as if her mind had switched off in despair. The Queen screamed again and brought her back to reality.

She looked again at the Queen's blood stained thighs. No blood now but as she looked more closely she thought she could see the top of the baby's head.

Definitely a baby's cry, she was going crazy. No blood because the baby's head is stopping the flow. Wey, will it drown in its mother's blood?

She had heard of healwitches cutting mothers to let the baby out. Nothing to lose now, Bertal was probably going to die anyway. She laughed. At that terrible time she laughed. She was prepared to do something unthinkable to the Queen and she hadn't got a knife!

Kneeling on the footboard between the Queen's knees she held Bertal's outstretched hand. Whenever the Queen drifted back to consciousness, she squeezed her hand and talked nonsense to her. The feeling of helplessness was overwhelming. There must be something she could do.

How long had it been now, a quarter? Bertal was dilating but not enough. Her father's friend had spoken of it, trying to save a cow. It had died! This was a person. Not just a person, this was the Queen.

So she saw herself do something she could not be doing, or at least she seemed to see herself, that way it detached her from reality a little. She tried to place the first and second fingers of each hand into the Queen, palms outwards. She was so afraid of damaging the baby's head that pressed against her knuckles. Blood streamed across her hands, released from behind the head. She wanted to press outwards but just couldn't do it. As she slipped her fingers away, Bertal contracted fiercely and almost miraculously, the baby's head appeared. Wey what had she done?

She gripped the head gently, the forefinger of each hand under the chin. Another contraction from the unconscious Queen, a gentle pull and the baby was in her hands, a boy. The afterbirth followed immediately and apparently completely.

The chord! She brought it to her mouth, closed her eyes and bit through it. Wiping her mouth on her shoulder she pressed Bertal's stained dress against her torn body. The baby, slippery with gore, slid from her other hand and fell to the footboard. Please somebody help me! As she grabbed it, almost convincing herself she hadn't just done that, the baby spluttered and cried. She removed her cloak from around her and wrapped the crying infant in one end, laying him beside his mother and covering her with the rest. The Queen was still breathing at least, but for how long she wondered; there was blood everywhere.

She climbed down from the cart and took a step back. The sun still shone and the frost was starting to disappear. It still wasn't far above freezing though, and she had sweated beneath her cloak and warm clothes with the trauma she had just experienced. That sweat now exposed to the cold air made her shiver uncontrollably, that and shock.

Now was the time to go for help. Patrikal! She screamed her name rather than called her. Where was she? And the dogs? They were probably still chasing the wolves, but it was not like them to stray far from the Queen. Did they sense her death?

She ran around the stack of salmon traps, looked under the cart. Come on woman get a grip.

The nearest thorn thicket. All the time calling. Patrikal was gone.

She ran to the Castle. It took her nearly a quarter watch but she didn't stop. The guard officer at the gates summoned General Gratax whilst still trying to calm Serculas and understand her gabblings as she tried to tell it all at once.

Gratax reacted instantly and a troop of cavalry raced to the Queen and baby, with Moreton and the King's personal healer, Ferlmun, close behind. The Queen was carried slowly back to the Castle on a litter, a gentle journey preferred to speed. She would live or she would die. The bleeding had stopped, but she had lost so much. The baby, still wrapped in the cloak, rode back in Moreton's lap at speed on horseback.

As Moreton rode back through the Castle gates, three more troops of Royal Guards rode out to begin the search of the riverbank for Patrikal. Heralds left for villages around to spread the word and to recall Rebgroth.

That was all a quarter watch ago now.

The King looked at Serculas, his expression surprisingly blank.

"My wife is most likely on the point of death; my daughter is missing, probably drowned or taken by wolves. My son however looks to be in surprisingly good health. I suppose I should thank for your part in that, and not admonish you for my wife's foolishness. I must also try to understand that in saving my son you lost my daughter."

He looked out of the window as if hoping to catch sight of Patrikal.

"I suggest, Rebgroth, that you take her to her chambers and clean her up, and keep her away from me until I do!"

Chapter 2

Patrikal was very scared indeed. She had jumped from the cart and run to examine the salmon traps, when she heard Serculas gasp and her mother scream. She turned towards the cart to see her mother seated, looking down and screaming with Serculas kneeling on the footboard in front of her staring into her lap. Mercifully, looking up from her short height she could see no more, except liquid dripping from the footboard.

As she moved towards the cart her mother fell back across the seat, still screaming and now clutching her stomach, but she stopped dead when Rowl growled and moved across her path.

To her left, three wolves had trotted round a clump of thorns then froze as they heard Rowl's growl, which was closely echoed by Rawl. The largest wolf, on the far side of the three, held a white bundle of cloth in his mouth. Rawl looked past the old mare at Rowl, as they eyed the wolves. There was a moment of stillness before the two dogs leapt forward across the ground towards the wolves.

Rowl took the foremost wolf shoulder to shoulder, their heads whipping round, their teeth slashing at the back of each other's neck. As they met, the other two turned to run. Rawl's teeth raked across the hindquarters of the wolf with the bundle in its mouth. It had been slightly slower to turn. It instinctively dropped its burden, spinning almost in its own length and snapping at Rawl's head.

They stood a lunge apart, growling and snarling, blood on Rawl's teeth from the wound on the wolf's hip. Rowl's opponent had cannoned off him unharmed and immediately fled after his other companion who was already half a field away. He left Rowl free to turn and come to Rawl's side.

This, the largest wolf, seemed prepared to take them both on. He was afraid but he wanted the bundle that he had carried so far and now lay just behind Rawl. It made a noise when he shook it and he knew there was food in it, but every time he thought about tearing it apart the thought drifted from his mind.

Rawl took half a step forward, Rowl moving slightly to his right. The wolf was not going to risk getting cut off from his pack and jump turned to his right, racing across the field after the others. Rowl chased him, allowing himself to lose ground but ensuring the wolf kept running. As he approached the middle of the field he slowed and stopped, not wanting to reach the thorns on the other side and be faced with all three wolves waiting for him. The wolf disappeared from sight.

Rawl walked back to the cart and stood beside Patrikal. Her head just reached his shoulder and she raised an arm gripping the fur on the back of his neck. He moved slowly towards the bundle left by the wolf with Patrikal at his side. Rowl was trotting back over the field and reached it just after them.

The bundle gave out a wail, then more distinctively, a baby's cry. The sudden sound made Patrikal start, her mother was still screaming and although she wanted to go to her, she was afraid of what she might find. The Queen had always told her that her boys would look after her, and they had.

She answered to the overwhelming urge she had to pick up the bundle. It was held together by an engraved silver brooch in the shape of a beach leaf. Unpinning it the bundle opened to reveal the face of an elfchild no more than three or four moons old. It had been swaddled in the cloth.

Patrikal had never seen an elf so to her it was just a live doll, still wrapped in a small white blanket. Neither, of course, did she know that elves could talk to you without speaking. Well not talk so much as put pictures and desires into your mind. Her mother had gone quiet for a while.

She knew immediately she had to head towards the sun, and that her mother would be alright without her. Once heading towards the sun she knew she must continue in that direction, although the sun would climb and pass over her right shoulder, finally setting from whence she had come.

The elfchild secure in her arms, she set off across the fields, Rowl to her right, Rawl to the left. She could not see to either side. With her head just reaching the dogs' shoulders, and them walking so close to her, all she could see was straight ahead. To anybody seeing them from a distance, all that was visible was two large dogs as her legs were lost to sight amongst theirs.

They walked for over half a watch, unconsciously following hedgerows and moving from copse to copse, seeking woodland wherever possible and avoiding any signs of people. The dogs were keeping a sharp watch for the wolves following them, but soon they were confident that they were not. Arriving in a large wood they approached a clear stream, its banks gentle grassy slopes, the water running shallow over gravel and stones.

Pratikal laid her burden down and unwrapped the child from the outer white blanket roll, pinning the silver clasp to her own coat. Inside the elfchild was bound in a small woollen wrap that was badly soiled and damp. She removed it and cast it aside, carrying the baby to the water and sitting her in the cold water's edge. She washed the child and dried her, thinking of bath time with Serculas, and trying to remember the last time her mother had bathed her.

She didn't have to think, something just told her what to do. She placed the baby face down on Rowl's back. The baby's fingers curled themselves tightly in his fur above his shoulders. Pratikal threw the blanket over him as he stood, then pulling it tight beneath his chest, she pinned it with the clasp. Walking to Rawl she lay along his back and clutched his fur, her legs down his sides and her toes tucked under his stomach. He too rose and looked at Rowl.

The dogs set off eastwards at a steady trot which they kept up all day, eating up the distance at a rate far faster than a child could walk, faster in fact than a horse could walk.

As it approached dusk they entered a wood of mainly conifers. On its southern edge where a small stream ran out into the fields, a conifer that had grown too tall too quickly had been blown over into the wood by a spring storm the previous year. The roots on the open side had torn out on the ground and snapped, the inner ones folding over but staying intact. Part of the upper branches still lived and mixed with the tree on which it lay, forming a thick canopy under which the dogs stopped and flopped down.

Patrikal climbed stiffly from Rawl's back. He moved towards the stream. When she had taken the elfchild from Rowl's back, he did the same and she followed. They all drank deeply, Patrikal laying on her stomach and lapping like the dogs, then cupping her hand and dripping water into the elf child's mouth.

They all lay beneath the tree and were quickly asleep, the children curled up with the dogs for warmth. They should have been hungry but were not, so they slept deeply until the dawn chorus in the trees above woke them at the start of another bright day.

Elves had evolved a form of telepathy as an aid to survival, although it varied in strength from elf to elf, and faded steadily in most of them as they grew older. The majority of male elves had lost all their capability by puberty, and almost all by the end of adolescence, in infants though it was often very strong. No elf of any age could converse in thought; it was more an ability to transmit images or ideas. Infants could communicate needs and desires, and the more gifted even emotions and feelings.

The ability was strongest between mother and child. It evolved because it meant that infant elves could communicate their needs to their mothers silently without crying out loud, a great survival advantage in the more dangerous forests of the past. The infant instinctively knew its mother and roughly where she was. It also recognised a threat, and could often persuade a predator that it was not there, or was something else. It only worked on the more intelligent predators though, the bigger the better.

A mother however could not normally communicate much to her infant other than security and love, and only over short distances, but she could certainly feel from afar if her child were alive, threatened or in need.

It was pure survival instinct therefore that had saved the elfchild. When the wolves had attacked the group of elves two days previously, the elves had killed many of them and the pack had scattered. The elf child's mother had been knocked to the ground and lost her grip on her child, who tumbled forward, a wolf grabbing the little bundle and dodging away. It was closely followed by two other males before it was far from the fight and together they ran quickly westwards, rapidly increasing the gap between themselves and the elves.

The elfchild instinctively blocked the wolves minds to her being food but was unable to exert enough power of thought to turn the wolves back towards her mother. For more than a day therefore the wolves had trekked westwards not really sure why they were carrying this bundle or going that way, hungry but not, thirsty but not, and very confused.

A night passed before the elfchild heard the dogs bark and she immediately sensed humans. She dropped her hold on the wolves and desperately tried to communicate vulnerability and need to the humans. Her focus landed on Patrikal as the most receptive, but she had also started to give out her rather stunted and rarely used elf cry to emphasise her needs to the humans close by.

When Patrikal picked her up the elfchild immediately sensed she was secure and could communicate her desires to the human child, and to some degree to the dogs. She knew her mother was somewhere to the east and hence Patrikal and the dogs had set off that way. She had sensed the fear and confusion in Serculas, and the pain in the Queen, but she strongly sensed the Queen would live and replaced the fear she felt in Patrikal with that thought.

The elfchild was feeling very hungry and uncomfortable by now though. It was easier to fend off tiredness and hunger in her saviours than in herself, but if she could just last out she knew she could get back to her mother.

The elves had taken a while to realise exactly what had happened as the elf child's distraught mother tried to explain the chain of events. They could not be sure which direction the wolves had taken and could not even look for tracks until the dawn.

When dawn came the search began, but the search was for tracks now, and many of the surviving pack had headed off in different directions. It took all day to follow each set of tracks to realise that they all eventually swung northward as the pack slowly gathered itself together and headed back to their home territory. All except one set of three of course, which set off westward and kept going.

The two elves that had followed these tracks did so for half a day before deciding they were not going to turn and heading back to report. Although their return was much quicker as they were not tracking, by the time all the search groups were in, it was late afternoon before the pattern was clear.

Despite the mother's pleas for speed, as she could sense her daughter was at least still alive, if not safe, the elves carefully selected a band of four to track the wolves. They included the two who had followed the trail so far, but as was normal amongst elves, did not include the child's father. Elves found the stress and emotion of family ties in such situations usually hindered efficient tracking. They ensured the party were properly equipped and had eaten before they left. They had decided that if any wolf carrying the child had turned north and joined the others, sheer numbers would have defeated the child's gift and she would be dead by now and eaten. The fact that these three had headed off alone was probably because of the child's instinctive defences.

They were of course correct, but it was with darkness closing in therefore, that the four elves set off at a fast pace, returning through the dusk and early evening to the spot where the two had turned back earlier. They could then only make camp and wait till the next morning, hoping any tracks would still be visible.

It was a very cold night, and the dawn found the ground covered in a bright white frost that whilst beautiful to the eye, made tracking impossible. It was late in the morning then that they made their slow progress westwards, picking up a sign here and there that gave them the confidence they were still on the trail, but it was painfully slow.

It was that evening that they made camp on the eastern edge of a large wood, not half a field from the elfchild, Patrikal and the dogs.

Chapter 3

Eilana would be fifteen in half a moon and she thought of the Maiden's Day she would have enjoyed if things had been different. She had risen at dawn, woken by the sounds of her father and brother preparing to leave and her baby's cries of discomfort and hunger.

Her father Harlada had been an ostler in the Castle's Royal stables since before she was born. He had been given a small terraced cottage behind the stables on his marriage to Eilenn eighteen summers past. All members of the Royal staff were given tied cottages within the Castle's outer walls on marriage. It was a custom begun two centuries before out of pure practicality. Castle workers simply could not afford to buy or rent property within the Castle, but if all the Royal staff lived at a distance, it became impossible to run the Royal Household efficiently. It also meant the properties were well maintained, which was particularly important when they were built into the Castle's outer walls and their roofs formed defensive fighting platforms.

Eilenn had borne him his son Harlmon within a year. It was a year before she conceived again, and Eilana was born early the following spring. She grew into an intelligent child but a dreamer too. Life was like living a fairy tale or in later years, a romance, the sort of stories the Castle folk would gather to hear minstrels tell in the square or taverns of Castlebury, the village just to the south.

She had cleaned and breast fed her child, young Harlada, and settled him back in his cot, then set about tidying the room before her mother awoke. She was still asleep under her blankets on the double bed in the corner. Mixing some oats, a little milk and water in a large pot, she hung it above the fire. Harlmon had taken some bread and cheese with him, but her father would be back in a quarter watch, after he had seen the royal visitors on their way and she would have his breakfast ready. She would wake her mother then.

Sitting by the fire she looked up at the ceiling, her mind drifting back over the events of the last nine moons or so.

A band of itinerant Jugglers and Tumblers had come to Castlebury and had sought permission to perform for the court, for the usual fee of course. The King was keen to entertain the visiting Elder Weypriests that were holding a gathering by invitation at the Castle, but had been stuck for something suitable. The celibate Weypriests were not appreciative of the more normal slightly lewd after dinner entertainment on offer locally, so this opportunity was sent by Wey himself.

A small party of the entertainers came up to the castle to reconnoitre the performing area and aquaint themselves with the space available for their show, which often had to be curtailed or changed if there was not enough room for the Tumblers.

Amongst them was Keffnon, a nineteen-year-old tumbler of classic physique and more than handsome features. He had travelled with the troupe for three years and broken many hearts along the way, so when he saw Eilana outside the stables, it was not only his interest that was immediately aroused.

Eilana caught sight of him, her knees weakening with a stirring inside her stomach she had never felt before. His friends were not surprised to see him disappear into the alley beside the stables, talking to a young girl. He would get them all into real trouble one day.

They sat and talked on the hay pile in the open barn for half a watch before Eilana heard her mother's calls. By this time it was too late, Eilana was hopelessly in love. Infatuation, adolescent crush, whatever you called it, it was love at first sight to her.

Keffnon was practised at his art. He told her how his heart had stopped when he saw her, how he could do nothing else but come and talk to her. He would return to the barn that evening after the show, and when the troupe left in a few days, she would travel with them and become his wife. It was just like the minstrels told.

That evening she washed secretly in the stables, using a bucket of fresh water she had fetched from the stable well. She was on fire with nerves. The butterflies in her stomach fluttered continuously and she tingled with anticipation. She was not so much nervous about what she was sure would happen rather than whether she would perform to Keffnon's liking.

Love making was something all the young maidens discussed freely amongst themselves, though they were mainly short on experience. Eilana had lost her virginity physically over a year before when riding with her father, exercising the mounts of some wealthy merchants who were staying at the Castle, but her sexual experience was limited to the personal sensual discovery of her own body, and observation of her elder brother.

She shared the attic bedroom with her siblings, her elder brother Harlmon, then fifteen, and her younger sister and brother. The young ones were usually asleep by the time she lay on her pallet, but Harlmon did not usually follow for a quarter or so. When he did she was usually asleep, but sometimes she just pretended to be, watching him undress and studying his body in the soft moonlight, which lighted him through the skylight above her.

It was pure interest that often kept her awake. She had seen her brother naked almost daily as they grew up, but as hair began to show on him and as his voice dropped in tone, he became suddenly shy and modest in front of them all. She had also noticed a change in his attitude towards her as hair began to sprout on her and her chest developed. She too had become conscious or her body, becoming more so as adolescent talk began to teach her of the world of love, and her mother had explained a few things when her bleeds began.

The pallet beds in the small attic were side by side an arm's length apart, barely enough room to move between them. The youngest, her brother Harlfel, was against the wall to her left, sister Eival next to him, her bed, then Harlmon's, against the right wall. If her other two brothers had not both died in their first year they would have been sleeping head to foot. Her parents slept downstairs on the large pallet that doubled as seating in the day, opposite the fireplace. The stone chimney stood out of the far wall of the attic, keeping it warm at night but meaning Harlfel and Eival had to climb over Eilana's bed to reach their own, as the wooden ladder entered the attic at the foot of Harlmon's bed.

She had often wondered exactly what Harlmon was doing as he lay beneath the rough woollen blanket that covered his bed. Her friends had told her the principle, but it was not the same as knowing for certain. His bed seemed to shake gently, his cover moved rhythmically and his breathing became heavier, until he gasped, sighed, and lay still, panting slightly and fumbling with the blanket, before dropping off to sleep.

One night in late summer she had come to bed, tired but happy after helping a friend and her family with the harvest at a nearby farm. The young ones were asleep as she curled up on her right side as she always did. Sleep did not come to her though, so she was still awake when Harlmon climbed the ladder and gently dropped the hatch into place. He slipped off his clothes quietly, standing between the beds.

Eilana had her left eye shut and was watching through her half open right. He turned towards her, looking across the beds, his right hand almost unconsciously fondling himself. His mind must have caught some thought for he drifted into a daydream. As he moved his hand slowly, he was no more than two forearms from her face. She was mesmerised, and whatever the thought in his head, he became quickly aroused.

To Eilana, it grew almost magically, standing straight upwards and outwards from his body, the foreskin rolled back revealing the helmet, that's what her friends called it. She almost jumped as Harlmon woke from his daydream and sat on the edge of his bed looking at her. She closed both her eyes, afraid he would see she was awake.

She half opened one eye as she heard him lay back on the bed cover, his feet still on the floor, looking up at the roof but with eyes closed. The moonlight gave his skin a slight sheen as she opened both eyes. He gripped himself almost like a sword she thought, but with loose little and third fingers. He rubbed himself steadily and quite quickly, speeding up slightly as his breathing got heavier.

It did not seem to take long. Eilana watched intensely as he held his breath for a moment, letting it out in a sigh of ecstasy as he seeded. She watched the thick liquid spurt then drip across his stomach. He moved his hand slowly, squeezing out the last drops that ran over his thumb and joined the rest. As his breathing slowed he reached for the edge of the blanket and wiped his hand then his stomach, collecting the liquid and almost gripping it in the cloth. He took another section of blanket and wiped up the rest. The first spurt had reached the hair on his chest and was harder to wipe.

Eilana had the presence of mind to close her eyes again as he raised his legs onto the bed and slipped beneath the blanket. As she half opened one eye again he raised himself on his elbow and looked across at her. A half smile flickered across his lips. Was it a moment of brotherly affection, or did he know she was awake?

She realised she was almost panting herself, not aroused exactly, in fact not at all, but quivering with excitement at what she had seen, added to the fear of discovery. Did he know she was awake? She fell asleep wondering, and was never really sure. Nothing was ever said of course, but that was not the only time it happened, just the first.

The next night when she went to bed she lay thinking of the night before. She had told her best friend Ereyna what she had seen. She was fascinated too. She said that her sister had told her of a friend who had seen something similar but had been discovered to be awake. She had helped her brother and they had experimented together, but eventually it led to terrible trouble within the family. They agreed they could never do that; they would just be too embarrassed anyway. It was that night however that Eilana began a slow journey of discovery about her own body, her own sexuality and sensual feelings. A journey she learned to enjoy.

She smiled to herself as she lay back on the hay in the loft above the rear barn. Keffnon would be there soon and she was glowing with anticipation. Would he like the feel of her, did she smell allright? She had washed, she would be fine.

Her hand drifted to her breasts. She could feel them through the light woollen top she was wearing. Her nipples came instantly erect. Wey she was so excited she thought she would burst. Would she come? She had discovered that drug herself, and with the love of her life it was surely inevitable.

The loft ladder creaked and Keffnon appeared in the half-light. He was sweaty after the performance and smelt a little, but she didn't care. Without a word they were in each other's arms, kissing passionately. His hands were inside her top before she realised it.

She trembled, overwhelmed by the blind passion of young love. She knew they would do it; in fact she desperately wanted to. The thought of pregnancy crossed her mind again, but she didn't care, she would leave with him in a few days anyway. This was wonderful.

His hand slid under her skirt and he smiled between kisses as he discovered she wore nothing beneath it. He touched her and discovered she was more than ready for him; she was physically, but not emotionally. As he explored her she fumbled at the laces of his codpiece with her left hand, the wrong one. She could feel him erect beneath his leather leggings, but when she had loosened the laces, she couldn't release him from them.

He impatiently withdrew his hand from her and did it himself. She gripped him. It felt so hard yet the skin was soft and warm. Her hand moved rhythmically, like her brother's did.

Keffnon was not one for foreplay however, and whilst certainly

23

experienced, had no interest in the pleasure of his partner. Suddenly he was above her, his knees between hers with her skirt around her waist. He entered her roughly and for her, painfully, and he was none too gentle thereafter. Her mind was in total confusion. It was supposed to be heaven, but this, her first time, was both painful and only potentially pleasant. She tried to move to increase her pleasure, but now he was panting in a way she knew only too well. He grunted gutturally as he seeded within her, in less time than it took Harlmon by hand she thought. She told herself it was probably her fault for wriggling about too much.

He collapsed heavily on top of her. She wanted to move a little to see if she could persuade him to stay with her. Her body was tense, aroused but now without stimulation. He rolled off her and lay on his back. She lay sideways and leant across him, kissing his forehead.

"That was wonderful," she lied.

"Me too, but now I must get back to the others," he whispered in her ear, "If I don't leave with them I'll be stuck in the Castle all night."

"When will I see you tomorrow?" she asked, disappointed but understanding why, and besides she would have to get back before she worried her family.

"I'll be here a quarter after noon," he replied, "We will need to plan to leave the day after." Tucking himself away and lacing his leggings, he rose, as did she, and kissed her passionately before leaving in the dark.

A moment later she followed him down the ladder and ran around the corner to the front of her house, her emotions in turmoil. Oh Wey it was running down her thigh! Her instinct was to wipe her leg with her skirt, but that would stain it wet. No, she settled herself and walked in.

Her father and brother were seated beside the fire, her mother by the table under the lamp. Looking up from her darning her mother spoke.

"We were just starting to wonder where you were."

"I've been with Ereyna," she lied again, walking directly to the ladder in the corner and beginning to climb.

"I'm going straight up" she explained, "I've had a long day. Goodnight."

"Goodnight my pet," her mother replied.

"Goodnight, sleep well," added her father. Her brother said nothing. He was carving something but she could not see what.

She pulled her top over her head and slipped out of her skirt. She smelt of sex she thought, sweat and juices. Pulling her nightshirt over her head she slumped onto her bed, pulling the blanket across her after using the edge of it to wipe Keffron's juice from her leg.

Lying on her back she stared at the ceiling, thinking of what she had just done. Had she been good for him? Did she live up to his expectations? He had come so quickly and had left her hanging; she still was. That was probably her fault for getting him so excited too quickly. She had not come herself. Would that upset him? Should she have pretended? She was not even sure he had noticed.

Did he like her body? She ran her hands across her stomach under her nightshirt, trying to imagine how it felt to someone else, then brushed them gently across her breasts. She pressed harder, feeling the firm flesh and erect nipples and realising how aroused she still was.

The young ones were fast asleep; she would feel better for it, more relaxed. She would never go to sleep like this. Her hand moved back across her stomach and between her legs. She was still very wet, both from her own arousal and from Keffron. Her wet middle finger slowly massaged herself, the point just dipping into herself but mainly just above. Her stomach began to boil and the tension rose steadily within her. Her eyes were closed and soon the centre of the world was at her fingertips.

The orgasm when it came sent three rhythmic vibrations of ecstasy exploding through her, then a fourth as she shuddered and groaned quietly, slowed and stopped, panting as gently as she could so as not to wake the little ones. She opened her eyes. Harlmon was standing by the bed looking down on her.

"I always said girls did it too," he grinned, his leggings clearly bulging at his excitement from watching her.

Eilana threw herself around in the bed, burying her head in the straw pillow. She heard Harlmon undress and climb into his bed, quickly setting about relieving his own tension.

Oh Wey! It should have been so perfect, her first time with the man she loved, a dream come true. Instead she felt confused, somehow slightly grubby, and sore. Her brother was having a better night than she had!

The next morning she went to the well for water and heard two guards discussing the previous night's show.

"Sad they couldn't do a show in Castlebury," said one. "They'ld have drawn a good crowd."

"Got to be in Gloff tomorrow night," the other replied, "they packed up over night and left with the dawn."

She dropped the bucket and ran to the Castle gates, her heart racing, a sick feeling in her stomach, and tears in her eyes. The troupe's encampment outside the gates was gone. She walked slowly back to the house, picking up her bucket on the way. She couldn't stop crying and her parents were at their wits end to help. She finally told her mother the truth, well some of it. She was surprisingly understanding.

Half a moon later her period didn't come and her misery was complete.

Nine moons later, a three quarter moon before her fifteenth bornbless, her son was born. She named him Harlada, after her father, in appreciation of his forgiveness of her for shaming the family. The Weypriest would do only a rudimentary Bornbless Ceremony, allowing no celebration.

Her father entered noisily through the door, jolting her from her thoughts. He had no sooner sat down at the table to eat his breakfast with Eilenn sitting beside him, when there came a loud impatient banging at the door.

Chapter 4

Harlada grumbled to himself as he rose from the table.

"No girl, I'll go," he ordered, stepping across Eilana's path to the door, "The only people who knock like that are in a foul temper or official."

He opened the door to a burly Royal Guard who filled the frame. He was certainly official, but more officious than bad tempered.

"Harlada the ostler?" It was more of a statement demanding confirmation than a question.

"Aye, I'm him. What business have you with me?"

The guard stepped back out of the doorway giving Harlada sight of two more guards standing each side of a finely dressed lady.

Harlada had never spoken to her, but he recognised Serculas immediately. She had been the centre of great excitement the day before, and most of the Castle folk were still trying to separate fact from rumour.

"May I come in?" she enquired.

"Of course Ma'am, please forgive my bad manners; I was surprised to see you. It is not often someone of the Royal Household has business with an ostler in his home." He had answered as he stepped backwards and sideways out of the doorway, bowing and gesturing her in.

She walked through the door, speaking as she entered. "No indeed, but it is your daughter I have come to see. I assume she is home."

Harlada pointedly pushed the door shut before the guards could follow, but before he could answer, Serculas saw Eilana standing in front of the fireplace.

"Can I offer you some breakfast Ma'am?" asked Eilana, bobbing slightly.

"No......Thank you." She added the courtesy almost as an afterthought. "I will come straight to the point. You have had a child recently?"

"Yes Ma'am, he is eight days old, and in fine health."

"I'm pleased to hear it. You are feeding him yourself and have plenty of milk?"

Eilana's mind raced as to where this was leading. "Yes Ma'am."

"Good, you will come with me now. You may bring your child. Master Harlada, you will see your daughter's belongings packed. I will leave two guards here who will bring them to the Royal Quarters. As from today your daughter is appointed to the Royal Household as wet nurse to the Prince Gudrick and my personal assistant as Nanny to the Royal Children. I assume you have no objection as I believe Eilana has not yet reached her Maiden's Day, nor will she now of course." The last comment was a statement of fact rather than a jibe.

Harlada was for a moment quite speechless. Eilenn spoke for the first time.

"Ma'am, we cannot thank you enough, it is such an honour."

"Expediency rather than an honour I'm afraid. Your daughter is here and in the right condition. However, your husband has been a loyal servant to the King for many years so we can at least be glad it is a happy coincidence." She turned to the door. "Come child, there is some urgency."

Eilana turned to the cot in the corner, picked up young Harlada and looked quickly at her parents. Serculas was already half way out of the door. She kissed them both quickly and hurried after her. The little ones were playing upstairs and Harlmon was at his duties as the new stable boy in the Royal Stables. She looked over her shoulder in the doorway then disappeared from her parents view. They looked at each other, both expecting to wake up.

It was only a hundred or so paces from the house to the gates of the Keep, the doorway to the Royal Household, but Eilana seemed to have to trot the whole way as she tried to stay with Serculas. Clutching little Harlada to her, she was out of breath when a guard held open the large studded gate and bowed to them, to Serculas, yes, but surely not to her.

Her pursuit of Serculas continued as she swept through the reception hall, along a corridor and up some winding stairs. She pulled back a curtain to reveal the side door to the Royal Nursery. Eilana followed her in.

"Give me your child," Serculas ordered, reaching towards her. She saw Ferlmun and Moreton standing by a large ornate cot in the corner, and realised she could hear a whimpering noise, a faint baby's cry.

"He is weak and needs to feed," Serculas informed her, taking Harlada from her. "He will not take milk from a glove and has lost weight since yesterday. Do what you can."

Eilana walked to the cot, smiling at the two men who stepped silently away. She thought she knew the Weymonk to be Moreton, she had heard of him, but she was not sure of the other.

She picked up the infant, lighter than Harlada. It was amazing how they grew, even in a quarter moon. When her son was born the Weypriest had told her, for all his formality, to concentrate on remembering young Harlada on his Bornbless Day, for it was easy to forget how small your child once was. It was good advice, she had forgotten already.

Looking around she saw a chair near the enormous fireplace and moved towards it. She made herself comfortable and looked up quizzically at Serculas, who was rocking Harlada, almost unconsciously, in her arms.

Suddenly understanding Serculas smiled, "Do not worry child, Moreton is a monk and Ferlmun a healer. Besides you are a Prince's nanny now, you can tell them to leave if you wish."

This time Eilana smiled and shook her head as she lifted her woollen top and raised the infant Prince to her breast. It took a few moments, brushing his lips across her nipple, which expressed some milk that wet his tongue. With a little more prompting he began to feed steadily.

Serculas grinned broadly at the men who looked overjoyed. Moreton left the room and Ferlmun came to the fire and began to question Eilana about herself as she fed the Prince. He also reassured her that she would naturally produce enough milk for both infants once she got into the rhythm of feeding them both. This satisfied her only real concern.

"How is the Queen?" she asked. She suddenly blushed, thinking she may have asked something above her station.

"She lives my child," smiled Ferlmun, "but today will tell I think. She lost a great deal of blood, but as she still lives, if no fever develops there is much hope, if it does then it will be Wey's wish alone that will decide, and perhaps a few of my herbs. Whether she lives or not though, I know she will owe you a great debt for helping the Prince."

Eilana was feeling more confident now. "Is it true what they say about the Princess?" There was a sudden tension in the room; she almost felt a blast of cold air hit her in the back.

"I'm sorry," she stuttered. Ferlmun put a gentle hand on her knee, looking over her shoulder and spoke.

"She is lost my child. While Serculas was helping the Queen and saving the Prince, she went missing. The Queen's wolfhounds are missing too. They are probably still chasing the wolves or may have even joined the pack by now, who knows? But the Princess cannot have strayed far, she is so young. The Royal Guard are searching the immediate area now but of course, we are very worried she may have fallen into the river. We can only pray for her safe return."

Strangely, as they spoke, Patrikal had just enjoyed the best tasting food she had eaten in her life.

Eilana looked over her shoulder. Serculas was recovering a little colour to her white cheeks; she had expected to see them flushed with anger. Their eyes met and Eilana seemed to see a deep hurt in Serculas, but also a kindred spirit, someone she could be friends with. She opened her mouth to speak but Serculas rode over her.

"It's alright my dear, I confess to being more than a little sensitive on the subject. I cannot believe that as Royal Nanny I lost the Princess. But for the King's mercy I should be in a dungeon awaiting my fate."

"Nonsense woman," boomed Ferlmun, "You saved the Queen's and Prince's lives, or so we pray. They would both be dead now without you at least, so shed this self-doubt and concentrate on now. We...."

He was interrupted by the main doors bursting open as the King entered almost at a run. Moreton was scurrying behind him.

"So, this is the wench. No...stay there." The King held a flat palm out to Eilana. "I can see you are busy. It took these idiots long enough to track down a young mother with a new born and you were right under their noses. Your father is our ostler I believe, I know of him. I sometimes wish he looked after my horses rather than our visitors', but I suppose it is right for visitors to have the best. Now young one, what is your name?"

Eilana's mind was in a spin. This was the King. She had meant to rise but with the Prince in her lap and suckling greedily, she hadn't been able to move before the King had ordered her not to. She was feeding his son, her breasts on show to all, and now he was addressing her directly when she had spoken to no-one more important than the Stable Master in her life. She took a breath and looked at him directly.

"Eilana, your Majesty. It is good to know my father is thought of so highly."

"Ah, a brave girl, excellent, you will have good strong milk for the Prince, which he appears be enjoying!"

30

She coloured at him staring at her breasts, but surely there were no sexual thoughts in his mind, she was feeding his son.

"Yes, your Majesty. I am so proud to be of service to you both."

The King laughed, then seemed to remember his troubles. He turned to Ferlmun.

"How is the Queen?"

"She sleeps Sire. Reassel is with her, with instruction to summon me if she awakes or gives any cause for concern. She woke and took some broth a while ago. She needs plenty of liquid to replace the blood, as does our young wet nurse if she is to feed both these babies."

"See to it Serculas," ordered the King, "and see she has some decent clothes before she meets the Queen. She must go to her as soon as the Queen can see her. I want the Queen to know her child is in good hands."

Serculas looked aghast.

"No no woman, I didn't mean it that way. For goodness sake, I can't keep walking on ice like this. See to it…Moreton, we must see how the search progresses."

He turned and stalked from the room, Moreton in his wake.

Eilana looked towards Serculas and saw the tears in her eyes. She lifted the Prince over her left shoulder to wind him and began patting his back. Serculas pulled herself together, holding Harlada tightly to her, and spoke.

"Right my dear, as soon as you have finished with the Prince we will sort a bath for you, then get you measured up. There are plenty of spare clothes around to keep you going until we can get some made to your liking. Ferlmun, perhaps as you leave you could ask Allaner to arrange a bath for Eilana."

Ferlmun took the hint, nodded and left by the main doors. The Prince burped and sicked a little milk onto Eilana's shoulder. She murmured something into his ear and put him to her other breast. As he began to suckle she looked around and took in her surroundings.

The nursery was a large room that looked circular but was actually twelve sided. The main double doors stood exactly opposite the fireplace. Immediately to the right of the blaze was the small door they had entered by, then three sides of window. To the left another small door led to a spiral staircase. As Eilana soon discovered, a few steps up those stairs was Serculas' room, a flight higher was her room.

Another doorway to the left of that led into the Queen's suite, which again joined the King's rooms, both through two doors, a porch between. The King's rooms, the Queen's and the Nursery, all had main doors into antechambers which in turn all opened onto a central hallway at the top of the main stairs.

The nursery contained a small bed, Patrikal's, and an ornate cot by the windows. A smaller cot had been placed beside it. There were two comfortable but upright chairs close to the fire and a central table surrounded by six stools. Heavy curtains hung beside the windows and tapestries depicting many domestic animals hung on any spare patches of wall.

She realised Serculas was speaking to her.

"The small cot is for your child when you are with the Prince. There is another in your room. You will take your child with you when you are not on duty, but may have him with you when you are. We will agree feed times for the Prince, then you must fit your boy's around them to suit. Understood?"

"Yes Ma'am. I am to have my own room?"

"Indeed. I will show you when you have finished with the Prince. No doubt he will sleep for a while when he is fed. He has not slept since yesterday." She laid Harlada down in the small cot. She had rocked him to sleep.

The day progressed as Serculas described. She had a wonderful bath beside the fire in the nursery. The tub was brought in by two footmen, who then returned many times with pitchers of hot water until the bath was full. A maid arrived with a large towel and some soap; the latter a luxury Eilana had never enjoyed before.

As she bathed, Serculas continued to aquaint her with Household etiquette, who was who and how to behave. It appeared that never again was a Royal child to leave the Castle without a nanny, a maid and at least two guards; a rule only to be over-ridden by the King himself.

She was embarrassed at first to bathe in front of Serculas, but she seemed quite unperturbed when footmen and maids came and went with more hot water, then food and drink. Later they brought rich clothes that fitted quite well, for her to wear until the Royal tailors could make some to measure, and measure her they did later in the day.

She fed Harlada, then half a watch later the Prince again. Luckily neither was taking much milk so hopefully she wouldn't dry up on them.

There was much coming and going all afternoon from the courtyard outside the windows as Cavalry Troops came and went, all part of the search for Patrikal, which was turning up nothing.

The Queen slept all day, or was unconscious, Eilana didn't know which, but she was not summoned to meet her.

So it was that she lay in her bed in her own neat little room in the Royal quarters, a small lamp on the bedside table beside her. Her own room! It was compact but it had all she needed, and now Harlada was asleep in the cot at the foot of her bed. She tried to take in the events of the day. It was all quite unbelievable.

She did not sleep for a while. She had never slept in a room alone in her life, and felt silly at her nervousness about turning out the lamp. As soon as she could she must return home and see her family. She had not even said goodbye to the little ones, or her brother Harlmon, and although they were only a hundred paces away, she had a feeling it would become an ever-widening gap, if she let it.

She missed her brother's company the most. Having got over the excruciating embarrassment of seeing Harlmon standing watching her by her bed that night, and his continued habit of ignoring whether she was awake or not when the moment took him, they became very close as brother and sister. They had after all shared each other's most intimate moments and had nothing else much to hide from one another.

When it was realised she was pregnant, he had become hugely protective of her and had been a tremendous support to her throughout its course, even holding her hand during the birth at her request. She wondered what he was doing now. She smiled to herself, she could guess!

She bravely turned out the lamp. A little light showed around the curtain over her small window from the torches in the Courtyard, enough to be comforting. Finally she slept, at least till the noise from the Courtyard woke her a watch later.

Chapter 5

Patrikal awoke slowly. She was stiff and cold, although not too cold. The heat of the dogs beside her had kept it bearable, and the elfchild clutched in her arms had also helped.

She was disorientated, why was she here? A wave of hunger swept over her and she tried to stand. The infant elf woke, her eyes suddenly open wide and staring at Patrikal, who immediately lost her hunger and limped to the stream. The dogs rose slowly and followed. They all drank and Patrikal cleaned the elfchild, wrapping her in the blanket again. It was starting to smell of baby.

With a dog on each side again, they started to move eastwards along the edge of the wood. They had not gone two hundred paces when Rowl stopped and growled, almost under his breath. Rawl did the same, his hackles even more raised than Rowl's.

Patrikal was suddenly overtaken by hunger and fear. The dogs seemed unnerved by something. She saw four shadowy figures turn the corner at the edge of the wood a hundred paces ahead of them. They seemed to merge with the background and were hard to see, but they appeared to be studying the ground at their feet.

The elfchild had sensed the elves at about the same time as Rowl had caught their scent. She dropped Patrikal and the dogs from her thoughts and screamed mentally at the elf men. Male elves were notoriously bad mental communicators; in fact it had become almost unmanly to admit to any sensitivity at all after puberty. This meant an opportunity was missed in selecting the four chosen to seek the child. A thought sensitive elf would not be specifically chosen, and a female elf would not be allowed to go, actually making the search harder.

One of the elves looked up however, coincidence he would say if asked, but something made him. He started to run towards them shouting behind him for the others to follow.

Now Patrikal was really scared, she hadn't recognised them as elves yet, and even when she did, she didn't know for certain they meant safety. The wolfhounds sensed her fear and took a few paces forward closing together slightly in front of her and the elfchild she carried.

As the first elf drew close he slowed to a walk, holding a hand in front of him at head height, palm down. He stopped and looked at the dogs, lowering his hand and speaking something Patrikal couldn't understand. The dogs lay down and placed their chins on their front paws. The others caught up and moved past him smiling. One spoke to Patrikal, and this time she could understand.

"Hello child, my name is Ranamo, do not be afraid. We have been seeking a lost child and some wolves that took her. It would seem you found her and saved her from the wolves, if it is her you carry."

"The dogs saved her from the wolves Sir, I just carried her, I just knew I had to."

"You have done well young elf-friend," he continued as he took the elfchild gently from her.

He turned and barked an order then handed the infant to one of the others. An elf spun on his heel and set off at a dead run eastwards, dropping his pack in the first couple of steps. Carrying the elfchild at as fast a walk as was comfortable for her, the second followed, again dropping his small pack.

Ranamo took Patrikal's hand in his and led her slowly back around the edge of the wood. They moved into the trees beside another small brook to a sheltered spot where the elves had just spent the night. He sat Patrikal down and gave her a flask of water he carried in his pack. His friend had picked up the dropped packs and called the dogs to follow.

"You must be very hungry," he said, opening a pack, "I have just the thing for you". He smiled and passed Patrikal a large soft biscuit, or was it bread, she wasn't sure, but it was bigger than her hand. "We will put some of this on it," he added, removing a glass jar with a large stopper. It popped loudly as he opened it in a theatrical manner that made Patrikal laugh, just as he had intended. She had already taken a large bite from the biscuit so there was a chunk missing from the side as she passed it back.

"Eat slowly my child or you will make your stomach hurt." How on earth could anything that tasted so good possibly make her tummy hurt?

He spread some of the contents of the jar over the biscuit and handed it back. It tasted wonderful. It was honey of some kind but with something added. She didn't care what, and as she munched steadily she looked round to see the dogs chewing on two chunks of dried meat that the other elf had produced from one of the other packs.

Ranamo grinned at her and explained that they had brought food enough for many days so now they had plenty to spare. He continued.

"Ralima has run back to bring the good news as quickly as possible to young Meyala's mother. Balida is carrying her back to her mother Meyas as quickly and comfortably as possible. My brother Ranor and I will bring you to Meyas. She and all other elves will wish to thank you."

Patrikal smiled but tears were suddenly in her eyes.

"How will I get home? I don't know the way, I don't know how we got here." Now she was sobbing loudly. Ranamo swept her up in his arms and held her close.

"I will take you home myself little one, you and your brave dogs. Fear not, you are to be honoured by elves and then I promise you that Ranor and I will bring you back to your home."

She wiped her eyes with the arm of her coat and smiled at the elf, her face in front of his.

"Thank you sir. Oh I have dripped honey on your jacket." Ranamo put her down laughing.

"Finish your food and we will leave. If you let me carry you on my back we will get there soon after noon if I run."

"Yes please," she replied, "That would be fun."

He put her back down and she sat again on a tree stump, steadily working her way through the biscuit. The elf brothers collected everything together again in the four packs. Ranor hung three around him whilst Ranamo looped one around himself so that it hung down his front. He knelt on the grass in front of Patrikal.

"Come on little lady, climb aboard, it's time to be going."

Patrikal climbed onto his back and looped her arms around his neck.

"Not quite so tight, I need to breath and I won't drop you."

He joined his hands behind his back, making a seat for her, and feeling more secure, she loosened her grip. He spoke in Elvish to Ranor and they moved cautiously to the edge of the woods, where they stopped and studied the landscape carefully. Satisfied there was nothing untoward in sight Ranamo set off at a steady run, Ranor just behind, the dogs beside them, one either side, Rawl on the left, Rowl on the right.

A steady run to an elf carries him over the countryside smoothly and faster than a man can sprint. It takes far less energy as well. They have a whole different relationship with the ground to man, and Patrikal enjoyed a smooth and exhilarating ride that ate up the distance relentlessly.

It was indeed shortly after noon that they reached the edge of the great forest on the eastern borders of Nisceriel. As they entered the forest Patrikal could smell the fresh clean air amongst the trees, rich as it was in oxygen and enriched with the smell of the forest. The dogs slipped into single file behind as they climbed a steep track.

For a short while they followed a barely discernable path that took them to the edge of a small clearing. It marked the centre of a large elven village. As Patrikal noticed movement around her she realised there were elves in the trees all about her. They all slowly moved into the open, forming a large ring surrounding the three new arrivals.

Ranamo gripped Patrikal's arms and swung her down from his back.

"Thank you," she said, smiling up at him.

"It is us that must thank young woman." The voice was soft but authoritative and belonged to Ranamo's uncle, Retalla, Chief of the Western Elves. He spoke as he approached them, flanked by a number of other older elves, and by Meyas, carrying her sleeping infant, now washed, fed and very contented.

"From the visions given to Meyas by Meyala you have made a remarkable journey, yourself and your dogs…"

"They are my mother's dogs, but they look after me," corrected Patrikal.

Retalla was not used to being interrupted, but he smiled down at the young human.

"I see, yourself and your mother's dogs. Well now we will eat and say thank you, then we will take you back to your home, but first we must know your name and where you live. Can you tell us child?"

"Yes sir, I am Princess Patrikal, daughter of King Gudmon of Nisceriel and Queen Bertal. I live at the Castle Nisceriel, near the River of Number, but I do not know the way. Ranamo promised to take me home."

"Then so he shall. Such a confident young lady could only be a Princess, I should have guessed. We are thus doubly honoured by your presence. Now before we eat there is one other matter to discus. It is custom for Elves to give anything within our power to anyone who has saved one of our number as you have done. It will be the duty of Meyas to provide what you ask as Meyala is too young. Is there anything you would ask of us?"

Patrikal thought for a moment, but it did not take too long to think of what she would like. It was a request however that would ultimately change the history of Nisceriel and cost many hundreds of lives.

"Sir, I would like to be able to eat that honey Ranamo gave me for breakfast whenever I want it."

Retalla was a little taken aback, but gathered his thoughts then spoke.

"Meyas will tell you how this will be done before you leave. Now we celebrate your visit and Meyala's safe return." He turned and walked away, his retinue close behind. As Ranamo put his hand on Patrikal's shoulder to guide her after the others, Meyas stooped and kissed her on the forehead. Saying nothing she turned to join the others.

Half a watch later they had all fed, all Elven etiquettes had been observed and goodbyes said. As Patrikal waited with the dogs at the edge of the clearing, Meyas walked towards her then knelt in front of her. She took both Patrikal's hands in hers and spoke to her softly.

"If you are to have your wish you must listen very carefully and remember exactly what I tell you." Patrikal nodded seriously, she had had this sort of instruction on how to behave from Moreton before now.

"The honey you ate was made by bees here in the forest, but it is very special honey, we do not add anything to it. The bees gather nectar from our sacred bushes and this alone makes the honey so special. It has great rejuvenating powers itself, but the berries from bushes, if squeezed freshly, produce the most wonderful fruit drink you will ever taste, and drinking it will keep you healthy throughout your life. Be warned though, never make wine from it. Wine made from a sacred fruit behests evil, and people who imbibe it lose all sense of right and can do great evil, no matter who they are. Do you understand me so far?"

"Yes Lady."

"Good, listen well then and remember more." She drew three seeds from a pouch at her belt, giving them to Patrikal.

"Plant these an arm's length apart in the walled garden within the Castle, on the north side, where the sun will be on them all day, but first you must wet them in your mother's tears, as cry she will when you return to her, her joy being so great. By autumn you will have your first crop of berries, but your bees will feed on the bushes and produce the honey you desire from late spring. Three bushes only will grow. You will never grow more, and they will only grow within the Castle, but three will produce all the honey and berries needed for all who dwell within its walls. Keep these bushes a secret, for they are sacred to elves and given only to you for the great service you have done us. Remember well."

"I will Lady, I promise."

"Good, then put the seeds back in this pouch and tie it to your coat belt. In the pouch is also a diced herb. Put it in hot water and give it to your mother. Meyala showed me what was happening when you found her, it will make your mother well. Bless you little man child, and thank you again."

She kissed her cheek as she pinned the silver beech leaf brooch to her dress. She stood, and turning, stepped back. She walked away without another word or a glance over her shoulder.

Patrikal saw that Ranamo and Ranor were stood behind her.

"Time to leave little lady," said Ranamo, gripping her arms again and swinging her up over his head and onto his back. "Ready then?"

He felt her nod and walked to the path that would take them back to the forest's edge, the dogs behind him and Ranor at the rear. As they entered the trees, Patrikal could not see any elves to wave goodbye to, perhaps elves didn't wave, perhaps they were better at saying goodbye than people.

It was almost a watch after noon when they left the forest. The Castle was some three watches away at a steady elven run, with a few short breaks. It would be some effort for the elves, but the dogs might have trouble staying with them. They would see.

The dogs kept up, and so it was that a quarter watch before dawn they stood outside the gates of Castle Nisceriel. Patrikal was asleep on Ranamo's back and the dogs were almost asleep on their feet. Ranamo hailed the Castle Guards and the dogs barked.

Chapter 6

The two guards that sat in the gatehouse looked at each other. It had been a long day following another longer one, and for them, a long night too. Midnight had arrived before the search was called off the previous day, but every able-bodied man was up and out at dawn again. They searched until it was called off half a watch before mid-night. The recall was sounded and everyone looked forward to some rest. The Princess had not been found and most had lost hope.

For these two though it was not to be. Rebgroth called his Third together and assigned the two of them to Gate Duty. He warned them he himself would be officer of the watch and to stay alert. Eight others were given lookout duties around the walls. The rest were dismissed.

It was just their luck to draw the short straws that night, still, they could rest all the next day if they could just stay awake long enough. They were playing word games with each other to try to stay alert, if Rebgroth walked in and found them anything else but, they would feel his wrath.

"Did you hear that?" asked one, "I could have sworn ...."

Ranamo's voice called out again. His voice was clear and loud despite his strong elven accent.

"Open the gate for the Princess Patrikal. She has returned."

The other guard jumped up and ran for the gates, shouting to his friend.

"Get the Second Officer quick, I'll do the gate."

He slid back the observation slat in the gate as he heard the alarm bell begin to ring. That would call out the guard and bring Rebgroth. It would most probably bring out the rest of the Castle inhabitants at that time of night too he thought. He saw two figures standing on the far side of the draw bridge, with two large dogs sitting beside them, one either side.

"The Princess Patrikal awaits entry, what delays you?" cried Ranamo.

"Where is the Princess?" shouted the guard, "and who are you?"

Ranamo swung the half awake Princess down from behind his back and stood her in front of him.

"We are Wardens of the Forest in the service of Retalla, Chief of the Western Elves. We have brought back the Princess Patrikal who has done us great service."

"Open the damned gate," shouted Rebgroth as he ran up behind the guard, the second at his shoulder. As the large locking bar was removed and the gate swung open, the rest of the guard turned out. Rebgroth stood them in a semi-circle inside the gate, swords drawn.

"Watch them," he hissed as he stepped onto the drawbridge, drawing his own sword, the duty guards in close support.

"Our lookouts did not see you approach," he called as he moved slowly forward.

"We are Elves," smiled Ranamo, a simple statement of fact offered by way of an obvious explanation.

"Lay your weapons on the ground and step away from the Princess," Rebgroth instructed, "There are bowmen at the weapon slits in the towers, move slowly."

Ranamo laughed, "We have no weapons, and I have carried the Princess on my back for three of your watches, at the run, I am hardly going to harm her now!"

"Do it," demanded Rebgroth.

Ranamo looked sideways at Ranor and muttered something in Elvish. They both stepped back two paces.

"Why is it that men distrust and fear all that they do not understand?" asked Ranamo, a note of distain in his voice.

Patrikal was now fully awake.

"Stop it, these are my friends, they have brought me home."

"Then why did they take you?" snapped Rebgroth. It was as well with his tone that Patrikal was only four, but she was still a Princess, as Moreton was about to point out to him.

"I will take control now, thank you Captain Rebgroth. Please have your men sheathe their weapons and come to attention to welcome the Princess and her guests home."

Moreton had walked up behind them listening to their conversation. Rebgroth looked at him with fury in his eyes, but he knew better than to argue with the Weymonk. Whilst he had no direct command over the Guard, he was the King's closest friend and advisor and carried his complete authority.

He couldn't trust himself to answer in a steady voice, so he bowed and stepped back, sliding his sword into its scabbard and nodding to the others who did the same.

"That's better," said Moreton as the Princess ran to him. He picked her up, the dogs at his feet. "Come my friends, I apologise for the discourtesy, soldiers are a strange breed but they are only trying to do their duty."

"You are kind Holy One, but I fear the suspicion shown by your Officer is probably just a small part of what we may experience if we stay. Goodbye Princess, remember us and visit us one day."

The speed at which the two Elves broke sideways and sprinted away in zigzagging arcs that met outside bowshot was astonishing. Their shadowy figures, which almost blended in completely with their surroundings, were hard to see, but they waved at Patrikal and turned away.

"You see Moreton, Elves do wave sometimes."

"Yes Princess, so I see. Now, we must go inside and you can tell us all about it. We have been very worried"

He carried her back through the Castle gates, up the main street and into the square before the Keep. It was almost full of people by now, who were all wondering what the alarm was about. As they saw the Princess in Moreton's arms a loud cheer went up, the level of noise remaining enormous as people babbled, trying to find out what had just happened.

Moreton reached the Keep gates as Serculas came from within. Tears streamed from her eyes as she grabbed Patrikal from him, hugging her tightly.

"Thank goodness you are safe," she wept.

"I was always safe," the Princess replied. "The dogs were with me and the Elves brought me home."

"Elves! My goodness you have so much to tell us." She turned, almost running across the hall and up the main stairs towards the nursery, Moreton close behind. At the top of the stairs the King stepped out of his room.

"What's this I here about elves?" he roared.

"All is well Sire," panted Moreton, "please do not jump to conclusions."

The King eyed him, went to speak, then just walked down the hallway, opened the door into the nursery anteroom and on into the nursery itself.

Eilana was standing beside the grand cot, Harlada, asleep in her arms. Patrikal looked at her but said nothing.

"This is your brother Gudrick," said Serculas, holding Patrikal over the cot, "and Nanny Eilana, who is here to help me." They smiled at each other. The side door opened and Ferlmun stepped quickly in, bowing to the King.

"Where's mummy," asked Patrikal, "I have some medicine for her." Ferlmun looked up sharply as the King replied.

"She is asleep in her room, my child, she is not well."

"That is why I brought some medicine for her, Meyas said she was ill."

"And who is Meyas little one?" asked Moreton.

"She is Meyala's mummy," she answered.

"I think you should tell us where you have been and what you have been doing." It was the King who spoke but Moreton butted in.

"Perhaps, Sire, I could sit the Princess on my knee and she can tell us her story?"

He didn't wait for an answer, he was already crossing the room to Serculas. He took Patrikal from her and carried her to one of the chairs by the fire. He sat down, resting her on his knee.

"Now little one, let's start from when you were down by the river what did you see?"

He skilfully took Patrikal through her story, prompting her and often asking questions to move the tale along. She told everything, as she had understood it of course, and so the journey east was more than a bit patchy, but Moreton helped her through it all, often holding up a hand to the impatient King, but even he could see the magic Moreton was weaving.

Despite odd gaps the main tale was clear. Moreton rushed her past the seeds and the herbs though, quite deliberately.

"You are a very grown up little girl for only four, my Princess," Moreton concluded.

"That's because I am nearly five," explained Patrikal. They all laughed. The relief of having her home was palpable.

"I think we should all let her rest now," Moreton suggested. "It is still a while until dawn, I think we could all do with some rest."

"You're quite right," agreed Gudmon, "come along, away everyone."

The room emptied except for Serculas, Eilana, and the children, but Moreton caught Ferlmun's arm in the anteroom as they left, stopping him to talk.

"What do you know about the ways of elves Healer?" Ferlmun looked at Moreton's eyes. They were bright and forceful.

"Very little I'm afraid. It is said they have great powers of healing from an ancient knowledge of herbs and fungi, but I have never met anyone with any real knowledge of them or their ways."

"Well you have actually, we have just never discussed it." Moreton explained to Ferlmun about elvish telepathy in the young, which made what happened to Patrikal so much clearer to him. That is how they knew of the Queen's illness, and if they have sent a medicine of any kind, I tell you healer we would be wise to treat it very seriously. They have powers of healing that you and I will never understand."

"If you say so Moreton, I can only bow to your knowledge of them, but what if there is some sorcery involved, some darkness?" Ferlmun looked back at the nursery doors. "Have they done anything to Patrikal?"

"Elves have not an evil intent about them, I assure you of that. Oh they can be manipulative and they would be extremely clever at the politics of the outside world, if they cared to be, but they would never meaningly hurt a human, particularly a child. No, if they have sent a medicine we must use it in good faith, but if it works as I believe it will, you must take the credit Ferlmun, the court is not yet ready to accept such a debt to the elves, the behaviour at the gates proves that."

"What about the consequences if it fails?"

"Then only you and I will know the truth."

Ferlmun leant against the wall.

"You play dangerous games Moreton, what hold do you have over the King?"

"No hold Ferlmun, he trusts me because I have proven my loyalty to him many times, but mainly, he trusts me as his only real friend."

"And are you?"

"He believes so, and I act as such, that is all that matters. We must talk to Patrikal." Ferlmun nodded and they went back into the nursery.

Chapter 7

Ferlmun entered the Queen's bedchamber carrying a large goblet of warm liquid. His dark robes brushed the twin doors as he pushed through them, not waiting for them to open fully. Moreton followed him in, rubbing his palms on the sides of his maroon habit, still trying to remove the oily feel of the potion he had just mixed. The two wolfhounds looked up but recognising the two men, relaxed.

Although dawn had just broken, curtains still hung over the windows. The room was lit only by two torches mounted on iron wall stands and the large log fire.

The Queen was still, as if sleeping deeply, although Ferlmun was sure she was actually unconscious. Allaner and Reassel, her Ladies in Waiting, sat close to the bed on light wicker chairs that looked somewhat out of place alongside all the heavy oak furniture in the room.

"I have prepared this medicine for the Queen," explained Ferlmun. "It will nourish her and help thicken her blood."

The women nodded almost in unison. They were both very worried, both for the Queen and for themselves. If the Queen did not recover, their places of honour as her Ladies would cease, and their positions at court would be lost.

Ferlmun sat on the edge of the bed. The Queen lay on her back, her hair spread over the wool pillow beneath her head. He dipped his forefinger into the goblet and wet the Queen's slightly parted lips. He did the same a number of times, the liquid running into her mouth a drop at a time.

Her head moved a fraction, almost imperceptibly, but then her lips parted slightly and her dry tongue sought the dampness of her lips. Ferlmun gently pushed a hand behind her head, lifting and pushing it forward. He placed the goblet to her lips and tilted it, pouring a small amount of the potion into her mouth. She swallowed.

He laid her head back, looking anxiously at her pale features, Moreton hovering behind him. Her eyes flickered open and the faintest glimmer of a smile crossed her face. Ferlmun repeated the process, then again. This time the Queen swallowed deeply and raised a hand tentatively to the goblet.

She tried to speak but the words did not come. Liquid gurgled in her throat and she coughed weakly. Moreton walked around the bed and put a hand under her shoulder. Ferlmun did the same on his side, and they lifted her into a sitting position. Her Ladies had removed her clothes and slipped a white linen nightshirt over her. She never usually wore anything in bed and now suddenly felt very uncomfortable.

Some of the colourless potion had run down her chin and soaked into the cloth. Moreton was slightly unnerved to see the linen turning a deep blue. He lent forward and smiled at the Queen.

"Welcome home Your Majesty; it is good to have you back with us." She smiled back at him, a genuine warmness in her expression. This time her voice worked.

"Hello Moreton," was all she said, but it was enough to bring tears to the eyes of both her Ladies, neither of whom could quite believe what they had just witnessed. Neither could Moreton or Furlmun if the truth were known.

"You must drink the cupful Your Majesty," instructed Furlmun, holding the cup with the Queen, "The potion will give you strength."

"It does so already Healer, I can feel it warming me from inside, what on earth is it?"

"An old recipe Ma'am, but I only had enough of the eastern herb for this one dose, so you must drink it all."

"I will inform the King of your progress Ma'am, if you will excuse me." It was Moreton who spoke.

"Don't rush Moreton, I could do with a little more quiet before the King comes barging in." Moreton nodded, the hint of a grin in his eyes.

"As Your Majesty wishes," he bowed, and turning strode through the doors, closing them behind him.

"What has happened Ferlmun? Tell me truthfully."

"You have a healthy son Ma'am. The King has named him Gudrick after his father. Serculas delivered him then came for help. Little Patrikal was lost with the dogs. She was found by elves. They brought her back safely, and she is well. Your Majesty should drink the rest of this for me and then rest a while longer. I will bring the children to you when you feel up to it."

The Queen reached for the cup, and taking it from Ferlmun, she drank the rest of the goblet in two large mouthfuls. Wey, she hated the name Gudrick, too late now. She felt slightly detached from herself as she passed him the cup. He took it back and rose from the bed. She wanted to see Patrikal now but just couldn't argue then.

"I will return in a while and see how you are." She nodded and lay back, feeling her senses swim. It felt almost as she was drifting just outside her body, sitting on her own shoulder almost, seeing herself lying on the bed. She closed her eyes but could still see everything in the room.

Ferlmun left, instructing the Ladies to leave her undisturbed until he returned, and as he closed the doors she saw the King arrive in the anteroom with Moreton. She heard Ferlmun telling him that he advised him to give her a quarter watch or so. The King agreed begrudgingly after Moreton added his persuasion and suggested they all get some breakfast.

She watched it all, saw it all so clearly, but part of her brain kept telling her she was in a different room and couldn't have.

It didn't seem like a quarter watch, only moments in fact, before Ferlmun returned, but it had been a quarter and more.

She opened her eyes and looked at him. She didn't just see him in his black and brown robes, she saw him, his inner self. She saw years of study, uncertainty in his talents, insecurity should he fail in his skills with any of the Royal Family, but above everything, an all enveloping desire to help people, to understand what made them ill and how to cure them, and a great sadness for the death of those he had failed with. This was very strange.

She sat up unaided as he approached, swinging her legs over the side of the bed.

"Careful Your Majesty, you will still be weak!" he cried, quickening his step and reaching out his arms as if to catch her.

"I am fine Ferlmun. Allaner, get some hot water so I can wash. Reassel, get some clothes. She looked at them each as she gave her instructions. In Allaner she saw relief at her position secure, and fear of her. In Reassel she saw envy, but also a great pride in her position as a Lady In Waiting. They both left the room about their tasks.

Standing upright, Bertal put her hands to her head. Ferlmun grabbed her shoulders.

"There, I told you to go steady Your Majesty."

"Stop fussing Ferlmun, it's my mind that's dizzy not my body!" He looked at her sideways.

"Yes Ma'am," he replied, stepping away. Then protesting he looked away, "Ma'am!"

She pulled the nightdress over her head and walked naked over to the fire. The Ladies had washed her while she was unconscious as best they could, but she still had dried blood on her. She sat on the fur rug in front of the fire.

"Don't be stupid Ferlmun, you're my Healer. You've examined all of me at one time or another. It certainly doesn't bother me, don't be such an old woman."

"No Ma'am, it's just if the King were to come in now he might not take it that way." He could not help but gaze at her naked back. She lifted both hands up to her hair and ran them back through it, pushing it away from her face and gripping it behind her head, as if to tie it back, her elbows wide to either side. Her breasts stood out wonderfully he thought. They were large at the best of times, they had been larger with milk that was now lost. She had dehydrated so with loss of blood, she would never now feed Gudrick herself.

She glanced back over her shoulder and dropped her hair. She saw confusion, gladness at her well being, and hidden beneath it a guilty and suppressed lust. She rose slowly, no matter how strong she felt she was still very sore.

"I am sorry Ferlmun. It is very unfair of me to tease you. I don't mean to, I feel so safe with you." She felt a flash of disappointment in him; he didn't want women to feel safe with him. More confusion. He did but, well was he that old and unattractive?

She returned to the bed and picked up a fur, wrapping it around her, making the excuse that the footmen would arrive with the bath shortly. She walked back to the fire and stared into the flames. Why could she see all this in people, she never could before, not this clearly anyway. She wasn't sure she liked this new ability.

Allaner opened the side door and came in. She was leading a footman who carried a metal bath.

"Here," ordered Bertal, pointing in front of the fire. The footman placed the tub carefully and bowed deeply, backing from the room, a man happy with his life, his station, very much in love and living life as fully as he could. Oh for such a simple life she thought.

"The children Furlmun, who's feeding Gudrick?"

"A Castle lass Ma'am, Eilana, daughter of the Royal ostler Harlada, she has a child of a quarter moon, also Harlada after his grandfather. She is feeding them both well for the moment."

A knock was followed by Allaner entering again with five footmen, each carrying two large pitchers of hot water. Bertal looked away, she didn't want to know about them, but as the last of them was pouring his pitchers into the tub, there was another, this time somewhat cursory tap at the adjoining doors to the King's chamber. Greardel stood framed in the open doorway.

"Your Majesty," he bowed, "the King has asked me to enquire about your health. He suggests you relax for the morning while he is hunting and see the children. He will return by noon and join you then, when he feels sure you will feel strong enough to see him."

Typical of him she felt as she turned towards the doorway and looked at Greardel. She stifled a gasp and almost took a step back. She was hit by a wave of hate, but disdainful and malevolent hate. Greed and spite were there too, in large doses. She would need to watch this man. Again her insight worried her, would she live the rest of her life like this, or was it just something to do with Ferlmun's potion? She realised they were all looking at her.

"Oh, yes Greardel, tell his Majesty that will be fine." He bowed again, a little deeper this time, "and Greardel." He stopped in mid turn. "The next time you enter my chamber, you wait to be called in, do you understand?" He looked over his shoulder at the Queen, then slowly turned to face her as etiquette demanded.

"Of course Your Majesty, my apologies." This time he backed out, closing the door behind him.

"I don't like that man Ferlmun, he will bring harm to my family." She almost heard herself saying it to the Healer. He looked at her thoughtfully.

"The King trusts him Ma'am, but I will pass on your fears to Moreton, he is more accustomed to such things."

Reassel came back into the room and curtseyed.

"I have laid out clothes in the robe room Ma'am, for when you are ready," she reported.

"Thank you Reassel. Now, Ferlmun, you be away and let me bathe and rest a while. I will summon you when I am ready and you can take me in to the children, and thank you."

He bowed and smiled then left the room, leaving Bertal with her ladies.

Allaner took the fur from her shoulders and Reassel supported the Queen holding the hand she had offered her as she stepped into the warm tub by the fireside. She squatted then sat in the water, lying back slowly so as not to splash water from the tub. She sighed deeply at the comfort of the warmth she felt over her whole body.

Reassel took the soap and began to gently wash her relaxed form. She was sore all right, but she felt so invigorated and strong. She knew she had so nearly died, she should be laid out for days. What had Ferlmun given her? He had said he had no more, and that it had been made from an eastern herb. She knew that was the truth, but she also felt it was not all the truth.

She began to realise that whatever the potion had done to her body, it seemed to be doing it to her mind as well. How long either would last was the question. She felt sure that it would support her bodily strength long enough for her to recover fully before wearing off, in fact she knew it would, but she didn't know how long it would affect her mind this way. She was worried whether it would leave her more or less mentally agile when it faded. Something told her not to worry and she closed her eyes and enjoyed Reassel's hands washing her body, slowly massaging her with soap.

She thought that Reassel might be enjoying this a bit too much, but then right now, so was she. She would file that thought away though. Reassel had been spending a lot of time with a young seamstress, apparently creating designs for the Queen's wardrobe. She smiled to herself and relaxed totally for a while.

Ferlmun walked through the anteroom to the Queen's chambers and out into the grand hall. Turning left along the first floor balcony, he had only taken a dozen steps before turning left again into the nursery's anteroom.

He could have used the connecting doors between the chambers, going through the one door, closing it behind him before opening the second, but it just wasn't done. The connecting doors were for the Royal Family only, which brought his mind back to Greardel. He had used the connecting doors between the King and Queen's chambers. He really was trying his luck that one, always seeing just how far he could push the boundaries of Royal patience, but always so fawning when reprimanded. He really couldn't see why he should not enjoy the same advantages as the Royals themselves.

Ferlmun dismissed him from his mind as he entered the nursery itself.

Moreton and Patrikal were laughing by the fire. He envied Moreton's closeness to the Princess; he could never communicate that easily with children, and always found it difficult when trying to understand their descriptions of their symptoms when they were ill.

Moreton was holding a small leather pouch in his hand, which he slipped under his belt into a hidden pocket.

"Ah, Ferlmun!" He looked up. "Patrikal was just asking after the Queen. How is she now?" Ferlmun smiled at the little Princess.

"She is very much better, my pretty one. She is having a nice warm bath and then she will be in to see you."

He looked towards the window. Eilana was seated feeding one of the infants, Serculas was holding the other. He couldn't tell which was which from where he stood.

"The Queen is looking forward to meeting you Eilana. You must speak directly to her, she likes that. Call her Your Highness if you address her, and Ma'am in reply, understand?"

"Yes Sir. Should I get up and curtsey when she comes in?"

"Normally yes, but use common sense, as you did with the King. If you are in the middle of feeding the children it is hardly practical now is it?" She shook her head, her infectious grin making Ferlmun smile back. "Good, but Serculas should have told you all this."

"Oh she did Sir, I am just so nervous I keep forgetting."

"I doubt that young lady. Have you seen your family since you arrived here?"

"No Sir, there hasn't been a chance to get away yet." Moreton entered the conversation.

"Well you will go this afternoon with little Harlada after the King returns. He will want some time with the Queen. I will entertain the Princess, we have things to do, and Serculas, you will look after the Prince if the Queen wishes it. I am sure she will."

Even Ferlmun sensed the disappointment that oozed from Serculas, it upset her plans with, and for, Rebgroth that afternoon. They would have to wait till that evening. It had been before all this started since she had been with him alone in her room. Her stomach fluttered at the thought.

Moreton had their attention still.

"The Queen is very much better, on the surface at least, but it is Ferlmun's medicine that makes her thus. She is still sick and does not need any pressure or troubles for a while, no matter how well she seems. Her body will heal as the

51

medicine wears off, but it will be a quarter moon or so before we can be sure she has recovered beyond relapse. I don't want to see her doing anything energetic with the children. Am I right Healer?"

"You are Sir," confirmed Ferlmun, "You are doing my job for me."

"Good, then we shall take our leave. I will return shortly after the Queen has visited you for a while. Then we will get on with the rest of the day."

He took Ferlmun's arm, steering him towards the door and out into the anteroom, closing the door behind him. He still held Ferlmun's arm.

"Your potion is very efficacious Healer," he whispered, "it is even stronger than I had hoped."

"Aye, the elves have a knowledge I dream of sharing, that is clear, but as you said in there Moreton, it is only superficial for the moment, she is still a sick lady underneath."

"The elves know their business my friend, do not worry. Now what else troubles you? I can see something is gnawing at you."

"Ha, you see too much you know. Oh it is just that man Greardel. He upsets the Queen and he sets my teeth on edge."

"One day he will go too far, until then the King owes him a debt of honour, or more so to Greardel's dead father actually, but I have said too much already, his time will come."

He laughed and thumped the Healer squarely on the back. "I will see you back here a quarter watch from now. I want to be with the Queen when the King returns,"

Ferlmun didn't ask why, he just nodded and left the anteroom with him before grunting a farewell and heading back to his rooms.

At that moment, the Queen was rising slowly to her feet in her bath. Reassel held her hands to steady her as she stepped out in front of the fire, and Allaner placed a large linen towel around her shoulders.

"Thank you Ladies, you fuss too much." They remained expressionless and each took a step away, then curtseyed. The Queen laughed. She stared at the fire. The last time she had laughed was with Patrikal and Serculas on that damned cart.

She rubbed herself gently dry and tossed the towel to Allaner, feeling the hot glow of the fire on her bare flesh. She walked naked across the room towards the small door to her dressing room, her robe room as the Ladies insisted on calling it.

They helped her dress lightly, in light white undergarments and a thin mid-blue woollen dress that clung to her figure, too much for her liking with her body still distended from her pregnancy. It would take a while to return to her normal slim waist and hips. Still, if it dampened the King's ardour for a while she would be more than happy, the thought of any kind of intimacy with him right now was unbearable. It frightened her a little that the thought ever flashed across her mind, that she felt that way.

Looking at herself in the mirror she threw a knitted shawl over her shoulders and walked back into her chambers. Reassel and Allaner followed her in.

"I am going to the children now. One of you take a quarter watch off, the other wait in the nursery anteroom in case I need something, then swap over. Decide to suit yourselves."

With that she headed for the adjoining doors to the nursery, opened the first, closed it behind her and stood for a moment in the dark, composing herself. She had said she would summon Ferlmun first. She felt for the handle, turned it firmly, and walked confidently into the room.

She stopped and looked at Serculas, who had come first to her eye, for she was standing looking into the cot. She saw strength and dependability, determination and honesty, but then she saw pain, a subject of violence, of rape, of despair. This did not make sense, none of this had happened to Serculas.....not yet.

The truth hit her like a blow to the head; this was the future she saw! She walked towards the cot in an attempt to hide her confusion, looking down at the two infant boys lying side by side in the large cot. She saw a great leader that men would follow, some to their death, others to victory and honour, and she saw a weak minded child that was born to follow, who would never love a woman, who would die childless. She picked up the baby nearest to her.

"Hello my little Prince," she said, "leader of men."

"Oh Your Majesty." It was Serculas. "I am so sorry, I was not quick enough, I was so pleased to see you. That is young Harlada, Nanny Eilana's child, the wet nurse, the Prince's milk brother."

She reached out and took the child from the Queen, before looking her in the face and realising she was a deathly white. She turned and handed Harlada to Eilana, who had moved up behind her. She bent into the cot, picking up Gudrick.

"Here is the Prince Your Majesty." She straightened to see Queen Bertal staring at Eilana," and this is Nanny Eilana Your Majesty." She saw the Queen pale further, though she wouldn't have thought it possible, before pitching forward in a dead faint. With Gudrick in her arms she could do nothing to catch her. She almost dropped Gudrick back in the cot as she cried for help. Eilana put Harlada down with Gudrick and crouched beside Serculas and the Queen, helping to sit her up and fan her face.

"Fetch the Healer," she shouted at Allaner as she entered the room, "Run!" Allaner was not used to a nanny giving her orders, let alone this fifteen year old who had only been here two days, but such was the command in her tone that she was running for Ferlmun's chambers without further thought. They eased the Queen up into a chair as she came round.

"Oh Your Majesty," cried Serculas, "are you all right, I think you fainted." Eilana shook her head imperceptibly, of course she's not all right, and bloody obviously she fainted, but why though? The Queen had looked her straight in the eye. It had felt like she was looking right inside her, and as she did so, fear flashed in her eyes, they rolled upwards and down she went.

"I'm alright, get me some water woman." Eilana got it, filling a goblet from the pitcher on the large table. She brought it to the Queen who took it from her and drank deeply. "I think I am weak with hunger you know, I haven't eaten for the best part of three days." Eilana could not help thinking what a strong woman the Queen was, when she heard a sob behind her.

"We will send to the kitchen for food Ma'am," offered Serculas, nodding to Eilana, but Eilana was cuddling Patrikal, who had sat down and covered her eyes when her mother collapsed. She had wanted to run to her when she came in, but Moreton had trained her that Princesses didn't do that sort of thing. Her mother had gone to the cot instead of to her, which hurt, and now she was ill again. This time it was too much for her, her adventure with the dogs and the elves, a new brother, and now this. She was sobbing her little heart out. Eilana carried her to her mother who sat her on her knee, the colour returning to her own cheeks. She cuddled the child and looked up at Eilana.

"Thank you Eilana. I will have to get to know you better, it looks like you are going to be here for quite some time."

"Yes Ma'am, I will look forward to it."

"I'm sure you will." Eilana had no idea what the Queen meant. Why did it look like she would be there for quite some time? Now her mind was racing. The Queen looked at her again as Ferlmun ran in panting.

"For Wey's sake catch your breath man and have some water. You look like the one that needs a healer."

"Your Majesty is obviously feeling better." He glanced almost accusingly at Allaner.

"It is not her fault, I fainted and it must have looked worse than it was. Hunger I think. Organise it Ferlmun, it's all the medicine I need."

"That was just what I was about to prescribe Ma'am," he smiled. He was so relieved. He reached for the bell cord by the door and pulled it twice. A footman entered a few moments later, and before he could bow and ask how he could be of service, Ferlmun was talking to him quietly by the door.

The footman left and Ferlmun turned back to face the room. Queen Bertal was still cuddling Patrikal with Serculas hovering beside her. Eilana had moved back to the fireplace and stood watching the Queen, obviously preoccupied with some thought or other. Both the infants were gurgling to themselves in the cot.

He was trying to think of something to say when the side door opened and Moreton appeared.

"Is all well again?" he enquired. The Queen looked up at him and hesitated before she spoke.

"All is fine Moreton. I am fine, but I think I would like a few moments peace to gather myself before the King returns. He will be back any time now." She stared at Moreton steadily as he replied.

"Indeed Ma'am. Come Patrikal, we have a job to do. Eilana, take young Harlada to see his grandparents. Serculas will mind Gudrick until his next feed when Eilana returns."

At that moment the food arrived. Moreton had it taken to the Queen's apartment.

"If you will excuse us Your Majesty, we will all be about our business while you dine and await the King." She nodded as Patrikal ran across the room and took his hand.

Everyone seemed to move at once except Bertal, then she too rose from her chair and went back to her chamber through the connecting doors. She sat on the cushioned chair by the fire with a plate of cold beef and a hunk of buttered bread. As she ate, her mind sought explanations to her visions.

She had seen Eilana, a woman, not the child she was now, dressed in a very fine ball-gown, dancing with the King. She had seen her with nothing on dancing horizontally with the King, and an infant in the Royal cot. She had seen a woman of great intellect and cunning, of great ambition for herself and her children. She had felt the power of life and death Eilana held over her.

This would also seem to tie in with her earlier vision of the children. Harlada would be a great leader, but her own son would sleep with men and avoid conflict and danger. Patrikal she had not seen, but knew she was there, and indeed she knew she would be there herself.

Should she fight the future? Could she change it? Should she insist Eilana was dismissed now before this went too far? Could she?

The only person she could think of to discus such things with was Moreton, but now she was not sure. She had had complete trust in him, but as she looked at him when he entered the nursery, the first time she had seen him since her power had manifested itself, to her surprise his whole figure glowed with a slight sheen, a sort of glistening shroud that moved with him, covering his whole being. She read it as a shield of some sort that stopped her seeing into his character, his past, or his future. It was certainly a protection of some sort, but why?

Her thoughts were broken as the adjoining doors to King's chamber swung open none too gently, and the King appeared, a large goblet of ale in his hand.

"Ah, there you are my Queen, I thought you might be with the children" Thoughts of how are you feeling now crossed her mind.

"No my dear, I came back in here to rest while I ate. Have you eaten?"

"Indeed I have. We have enjoyed some ham and ale before I came up"

"Good, then forgive me if I finish this while we talk." She looked up at him for the first time as he consented. He crossed the room to sit beside her.

She saw a basically kind man, arrogant, but it would be hard for a King not to be. She also saw a deep sadness, something missing in his life, warmth, love. He moved closer, putting an arm around her and nearly knocking the plate from her knee.

"You are looking better my dear, how are you feeling now?" She felt like shouting at last, but replied quietly.

"Much better, thank you, but very tired. I need to lie down for a while."

"What a good idea!" he laughed, giving her a squeeze and kissing her cheek.

"For Wey's sake Gudmon. I am exhausted and very sore," she snapped back at him. "It was a moon after Patrikal was born, you'll remember, before I felt ready, and that was a normal birth. What has got into you?" He stood, looking angry rather than hurt.

"I just thought…"

"No you didn't Gudmon. That's it exactly, you didn't think, not beyond your crotch anyway." Now he looked angry and hurt. "Just sit down here and talk to me for a while."

He sat back down somewhat sulkily and she snuggled up to him. Now he was confused, after his formal Royal upbringing, he found it difficult to separate an affectionate cuddle from sex.

"Now, how did your hunt go this morning?"

He talked for what seemed an age of his morning in the saddle. She listened with the occasional grunt of understanding or feigned disbelief, until the moment was right.

"I am pleased you had a good morning. You must have had a worrying few days."

"It has not been easy," he agreed, then led her in perfectly, "but Moreton was a pillar of strength, as always."

"He is a very old friend of yours, I know, but in the five years we have been wed, you have never told me anything about him, or where you knew him from."

"There is nothing much to tell. He was the son of my father's falconer, born a day after me. The King looked on his father more as a friend than a falconer.

"They went hunting with the birds up beyond the northern borders early in the spring, just before my first birthday. They were attacked by some tribesmen when separated from the main group. The King's horse was killed by an arrow and fell sideways, trapping his leg. Moreton's father jumped from his horse and sword drawn, stood astride the King. There was one other Niscerian with them, a young soldier of the Royal guard, Greardel's father. He too stood over the King, sword drawn, ready to honour his oath to defend the King to his death.

"Back to back they fought off the tribesmen until the noise of battle brought the rest of the hunting party at the gallop. They drove their attackers off. Greardel's father was still standing, an arrow through his gut. Moreton's father was already dead, three arrows in him, the last taking him in the throat as the tribesmen fled, a final hasty shot.

"The King was unhurt, apart from a badly bruised leg. They lay the soldier on a litter and dragged it back behind his horse. Moreton's father's body was tied upright in his saddle and rode back beside the King in honour.

"They stopped on the way back, camping overnight. Greardel's father died early next morning after a night in agony. The King was with him and promised him in gratitude he would look after his wife and baby son. He took her into Royal service. Greardel grew up and was trained as a body servant from a young age. He was appointed to me on my Sire's Day. He has been with me ever since, I had to promise my father that.

"Moreton's father was a widower. His wife had died shortly after the birth and his sister struggled to look after Moreton when his father was on Royal duty. The King took Moreton in as my play friend. He lived with me, shared a bedroom and schooling until our Sire's Days. Moreton left then. His aunt had received a letter of some sort I was told, but I think my father had done some deal with the Duke of Merlbray. Anyway, Moreton set out for the east but never arrived. Seven years later, eight years ago now, he suddenly appeared at the gates, a Weymonk, returned from the dead it appeared.

"That's it really. He was, and is, my closest friend, my only real friend, who doesn't care that I am King, and never expects anything of me but my friendship in return."

"Where was he those seven years?"

"He never told me exactly and I have never had reason to question him. He was caught by bandits, rescued by a monk I think, who lived in the forests or something, but basically he trained as a Weymonk and returned when he had completed it. I have never understood what training that might have been I must say. The training for a formal Weypriest is rigid and set in the teachings of the Church, but these Weymonks are more mystics, maverick holy men. They are not celibate, which annoys the church enormously, and are therefore not recognised formally as Priests, but what training they actually receive is a mystery to me. I have never delved deeper and shall not. I just thank Wey he is here for me to rely on."

"You are lucky to have him, he is a strength to us all." She dropped a hand to his crotch and gave it a gentle tweak. "Now I am off to my bed. The more rest I get the sooner I will be healed for you."

He struggled up, thinking he must lose some weight, and helped her to her feet, leading her to the bed. She pecked him on the cheek and lay down. He leant forward, lifted her hand and kissed it. He would lose weight; he couldn't bend down far enough to kiss her cheek. Smiling down at her he left through the adjoining doors.

She watched him go, her mind working on what she had learnt.

Moreton was a mystery still. He obviously had the power to protect himself from anyone reading any of his traits, his past, future and probably thoughts. But why should he? He did not know of the onset of her gift, or perhaps he did. If not, who was he protecting himself against?

She had actually learned more about Greardel, and could start to understand his bitterness.

His father had been killed alongside Moreton's, protecting the King. Despite the King's personal friendship to Moreton's father, he could not see why he was brought up as a servant and Moreton as a prince. Worse still, he still was a faithful servant after all this time, whereas Moreton had disappeared for years and been welcomed back, again becoming the King's trusted friend, with more power than any other man in Nisceriel.

She fell asleep, sleeping soundly until dusk, only waking to the sound of Reassel putting some more logs on the fire as quietly as she could.

Eilana went to her room to collect a shawl before leaving for her parents' house. She laid little Harlada down in his cot whilst she opened her chest and found her shawl. For no specific reason she stood at the foot of her bed, lifted the curtain aside and looked out of the small window that provided the only natural light to her tower room. Serculas' room was directly below hers but was considerably bigger, as the tower tapered towards its spire.

She looked down on the Castle's walled garden. It had not been originally designed as such, but two walls, taller than three men, ran to the outer walls from doors at each end of the Keep's south wall, allowing defenders to move between the outer walls and the Keep if the Castle's integrity was breached. These formed a square walled area that had naturally become a secluded space for the Royal family to use, and almost inevitably a garden.

As she looked down, Moreton entered the garden, leading Patrikal by the hand, although mostly she was pulling him. They stopped right below her window, on the north side of the garden, where the sun shone most of the day, if it did at all. She had to climb on her bed to lean out far enough to see what they were doing.

Moreton drew a long pointed object from his habit. For a moment at a distance she thought it was a knife and almost cried out, but then she saw it was just a rod of iron, a finger thick and a forearm long. He pressed it into the grass, as deep as he could into the frost hardened ground. The surface was soft now but it was still hard just underneath. He pulled it out and Patrikal dropped something into the hole.

They repeated this twice more, about an arm's length apart, Moreton standing and pressing his foot down hard on the holes afterwards, sealing them and enclosing their contents.

It had to be seeds she concluded, correctly as it happened, but all she could do was wait to see what grew there in time. Intrigued, she swung her shawl around her shoulders, picked Harlada from his cot, and descended the spiral staircase to the foot of the tower. A stone corridor led to the Keep's courtyard, which she crossed to the east side where the main gate led into the Castle's inner grounds.

She crossed the main square at a brisk walk. She would have to be back within half a watch as the Prince would wake soon after that for his late afternoon feed. Serculas would only get in a temper if she was late.

It only took a few moments to reach her parents' little house beside the stables. She knew her mother would be there, but she was delighted to find her father too. There were no visitors at the Castle so work was slack for him. He had found time to return for a bite between helping with the general running of the Stables.

They greeted her enthusiastically and questioned her on everything she had seen and heard in the Royal Household. Had she met the King? How was the Queen? Her mother positively glowed as she cuddled her grandson and talked with her daughter whilst the younger ones sat on the floor by the fire and absorbed it all.

The time slipped by so quickly. Harlada got up and headed for the door.

"I will send Harlmon back to say hello, he misses you I think. I'll cover his duties while he's here."

Eilana got to her feet too, donning her shawl and taking a contented little Harlada from her mother, who she kissed and hugged with her free hand. She kissed her younger brother and sister, saying her goodbyes and closing the door behind her.

Harlmon was just coming around the corner from the stables, but even in the half-light it was clearly him. They embraced around Harlada in her arms, then he led her back around the corner where two hay bales were stacked outside the stable. He pulled the top one down beside the other. They sat down side-by-side and held hands, her free hand clasped in his.

"It has been very strange without you pretty one," he began. She agreed and explained how scary it was sleeping alone. She only really realised herself at that moment how much she had grown to rely on him during her pregnancy. He was the only other person who knew who little Harlada's father was by name. A secret she kept even from her mother.

As they parted after precious moments together, Harlmon put an arm around Eilana and whispered in her ear.

"I will never let anyone hurt you pretty one, you let me know if anyone or anything bothers you, I will sort it for you." She felt a girlish surge of emotion wash over her, and tears welled in her eyes. She kissed him and walked away before she cried.

When she got back to the nursery Serculas was delighted to see her. Patrikal was playing with some carved animals at the table, and Gudrick had just dropped off following a fractious quarter. After a brief exchange, Serculas disappeared to find Rebgroth and finalise their arrangements for later that evening.

Eilana sat by the fire and fed Harlada. He had been awake all afternoon and would sleep well after a feed. Patrikal rang the bell for her and Eilana had the footman light all the candles. Combining with the flickering light from the fire, they added a warm glow to the nursery. More logs were brought for the fire before a meal of hot beef and vegetables was served for them both. They ate talking and laughing before Eilana woke Gudrick for his evening feed. With luck both babies would sleep through to dawn, they had both done so once.

With the Prince in his cot asleep, and Patrikal tucked up in her bed, Eilana gently lifted Harlada from his cot so as not to wake him. She opened the door to the anteroom and spoke briefly to the young maid who slept there at night. Patrikal would go to her if she wanted anything, and if the Prince cried, she was to come and fetch her. It was her night tonight, she alternated with Serculas.

Eilana walked back across the nursery and through the little door onto the spiral staircase. She climbed a few steps passing the door to Serculas' room. A line of light escaped from below the door and she heard voices laughing within. Serculas had brought Rebgroth up the back way of course. Technically, such a liaison between members of the Royal Household was not permitted. Everyone seemed to know about them, but if they didn't flaunt it, it was apparently something people turned a blind eye to.

Eilana smiled to herself and continued up the spiral stairs to her room above. She fumbled in the dark with the handle and pushed the door open, entering and kicking it shut. As she moved towards Harlada's cot she tripped on the rug that covered the floorboards in the centre of the room, folding it back and almost falling headlong. She caught her balance and in the glow from the embers of her little bedroom fire, she laid Harlada, still fast asleep, in his cot.

She placed a large log on the fire and turned to spread the rug back flat. In the darkness of the room, lit only by the fire as she hadn't lit candles or her lamp yet, she saw a shaft of light rising straight from the floor where the rug had been. There was a knothole in the floorboard the size of an eye.

All the rooms in the tower were the same. Their roofs were formed by parallel beams a forearm apart. They ran across the circular gap left by the stone fighting ledge that extended inwards for an arms length all the way around the tower at each level. The middle beam was the longest as it spanned the entire diameter of the gap. To each side they reduced in length as they moved closer to the edge. At right angles to the beams, planks were laid as floorboards, forming both the ceiling from below and floor from above. Looking up, the beams were visible and the underside of the floorboards laid across them. As a barrier between rooms, they were not too sound proof.

Eilana was only human. She knelt and put her right eye to the hole. It was directly above Serculas' bed. She could see her face, her eyes closed, her arms around Rebgroth's naked back, and her knees either side of his buttocks, which were driving rhythmically as he moved inside her.

She looked up at her wall, embarrassed by what she saw; embarrassed but fascinated. Surely if Serculas opened her eyes she would see her eye peering down at her, but she realised that as long as her room was dark, as it was, the hole would just be a black mark on the ceiling as it had always been under the rug. Her eye went back to the hole as if attracted by a magnet.

As she watched, Serculas' head bent back with a stifled cry, her back arched, thighs contracting against Rebgroth, her fingers digging into his back as she clutched at him. He grunted, satisfied, then coughed on her shoulder. He rolled off her onto his back and they lay panting, a hand on each other's stomach. Eilana watched his ardour die as they spoke. She could not hear what they said. She sat up and put the rug back.

She undressed and lay on her small pallet bed. She didn't feel aroused exactly by what she had seen, not by the few moments she had watched, but it did awake in her a realisation that love making had not been part of her life since she had become pregnant, apart from occasionally watching Harlmon's self gratifying antics, and now she recognised a latent desire. She hadn't shuddered herself since that night Harlmon had watched her.

To her surprise, the next thing she knew it was almost dawn and Harlada was grizzling in his cot. She rose and fed him, and had only just finished and dressed when the maid tapped on her door, calling her softly.

Chapter 8

Spring ran its course and the summer raced by. At the Royal Castle Nisceriel, relationships and routines had settled for a while, but the foundations of the changes to come were firmly laid.

Eilana's curiosity was answered when three small bushes sprouted quickly from the three seeds she had watched Moreton plant with Patrikal. They blossomed when they were no more than a hand high, and by autumn they were a man's shoulder high and laden with winter berries. With any other bush, Moreton would have predicted a bad winter ahead, but all the other wild bushes around the Castle only carried an average yield of berries, from which juice drinks and wine were made by the locals. In fact, Nisceriel was renowned for its fruit wines, producing some of the finest a connoisseur might find. Grape wine alone was brought from afar, shipped by merchants and popular only for entertaining and banquets, when visitors were unused to the local fruit wines. Ales and particularly local apple cider were the favourites of the local villagers.

These new bushes were constantly at the attention of the Castle's bees. The Royal apiarist had a line of eight hives, just over the west wall of the walled garden, and the Guards on the battlements even commented on the almost constant stream of bees that rose over the wall and gathered nectar from Patrikal's bushes.

It was the bees that finally named the bushes, a bush never known before. To little Patrikal, the visitors to her bushes were bumblebees, and it wasn't long before the bushes became Bumbleberry bushes. No one could actually be certain who first called them Bumbleberries, but they became recognised as such almost overnight.

The beekeepers noticed a gradual reddening tinge to the honey they removed from the hives over the spring, and so it was that at her fifth bornbless party, Patrikal got her wish of eating the honey she had tasted with the elves, what seemed to her, an eternity ago.

The honey was much sought after and very popular within the Castle. Strangely, whenever the Royal apiarist decided the time had come to sell this exquisite honey outside the Castle, they seemed to run short and decided to delay doing so, but then again despite their fears, there always seemed ample for consumption within the Castle.

The same was the case after the first harvest of Bumbleberries. As they freshly squeezed the berries, the juice produced was nothing short of divine. Moreton put his foot down firmly in an area that normally was not his business, in insisting that there were not enough berries to use for wine making and forbidding it flatly. Just like the honey, there was plenty of juice for Castle consumption, but never enough to think of selling it to others.

As visitors came and went from the Castle, they all told of this fabulous juice they had drunk. On Moreton's strict instructions, supported by a personal Royal order from the King, the source of the juice was kept a secret, and visitors were told of a secret recipe, blending four local berries, that produced the drink.

Queen Bertal returned to full health within a moon. The visionary powers she had gained wore off within a few days, to the point where she could not really be sure they were ever there, and the memory of what she had seen faded with them.

Eventually she shared her experience with Moreton, one evening as darkness grew, sitting in the Royal day room. He laughed and assured her that what she thought she had seen was just the hallucinatory effects of Ferlmun's medicine. His fears were confirmed though, they were very much the effects of the elven medicine, but they had been very real. He had been right to screen himself.

One legacy of the Queen's experience was to have a very significant effect on court life however. She had a vision of the King in her mind rutting with another woman. She could not make out who it was. She kept almost seeing the face, but it twisted and writhed so the features were blurred to her. What it did however, was to turn her off sex with the King completely. She had been brought up strongly in the ways of a wife's duties to her husband, but the first time the King came to her, a three-quarter moon after Gudrick's birth, it was a nightmare to her.

She was not ready in her mind yet but Gudmon was unstoppable. He was basically a man of simple male desires, but he had never gone so long without a woman since his first marriage, and somehow self-gratification seemed unkingly to him. It was purely a power thing, but as King, he could have any woman in the Kingdom he chose, but he didn't want any woman. Probably because he could, he had never been one for wenching, for bedding any woman that took his fancy, so he had been agonisingly celibate since Gudrick's birth, and hadn't entered a woman for moons.

This was really what he couldn't understand. When Bertal was pregnant with Gudrick, she had enthusiastically found ways to satisfy his needs, and he had loved her all the more for her unselfishness in wanting to please him. So what had changed now? She didn't seem to want him near her, let alone offer to please him in any way. It hurt him but made him feel guilty of such selfish thoughts at the same time.

He had entered her room a little drunk and determined to have sex with his wife. She had been totally reactionless, not exactly fighting him off but in no way encouraging him or showing any sign of desire or enjoyment. He found that a turn off in itself, but it had been so long. Foreplay was totally absent therefore, and when he entered her she was in no way ready for him, which made it painful for her and difficult for him.

Luckily for them both, after so long out of the saddle, he seeded so quickly it was all over in a few moments. He felt guilty and cheated at the same time, she felt sore and disgusted. From that day on, sex between them became something he took and something she endured, and from that moment love began to die, resentment growing rapidly on both sides. Both were aggrieved, and both to blame, but their growing coldness to each other meant they couldn't talk about it, and so things grew steadily worse as the summer slid by.

Eilana became rapidly established as indispensable. By the end of the summer, both infants were onto solid foods and her main reason for being there had ended, but there was never any question of her leaving. She had become an invaluable member of the Royal Household and an independent young lady.

She spent many an evening with her eye to the knothole in her floor. She watched Serculas and Rebgroth make love and do the most astonishing things to each other. They were enthusiastic lovers. They were very much in love, enjoying the thrill of pleasing each other unselfishly, and far from becoming used to each other or bored with their lovemaking. She learned an enormous amount about sex, how to please a man, or a woman for that matter, from watching them.

She learned many pleasing positions, picking the best in her mind, seeing which were the ones Rebgroth enjoyed most. She discovered lovemaking with lips and tongue, which was something they both seemed to enjoy the fruits of tremendously. She was not sure how much either of them enjoyed doing it to the other, but it was the unselfishness of it that enamoured her to it.

They both had a healthy understanding of each other's private parts, and what felt good to each other, mainly because they told each other. It also taught her that honest sex between two people was not something that worked perfectly every time, indeed more often than not, they did not finish perfectly in unison as her friends and naivety had taught her to believe. Her own experience with Keffron had taught her that already, but these two understood each other and were honest.

On many occasions, Rebgroth came before Serculas. If he could not stay with her, he would roll off her and use a hand or his tongue. Even then sometimes, Serculas was just not going to get there, but she was happy that he knew and had tried, not just leaving her hanging.

What most intrigued Eilana was on some of these occasions, Rebgroth would sit up with his back to the bed head. Serculas would sit with her back to him between his outstretched thighs, lying back on him, her head on his chest, her thighs apart inside his, her knees bent. His arms over her shoulders, he would caress her breasts gently, kissing her forehead, until eventually, Serculas' own hands would drift down between her thighs, bringing on her own shuddering climax.

On just a few occasions when Serculas was not feeling well, or just too tired to do it for him, she would massage his stomach gently, her head on his chest, while he lay back and brought himself to seed. It always made her laugh and moan at him for the mess he had made.

Eilana learnt so much that would be invaluable to her in the near future, but only occasionally did watching them arouse her, to her it was more like a study course than voyeurism. Just sometimes, when they did something she found particularly touching more than erotic, she would slip into her bed, a flutter in her stomach. Her hands would seek her full breasts. Her nipples erect, her hands would run lightly across her stomach and hips until after a time, her right palm would settle over the patch of hair where her legs parted. Her first and second fingers would set about their business, wet and slippery from her juices, until her pleasure was complete. Afterwards she would open her eyes, half hoping to see Harlmon looking down at her and smiling, he always said girls did it too!

She would sit by the fireplace in the nursery talking to Serculas for many a watch on spring and summer evenings. Although on many days the fire was not lit, the two chairs were a comfortable place to share quiet conversation as the darkness fell and the children slept. More often than not, Harlada would stay in his cot beside the Prince.

They slowly became firm friends. Of course Eilana never even hinted at what she had seen, but she did get Serculas to talk about her relationship with Rebgroth, about sex and men in general. They would giggle and run men down in an affectionate way, but again, all the time Eilana was learning.

She pressed Serculas most about what made her relationship with Rebgroth so good. Serculas was always hesitant about replying, not because she didn't want to talk about it, but that she wanted to be sure about her answer. She finally decided it was their honesty in talking to each other, about their feelings, about love making, everything. She was sure that once a couple reached the stage of hiding things from each other, or being embarrassed about sexual feelings, they were on the decline.

Serculas explained how she had needed to cast off some inhibitions about intimacy herself. Her upbringing had taught her, wrongly she knew now, that certain aspects of it were taboo, dirty somehow. She had been taught that men gratifying themselves was not very nice, women worse, but she was sure now that was for her two brothers' sake, else they would have been doing it all the time. Eilana told her that her brother Harlmon did do it all the time, at least daily it seemed. They laughed together.

"There is nothing dirty about it, certainly not when done within a loving relationship. You have to try and understand each other. When either of you gets selfish, starts just taking, and only wants sex when it suits you; when it becomes more bother than the desire to give your partner pleasure, that is when things start to slide. Besides, there's been many a time when I've not really felt like it, but gone along willingly to make him happy, and ended up enjoying some of the best love making ever. At the hub of it all, if your man needs it more than you do, and he doesn't do it himself, he'll do it with someone else. Better to help him, have him do it where you can see him I guess."

Eilana felt a little guilty about her voyeurism, especially now she knew Serculas so well, but she realised how much she had learned, and how many people could go most of their lives and never experience any of what she had learned. She wondered about her parents' relationship, but only wondered, every child knows their parents don't do it!

One evening as they chatted about the day in general, Serculas mentioned that a showman had been at the Castle that day. A troupe of tumblers and jugglers was back in the area. They were not required by the Castle, apparently the King was not in the best of moods when he came, he's often not of late as she knew, so as they had no guests in the Castle, he refused to let them perform, which was a shame as they had been so good when they had been some fifteen or sixteen moons ago.

Eilana wouldn't have seen them of course because it was before she came, but they were going to do a show in Castlebury as they had not been able to last time, and if she wanted to go, Serculas offered to be sure to be on duty that afternoon.

Eilana's heart raced for a moment, anger not excitement. No, she would not go, but it was a kind offer.

Grendal was no naïve maiden, she was nineteen and had enjoyed men for a number of years. It was five years to be exact, since she had fumbled in the hay with her brother's best friend. She had done it for a dare and it had all gone further than she had meant. Not that she regretted it, she had been enthusiastic then and she still was, in fact she had been enthusiastic with more than twenty men that she could name since then, and quite a few she couldn't.

Her tally was made up of a few local boys, which always seemed to lead to complications, but mainly of soldiers or travellers as they passed through. Some of them gave her money or gifts afterwards, which was a welcome bonus, but there was never any comeback, they moved on and forgot her.

She had never become pregnant in all that time and whilst pleased about it in one way, she was a little worried she might never. She told herself that when she settled down with the right man she would conceive easily enough.

That was the problem, the right man. The local boys were all so boring to her, so she developed a vague strategy that one of her passing lovers would eventually prove to be rich and lonely, and would take her away from village life to a large country home somewhere, or even a castle, so the more she tried the better.

When the troupe of jugglers and tumblers entered the village to much local interest, she knew none of them were for her long term, none would have enough money. Her eyes did fall on a well-built young man of about her age, or a little more, whose muscles rippled beneath his tight linen shirt as he walked, waving in the parade.

They were shouting the time and place of their performance to the crowd that was slowly gathering along the roadside, between the small houses, as they made their way to the village square.

She was admiring Keffnon as he turned his head her way and looked straight at her. Their eyes met and he waved, blowing her a kiss. She smiled and began to walk along the roadside behind the watching villagers, keeping pace with the parade. Keffnon was aware of her but continued waving to the crowd as he walked.

When they reached the square there was a flurry of activity as the troupe began unloading equipment from the two carts that had followed the parade into the village. They had made camp on the outskirts, their travelling homes in a loose circle, their carthorses tethered within and attended by the troupe's wives and children.

With everything ready and a quarter to go before the show, the troupe dispersed. Most headed to the local Inn, run by Grendal's father, but none of them was surprised to see Keffnon talking to a pretty girl.

Grendal and Keffnon arranged to meet a quarter after the show. She had a small and cosy room of her own at the back of the Inn. It was a stone lean to added to the back as storage originally, but as she passed her Maiden's Day, her parents were only too glad to have her move into it, giving them more space and a bit of privacy themselves. A small blue door was the only entrance, and a small window was the only source of natural light.

Grendal lit a fire in the tiny fireplace, in case it went off cold with the dusk. She liked to do things properly and wanted to be sure the room was warm enough, she wasn't going to give him any excuse to keep any clothes on. She left to watch the show.

It was a quarter after sunset as Grendal lay on her back on her pallet bed with Keffnon above her, as naked as her. She was thoroughly enjoying herself. Keffnon was proving an excellent lover, after she had slowed him down a bit, and now his slow rhythm was hitting all the right spots.

The room was dark, her eyes closed, and her mind was concentrated on her body's enjoyment of the moment. He too was concentrating hard, on anything except what he was doing. For once in his life he was thinking of his partner's enjoyment, and in his mind he was running through a sequence in the show. If he thought for a moment of what he was doing he knew he would finish, too soon for Grendal.

Neither of them therefore, heard the door latch lift very gently, nor the quiet creak of the hinges as it opened just enough for a person to slip through, nor did they hear the soft footsteps of bare feet across the floor.

All Keffnon felt was a knee drive down in the middle of his back, just below his shoulder blades, as a hand grabbed his hair and yanked back his head. He didn't realise what the pain was that he felt across his neck, as the knife cut deep into it, slashing across through his jugular and wind pipe, in fact he was dead before he could work it out.

All Grendal felt was a sudden increase in weight on her, and as she opened her eyes and her mouth to cry out, they were filled with warm liquid. She blinked, her hands flying to her face, and coughed as she choked, Wey she was drowning.

Although Keffnon's full weight was on her, it lightened, and she heard a man's voice say,

"That's for my sister."

She tried to scream but her mouth was still full of liquid. She heard the voice again,

"Keep quiet and I'll not harm you."

She couldn't see properly but heard footsteps this time. The door opened and closed. She could hardly move for Keffnon lying on her.

"Get off you fool," she cried, grabbing his head and pushing it off her face. This time she did scream as the head just went back in her hands, opening the huge gash across his throat, and pumping another surge of the little blood he had left in him, full into her face.

She rolled half sideways, as far as she could with his dead weight on her, screaming hysterically, blood everywhere, the bed soaked and herself covered.

The door burst open and a passing neighbour looked anxiously into the gloom. She too screamed at the sight and ran out, shouting for help. Grendal lay back, sobbing hysterically.

Moments later her father ran in, accompanied by two Castle Guards who had been watching the show and drinking at the Inn afterwards.

"Great Wey above!" he swore, grabbing Keffnon's blood slippery shoulder and rolling him off her. The body lay on its back, shoulders over the edge and head right back, wound gaping. The guards pulled him off the bed, dropping him in a heap in the corner.

"Throw those clothes over," ordered one. The other picked the pile of Keffnon's clothes off the chair and tossed them to him. He covered Keffnon's body as best he could.

Grendal was literally covered in blood from head to waist. Her father went to wrap the woollen bed cover around her but realised everything on the bed was soaked through. He stood her up, an arm around her as she sobbed, still babbling hysterically.

"There." He pointed at the door curtain. The first guard understood immediately and tore it down, passing it to the Innkeeper. He flung it around his daughter's shoulders and led her out and round to the side door of the Inn, through the crowd of inquisitive neighbours that was rapidly gathering.

The two soldiers remained outside Grendal's door, both uniforms splashed with blood. After a brief conversation one turned to leave for the Castle when three other Guards, these on duty, came around the corner having been summoned from the square.

The Castle Guard were responsible for civic order throughout the Realm, with the help of locally stationed troops in outlying areas. The investigation, which never reached a conclusion, was about to begin.

The news spread like wildfire. There was occasionally petty crime, but a murder this close to the Castle was very rare indeed. Rumour, as always, grew and inflated the story, which was horrific enough anyway. Rebgroth learned the real story of course, and told Serculas, so Eilana heard it pretty exactly, particularly the victim's name and the killer's words.

Her heart and mind raced together as she listened to the story, and she desperately tried to look composed. "How awful," she heard herself say, and hoped the flutter in her voice would be put down to the shock of such a terrible event.

She could hardly wait the half watch until she could get away from the nursery. Leaving Harlada with Serculas, she hurried to the stables. She could see Harlmon through the large open barn doors at the front of them, but she had to do this subtlely.

She walked by slowly. Harlmon saw her, put down his pitchfork and walked to the doorway, only to see Eilana disappearing around the side of the stables, towards their parents' house, but he noticed her left hand gesture fleetingly at him as she went. He went back into the stables to make an excuse to leave for a moment, but the Stable Master was nowhere to be seen.

He stepped out of the rear door to find Eilana standing there. She took his hand without greeting him and led him into the back barn and up the stairs, the same hayloft where she had lain with Keffnon.

"What in Wey's name have you done Harlmon? It must have been you." Her voice was a fierce accusing whisper. He knew exactly what she was talking about and didn't try to hide it.

"I did it for you pretty one. I told you I wouldn't let anyone hurt you." They were still holding hands. He clasped her hand in both of his. "He deserved it for what he did to you." To him it was a statement of fact.

"You're a bloody bloody fool. Who knows you were away yesterday?"

"It was my day off, I went fishing as usual as far as anyone knows, really, it's alright."

"You were doubly stupid to say anything; you said it was for your sister!"

"But they have no connection between you and Keffnon, no one knows except me. I would have killed her too but she didn't see me."

Eilana looked at him in horror. Had she just heard him say that?

"A good investigator might try to find out if anyone had a baby nine moons after their last visit here, and if she has a brother, the only hope is they would dismiss the thought on the grounds that no-one except my brother would be stupid enough to kill him on his own ground."

She flung herself around and walked to the top of the ladder, staring down. He was under threat of his life, not her, he would never implicate her in the killing if he was caught, but it would probably mean she would lose her position in court. She suddenly realised how important that was to her. She suddenly realised that subconsciously she had been planning a future at court for herself, and Wey forgive her the thought, here was a man that would kill for her. She frightened herself with the fact she could even think it, but she had.

"I talk to Serculas often about very personal things, my friend and senior Nanny. Little Harlada was born three quarter moons early. I will confess to her that you are his father. I will tell her how a stupid adolescent game went wrong, making me pregnant. I can date it as a moon before the Weypriests were here, that would make Harlada a quarter moon late. I can talk about a difficult birth with a large baby. She will tell Rebgroth it couldn't possibly involve me if it is ever suggested. Do you understand me?" He nodded, almost sheepishly.

"Yes, I'm sorry…… but I would do it again." Then he added, "It was very easy."

"I know you would." She stroked his cheek. "And you never know, I might want you to, but you never do anything like it ever again without my say so. Do you understand that?"

"Yes, pretty one."

"Don't call me that you dumb oaf, now get back to work before you're missed." She kissed his cheek and climbed down the ladder. Wey, if my brother's that crazy, am I too?

Chapter 9

By the end of the autumn the investigation of Keffnon's murder had petered out. According to the members of his troupe, he seemed to have so many potential enemies, so many potentially aggrieved brothers, that someone could well have had the motivation to travel far to commit this crime.

Beneath it was a belief that no-one from Castlebury could possibly have done such a thing, and anyone from the Castle itself was obviously beyond suspicion. This after all was the just death of an itinerant performer.

Eilana told Serculas her story though, just in case, one autumn night as they talked in the nursery by the fire, the little ones all asleep. The conversation had got back to children. Eilana asked her if she looked forward to having some herself. Serculas had laughed. Of course Eilana knew all about Rebgroth, so she joked about how awkward it might be to explain at the moment, but then said how lucky Eilana was to have Harlada, and asked did she regret not being with the father.

Eilana surprised herself by what a good liar she was. Tears came naturally as she played the part, in fact it was heart rending. Serculas cuddled her, touched that she had told her and swearing secrecy. Eilana was sure now that their friendship was strong enough that she would break that promise to protect her. A job well done.

The winter dragged by as always. The long nights meant people generally went to bed earlier, rising with the dawn after a good sleep, but it was a time when things were quiet, boring to the gregarious.

The King and Queen continued to grow further apart. He would go to her room at night two or three times a quarter moon as had been his habit before

Gudrick's birth, and still Bertal did not resist him, but in no way encouraged him.

Gudmon was hurt. He was not angry, but when he touched the Queen she flinched, tightening her body in obvious dislike, and in obvious passive submission. It hurt him, so that often his ardour died, he felt he was forcing himself on someone who disliked him but was suffering her lot. Only when his desire had grown to bursting did he force himself upon her. What was worse was that she just lay there and took it.

After a time he found he was just visiting her every two or three quarter moons, much to her relief. He wondered if she was having an affair with someone in his court. There was no doubt that she flirted outrageously with all the young officers of the guard at formal functions, to annoy him he was sure, but he had had her watched every moment of the day, and she seemed innocent of any such suspicion.

He found it was almost worse that she wasn't, at least she would have been enjoying love making with someone. It should have made it better, but to be married to a woman that had just gone off it seemed a life sentence.

The drudgery of his marriage moved steadily on, and he lost weight steadily too, needing clothes altered moon by moon.

Most Kings would have just wenched around, demanding sex from any woman that took his eye. Who could refuse him, and many would welcome the chance of catching his fancy in the longer term, but this was just not his way. All he wanted was a secure and loving marriage, a wife who he could live out his years with happily.

His mind would drift back to his fifteen Bornbless day, his Sire's Day, the day before Moreton's. His father King Gudrick had arranged a court celebration for him, as all would have expected, but he had insisted on Moreton's celebration being combined, they were almost like twin brothers after all.

The King gave a speech early in the evening, before too much ale and fruit wine meant no-one would listen or be interested, praising his son and including Moreton in his words. The speech ended with the normal conclusion of a Royal Sire's Day. Gudmon was formally recognised as Prince Gudmon, heir apparent, and in recognition was granted a body-servant, duly trained in the needs of a Royal Master.

Greardel was called forward, applauded by the court, and officially appointed with full ceremony. He glared at Moreton throughout, hardly able to disguise the contempt he felt for the whole proceedings, and the jealous hate he felt for him, which inevitably spilled over onto the Prince. His father too had died to make this possible, yet Moreton stood beside the Prince, whilst he now served him.

The celebration progressed from evening to night. It was the first day that Gudmon and Moreton could legally drink ale or wine, and as the evening wore on they steadily became the worse for wear, to the point where the next day there were long gaps in their memory of the night.

One memory had stayed in Gudmon's mind ever since, however. It was a memory of one of the few moments of affection he had of his father, one of the few moments when they had communicated as men, together.

He was with Moreton as always, filling their goblets with ale in the Great Hall annex, the wine came later. They were enjoying a few moments out of the public eye. The King strode towards them, the worse for wine himself. He threw an arm around each of the boys, slopping wine over Gudmon's fine tunic.

"Well my boys, you're men now, from now on you enter the realms of those fearsome creatures, women." He laughed loudly, "As long as you know them lads, you'll never understand them! Tell me, both of you, have you tasted the forbidden fruit yet?"

The two young men looked at each other, enough ale inside them not to be as embarrassed as they would have been.

"We have Sire," replied Gudmon, "but only with the daughters of very fine gentlemen."

"Well I don't want any very fine bastards in my Castle, you hear? Life gets too complicated with Royal bastards. Let me tell you, don't use a woman to pleasure yourself into."

Gudmon and Moreton looked at each other in disbelief.

"I'm sorry, Sire, I'm not with you exactly." It was Moreton this time.

"What I mean is, if all you want to do is get rid of a little seed, do it yourself, just relieve the need in a quiet moment, don't complicate life by doing it into girls you probably won't see or speak to again. They have a habit of coming back and biting you. Only do it with girls you care for."

"Have you always thought that Father?"

"Not when I was young I didn't, had to learn the hard way. The real enjoyment of love making is pleasing a partner, in fact, if you just do it with a woman your attitude is all wrong; make love to them, that's where real pleasure lies. That's what I mean lads, do it with yourself, make love to a woman." He laughed at his own drunken ramblings. "But don't tell your mother I said that, she'll think she's safe."

"But surely that can only work when you're young?" questioned Gudmon, "What if you felt like it and mother was away, surely you don't...."

"Of course I do boy, so does every man, or he's a liar. I may have lived thirty-eight years, but in my head I am still in my teens, I still feel just the same, it doesn't change boys, remember that."

He turned and walked away, a little erratically. The two young men looked at each other and laughed. They were both quite touched, and intrigued by the King's philosophy and admissions of his basic humanity.

With this in his mind, the King eventually bowed to the inevitable, and waking one morning greatly aroused, he relieved his tension. He still felt it a little unkingly, but he settled into a rhythm of two or three times a quarter moon, whether with the Queen or himself, and although he would not admit it even to himself, with the Queen behaving as she was, it was better by himself.

He resented the fact that it was that way though, that he had been forced into that position, and the rift between them grew.

The Queen endured her life. She knew that any sort of separation was impossible, and she would never risk losing touch with her children. Wey forbid, the only reason she let the King near her was her memory of the history told of Queens being murdered to relieve their husbands of such problems. She couldn't imagine Gudmon would contemplate such a thing, but she didn't feel that confident, he was changing, becoming more aggressive by the day.

She had no real friends, and Allaner and Reassel became more important to her, companions more than Ladies in Waiting, and their status grew within the Court accordingly.

Eilana had decided to try and understand the workings of the Government of Nisceriel, who did what and how it all worked. She gathered information slowly, and she had a natural ability to understand the politics of the court, but government of the people, taxation and the like, were things she had never thought about.

She had not embarked on a particular scheme or plan for the future; she was just reacting to instinctive desires to gather knowledge of the ways of the court. It was of course an unconscious ambition that drove her, but it manifested itself in her looking at every level of administration and realising that she could do it, there was nothing difficult about it.

Nisceriel was governed by a system set up generations before that had worked well for a number of reasons, but mainly that it was simple and it gave strength to the whole.

The Chancellor was responsible for taxation and public order. He had five deputies, Ministers of the Crown. Each of these was responsible for an area of the country called a Counting, having just been increased from four to five some years before, after Moreton had reviewed the situation at that time. The steady if slow increase in population had made it necessary.

Each Counting was divided into three Hunders, each of which was ruled by a Hundert, appointed by the Crown. These men ruled within the laws of the land, but over the years, corruption and nepotism had almost led to a ruling elite becoming self perpetuating, as there was great wealth to be made if one was to take advantage of the position.

Moreton had weeded out some corrupt Hunderts from the twelve there had been, increasing the number to fifteen and appointing capable and at least for the moment, honest men to the positions. The eight that survived the cull had seen the fall of their colleagues who they knew had abused the system. Some were thankful suspicion hadn't fallen on them, others were pleased to see their honesty recognised, but all realised the realm, now largely under Moreton's control, would not tolerate anything but the highest standards.

It was the duty of each Hunder to be able to call up one hundred trained fighting men as required. This meant that each one was allocated two full time infantry Sergeants for training the local male population in arms.

At any one time, ten local men would be under training, living in the Hunderhouse, the local administrative centre. Whilst training they were also responsible for upholding the law under direction from the Hundert, and most importantly, the collection of taxes.

The taxes were not heavy, but they were enough to fund the administration, the Sergeants, maintain weapons for one hundred fighting infantry, and compensation for the ten trainees at any time for not being able to work their farms or do their jobs, with twenty percent also going to the Crown.

The hundred infantry men must have at least twenty trained archers, and tended to be about three quarters of the male population past their Sire's Day at fifteen. Each Hunder tended to contain a population of around three hundred adults and about five hundred children. Each Counting therefore had a total population of around two thousand four hundred.

The Castle Nisceriel had a resident garrison of two hundred Royal Guards, all trained Cavalry, which was very rare in those times. The cost of horses was prohibitive to all but the richest kingdoms, to which Nisceriel belonged. The Castle also housed some four hundred adults and children, being effectively a walled village itself.

The Kingdom had a total population of almost thirteen thousand, a population that was not rich but saw little real poverty. They were well protected in that they could field a trained army of fifteen hundred infantry, including almost three hundred archers, and two hundred cavalry, a very formidable army for its day, and well led.

The system was simple but very effective, but more to the point, thanks to Moreton it was running smoothly and legally. The people of each Hunder felt they were a useful and contributory part of the whole.

Understanding it now, Eilana realised what an excellent form of government it was, and could not help but admire the old Kings that had built it.

It was while she was sitting in the nursery one late winter evening thinking about it, and also contemplating Prince Gudrick's and Harlada's first bornbless days, which were rapidly approaching, that Reassel came in with a message from the Queen. Eilana offered her a drink and they sat talking for more than a quarter watch.

Eilana was keen to make a friend of someone so close to the Queen. This was again an instinctive move, not consciously planned, but one that felt right. She thanked Reassel for her company as she left and invited her to join her whenever she liked.

Reassel became a regular visitor throughout the spring, although she never stayed if Serculas was around, but as the summer drew closer, Eilana felt she had made an important friend.

The summer was one of the best for many years and spirits around the Castle Nisceriel were mainly high. The King was generally surly and bad tempered, the Queen withdrawn and insular, but everyone else was lifted by the sun and the warmth that set in for over two moons.

Life in the nursery was busy and time consuming. Prince Gudrick and Harlada were well into their second year; their first bornbless days being celebrated boisterously by the adults in their lives whilst passing them by. They were both crawling and needed constant attention to keep them from the day-to-day hazards of Castle life. Harlada could stand, pulling himself upright on a chair or table leg. Gudrick didn't seem to be bothered to try; he got around as he wished, following Harlada's every move. They were becoming inseparable even then.

Patrikal was a lively six and taking more and more entertaining to keep her active mind occupied. Moreton still took some of the load, mainly telling her stories of Kings and Queens of the past, of battles between countries and romances between Princes and Princesses.

Eilana often listened to his tales too. She quickly realised that Moreton was teaching Patrikal a great deal of history without making a fuss about it, but most interestingly, conditioning her mind, influencing her thinking in a very subtle way. Moreton was a very clever man. He could be a valuable friend or a challenging, dangerous enemy.

She had turned sixteen half a moon after the boys' bornbless party, but the day passed quietly. She had not told anyone in advance, only telling Serculas that evening. Serculas was devastated she hadn't known, and hadn't been able to give her a bornbless gift, but Eilana laughed it off, her friendship was the only gift she wanted. It almost sounded convincing to herself!

Reassel visited the next evening and Eilana dropped it into the conversation then. Reassel laughed loudly and hugged her.

"It was mine ten days ago," she confessed, "but I didn't tell anyone either. I don't think the Queen is in the mood for parties. Are you free tomorrow evening?" Eilana thought for a moment.

"Yes, Serculas was off last night and tonight, so I will be tomorrow. Harlada sleeps with the Prince now so I don't have to look after him."

"Great, so am I. You must come to my room after supper and I will get a jug of wine, we can celebrate together. You know how to get there?"

"That would be lovely, yes, your room is the same as Serculas' above the Queen's room isn't it?"

"That's right, just go down the stairs from yours, a door along and back up, you can't miss me."

"I'll look forward to it, thank you." She hugged her again and they kissed cheeks. Reassel left, twiddling her fingers in a little wave as she stepped through the door.

The next evening, just after supper, Reassel descended the main stairs into the cellars to fetch some wine. In her position she could collect what she wished at any time. As she approached the door in the torchlight, it swung open in front of her and Greardel stopped in the doorway. For once he actually grunted an apology and stepped back to let her in. She thanked him as she walked through and he stepped out behind her letting the door swing shut.

Apart from his apology she felt there was something odd about him, but it wasn't until she was leaving herself and reached the door with a jug of fruit wine, holding its weight in one hand as she opened the door with the other, that she realised what it was. He had not been carrying any wine himself and it was an odd time to be there if not collecting wine for some event or other, but it was none of her business. She had her mind on that evening.

She arrived back in her room a short while later, panting slightly after the long climb up the spiral staircase. She had been back only moments and was just lighting her lantern in the gently fading daylight when Eilana knocked at the door. Her heart and stomach fluttered as she let her in.

Eilana looked around at the room. It was identical to Serculas' in shape, although the furniture was laid out differently. Her knothole would have been useless here she mused; the bed was against the other wall.

They sat in front of the fireplace, but no fire was lit in mid-summer. Reassel poured some wine and they wished each other good health and happiness.

The conversation covered many things, but eventually moved on to more personal areas they had never discussed. Eilana told Reassel of her childhood as an ostler's daughter, and Reassel told of her upbringing in the house of a wealthy landowner, a Hundert of some renown and close to the court; hence her position of Lady in Waiting.

Reassel asked of Harlada's father, if Eilana missed having men around her. Very aware of the rumours regarding the blonde seamstress, Eilana told of her closeness to her brother, of always having male company, of a childhood mistake that lead to Harlada's birth, but not the full story she had told Serculas. On a mischievous whim however, she added that she had found men such clumsy lovers in her experience, having claimed it much wider than it was, then asked Reassel of her experience with men.

Reassel looked at her for a moment, probably assessing whether Eilana knew about her preferences.

"I have had my share of men," she replied, "and I find them unsubtle and selfish lovers. Perhaps one day I will find a man who can please me and understand a woman's body, until then…well, I will do without them."

Eilana could feel a tension in the room. Reassel nearly let her secret go, but was obviously still not sure what reaction she would get from her. Eilana, for her part, had decided she would keep Reassel on a string for a while.

She had been there a quarter watch, the wine was drunk and she made her excuses to go. They kissed cheeks affectionately as she left, fascinated by the evening. She was sure that if she had expressed the slightest interest in women Reassel would have made a play for her. This could be very useful in the future; she must consider it further.

Greardel had had a quiet start to the evening. The King was dozing, sleeping off the effects of too much ale consumed whilst playing cards that afternoon with his three hunting friends, each a Hundert of nearby Hunders. He called them his friends but really they just pandered to him in the hope of further advancement, and basked in the prestige of being in the company of the King.

They had left before supper and the King laid back on the couch in his study. He was asleep in moments, snoring gently but persistently.

Greardel left for the wine cellars. He had business to discuss with a young assistant vintner he had caught trying to sell Castle wines to local tradesmen. He hadn't reported it, just made it clear that he would expect favours when he required them. He was going to call one in now.

He collected a cloth bag from his room on the way. It was the size of his pillow and contained bumbleberries, stolen over a few days from the kitchen store, a handful at a time. Moreton had ordered that under no circumstances should wine ever be made from bumbleberries and Greardel had to know why; any fruit that tasted that good had to make excellent wine.

He suspected that there was not enough for general wine use so a small amount was being secretly made for the King, Moreton and their cronies, and he should be able to enjoy the best too. By the time he reached the cellars he had worked himself into foul envious temper, a fairly common state for him these days. He sought out the young vintner, Fenlon, whose duty it was that evening.

"Right young man, I have a task for you," he said as he dumped the bag of Bumbleberries on the wooden sideboard of the cellar office. "Did you find out if any wine was being made that is not for general use?"

"No Sir, I mean yes Sir, I did and there isn't." Fenlon was simply scared of Greardel and not very bright. "I've searched everywhere, and no-one speaks of any."

"Good, you had better be right. Now you are going to make some, there is only a little fruit and you will have to press it yourself. Is that a problem?"

Fenlon opened the bag, peered in then felt its weight.

"There may just be enough for a couple of bottles," he judged, "It would be much better if you could get some juice, save time too."

"Listen my young friend, there is no juice I can get my hands on. Do you know what they are?" Greardel looked at him menacingly.

"No Sir. I have never seen its like."

"Well I'll tell you then, they're bumbleberries, and you are going to make as much wine as you can from them. Two bottles will be fine."

"But Sir," Fenlon protested, "the Royal decree, I will get into terrible trouble if…."

"You will be in far worse trouble if you don't my boy, and that is a certainty. Now how long will it take to do properly, and I don't want a snivelling lecture on wine-making, how long?"

Fenlon was on the point of tears. "This time next year at the earliest Sir; and better the year after that; these Berries are not fresh, they may not make good wine."

"They are fresh, the bushes carry berries all the year round, they are quite extraordinary. Now do your job, keep it well hidden and totally secret, or you will suffer considerably for it, do you understand me?"

"Yes Sir." Fenlon looked like a condemned man.

"Good, you will be well rewarded when it is done." With that Greardel turned his back and walked quickly from the room. Fenlon picked up the bag and dropped it in fright as he heard the door open again.

His heart was thumping when he realised it was Reassel, and he grinned at her in welcome in an effort to look relaxed. This was going to be a long two years.

Chapter 10

Autumn and winter raced by. The toddlers turned to boys, walking, talking and beginning to get into everything, and now totally inseparable. They shared a bed, eating and playing together all day; a total handful and typical terrible twos.

Patrikal turned seven at the start of the spring, and her education started properly. Every day she attended classes with three other children of Castle based nobles, all seven that year, but when she was in the nursery, she helped with the boys and enjoyed it.

The King had lost all his excess weight. He didn't eat much and drank heavily, to excess most nights. Moreton had tried to slow his drinking down, but had failed in the main. The King was just terribly unhappy, a man who had everything he could want except the affection he craved. He only visited the Queen's bedroom every three or four quarter moons, usually drunk.

Bertal dreaded his visits. She had grown to hate him, the love she had once felt had soured, turning his habits that she had once found endearing, into objects of disdain. When he entered the bed she tensed and let him do as he would, which infuriated him. Sometimes his anger overcame his lust and he left, other times it fuelled it and he took her roughly. Unfortunately for her, his consumption of alcohol tended to prolong the ordeal, raising his passion but delaying his satisfaction.

Eventually in late spring he became so angry in his drunken state, that when she tensed herself as he was about to enter her, he pushed himself back onto his knees, kneeling between her thighs. She opened her eyes and looked up at him. He looked vaguely ridiculous, his erection thrusting upwards from his open codpiece, his scrotum wrinkled as it hung entangled in laces.

She half laughed at the grotesqueness of it all, until he slapped her hard with his right hand, and as he backhanded her on the return swing his fingers bent into a fist, striking her a glancing blow with knuckles rigid.

"You bastard!" she screamed at him, but he punched her hard on the cheek, splitting the skin across the bone. She sat up suddenly in a fury as his hand swung back again, her hands clawing for his crotch. His punch swung behind her head which she flung forward in avoiding the blow, only to catch him squarely in the mouth with her forehead, totally unintentionally, as her fingers caught and squeezed his genitalia with all her strength. Stifling a cry of agony, his forearm crashed into the side of her head, knocking her senseless from the bed, her hands tearing free.

He swore and stood over her prone and bleeding body.

"You damned bitch," he swore again and stamped on her stomach. She arched sideways clutching herself and sobbing hysterically. "I am your King and your husband, you can hate me as you do, but never laugh at me bitch." One hand held his aching scrotum.

There was so much she wanted to shout back, her hate, her anger, but she was afraid. Whatever had happened in the past, he had never hit her. She cried, shaking on the floor as the door opened. Allaner had heard the row and the blows. It might cost her place as a Queen's Lady but she could not ignore what she heard. She knocked and opened the door.

"Did you call Ma'am?" It was all she could think to say. The King spun round to face her.

"Get out woman!" he shouted. She could not help but see his now drooping erection hanging over the hand that held his throbbing balls.

"Sire," she curtseyed, and stepped quickly back through the door, but she had done enough. The King stumbled from the room, slamming the connecting doors, and Allaner ran back in to help the Queen, who had been hidden from her behind the bed.

"Oh Your Majesty," she exclaimed, as she bent to help her sit up. Bertal straightened herself very slowly, her stomach wanting to stay curled where he had stamped on her.

"That man will never do that to me again," she said as she crawled to sit on the edge of the bed. Allaner held her handkerchief to Bertal's cheek.

"He is the King Ma'am." It summed up Bertal's predicament perfectly.

"Wey, I hate him," Bertal continued. "You are right though, but one day he will regret doing that, one day when he needs me, I'll remind him of this night."

In his room the King too sat on the edge of his bed, as best he could. He hurt worse now, and had that sick feeling in the pit of his stomach.

"Bitch!" he murmured under his breath, but he felt ashamed of what he had just done. Allaner staring at him in shocked disgust had sobered him instantly. Wey, what had he become, a drunk, a wife beater, why didn't she love him any more?

He did something he hadn't done for years. It started with a wave of emotion that built in his chest, his shoulders hunching once, then again, then repeatedly, rhythmically, as the weight in his chest burst forth in deep sobs. He cried his heart out.

A quarter later he lay on the bed. His mind was dazed, numb. He had cried himself back to reality, for a time at least. He realised how fundamentally unhappy he was. He was drained, emotionally exhausted. He begged for sleep, but it was a long time before it came, whilst his mind seemed switched off. He lay conscious just of being, but without a rational thought in his head, his mind an actual blank.

When he woke the next morning he felt drained, his chest aching from the wrenching sobs of the night before. He walked across his room and into the anteroom where Greardel sat awaiting his call. As he moved towards the hall Greardel jumped up and took his elbow, steering him back into his room.

The King would normally have snapped at him for touching him uninvited, but he didn't.

"Sire, you are not dressed for breakfast." Gudmon looked down, following Greardel's eyes; a year before he could not have seen around his stomach, but now he saw his genitals, in all their wrinkled splendour, still hanging from his open codpiece.

"You're right Greardel," he smiled, "I am not. Perhaps we had better go and get me washed and changed. I have some thinking to do."

Despite his efforts, life seemed to do everything it could to be difficult. The more he tried to relax, the more things went wrong; silly things that he would have laughed off before, until even his favourite pastimes became an effort and failed to amuse him anymore.

The Queen ignored him totally, in fact she only ignored him when she had no choice but to be in the same room as him, otherwise she would leave any room she was in that he entered. Her affection for him, for it had never really been love, had turned to a bitter resentful hate.

He became withdrawn and sat in his room alone for most of the day, letting matters of state pass him by, to the point when the King's Council effectively ruled the country without his participation.

The Council was made up of eight Lords appointed by the King. Two were powerful men. Lord Gratax, General of the King's Royal Guard, was one. His position put him at the head of Nisceriel's army, a job at which he was extremely good. The Chancellor, Lord Bradett, was the other. He ran the administration of the country and most importantly, the Treasury.

The six other Councillors were the five Ministers of the Countings and Guard Officer Rebgroth, second in command to Gratax.

It had been originally set up by Gudmon's grandfather as a formal advisory body to the King's absolute rule. He had inherited a system based on cronies rather than wise heads, and corruption mingled with the politics of the King's ear. The Council had stopped all that and had done its job well ever since, but it had never been intended to exist in its own right as it now effectively did. There was no hierarchy within it, and no laid down procedures. If Gratax and Bradett agreed, it happened, and so far they had not yet disagreed, though it was only a matter of time.

Moreton set about rehabilitating the King. He had seen such depression in others before and knew that healing was a matter of time and encouragement. Patrikal was in fact the key. He involved the King in her education, often leaving the King to teach his daughter bits of history, or to tell her the ancient tales and legends from prehistory.

Over the course of the summer the King slowly returned to his old self, Patrikal making him realise there was a future for him and all his people. He did not make peace with the Queen, and never even visited her room. He had never felt the desire to either, so had never tried.

His desires generally, however, returned. He rediscovered personal gratification as his desire for women grew; one which he did not satisfy but one that grew steadily and would one day burst out.

In early autumn, Moreton came to the nursery to collect Patrikal. The King was presiding over the Council for the first time for many moons, and Moreton had promised her that he would take her to the gallery to see her father at work, now that he was better.

Eilana was just handing over to Serculas as Moreton entered.

"Good morning ladies." He greeted them with a half bow and a flourish of his hand that amused Patrikal. "Are you ready my girl? We must not be late. If we are not in the gallery before the King arrives we may not enter."

"I am ready," Eilana heard her reply, and before she could stop herself she asked,

"Do you think I could come with you?"

Moreton looked round at her slowly. He seemed to look into her, through her eyes.

"So it begins," he said, almost beneath his breath, "You are welcome Nanny Eilana, I didn't know you had any interest in matters of state."

"I don't think I have really, I am just curious." He nodded gently.

"Yes, of course, come quickly, both of you then, we cannot be late," and he hurried them through the door.

They went down the main staircase to the hall and into the Great Hall anteroom, where a small single door with a rounded top opened onto a small spiral staircase, which led up to the minstrels' gallery. On each side of the hall a narrow banistered gallery ran along its length to a second tiered gallery, that stepped up with padded benches.

They walked the length of the hall and sat on the front bench of the empty gallery. Below and in front of them, a large rectangular table of heavy oak was surrounded by heavy brocade padded chairs with carved arms and ornate legs. There was one set at the head, which was larger than the others, and four down each side.

Almost before they had settled the door underneath the gallery opened and eight men of varying ages entered the chamber. They were all finely dressed in colourful embroidered tunics and tight woollen leggings, as was the fashion amongst those who could afford it.

Lord Gratax was armed with his ceremonial sword, a light but formidable weapon, excellent at close quarters in confined spaces. On the field of battle however, he preferred his two handed broadsword, which he was more that adept at handling. None of the others was armed except Rebgroth, and he only with the cavalry sabre carried by all the Royal Guard when on duty.

Chancellor Bradett wore a wide light blue sash over his tunic that ran diagonally across his chest and around his back. On his right shoulder, pinned to the sash, was a large gold brooch in the shape of a handled basket, signifying his role as provider to the country. Each of the Ministers sported light blue sashes, but much narrower.

They talked loudly and almost theatrically as they entered the hall, making polite conversation, but without the genuine warmth of friends. Eilana sensed this immediately, and was intrigued by the way they casually took places at the table.

Gratax moved directly to the chair to the right of the head. She expected Rebgroth to sit next to him, but he moved to a couple of chairs down on the opposite side. On this side sat Bradett, but he placed himself four chairs down, and he pulled his chair sideways as he sat, almost facing the end of the table, as near as possible without actually moving across the opposite end.

The Ministers spread around, filling the gaps so four chairs were filled either side of the head. Eilana wondered if the sides the Ministers sat determined their affiliations or not. Her instinct told her not; that would be too simplistic. She was right of course. Rebgroth deliberately placed himself to break up Bradett's side of the table, clearly placing the militaries' influence on both sides, but the Ministers sat at random, all too experienced to be so obvious.

The door opened again and the King entered the room. All of the Council stood, most immediately, Bradett noticeably slower, but not impertinently so.

The King sat at the head of the table, and as he did so he spoke.

"Please sit Gentlemen." He looked steadily around the table as they took their seats. "I wish to thank you all for taking care of state affairs whilst I have been indisposed. Wey decided I needed time to ponder on some issues, and this I have done. I promise you gentlemen, I am now stronger of purpose than I have ever been, and I know you will be the stronger as a team for carrying on without me. Together now we will rule the finest Kingdom known to man, or Elf come to that. Can I count on you all?"

A general hubbub of approval resounded, with them all clapping and shouting support. Eilana was trying to measure how much was genuine.

"Thank you my Lords," said the King, having allowed a perfectly timed reaction from the Council, just before the noise died away. "So, to the first business of the day. My Lord Gratax, what of matters Military?"

Eilana sat and watched enthralled. After a while Patrikal climbed onto her knee, starting to become bored, but calmed by Eilana's cuddles and shushes as she listened.

The politics of the Council was so obvious to her that she did not realise it came from a gift she had for understanding such things. The conflicts between the Military and the Civil factors were all down to the financial constraints and how the wealth available was distributed. The Civil needs were all immediate, the Military all 'what if's'.

After a quarter Moreton quietly gathered Patrikal into his arms from Eilana's lap, where she had fallen asleep, and carried her silently along the balcony and out of the hall, leaving Eilana to listen on. She had made to rise but he had pressed a hand down on her shoulder; a clear signal to stay. She could not come to terms with him in her mind. She kept feeling he was a threat to her well being in the long term, but he was so supportive of her at the moment. It troubled her.

She stayed for another half watch, until the Council broke up. Business done, the King formally closed the session and as they rose from their seats, Gratax pulled the bell cord beside the door. Almost straight away, servants entered carrying food and jugs of wine, goblets and plates, and spread them over the table.

As Eilana stood and walked along the balcony, she felt eyes watching her. None had been aware of her until then. Those who knew her were curious on seeing her as to why she was there, those who didn't for other reasons, but she didn't look back.

Moreton was with Serculas in the nursery when she got there, just ordering lunch for them all. He smiled at her as she entered, increasing the order.

"Did you enjoy your morning Nanny?" he enquired. He sounded formal to others but Eilana detected a genuine question.

"Very much so," she replied. "I was interested how um, opinions were divided around the table. It didn't always seem to follow the logic of the debate."

"Ha, you see through their words my dear. I can see you are a clever young lady, perhaps one day we should spend some time talking of such things, but first, I am afraid, I now know I must leave Nisceriel for a while, so I need you both to promise to look after these little ones whilst I am away, I know you will." He held out an arm to include Serculas in his meaning. They both nodded, promising to do so and protesting at his words.

"I go to the King now to tell him. Stay faithful to him. Much will happen while I am away, to you both. Your futures are both clear and clouded to me, but you both have important parts to play in both the King's and the Country's future, for better or worse, but protect the young ones, it is for them I sense the most danger."

Eilana realised he was staring at her. He seemed to realise it also and looked away, moving to Patrikal and hugging her, her eyes brimming with tears as she realised he was leaving them.

He hugged the boys also, both of them, before striding to the door and closing it behind him. It was seven years before they saw him again.

That night Eilana tucked the boys into their bed, Patrikal's old bed in the far corner of the nursery, pulling the curtain around them. At seven Patrikal graduated to her own room in the children's quarters along from the nursery, which she took to happily.

Nothing had been formally announced to her knowledge, but the servants now took orders from her as they did from any senior member of the Royal household. She was certainly looked on as an equal to Serculas, although she ostensibly bowed to her in public. Their friendship had cemented further, they had almost become like sisters, in fact more so really as they both worked at being so.

Her friendship with Reassel had grown too, but behind it was a clear feeling within her that Reassel's interest was more than platonic, which indeed it was. Reassel had fallen madly in love with Eilana over a year before. She remained in a relationship with her seamstress, more for sexual gratification than anything else, and a sense of stability, but Eilana was her love, and unrequited love was painful to carry.

Throughout the royal Household Eilana was treated now as an equal, and the servants therefore treated her as such. So as the autumn turned to winter Eilana grew into a habit that would change her life in two very significant ways over the next few years.

Each evening she was on duty, when the boys were asleep, she would order a bath be filled in front of the fire. It was the one luxury of Royal Household life that stood before all others, coming from her sheltered background, and as she lay back in the warm water, she thought back to her early life. She was only seventeen, eighteen in a few moons, but she had risen in the world at a heady pace; firstly by pure luck, but after that by instinct and a political guile she was only just beginning to recognise she had.

She thought of her family. She visited them as often as she could, but not really often enough she knew, and her parents were always so pleased to see her and talk of Royalty. She saw more of Harlmon than her parents though, choosing to seek him out in the stables when she could, without her father knowing. They would talk of their childhood together and their lives since, and sometimes, as she lay in her bath, she would think of those nights in their bedroom, of watching him, and of opening her eyes and seeing him there. At those times she would shut her eyes and imagine him looking down at her, a tingling would touch her stomach, butterflies would awake within her, her hands would drift across her body, soaping, stroking; her breasts, her stomach, and then the heart of her desire; yet when her fingers had done their work, when the waves of pleasure eventually pulsed through her, and she would open her eyes, he was never there.

Winter was ending, the spring just starting to show itself again. The boys had turned three and Patrikal was almost eight, and looking forward to her Bornbless Day party.

The atmosphere in the Castle Keep had changed since Moreton's sudden departure. It had somehow lost some of its balance; life was not as calm as it had been.

The King, back in good health, almost looking slim again, was full of energy he had not felt for years. He was eating heartily but not regaining the weight he had lost. In fact everybody in the Keep was in very good health. Patrikal said it was the bumbleberry juice they all drank with breakfast, and often throughout the day, that kept colds away and made everybody feel so fit. They all smiled at her child talk and nodded, but of course she was right.

The Queen had almost a separate household within the Royal apartments, meeting the King on formal occasions only, when she had to, but otherwise living a life on her own. Her only contact with the world outside was through Allaner, who had grown particularly close to her, and Reassel, a close confidant too, although at a little more distance.

Eilana carried on her duties as thoroughly as always, and three or four nights a quarter moon, enjoyed her bath by the fire. It had become quite a joke with the servants, the footmen in particular, who joked about the cleanest lady in the Castle, but a little more crudely. Eilana heard of it from one of the housemaids who was cleaning the nursery one morning, and was genuinely amused, but it had become her quiet time when she could think, put things into place in her mind.

She continued to visit the Council sessions on many occasions, to the surprise of the Councillors who found much of it tedious. The King had resumed total control, and they had become merely advisors again. It was far less stimulating than when they had actually ruled for that now, seemingly short, summer. There were no rules about who could be present, and she was tucked away from sight so that they were often not sure if she was there or not, but basically, if the King was not concerned about her, neither were they.

She absorbed huge amounts of information and learnt of aspects of running the Country she had never thought about. The Treasury and finance matters were a vast ocean of detail which she struggled to stay with for quite a while, but it clicked into place eventually. It was the general logistics of food production, transport within the Kingdom and suchlike that she had never considered before.

In her bath was where it all came together as she luxuriated in its warmth.

It was one such evening that Reassel put her head around the door as the usual posse of footmen were filling her bath. She had a jug of wine and two goblets in her hands.

"Oh I'm sorry," she said, "I thought you might like to share a glass or two with me, but I didn't realise you were about to have a bath." Be damned you didn't thought Eilana, but something told her now was the time to call her bluff, if bluff it was. She had no idea how she would react if it wasn't.

"No, no, come in, it's just what I need. The lads have been a nightmare today; I've only just got them to sleep and could just do with a glass." It was partly true but mainly politeness. "How has your day been?"

Reassel told her as they sipped wine, seated beside the table whilst the bath was filled. Eilana poured another goblet each as the last footman left the room, and took a sizable gulp.

"I had better leave you to your bath," Reassel smiled, rising from her chair and reaching for her goblet. "I'll pop back later perhaps?"

"No stay, we're friends. You can scrub my back!" You're pushing this she thought.

"If you're sure," she smiled, sitting back down before any answer.

"Of course, make yourself useful and grab a towel out of that chest there," pointing to the far corner of the room. Reassel crossed the room and opened the chest, removed a large off-white towel, closed it and turned back across the room.

Eilana had slipped the light woollen dress she had been wearing off her shoulders and into a heap at her feet. She was just stepping out of her underclothes as Reassel looked back at her and saw her naked by the fire.

Reassel faltered in her step then came on holding the towel out in front of her. Eilana took it and tossed it over a chair back, stepping into the bath.

"Pull up a chair where I can see you," Eilana smiled, "we can chat while I soak," and they did. Eilana leant forward and over the edge of the bath, picking up the soap from a small dish on the floor.

"This is all I really have a bath for," she confessed, "it is the one luxury of Royal life that I would really miss if I were to leave."

"Surely you're not thinking of leaving?" cried Reassel, a little too concernedly.

"No, no, of course not, I enjoy life here far too much, the children, my friends, my special friends like you, and Serculas."

"She can be a haughty madam sometimes," said Reassel, more than a hint of jealousy in her tone. Eilana laughed.

"Indeed she can, but she always means well." Eilana could feel the jealousy oozing from Reassel now. She obviously felt Serculas a rival for Eilana's affection, "and she is so in love with Rebgroth. Goodness, the noise they make when they are at it beneath my room at night, sometimes I can't sleep!"

Reassel laughed out loud, much relieved by Eilana's affirmation of Serculas' heterosexual habits.

"Men can be so loud and clumsy," she confirmed, "unsubtle, no finesse."

"Very true," agreed Eilana, as she began to rub soap slowly over her body. Reassel sat mesmerised as she watched, her hands moving slightly on her knees, unconsciously in time with the bar of soap. A red flush had appeared on her neck, and Eilana could not help noticing the shape of her now erect nipples, pushing at the front of her linen blouse. For good or bad now was the time, Eilana knew, and Reassel would be hers and with her, her way to the Queen.

She sat forward, handing Reassel the bar of soap.

"Come on, you can scrub my back, can't reach myself." As Reassel took the soap, Eilana leant forward, her elbows on her knees against each side of the bath, her hands together, her chin resting on them.

Reassel wet her hands and the soap and began to rub it slowly over Eilana's back, then replacing it in the little dish, she knelt behind the bath and gently massaged the soapy skin with both hands. They moved in small circular motions around Eilana's shoulders, moving steadily down her back and sides.

Reassel turned her hands, fingers pointing downwards, covering Eilana's lower back, her fingers entered the water, brushing across the cleft that began there. She reached again for the soap, and as she moved steadily upwards again her hands began to turn, but only halfway, her fingers pointing forward. Reassel's palms moved around her sides, and Eilana felt the fingers lightly brush the outside of her breasts, sending a tingle of anticipation running through her, despite herself.

Reassel was massaging her shoulders again, and she gave way to the gentle backward pressure she felt, more inviting than demanding. She leant slowly back against the bath, her neck on its edge, her head on Reassel's chest. Her elbows had run up the edge of the bath, her hands on her knees, still also resting one on each side.

Reassel picked up the soap again and started sliding it slowly over her shoulders.

"If I was a cat I'ld be purring now," she grinned, looking up at Reassel's face just above hers.

"You don't want me to stop yet then?" Reassel asked, still rubbing gently but more on the front of her shoulders now.

"No not yet thank you, not for quite a while yet I think." She closed her eyes as she said it and relaxed her neck further back. Reassel's hands and soap moved slowly down, excruciatingly slowly for Eilana. She had never experienced any sexual contact with a woman, not even with her closest childhood friends, and although she didn't feel the least sexually attracted to Reassel she could feel herself tensing, the blood building in her breasts, so that when Reassel's soapy palms slid gently over them, her nipples were instantly erect.

Reassel had obviously done this before, and was in no hurry either. She moved her soapy fingers slowly around Eilana's breasts for a good while, the tension building within them to bursting point, until Eilana's pelvis began to lift from the bottom of the bath, her pubic mound lifting from the water as she sought attention.

Reassel shifted slightly around the bath, still at work with the soap, but she put it down with one hand, replacing it on Eilana's stomach, where her soapy palm circled, pressing lightly downwards against Eilana's lifting hips.

As her left hand still caressed each breast in turn, her right slid across the mound of dark hair, much darker than anywhere else on her body, something Reassel would make light of often in the future.

Her fingers reached their goal, and Eilana moaned softly. She could feel Eilana warm and wet, even in the bath water. Woman to woman she knew exactly the right spots for maximum effect, but had not realised just how ready Eilana was for that moment. It seemed only a moment more before Eilana was contracting under her fingers, her gasping pant turning to a deep moan at a final shudder.

Eilana opened her slightly glazed eyes and looked up at her, completely speechless. What did one say at such a time?

"Thank you," she muttered, still breathing heavily. It sounded so stupid to her, but it was all she could think of. She had expected to try to fake enjoyment, but there had been no need for that! Reassel leant forward and kissed her on the forehead, grinning mischievously.

"You can do the same for me one day," she suggested, and stood, reaching for the towel then holding it out. Eilana pushed herself to her feet on slightly wobbly knees, stepping out of the bath and into the towel. She wrapped it around her, moved to the table and sat back in a chair, as Reassel spoke.

"I'll be going now, I'll see you tomorrow no doubt," she said as she moved to stand in front of Eilana, putting her hands on her shoulders and leaning forward to kiss her fully on the mouth.

Eilana's hands went to Reassel's hips, holding her in the kiss and pulling her forward so her legs parted around hers, then her hands pulled up the woollen skirt and underskirt, her right hand moving between Reassel's thighs, As she expected, Reassel was almost as excited as she had been, but had not been going to assume anything.

Her fingers set about their business, not as expertly as Reassel's; she had only done this to herself and watched Rebgroth with Serculas, and indeed Serculas with herself; but she was just as effective in the end.

Reassel's kiss had ceased as her breathing became heavier, and when she climaxed, her knees gave and she knelt against the chair, sitting astride Eilana's lap, lying forward on her and panting in her ear as she recovered her breath.

"Now I must say thank you." Her tone conveyed her smile as she finally pushed herself off Eilana and the chair.

"It was my pleasure," quipped Eilana, "in fact both our pleasures." They laughed as Reassel stood and gathered herself. Eilana raised herself stiffly from the chair, realising how squashed she had been. Reassel held her shoulders and kissed her softly.

"I will see you tomorrow," she said and almost skipped from the room.

Eilana got back into the lukewarm water, washing her hands of Reassel's juices and washing her own juices away too.

She lay back and stared at the ceiling, despite washing she felt almost dirty. She had felt that way before, after Keffnon, but not nearly so intensely. Certainly her body had enjoyed it. She had just reacted to enormous stimulation, but she didn't enjoy being with another woman as a choice.

That was the problem she realised. When she had been receiving pleasure, she had been able to ignore who was giving it and just enjoy the moment, but when she had been pleasuring Reassel it had just been a means to an end; there had been no question of giving pleasure to a loved one, just doing what was needed to achieve the end.

She knew however that Reassel was now hers. She would do anything for her now, and all she had to do was pretend every so often, not too often she thought, keep her wanting, and she could question her about the Queen in those intimate moments, her actions, her ambitions.

Inside though, she didn't like herself very much. She pushed the thought away and wondered what Harlmon would have made of it. She smiled as she realised exactly what he would be doing now if he'd watched them, and laughing to herself she climbed out of the bath for the second time that evening.

Chapter 11

Patrikal's party was enjoyed by all. Everyone was served with Bumbleberry juice of course, at Patrikal's insistence, but nobody was arguing, it was truly superb. It blended perfectly with the toasted bread, smeared with butter and covered with the Castle's slightly pink honey, Patrikal's favourite.

The reputation of the juice was spreading, and how it was only available within the Castle itself. Although Moreton had been gone for nearly a year now, his instructions had been strictly adhered to and the secret of the Bumbleberry bushes kept. Despite the story of the secret blend of four local berries that made the recipe for the juice, rumours spread, of the magic and sorcery that had led to the excellent health everybody now seemed to enjoy within the Castle walls.

It was a moon later that Eilana lay on her side next to Reassel, head on her shoulder and left arm lying across her stomach. They lay naked on a loose pile of furs by the fire in Reassel's room. Eilana did not let Reassel come to her room, saying it was because she did not want Serculas to realise their closeness in case the knowledge of it affected her own position. She was concerned how Serculas might react if she found out, and was certain the King or Queen might object if either of them found out.

Reassel understood this, and indeed her position could have been at risk too. The rumours of her relationship with her seamstress had caused some friction until hotly denied. She still saw her occasionally, but really only when she was angry that Eilana did not come to her, so the relationship had soured somewhat.

The real reason however was that it allowed Eilana to control the relationship, to ration her visits. She had become used to their lovemaking, but still did not really enjoy it. Her body reacted but her heart was not in it. She had learned quickly that you could not fake things with another woman, Reassel understood her body in a way a man never could.

She hadn't been sure why she had taken this course, only that instinct told her it would be advantageous, and that evening it started to be.

They began to discuss their days as they lay together. Eilana spoke of how the children had been impossible after a long walk that afternoon, the boys in particular, bad tempered and crotchety until she had finally got them to bed, together of course.

Reassel cuddled her tighter and spoke in a whisper, almost overdramatically,

"You must promise never to tell a soul, but I discovered something really astonishing today, and I can't quite believe it, in fact I am more upset that I didn't know before because I think Allaner has known for a moon or two. I can't understand how I didn't realise before, it's so obvious now"

"Oh for goodness sake what is? You can't start like that and just prattle on, what?"

Reassel was looking up at the ceiling as Eilana, still lying beside her, lifted herself up on one elbow and looked down at her face.

"Well, I was in the Queen's ante-room with Allaner this afternoon. I thought I heard a door close quite loudly from inside the room, but dismissed it because I knew you were out with the children, and it wouldn't be the doors to the King's rooms now would it, you know what they are like together, all the rowing they do, the Queen always......"

"Reassel; for Wey's sake what?"

"Sorry. Yes, well, it was quiet for a while. I thought I had heard a voice or two but couldn't be sure, anyway, the next thing there were raised voices coming from the room, a man and a woman's, shouting, some sort of row. 'Should we knock?' I asked Allaner, 'it might be the King.' She shook her head. 'It's not the King' she said, and at that moment the door burst open and Gratax stormed out of the Queen's room and passed us, carrying his helmet, breastplate and sword, and swearing."

"Gratax! What was he doing in there?"

"Well that's just it, I realised he must have gone in through the panel door that leads onto the back stairs up to this room and Allaner's. They had some sort of row about something and Gratax must have forgotten himself and stormed out the main doors. Anyway the Queen called us in, she was half dressed and the bed was a mess. She glared at us, 'You did not see this,' she said, 'It did not happen, you understand.' We both nodded, 'Of course Ma'am'

'Good' she said, 'If you hadn't already worked it out, Gratax has been satisfying a few of my womanly desires, which have returned to me of late, but I'm afraid we've just had a little lover's tiff.' I just couldn't believe what I was hearing. 'Now as my personal Ladies you are the only people other than Gratax and myself who know about it, so if anyone finds out it will have come from one of you. Not only will that upset me because you know I am fond of you both, but doubly so as I will have to dismiss you both, knowing that one of you is innocent."

"What else did she say?" pressed Eilana.

"Well nothing really, she ordered a bath, then ate. It dawned on me though that Allaner had said it wasn't the King before Gratax burst out, she had known and not told me. I asked her later and she admitted to seeing Gratax on the back stairs, twice in the last moon. He had not seen her around the spiral, but she had just caught sight of him as he entered the room. She hadn't told out of loyalty to the Queen she said, and that she hadn't been sure. I told her I thought we were friends. Anyway that's it."

"The Queen and Gratax, mmm, I suppose he's an attractive man for his age, I quite like older men!"

"As long as you don't go for older women," snapped Reassel. Eilana leant forward; resting her head on Reassel's breasts and giving her an affectionate hug. She kissed both nipples lightly as she pushed herself up off the floor, turned and reached for her clothes that she had cast carelessly across a chair.

"No chance of that," she laughed, but not for the reasons Reassel thought, because she didn't really like younger women either.

"I'll see you in the morning."

"Why don't you stay? You can leave at dawn," Reassel pleaded.

"No, I'm on call from midnight if the boys wake," she lied, "and you've had your fun for tonight."

Reassel laughed as she stood and kissed her goodnight. She wasn't really happy though. Eilana was, at last it had paid off, and she hadn't gone through it all for nothing.

A moon later the Great Hall echoed with the sound of voices and laughter that all but drowned the jolly sounds from the musicians in the gallery. In the centre of the Hall, fifteen or sixteen couples were dancing to what they could hear above the general noise of merrymaking. It was the King's bornbless party, his thirty-third.

Along the outer wall ran a long series of tables. Towards the main doors they were laden with food, but that would disappear quickly enough when the time came, and towards the Minstrels Gallery there were at least fifty flagon jugs of wine and four times that many goblets; or at least there had been, as many were in the hands of the numerous guests, everybody who was anybody in Nisceriel, and as most of them had been filled and emptied a few times by now, many of the jugs were empty or half full. The empty ones were collected by brightly liveried footmen and taken to the cellars for refilling, although the quality of the wine was steadily dropping; the King always felt no-one noticed after the first few, and the majority of those present had consumed at least a few.

Greardel surveyed the guests below from the gallery and smiled to himself. There was one flagon of wine that would not be drunk that night. It sat on the mantelpiece above the fireplace in the King's reception room next to the Royal bedroom. It was his bornbless present to the King.

It was not unusual for personal servants to give their masters or mistresses such presents, in thanks for letting them serve them. In fairness, it was a custom that had grown up when service to a master usually meant far better food and shelter than one could ever expect otherwise, and hence carried status outside the master's home.

Greardel had presented it with his usual display of humble respect and subservience, both of which were appreciated by the King, but inside Greardel both laughed and was consumed with curiosity. He had explained that it was a rare and excellent wine he had ordered from an importer who had brought it from across the sea to the east, sailing far around the southern coast of Deswrain and back to Ffonhaven, the port village at the mouth of the Ffon on Nisceriel's southern border.

It was actually the wine he had bullied Fenlon into making from the bumbleberries he had collected over the first summer they had grown. Moreton had ordered none should ever be made into wine, and knowing Moreton as he did, there had to be a reason for it. Had it produced good wine he was sure some would have been made, so it had to be something else, something bad, he was certain. Fenlon had sampled it, and from the sip that he had rolled around his mouth and spat out, he said it tasted superb. He had been in a foul temper when he delivered it to Greardel though, and returned to the cellars after a very sharp exchange of words, and somewhat chastened.

This was going to be at least a little revenge on Moreton and the King, but

Moreton had gone away of course and that had spoilt things a little. He would still enjoy seeing what it did to the King though.

His thoughts were interrupted by a loud banging on the table at the head of the room. Chancellor Bradett stepped up onto a small dais and formally proposed the toast to King Gudmon on his bornbless day, and may there be many more of them.

Everyone cheered and joined in the traditional bornbless song, a formal nursery rhyme sung in a boisterous and somewhat slurred manner by the guests. The King waved with feigned embarrassment, enjoying every moment of his evening.

Eilana sung with the rest. She had drunk two goblets of a deep red wine, she wasn't sure what sort, or even if they had been the same. She held the goblet in one hand, a little wine still in it. Her other hand leant on a side table. The wine was strong and she knew she had had a drink, not drunk but slightly light-headed.

She saw Serculas laughing with Rebgroth and set off across the room towards them. She had been cornered by a Hundert from Gloff who had become more self-important the more wine he drank. He had swayed away in search of a refill and she didn't wish to be there when he returned, if he did.

Just as she approached them and caught Serculas' eye, a large hand slapped down on Rebgroth's shoulder.

"Well my boy, are you enjoying the evening?" asked General Gratax.

"Oh uh yes, thank you my Lord," stammered Rebgroth, a little surprised by his Commanding Officer's informality. "It is nice to see so many people enjoying themselves on such a great occasion."

"Don't talk nonsense to me my boy. They are all here because it's the place to be seen. They'ld all have been mortified if they hadn't got an invitation, and they're only enjoying it because they've all had too much free wine!" It seemed fairly obvious to all three listeners that Gratax had too.

"So this is your wench is it? What's your name my dear? Can't think of it for a moment, know it so well really." Serculas couldn't quite believe what she was hearing, but before she could reply Rebgroth spoke.

"May I present the Royal Nanny Serculas, my Lord." She held out her hand formally and the General took it in his, raising it to his lips and kissing it in an automatic reaction.

"Of course, of course, forgive me, you lost the Princess a few years ago, Wey, that was a night or two that was. Ended up with those Elves she did, and we got those bloody bushes from it." Tears welled in Serculas' eyes.

"My Lord forgive us, Serculas must get back to the Prince and Princess now, please excuse us."

"Of course my boy, away now and look after your Nanny." He slapped him on the shoulder again and gave a large theatrical wink as Rebgroth gave a half bow and steered Serculas away.

Eilana had stood amazed at what she was witnessing. General Gratax was just one of those people whose appearance made her squirm just to look at. It was nothing particular, but she disliked him to look at without ever having spoken to him. It may have been listening to his arrogance in Council, but his confident manner oozed his belief in his natural superiority over others, and he had long forgotten the social and political skills that he had employed to become a General.

His eyes fell on Eilana as he turned away from his retreating second in command.

"Ah, another Nanny, a brace is too much for any man, too bossy, nannies, too used to handling children." He grinned leeringly at her. "But of course you're our audience at the Council, do you see yourself a future Councillor?" He laughed at the very idea, "Or is it that you are attracted to powerful men?"

"My Lord flatters himself I'm afraid. I merely became interested in the workings of Government. When I first saw those who advised the King, I realised there couldn't be much to it."

She might as well have hit the General with a stick. He swayed back a step, his smile suddenly fixed in a more menacing glare.

"Well well, a vixen with a sharp tongue. You would do well to remember to whom you speak my girl. I can see to it that your time in the Castle ends very shortly. I am sure an ambitious young thing like you would regret that. You should learn to control it my girl."

When Eilana spoke she had no idea where the words came from. They were not spoken from anger, or from a conscious strategy, but from the same instinct that had kept driving her these last few years.

"My ambition has never led me to sleep with Royalty My Lord."

His hand swung back to slap her face, but the back stroke caught a merchant stood to his right, knocking his wine from his hand and over his wife's dress. A flurry of apologies followed that allowed Eilana to step away, but not too far. She realised if she left things as they were the Queen would hear of it and that could lead to reprisals on Reassel and Allaner if they were truly the only ones to know.

The General saw her and walked steadily towards her, now very sober.

"So my little minx, what did you mean by that?" He growled more than spoke.

"I have seen you enter the Queen's apartments from the rear stairs when visiting my friend, twice now, and have listened at the door. The second time you did not shut the door properly and I saw you kissing the Queen, and from the passion of it you must be lovers."

"You are on very dangerous ground young lady, very dangerous. If the Queen found out you know you would be banished from the Castle at least."

"And if the King found out you would hang!" she snapped. "I have written all I have seen in my diaries which are hidden where only a few close friends and I know. If anything happens to me they will read about you and know what has happened to me. I suggest we keep each other's secret My Lord"

She curtseyed and turned away before he could answer. He watched her closely as she walked across the room. She was too high profile to just disappear. He would have to start looking into this young lady's past and present. He needed to find something about her that would lead to her dismissal that was independent of him, but first he must have her watched and find her diaries.

He looked down the Hall. The Queen was talking to a gaggle of women, wives of the great and good who hung on her every word. The King was at the other end of the Hall, downing another goblet of wine and obviously enjoying his party, or getting drunk at it anyway.

He decided not to tell the Queen, she would only panic. Discovery would endanger her too. No, however long it took he would get that damned nanny away from the Castle and removed as a problem. Her sharp tongue had ensured an early end to her life.

That morning, Eilana had had a furious row with Reassel, a lover's tiff. She laughed at the thought. She had tried to explain to Reassel that they could not continue as they were. She had told her about Gratax, of their exchange, and how he would be looking for any opportunity to have herself thrown out of the Castle at the very least. She was not going to hand it to him on a plate.

It wouldn't take much thought for Gratax to realise that only Reassel and Allaner lived on those back stairs above the Queen's apartments, so if she had seen him going into them through the rear door she must have been visiting one of the two. At least they both knew of the affair as well so there was no added risk to him there, but he would be concerned that one of them was close to her.

She was fairly sure he wouldn't have told the Queen, and that Reassel and Allaner would be safe until he could be sure which one was her friend. Even then they were too high profile to be at too much risk, unless he discovered her relationship with Reassel, which would be the perfect excuse to get rid of them both. All he had to do was have someone discover them together and then have them tell the King.

She determined to see Gratax and let him know for once and for all that if anything happened to her or her friends, or indeed her family, the King would find out about his affaire with the Queen: in fact rather than threaten her, he had better make sure they were all safe in case she misinterpreted an innocent event and told the King anyway.

Reassel of course had been her usual emotional self, declaring her love and saying they would be best to leave the Castle, leave Nisceriel, and make a life together somewhere else. Eilana had told her quite simply that was not an option. She had been poor once, and once was enough. Gratax could take no action without endangering his own position, and indeed his own life, but they would have to restrict their time together to a few safely planned moments rather than the current regular pattern. A footman knocked at the nursery door, looking for Reassel; the Queen was ready to leave; she had stormed out.

Reassel had left with the Queen and Eilana was laid back in the warm waters of her bath, where she always thought best, and for the second time in her life her habit was to change things. This time more fundamentally than she could ever have imagined.

She opened her eyes and sat forward a little to retrieve the soap from the dish on the floor beside the bath. Stretching one arm over the side of the bath and reaching down, her breasts lifted from the water above the level of the bath edge.

She caught the tiniest movement in the corner of her eye but didn't react. Her heart raced with the serge of fear that entered her body. Surely Gratax could not be that reckless. There was no movement or sound now. Her eyes moved rapidly, her gaze searching out a weapon, anything that might help. Perhaps she should now just casually get out and dry herself within easy reach of the heavy poker that lay in the grate, in fact the fire could do with some air to it; she should just get out and poke it; at least then she would have something hot and heavy in her hand.

Just as she was about to move she glanced across the room to her left. The curtain that pulled around the cots in the corner was permanently pulled back since the boys had graduated to their bedroom, and this exposed the mirror above the chest beside the cots. By a quirk of coincidence, the mirror angle let her see the room behind her quite clearly, if a little distantly.

Someone was standing in the space between the two doors into the Queen's chamber. The Queen had left with some ceremony to visit her parents, the King and Queen of Deswrain, earlier that day, with a Royal Guard led by Rebgroth. He was only too happy to be going as everywhere the Queen went, so did her Ladies-in-Waiting, and her children. This meant Serculas accompanied the party, but only her, leaving Eilana free for over a moon at the Castle, the first break of any kind she had enjoyed since joining the Royal Household.

Harlada had gone too, Prince Gudrick simply would not be parted from him, so it was easier all round with everybody for him to go. They would travel by road to Ffonhaven that day, then by boat the next day down the Coast to Deswrain. To go the whole way by road meant a trip very many days inland to skirt around the southern marshes, taking twenty times as long as sailing down the coast.

Whoever was there was peering through the long crack down the hinged side of the door, getting a three-quarter view from the rear of her back in the bath. Her stretching for the soap had brought her breasts into full view and the movement she caught had been the door opening a fraction more, widening the crack through which her watcher could see, but it also meant that she could now see their outline in the mirror from the side through the wider gap of the open door.

She realised now that if this person rushed her she was terribly vulnerable. The weight of water if she moved suddenly would be too great, then to step out of a slippery bath quickly and try to grab a weapon; it was just not possible. Plan B it was then.

She rose slowly from the water, her naked rear towards the door. She felt as much as heard the tiniest creak as the door moved a fraction more. She was suddenly confident this was a peeping tom rather than an assassin; so now to try and see who she was dealing with, her fear turning to excitement.

She stood by the fire and dried herself slowly, then spread the towel on the chair and sat naked beside the fire. The chair was sideways to it, a quarter off facing the door, and a glance to the right let her see the man more clearly now.

She leant back in the chair, her head on its back, her dark wet hair down over her shoulders almost to her breasts. Her half closed eyes would have looked shut from the door, but she could see the mirror clearly.

Again the door moved a fraction. The crack was at its widest possible now, any more and it would start to narrow again, but it was enough for her. The King's bright yellow velvet half jacket was enough to tell her of her Royal voyeur. This needed to be the show of her life. Just pretend it's Harlmon was her thought, as her hands started to move gently over her body.

The King was slightly drunk and very lonely. It was crazy that he was missing the Queen, the woman that made it quite clear to him that her love had turned to hate, no worse, contempt. He thought he was used to it by now, but her actually leaving the Castle brought it all back to him.

He was walking aimlessly around the Castle, trying to take his mind off his misery. He entered the lower Keep from the walled garden to find a succession of footmen carrying large enamel jugs of hot steaming water across the corridor and up the back spiral stairs. He stopped the nearest.

"Who are these for my man?" he asked and smiled in genuine mirth as the poor footman desperately tried to bow without dropping or slopping the jug he had supported on his shoulder. He had never spoken to any member of the Royal Family before, or even been in direct contact with one.

"Sorry Your Majesty, they are for…." A large splash of water slopped out of the mouth of the jug and splashed to the floor between them, soaking both the King's foot and his own. "Oh Wey! What have I done?" wailed the footman, "Oh Sire, Your Majesty, I am so sorry." He struggled to put the jug down without spilling more. It banged down beside him.

"Calm down, no harm done, it's only water. Now answer my question," ordered the King, his humour much improved by the poor man's buffoonery.

"Yes Sire, I mean Your Majesty, oh no!" He kicked the jug in his efforts to bow and step back deferentially, slopping more water.

"Pick it up and get upstairs you oaf," thundered a voice well known to the King. It was Greardel walking back from the kitchens after arranging the next day's meals for the King. He swung a foot at the rapidly retreating backside that raced thankfully across the hall and up the stairs.

"He never did answer me," laughed the King.

"What was the question Sire?"

"I merely asked him who the water was for and he completely went to pieces."

"He is not known as the brightest amongst the staff Sire, although he does try!" Greardel actually smiled as he said it. "The water is for Lady Eilana Sire. I understand she often takes a bath during the early evening in the Nursery, beside

107

the fire. All the servants know not to enter around that time without knocking."

"I see, thank you Greardel, carry on."

"Thank you Sire," he said bowing and backing a few steps before turning and continuing down the hall. Another two footmen crossed the hall as two more returned, including the one with a wet foot. They all bowed acknowledgement as they passed. The King half raised a hand and walked to the next stairs before turning and climbing the spiral.

He reached the rear door to the Queen's apartments and strode through it. He stood in the large bedroom. He hadn't stood there for over a year. He really could not help himself. He walked towards the connecting doors and very gently turned the handle to the first. He stepped into the gap between the doors, carefully closing the first door silently behind him. It turned the small space pitch dark, but as he could only just turn around comfortably he was hardly going to get lost.

His hand moved gently, searching for the handle to the second door in the dark. His left hand found it and very slowly and gently, turned it clockwise. When it stopped at a full turn, he moved the door fractionally open and slowly returned the handle against its spring.

His hand was trembling with the prolonged steady effort. His heart pounded with excitement. This was like escaping from his bedroom as a child for a nighttime adventure, but his motives this time were very unchildlike. What was he going to say if the door was opened now and he was discovered? Nothing, he was the King!

Light showed as a line down the hinge side of the door and more brightly down the handle side that stood open only a finger wide. He put his eye to the crack and could just see Eilana's naked back as she sat down slowly in the hot water.

She lay back and stared at the ceiling for what seemed an age. She was three-quarters back to him so he didn't have a very clear view of her. After a short while he was feeling braver and gently pushed the door open another finger or too. The hinge crack opened a little wider. He couldn't use the open side of the door to see without actually sticking his head out around the end.

He pushed the door another touch. It gave a tiny creak and he swore under his breath, but his view was a fraction better. Eilana sat up and reached for the soap, her breasts rising from the tub. He was mesmerised and eased the door more. It was open a forearm now and the crack was at its optimum. She stood up in the bath, stepping out and drying herself in front of the fire.

He had not seen a woman in the flesh for well over a year and he felt the tension rising in his leggings as he grew within them. His hand moved unconsciously to rest over his codpiece.

Eilana spread the towel on the chair and sat down almost facing him. This was too much; he was embarrassed for a moment, ashamed of himself, but only for a moment, as her hands began to move slowly over her skin, her stomach, her thighs, up to her breasts. Wey this wasn't happening; he was hard within his leggings.

As her hands brushed her breasts her knees parted, and the King's fingers loosened the laces of his codpiece. By the time her right hand had moved back down across her stomach and begun its work the King also had himself in hand.

He could not believe what he was seeing. Somehow watching Eilana do this to herself showed that she enjoyed sex, something he had begun to doubt women did, and it was so stimulating.

With his eye glued to the narrow crack he heard her begin to moan. He almost forgot where he was as his hand moved in time with hers and as she moaned loudly, her knees moving together and gripping her fingers in her thighs, his seed spurted over the back of the door. He tried to keep his breathing quiet as he realised what he had done. He pulled the door slowly shut. She was facing the door but her head was back looking towards the ceiling, her eyes closed. Surrounded by the dark again he felt for the door handle behind him, opening it quietly and backing into the Queen's bedroom.

He closed it, his mind a confusion of guilt, excitement, shame and pleasure. His hand was covered in his seed, as was his surprisingly still alert erection. He walked over to the Queen's bed and wiped his hands in the soft cover, then raising it from the bed, the rest of him. He smiled ironically to himself. It had been a long time since there had been any of that on the Queens bedding! He tucked himself awkwardly back into his leggings, lacing the codpiece firmly and looking at the empty bed. As he straightened the cover he had disturbed, he realised he was cured, free of the damned woman. She was gone for over a moon and Eilana was here.

Then his spirits dropped again. He was being a stupid old fool, she may enjoy sex, but with him? He doubted it. He was an old man in her eyes, thirty-three summers, and she was probably no more than eighteen or nineteen, but then again he had to try. He would make a complete fool of himself he knew, and be totally embarrassed and feel worse at the rejection afterwards, but he knew he had to try.

Eilana opened her eyes and stared upwards, a satisfied smile crossing her lips. Not sexual satisfaction, she was almost totally unaroused, her concentration on her acting abilities had suppressed that, no, she was pleased with herself.

The King had reacted just as Harlmon would have; his brain in his crotch. Her hands had not dwelt long over her breasts, not nearly long enough to awaken her these days, and with the heel of her hand resting on her pubic mound, the fingers that appeared to be doing their work hardly touched her, and when they did it was with the cool realisation of what they were doing to the King, not her.

Watching the King from the side with the aid of the mirror, her timing was perfect. The excitement she knew he felt from the noise that he didn't realise he was making, brought him to a conclusion quickly. Her act had to be much shorter than the real thing. The King's breathing, he had thought so quiet, had been her perfect guide, just like Harlmon's or Rebgroth's. Reassel was right really, women were much more sophisticated in their lovemaking, but then sophistication wasn't her thing.

She straightened up out of the chair and walked quietly on bare feet to the door, putting her ear to it. There was no noise. She gently opened it. In the light the King's seed was in runs down the inner panels, making its way to the floor, where some had obviously landed directly. She ran her hand across the wood, gathering some on her fingers and rubbing it between them. It clung to them and to itself, stretching between them as they parted before breaking into separate globules.

She walked back to the bath and rinsed them in the tepid water. It was only the first of a great deal more of the King's seed that she would wash from her body in the years to come.

Chapter 12

Gudmon, King of Nisceriel, lay on his back beneath a soft linen sheet on his bed. He was the happiest man on earth, although at that moment he could easily have been persuaded he was in heaven.

For the first time in his life he was totally, completely, helplessly, head over heels in love, and it felt wonderful. He ignored the nagging doubt in the back of his mind that this young thing was only pretending to love him, only after what being the King's mistress could bring her, but frankly he didn't care, he just thanked Wey for his good fortune.

He leant his cheek on the top of her head, smelling her hair and her body next to him. His right arm around her, she lay on her left side, her head on his shoulder, hers tucked into his armpit, her right arm thrown across his chest, her right leg curled over his hips. He bathed in her warm nakedness against his skin and almost cried with happiness.

She stirred slightly in her sleep and cuddled into him. It was a moon since he had watched her in her bath. He had almost run back to his room that evening, waves of embarrassed guilt washing over him. What had he thought he was doing? Had she heard him? If she had, did she know it was him?

What he did know was that he couldn't get her out of his mind. He seemed to dream of her every moment of the little sleep he got that night, and when he was awake, all he could see was her sitting on that chair and the overwhelming ache he felt for her.

He looked for her the next day, trying not to make it obvious, but with increasing agitation when he couldn't find her. She had gone to visit her family, quite deliberately; confident that he would be searching her out, and knowing full well that making him wait to see her would work in her favour.

She returned that evening and contemplated another bath. No, that would be too obvious, too unsubtle. She ordered food brought to her room and retired early. Just before midnight she thought she heard movement on the stairs outside her room and lay motionless in her bed. If it was the King she would not make it easy for him.

A strip of faint candlelight showed under the door, confirming someone was out there, but she heard no more sounds for at least half a quarter. The King could not pluck up the courage to knock on her door, for indeed it was him. He sat on the top step of the spiral stairs and gazed at her door, mesmerised by her closeness but not daring to disturb her.

His emotions swayed rapidly. He was afraid of rejection, of looking stupid in her eyes; after all he was almost twice her age. Then anger would strike, he was King for Wey's sake, why was he cowering outside some upstart peasant's door; he could have any woman in the Kingdom, except he wasn't that type of man. Next a self-contempt at his own stupidity, here he was a man of thirty-three acting like a love struck fifteen year old. Love struck! He couldn't be; lustful undoubtedly, but not in love, not yet surely.

He watched the door, willing her with every fibre of his body to open it and find him there, but of course she didn't. Even if she had felt the call of his mind she would not have. He must wait.

Eventually she saw the light fade as he stood quietly and crept down the stairs, feeling very foolish. Later, as Greardel pinched out the candles in his bedroom and wished him goodnight, he resolved to get the stupid bitch out of his head, and if that meant out of the Castle, so be it. He knew he didn't mean it though, and as he shut his eyes she was sitting on that chair in front of him.

He fought it for a while, but the vision had aroused him and sleep would not come, so in a typically male response to his problem, he relieved his tension, hoping it would relax him into sleep, and as usual it worked.

He woke early though, called Greardel and dressed, then headed for the gardens and a walk before breakfast. As he passed below her window he looked up and thought he saw her face, but no, he was seeing her everywhere now.

In fact he had. Eilana had looked out to admire the early autumn light on the river. Looking down she saw the King and jumped back from the window. She grabbed her clothes and dressed quickly. Actually, there was a lot of thought behind what she grabbed; a snug fitting linen dress that was cut low enough to display her assets without being obvious. The cold morning air would do the rest.

She raced down the tower's spiral stairs, slowing towards the bottom to compose herself and get her breathing back to normal, before stepping out into the walled garden and looking around for the King.

She decided he must have walked around the Keep wall and hence was out of sight, so she moved in that direction until she came to the three bumbleberry bushes that were laden with autumn berries. She stopped, pretending to admire them, knowing that the King would eventually walk back around that way as there was no way into the Keep or out of the garden further around.

She did not have to wait long. He was looking at the ground a few steps in front of his feet and obviously his mind was not nearby, but as he came closer he was suddenly aware of someone and looked up. Seeing her he stopped and stared for a brief moment, then smiled.

She curtseyed as he moved towards her.

"Good morning young lady," he greeted, "a beautiful start to the day." He couldn't believe he had come out with something so crass.

"Good morning Sire, it is indeed."

"You are admiring our bushes I see. Do you like bumbleberries?" What a damned stupid question, everybody does.

"Oh yes Sire, they are very special," she replied.

"Then we shall share some Nanny," he said as he picked a bunch of berries from a bush and offered them to her.

"You spoil me Sire," she smiled taking the berries and making sure their hands touched as she did.

"Someone as pretty as you should be spoiled occasionally you know, and it gives me pleasure to do so."

Eilana pretended to be embarrassed as she popped two berries into her mouth. Then she broke two more off the bunch and stretched her hand out towards the King's face, hesitating. As he smiled he opened his mouth and she placed the berries between his lips. He took them from her fingers, his lips touching them as he did.

As he ate them he took her by the arm and led her down the garden. They sat on a stone seat and talked, interrupted by short silences as they finished the rest of the berries, which were truly delicious.

They talked for almost a quarter. At first about mundane things, but then the King commented on how often he had seen her at his Council, asking of her interest. She explained her fascination with things of state, and of how she had been determined to understand.

"You are a very unusual lady Nanny Eilana; not just beautiful but intelligent too, I must learn more about you, get to know you better, if you would not mind."

"That would be a great pleasure Sire, I would enjoy that also."

The King smiled at her, a glimmer of hope in his heart. He asked her of her child Harlada, expressing his delight that Gudrick had such a good friend, how it reminded him of his childhood with Moreton, and how he wished Moreton was in Nisceriel now.

She asked if the King knew where he had gone. He thought he had probably gone far to the north, a moon's journey to the monastery that was the home of his order of Weymonks. Moreton had told him of it once, a small island just off the northeast shores of their land that could be reached by a causeway for a short time at each low tide, where stood a large monastery that looked more like the castle it actually was, at the top of the island's single hilltop. All around the hillsides sloped down to the rocky shore except facing the mainland where a wagon track wound up a slightly gentler slope to the drawbridge, portcullis and studded gates. As for how long, he could only guess. The last time he had disappeared and been away for seven years, he had a sad feeling it may be as long this time.

"Has Harlada a father?" He had asked it before he knew what he was saying, unintentionally speaking his thoughts. What he was really asking was if she had any emotional ties, which she immediately realised.

"No Sire," she sighed, "I was a stupid girl led astray by a boy I hardly knew and who I believe to be dead now. I have just my family, my parents, two brothers and a sister, but there is no love in my life." She thought of Reassel for an instant, but that was not love, nor lust, merely a means to an end, and probably already reached.

"I am not lucky like you Sire, to have married and to have two such lovely children in a secure home." The King gave an ironic laugh, and suddenly it all poured out of him.

"I have no marriage, Nanny Eilana, I am at the centre of a sham. I am a King, I am wealthy, I wield great power and can have almost anything I desire, but I am lonely and miserable with a wife that has grown to hate me, and who has made it even harder than it normally is as a King to be close to my children. I am thirty-three, as old as many men live, and can see no way back to happiness, for who would genuinely love me now? A King can trust no-one completely; so many people just want to be close to you for what they can get from it.

Moreton is the only person I know who is a real friend, a friend of Gudmon the man, not of Gudmon the King."

He looked at her. She was staring into his face, a look of almost pity in her eyes.

"I am sorry, I shouldn't have said all that," and he looked away.

"No Sire don't be, I had not thought that a King could feel as you describe. I forget the King is a person too, even when I work so closely to you." She did actually feel genuinely sorry for him.

"A person who can sometimes be unsure and vulnerable my dear, and as flawed as any man." In her mind she could not help adding, with a brain in his crotch, just like Rebgroth and her brother.

"You are too hard on yourself Sire. Of course you are a King, which is enough to turn any woman's head, but you are an attractive man too, and as I know now, sensitive and caring. You have a lovely smile and you know how to laugh, even at your own expense, which I find very attractive in a man."

He had been gazing across the lawn as she spoke, but again he turned to her, looking slightly down on her face as she sat beside him. Her eyes were on him and seemed to be filled with genuine warmth. His eyes moved down, inevitably stopping at her breasts, which he could see so clearly in his mind but were now held inside the tight linen, cleavage showing and nipples very obvious in the crisp morning air. He took her arm.

"Come, you are obviously getting cold sitting here, we will share some breakfast." She laughed and squeezed his arm affectionately as he led her back into the Keep and to his dining room. Greardel had another place laid as soon as he saw them enter together, smiling at her in a very guarded way.

They ate, and they laughed together while they did. They washed the fat from their mouths with a glass of very fine red wine and the King ordered two horses saddled.

"You do ride? I never thought to ask," he said apologetically, "We could always just go for a walk."

"My father is your ostler, Sire. I was riding almost before I could walk."

"Yes of course, I knew, it's just my brain doesn't seem to work properly when I am with you, you have a very strange effect on me you know?"

"I am beginning to believe I do Sire, and you on me."

They looked at each other across the table. Gudmon's heart was fluttering, his stomach full of butterflies and a yearning ache in his chest. They stood and made their way to the courtyard where of all people, Harlmon was holding two magnificent horses, tall brown geldings, saddled and ready.

The King helped her up and into the saddle, then lithely and with a confident ease, mounted his own. Harlmon released the bridles and stared at his sister, an enquiring look on his face. She winked at him and turned her horse to follow the King towards the Castle gates. She was amused to see a troop of twelve guards follow them out at a discreet distance. The King caught her look and laughed. He kicked his mount and led Eilana at a trot northeast from the Castle, taking a track that led from the road towards a distant hill.

They were over a watch and a half in the saddle before they reached a path that led steeply upwards into the trees. The King pulled up and waved to the guard, some fifty paces behind, then started up the slope. As they reached the tree line Eilana looked back to see the troop splitting and starting to deploy around the hill, spreading themselves at equal distances along its base. Eilana was confident they wouldn't be disturbed by anybody human at least, but in the woods there might be the odd animal upset by their presence.

Just as they approached the summit the trees ended and they rode out into a large clearing that crowned the hilltop. The view to the north looked over Gloff to the distant wooded hills beyond. To the west one could see past the Castle Nisceriel and way over the River of Number, deep into the wild realm of Whorle. South could be seen most of the Kingdom as far as the gentle slopes of the hills through which the Ffon had cut its deep gorge; all a rich pattern of woods and farmland. Behind them to the east a range of wooded hills rose, slightly higher even than the hilltop on which they stood. They seemed very close, as indeed they were; a single wooded valley away, and marking the border with the realm of the Elves.

Eilana had never seen an elf. The nearest she had been to one, that she knew of at least, was when two had returned Patrikal to them three years before, but she had not seen them. If the stories of their eyesight were true, they could easily be watching them now. Well they would probably be in for quite a show then she thought.

The King dismounted casually and held her horse's bridle as she slipped easily to the ground. She thanked him and he let the horses go, their reins hanging to the grass. They would not move far.

He led her to the edge of the flattened clearing, looking across to the west. The autumn sun warmed the wind that blew gently in their faces as they sat on the soft grass that smelt divine.

They talked a while, hand in hand, although neither of them had been quite conscious of doing so. It was no surprise to either of them when the King finally kissed her tenderly, desperately resisting the temptation to crush her in his arms as he desired.

Eilana was totally responsive to him, indeed subtly proactive, and it was not long before they were semi naked, making love on the soft ground; and as she thought afterwards, making love it was. He was tender and thoughtful, using all his experience to ensure her pleasure as well as his own. There was none of the clumsy thrashing about of Keffnon, and so much more feeling than with Reassel. There was something about a man inside her that felt so right, and this man was very good. She could get used to this!

They lay and talked softly, laughing often, for most of a quarter watch. She was laying half on top of him, their faces close, eyes enjoying the sight of each other. He pulled her down and kissed her firmly but gently. She lifted away and smiled, pecking his nose, then remembering what she had watched Serculas do so often, she slid down him and kissed his stomach and thighs. His body tensed as her lips and tongue moved around his thighs until they reached their goal, which was now fully recovered from their earlier activities and eager for more.

As she took him in her mouth he looked upwards, staring at the sky, at the few wispy clouds and at a lone buzzard that circled high above them. He could not believe this was happening to him, it was all so perfect. She worked at him for a while as he lay worrying that after all she was doing for him he wouldn't make it again so soon, he wasn't as young as he had been, but he need not have worried and he moaned ecstatically as he filled her mouth.

"Very salty!" she chuckled as she swallowed. He reached for her and pulled her close.

"You are too good for me you know?" He sighed as he hugged her.

"How can you be too good for a King? Hey?"

She cuddled him closely and they lay there dozing in the sun for a while, much as they were now in his bed. Their ecstasy had continued for over a moon now, and it just got better. Even Eilana was surprised at her feelings for him. She wasn't sure she had fallen in love with him, but she had certainly grown very fond of the old fool. He was very attentive, considerate and a very unselfish lover. It was not a chore to make love to him, in fact she positively enjoyed it, finally understanding that Serculas' and Rebgroth's apparent excesses were not so at all, just a natural desire to find new ways of enjoying each other.

For the first time he had someone who wanted to make love to him, someone who started lovemaking when she felt like it, and taking the initiative occasionally. It made him feel so wanted, so loved. Even when times were good between Bertal and himself, he had always had to initiate things, always going to her room, but Eilana would just as likely come to his room in the middle of the night because she wanted to make love to him, as he go to her. In fact the first night he had lain with her in her tiny bedroom, he had left her in the early quarter and returned to his rooms. Within a quarter she was slipping into his room and kissing him into wakefulness.

Now they just slept together every night, in the King's bed. Greardel knew, but no one else was supposed to. It must have been obvious to most however, as they spent so much time together in the day.

He did not care, he was in love, he was happier than he had ever felt in his life, and Wey help anyone who came between them.

Gudmon was woken by a persistent banging on the main doors to his chamber. It was Greardel's "Your Highness' pardon" knock. He was aware of the daylight surrounding the hastily and only partially drawn window covers. Eilana stirred in response to the knocking, firstly cuddling into him, then by pushing herself up on one elbow and smiling at him sleepily.

"No peace for the wicked!" she croaked, her voice refusing to function properly. "For goodness sake see who it is," she demanded as the knocking continued, throwing herself theatrically back onto her side of the bed and burying her head under a pillow.

Gudmon laughed as he stood and wrapped a large fur bedcover around him and shouted for whoever was knocking to enter. It was Greardel.

"Your Highness' pardon, an Envoy has arrived from Deswrain Sire; I felt it might be important and that I should wake you." He glanced at the shape under the furs and soft sheets on the bed and added, "I thought it might be an urgent message from the Queen."

The King looked hard into his expressionless face.

"Yes, thank you Greardel. My clothes...."

"Are laid out in your robe room Sire, I prepared them earlier. It is quite late Sire, later than you usually rise." He glared at the bed that quivered as Eilana giggled beneath the covers.

"Then let us get me dressed Greardel. The Lady Eilana can then arise at her will. Come."

The Lady Eilana is it, thought Greardel as he followed the King through the side door, that should interest the Queen. He determined that the envoy would carry an unofficial message back along with any formal reply.

King Gudmon was seated on his throne to receive the Envoy who had arrived in formal attire, and had therefore to be met formally, as diplomatic etiquette demanded. The double doors to the throne room were opened by two Royal Guards who positioned themselves each side of the opening. The Envoy stood in the anteroom facing the opening and bowed deeply. As he stood Gudmon beckoned him forward into the room.

"You are welcome my Lord," said Gudmon as the Envoy walked towards the throne, stopping and bowing again a few paces before the King. "Identify yourself and join me in some refreshment."

"Your Majesty is very kind," replied the Envoy, "I am Lord Mendel, Sire, Envoy to King Gabral." Two goblets of the best local fruit wine were served to them on a silver tray, the Envoy being given a choice of either goblet. The King drank first. When they had both drunk from them and hence the formalities completed, the King spoke again.

"What business do you have with us my Lord?" he asked.

"I bring a message from Queen Bertal Sire, on the instructions of my King Gabral."

"And what has she charged you to tell me my Lord?"

"She has instructed me to inform you Sire that her father, King Gabral, is very sick and lies bedridden in Castle Deswrain. As his only surviving daughter, she feels honour bound to attend him; concerned as she is that he may not survive his illness. She realises that any delay in her return would risk a difficult and dangerous winter voyage, to which she feels she could not subject Prince Gudrick and Princess Patrikal. She also realises that a winter journey home by land would be almost as great a risk to their health. She instructs me therefore Sire, to inform you that she does not intend to return until the spring."

"I see, is that all?"

"From Queen Bertal Sire, yes, but Prince Kadrol has charged me with conveying his promise to you Sire, that he will protect your Queen, your family and their entourage as if they were his own, whilst they remain in Deswrain."

King Gudmon had kept a diplomatic blank expression throughout the exchange as his Royal training had taught him, and hence Mendel had no idea of his reaction to the message, other than he hadn't flown into a rage as he had half expected, and as he had been warned he might by Queen Bertal.

General Gratax however looked apoplectic. He was shaking and bright red with fury. When the Queen had told him of her intention to visit her family in Deswrain he had pleaded with her to let him go, but she forbade it. It would be normal for Rebgroth to command the guard on such a trip, and so it would be. She had insisted that they could not have carried on their relationship as guests in Deswrain anyway, and she would be only gone for two moons at the most. Now she would be gone for half a year at least, more probably, and he feared he might lose her affection. Two moons he was happy would mean absence making the heart grow fonder, six or seven could lead to out of sight, out of mind, and meanwhile he had to bear seeing the King dote over that nanny whore, who was now definitely beyond his reach and yet more dangerous to him.

Mendel moved his gaze from Gratax to his drink, and then looked up from his goblet as the King spoke.

"Thank you my Lord. Now you must rest from your journey. A room has been prepared and you must join me in a luncheon at mid-day, after which I will give you a formal reply for Prince Kadrol and for my Queen. Until then my household is at your service my Lord."

"Your Majesty is most kind." Mendel bowed, took five paces backwards and turned towards the door. Gudmon watched him leave the room, a smile breaking across his features as his genuine delight finally broke his self-control.

The Queen would not be back for at least five moons and he wouldn't have to go through the traumas of her return until then. He rose and almost ran to share the news with Eilana.

Mendel stayed another two days as good diplomatic manners demanded, then set off for Deswrain by land this time. The river of Number had a reputation for autumn and winter storms that could blow up suddenly, turning its deep running tidal currents and notorious shallows into death traps for even the most experienced Captains.

The tide rose and fell by the height of nine men, and although the estuary was some twelve fields wide at the mouth of the Ffon, the deep channel wound its way between treacherous mud flats in sweeping meanders. The tide raced in and out across the flats, and if the wind was up and the water rough, a ship that strayed or was blown slightly off course could be picked up and banged down disastrously on the unforgiving sand, or at least stranded whereby its hull shape would tip it sideways as the water rushed away around it. A large ship was doomed; if not flooded as it tipped, when the tide rushed back in a ship would fill with water and never right itself, remaining capsized and then often pushed upstream if it did not get seated deeply in the sand.

The estuary was so large that a huge amount of water flooded and ebbed at every tide. The speed of the current itself could mean that if there was too little wind, a ship could not make headway upstream on an ebbing tide, nor downstream on a flood. Indeed to tack when the wind direction was difficult, meant the slightest misjudgement could spell disaster, and it had done so many times in living memory. The deep channel was very narrow at times, and at its narrowest, just below Ffonhaven, it ran along the rocky shoreline. With so little room between the rocks and sand bank, to tack in bad weather was almost impossible.

It was a wise if cautious decision therefore that Mendel had taken, particularly as he was not the best of sailors either.

He carried three messages back to Deswrain, although it would be mid-winter now before he arrived. The first was one of formal thankfulness to Prince Kadrol for his promise. The second was a somewhat ambiguous 'stay as long as you like' reply to Queen Bertal. The third however was going to be extremely difficult to deliver.

Greardel had cornered Mendel after breakfast on the second day of his stay to advise him of the King's blossoming relationship with the Lady Eilana before he put two and two together himself. He only did so, he explained, so that Mendel would understand the situation as it was rather than perhaps convey a distorted picture on his return. Whilst the King would certainly never harm his children, there just might be a risk to Queen Bertal, should he be persuaded into an uncharacteristic action by a lover that seemed to have already turned his head completely.

Greardel lied convincingly of his devotion to the Queen. He just wanted to be sure she knew the situation and could make an informed decision about returning, if at all. Lord Mendel was no fool and realised there was more to Greardel's motives than love of the Queen, but he did not know him or the situation well enough to see through them. Was this the King speaking through him, or something more devious for his own benefit?

His real problem was who he should give the message to. However he would have plenty of time to contemplate the situation on the return journey.

He was only half way home when Gudmon and Eilana were lying by the fire on a bed of furs.

121

The evening had been an ideal one for Gudmon. They had eaten early and he had soaped Eilana thoroughly in her bath. They had made love slowly and gently on the furs while she was still wet, but now they sat crossed legged beside each other, the heat from the fire making them drowsy.

Gudmon uncrossed his legs and lay behind Eilana. She eased back against his chest and put her arm around his head as he pushed under it and kissed the side of her breast. She flinched slightly.

"Oh I'm sorry," he said, concern in his voice, "did I catch you wrong?"

"No my love," she replied, "it is very common for a woman's breasts to be tender sometimes in early pregnancy."

It took a moment to sink in. Gudmon pushed himself round suddenly, sitting up beside her, facing her with his back to the fire.

"Pregnant, did you say pregnant?" His eyes held hers expectantly.

"I did my love, are you pleased?" He threw his arms around her, hugging her and kissing her cheeks and neck.

"Of course I am, I am very happy about it." In the back of his mind his father's words came back to him. Something about the complications of royal bastards about the Castle, he couldn't remember exactly and he didn't care anyway. He was genuinely delighted to be having a child with the woman he loved so much.

Eilana hugged him back and felt the wetness of his tears on her cheek as he cried with happiness.

Chapter 13

When Mendel arrived at Castle Deswrain a few days after midwinter's night, ending a tedious and uneventful journey, the Castle was in mourning. He had crossed the borders of Deswrain just as news of King Gabral's death reached the far ends of the realm, and he had ridden at speed the rest of the way in a vain attempt to reach the Castle in time for the funeral, but he was not surprised to discover he had missed it by days. He was in time however, for his good friend Prince Kadrol's coronation as King.

Mendel had crossed paths with Heralds sent to carry the news to neighbouring lands, but Kadrol had decided to go ahead with his coronation promptly, rather than wait until the spring when guests could more easily and practically travel to Deswrain. He did not feel the need for, nor wish the expense of, a lavish ceremony.

He slapped Mendel on the shoulder with genuine joy at his return.

"What of that bastard Gudmon my friend, my sister will want news of him?"

"He sends his greetings Sire, and thanks you for your promise to protect his family. He sends greetings to his wife in understanding of her dilemma, and his blessing to remain here until the spring, but there is more I should tell you Sire, perhaps when we are alone." His face had a serious look about it.

Kadrol glanced at the courtiers standing around them, all at a respectful distance but not necessarily out of hearing. He threw a comradely arm around Mendel and led him through his library door, closing it behind him.

"You cannot intrigue me like that old friend and expect me to wait to hear what you will not tell me in front of others, not with such a concerned look in your eye."

"I am sorry Kadrol, but it is not easy. I have thought much about it and there is no better way than to tell you and ask your advice." All pretence of rank had ceased between them now they were alone, and Mendel sat heavily on a soft chair with an air of weariness about him.

"That bad eh? Well you'd better spit it out then." Mendel looked up at him from the chair.

"It involves King Gudmon and your sister."

"That doesn't surprise me, what of them?"

"Well we knew they weren't getting on, and that they were living apart at Nisceriel, but since Bertal has come to us here, he has taken himself a mistress, a Lady Eilana, a Nanny with Serculas to Patrikal and Gudrick. At the moment they are inseparable and I fear for Bertal on her return."

"Gudmon would never dare harm Bertal, it would mean war between us, he would never do it."

"Probably not Kadrol, I agree, but this much I was told by a servant of Gudmon who says he is loyal to Bertal, not that I believe him. What I learned elsewhere though through a large bribe to a guard was that he is not the only one in the mist of a steamy affaire. It would appear that Bertal is heavily involved with General Gratax of the Castle Guard, who had ordered a constant watch on Lady Eilana. I just fear that in all this intrigue there lies danger for Bertal. Were she to be pregnant by Gratax, or this Nanny by Gudmon, it could all add up to real trouble."

"Thank you my friend, as always your interests are with me. Now then, I am sure Bertal is not pregnant. She has been here three moons and more, and with her slim figure I am sure we would have seen the signs by now, but should this mistress woman of his have a child, the problems would start if there was any threat to my nephew Gudrick as heir to the throne of Nisceriel." He held out a hand to Mendel and pulled him to his feet.

"Come, we will eat and drink to celebrate your return. I will think on all this, and I have until the spring at least to do so. I fear though that we will just have to see Bertal returned safely to Nisceriel, knowing the situation. We will also need to get a clear message to Gudmon of the consequences of any harm coming to any relative of mine, but that bit my good friend, will be down to you."

He laughed and hugged Mendel, then led him back into the reception room.

So it was that when Queen Bertal and her entourage boarded ship in the late spring she knew what she was returning to. Forewarned was forearmed her brother King Kadrol had told her, but all she could feel was a strange sense of relief. She was no longer the one that had been unfaithful, and if he wished it, she would declare her love for Gratax. If she knew Gudmon, he would have his whore installed permanently in his suite by now, if not in hers, which would actually suit her as she could establish herself in the dowager wing where she had moved temporarily after their rows. In a strange way she was happy for Gudmon, and if he left her alone, things could be quite settled.

She was perfectly correct about the arrangements at Castle Nisceriel. At first Eilana slept with Gudmon every night, but as her pregnancy advanced she was often tired and needed to rest. If she retired early, the King would often wake her accidentally as he came to bed, often slightly drunk.

He suggested he have the Queen's chambers renovated for her. The Queen could have the dowager apartments she had been using happily enough before she went, and now if they retired together they would sleep together in the King's bed, if Eilana went early on her own she slept in her new apartment, in the Queen's old bed, but Gudmon never slept with her there. They never made love together on that bed.

The day the Queen set sail from Deswrain they had a very narrow escape, although they did not realise it. It was early evening and Eilana was sitting by the fire. Although it was spring the weather had not been good, wet, cloudy and miserable, so Eilana had ordered it lit.

Gudmon suggested a drink and was about to order some wine when he saw the bottle on the end of the mantelpiece that Greardel had given him for his bornbless present. It seemed an age now.

He reached it down, and he did have to stretch up for it. As he did so he said how he had forgotten all about it and that they should try it. When he said who had given it to him Eilana almost shrieked no. She tried to explain that she couldn't help it but she just couldn't stand Greardel and couldn't possibly drink anything he had given him.

Gudmon pushed it back with a flash of temper. They had been through this a dozen times, and stupid though Eilana thought it, he was loyal to Greardel and he would not dismiss him, but then again, he couldn't stay angry with Eilana for more than a few moments. He laughed and rang the bell, ordering the finest grape wine for his beloved.

It had been a calm if wet evening, but the wind veered round to the northwest, growing quite suddenly into a gale that drove rain almost horizontally at the Castle walls. They lay by the fire and made love gently with a quiet passion, warm and safe from the storm.

At that moment however, Queen Bertal was wondering if she would survive to see Niscerial again.

Bertal had complete faith in the Captain of the ship she travelled in, the Lone Hart. He was a legend at twenty-two, but even his infamous seamanship could not give her comfort just then.

Captain Nordrall had sailed the waters around Deswrain and Nisceriel for all his life. His home port, where he had been born, was Ffonhaven, and the treacherous waters of the estuary had been his home since birth. No one knew them better.

His father had plied these waters too, passing on his knowledge and skills to his son. At eighteen years old, Nordrall was given command of a converted lugger and sent on a trip of exploration. The crew were all volunteers, all young sons of sailors, and all determined to make a name for themselves. His father stood proudly on the quay and waved them off.

They sailed west down the estuary then changed tack, running north of west and hugging the coastline to the north of them. When it came to a craggy end they turned north to follow it wherever it took them, and to try to record and chart their journey.

They carried a pointer stone, a sharpened piece of ore that hung balanced on a thread within a glass lamp, firmly attached to a wooden barrel top in front of the tiller. Wherever they sailed it pointed to the North Star. They had learned of such stones from the wild seamen of the east who his father had befriended years before, but whilst they had learned to use them, they never understood them.

They headed slightly east of north for a day, but found themselves boxed and had to turn a little south of west until they could head north again. A day later the coast took them westwards again for over a watch before the shoreline swung north.

They anchored and camped ashore occasionally. When they did they lost the odd crewman to the women of the area, but they gained an adventurer or two on the way. They often had to overcome a language barrier at these times, but it never proved insurmountable.

Eventually they were pushed west again, driven into some blind bays trying to force their way north, but when they did set a northern course they were caught in a storm that forced them west. As they finally turned north again, in search of a shore to the east, a lookout called land to the west.

The swell was too long to be caught in a bay, so Nordrall pressed on northwards until he picked up an eastern shore again, but for the next moon he struggled north along cliff lined shores, into blind bays and around islands, into deep valley inlets from which he had to turn directly back, and all the time the hills inland got taller and more mountainous. Quite suddenly there was nothing to the north but sea, and the coastline turned east again.

They followed it east then turned sharply south into a deep bay and anchored for many days. They ate well on local wild goats and sheep they hunted, and made brief contact with a strange red haired people. They spoke in a shrill guttural tongue, but whilst looking fearsome, they were hugely welcoming, at least the very few they met were.

A day's steady sail east and they turned south for the first time, south west in fact to follow the coast, but this was another blind course, and they had to tack back east again for almost two days before once more swinging slightly west of south.

After a brief sally into a fairly large estuary, they moved further south to find a large southwest running estuary not unlike their home, but inverted. Here they chose to rest again, and here they met the only real trouble of their journey.

They anchored as the estuary turned to the north, leaving them in very sheltered shallow water. Above a small beach stood a village and the inhabitants, about a hundred men, women and children, lined the water's edge waving happily. The crew of twenty-four waded ashore, all armed but expecting no trouble. The villagers were farmers in the main, and only four of the seventeen or eighteen men wore swords, but then here a sword was a treasured and rare possession.

Nordrall gave presents to the villagers, mainly lengths of thick woollen cloth, for which they were very grateful, and that night the village held a celebration of their arrival that involved everyone.

Day broke and the village awoke as normal, Nordrall and his crew dragging themselves from sleep after a late night, but they were shocked into wakefulness by a loud metallic ringing as a hammer was crashed rapidly on a hanging shield. Most of the crew were with him, having slept in the large round house that had been the hub of the previous night's activity. Three of them were missing. They had been befriended by local girls and had slipped out of the party during the evening.

A villager ran in, pulling Nordrall's arm and pointing outside. His words were meaningless noise but the urgency was clear.

"Arm and head for the beach," he ordered as he was dragged out, shouting over his shoulder.

Villagers were running in all directions, but the men were moving generally towards the shore, armed with whatever farming implements they could wield as weapons.

His eyes followed the villager's pointing finger to see a strange boat moving towards his own. This craft was longer than the Lone Hart by at least two men, and it was a man narrower in the beam. The bow rose up in a neck and head of some angry beast, and the stern as a pointed tail.

It had a single steering oar lashed to the stern and a coloured square sail rigged on a single mast which rose from the centre of the boat. A row of eight oars ran along each side and rowers sat on cross benches, breaking the line of the single deck that was raised only at the stern as a steering platform.

The speed at which it approached was astounding to Nordrall. He watched helplessly as it passed astern of his boat and half a dozen torches arced across the space between the craft and fire caught in the sail. He realised there was no hope of saving the Lone Hart, and he turned to catch his men before they left the building. The missing crewmen arrived as he did so.

He spoke rapidly to his crew, a plan in his mind, and they left the landward side of the building at a trot.

To give the villagers their due, they rallied on the beach, sparsely armed as they were. In the south, villagers would probably have run into the woodlands inshore, but as Nordrall looked across the open rolling hillsides around the village, he realised that for these people there was nowhere to run to or hide.

The men formed an eighteen strong fighting line, their women and children behind gripping wooden clubs and brooms, anything they could at least try to defend themselves with.

The raiders were clad in heavy leather armour and many had metal helms. As they swung around the burning Lone Hart, they ran their craft fast at the beach. As it grounded the sixteen oarsman shipped their oars and took up their weapons, the seven other crew leapt ashore ahead of them.

If they had grouped first, they would have cut the villagers down quickly, but this was going to be easy, they had done it many times, and the first seven ashore ran shouting fiercely at the villager's line. The line inevitably buckled inwards in the centre as two villagers died immediately, cut down horribly, one by a blow from a battleaxe that cleaved through his shoulder and stopped halfway down his chest, the other by a sweeping blow from a two handed sword that all but decapitated him.

But suddenly the attackers found themselves isolated, the line that had buckled broke in the centre, swinging inwards, and now the seven raiders had a line of villager men on each side and the women ahead. Which ever way they turned to face a villager, there was another one behind them. The villagers had not planned it but it was a devastating tactic. Six of the attackers went down, hacked down from behind as they defended their front. Three more villagers were down too though.

The surviving raider ran back to the fighting line of the other sixteen of his companions and turned to face the villagers. They were less reckless now, and doubly dangerous organised. They all had a merciless look in their eyes, angered as they were from the loss of their comrades.

The villagers too realised that any hope of quarter was now gone. None expected to live, but they would not run. They straightened up and faced the raiders, line for line this time. They both moved forward across the beach, but as they were about to clash, a large fighting cheer rang from behind the raiders as Nordrall and his crew broke from the cover of the small round houses beyond the raiders' boat.

Sandwiched between the two, and outnumbered more than two to one, the raiders used their superior arms to good effect, but they did not survive. Given hope by the Lone Hart's crew entering the fight, the villagers fought far better than they might have, and Nordrall's crew were well trained if not too experienced.

As the last raider went down, another twelve villagers were dead, seven of them women, and five from the Lone Hart. There was a number of wounded too, but none too seriously. In that fight, a bad wound meant death anyway, just going down invited a killing blow.

If the raiders had formed a tight circle and fought more as a unit, they could have won the fight, but their culture was obviously one of heroic individuals, which had this time gone against them, allowing a single combatant to be cut down from front or back by superior numbers. They had raided this village on the wrong day.

The eight surviving village men hugged Nordrall and his men, not knowing whether to laugh at their victory and their own survival, or to mourn the loss of so many of their own.

The remaining village women and children knelt crying over the bodies of their men or stood with their surviving partners and parents, equally numbed by the experience.

A grateful village girl bandaged a cut on Nordrall's right forearm, the result of a loose parry, his opponent's blade connecting hard enough to cut through shirt and skin, but not deeply.

He surveyed the scene. The locals were gathering the bodies of their dead and carrying them to the burial mound on the landward side of the village. He ordered his men to lay out their dead for burning at the far end of the beach.

The women of the survivors set about stripping the dead raiders, and soon there were twenty-three naked bodies in a pile on the beach. Their clothing had been plundered by the villagers, but their weapons, helms and leather armour lay in separate piles beside them.

Nordrall was in shock to an extent, not from the fight, but from some of the scenes afterwards. As the village women stripped the bodies they drew their small work knives from their belts and mutilated the corpses, cutting the genitals from them with great glee, and waving them at each other, laughing in delight. It made him feel quite ill.

A somewhat farcical sign language exchange then took place as the village leader tried to explain what was going on. It was clear enough though, had the raiders won, the children would have been slaughtered and the women raped and killed, or taken off in the boat to be frequently raped by many of the crew until eventually murdered and thrown overboard as they neared home. Now the women waved the body parts that would have abused them above their heads.

This was the villagers' way of atoning for other villages attacked and wiped out over the years, their women cruelly defiled, but it didn't make it any pleasanter to watch. Nordrall finally turned away as the women began to nail these parts of the raiders' anatomy to their doors.

He called his crew together and they examined the burnt out wreckage of the Lone Hart. Although the hull was charred, it was intact, but it would take a mammoth effort to strip and rebuild the gutted fittings and mast. The raiders' boat however was untouched by the fight and in perfect order.

The crew stripped it of the raiders' personal belongings that were of no use to them, and began to settle themselves aboard. At the village leader's behest, they had chosen the pick of the weapons and armour stripped from the dead raiders. Nordrall had just taken a fairly light oiled leather tabard, waisted and belted that protected the torso but allowed plenty of movement of the arms and legs. He really hoped he would never have to fight on land again, and at sea, anything heavier would mean certain death if one went overboard.

The rest of the crew tended just to upgrade inferior weapons, but interestingly, nobody took a helm, even for a trophy.

The morning was spent building funeral pyres at the far end of the beach from the village and sending their dead back to Wey with due ceremony. Five plumes of fat smelling smoke arced away to the east, merging into a single dark column that finally dispersed high above them.

That afternoon their low spirits were lifted as they took the raiders' boat out on trial. It rowed well, an added bonus for them, as their own boat could not be easily rowed. It did take some effort to get a sensible rhythm going however, and Nordrall realised the significance of the drum he had tossed onto the beach. He would retrieve it later.

The square sail was new to them too. Theirs had been triangular, and for their design of boat probably better, but on this sleeker design they soon learnt to handle it and see some advantages, but most significant of all, this was the fastest boat any of them had ever sailed. It would leave any other boat they had come across standing.

They sailed back into the estuary and beached the boat as dusk settled on them. That evening was a mixture of celebration at their victory and mourning for the dead. As they settled down to sleep they were astonished as the wives of the living moved among them to offer sexual favours, the traditional way for these people to express thanks to fellow warriors.

Stunned and embarrassed at first, the crew were hesitant, but as red blooded men who had been away from home for many moons now, they soon entered the spirit, and even Nordrall lay with the village leader's wife before she moved on to two others of the crew.

The next morning they waved to the villagers as they sailed down the estuary, turning south and west. For almost a moon they sailed steadily, stopping and sleeping ashore every few days, replenishing water supplies and hunting. They tried to avoid contact with local people, as they were rumoured to be less than friendly, and with their experience further north, Nordrall could understand why they might have a standing fear of strangers, particularly in this style of craft.

After the first few days they had sailed past a mountain island with a castle perched on the top. It looked a formidable fortress, and a large white flag flew from each of the four towers, the central one larger and higher than the others.

On reaching a large bay as the next full moon lighted the night sky, they had to turn east again for a day before the shore turned gently to the south, its large sand dunes and sandy beaches deceptively inviting, but Nordrall sailed well off to avoid the danger of hidden sand banks.

The new Lone Hart almost flew across the sea, in light weather, and cut through the swell when it was rougher. She was a truly magnificent craft.

After another day's sail to the southwest they reached a shoreline that cut across their bow. Another day sailing slowly to the east and the coast led them southwest again, huge white cliffs to the right of them. Nordrall was sure he could make out land far to the east.

Another few days and he knew where he was, sailing down the coast south of Merlbray, and eventually reaching the familiar waters of south Deswrain, and the port of Dorthaff. Here they were greeted enthusiastically, and as they told their story of the first sailors to sail right around what they now knew to be the large island on which they all lived, they were hailed as heroes.

Their maps and mapping materials had all been lost in the fire on the original Lone Hart, so they could only describe their journey and adventures. After two day's rest, Nordrall and his crew sailed on southwest. They turned northeast around the rocky cliffs where the land ended and back along the north coast of Deswrain. Here they entered the estuary of the River of Number, eventually reaching Ffonhaven. Their story had arrived before them, and by now they were legends. They had fought sea monsters, defeated a fleet of North Raiders, and spread their seed around this vast island.

Nordrall himself became a legendary Captain, his personal adventures, all made up by the tellers, were told of across Deswrain and Nisceriel. He became the first choice for Royalty and Nobility for sea passage, ensuring his fortune, but with good reason. He sailed the most seaworthy craft available, and fast enough too to outrun any attacker. Although many tried to copy the design of the vessel, a great deal of its strength was in the way it was built, and that took generations to understand.

He had experimented with sails, and now had two rigs, the square had advantages down wind, but a triangular rig allowed the boat to sail much closer into the wind, so now he chose which his crew would rig before any journey, dependant on the wind direction and his experience at forecasting the weather.

On that night twelve years later, however, all his skills were to be tested to the full.

Chapter 14

Nordrall stood on the steering platform at the stern of the Lone Hart and looked up the granite cliff at Castle Deswrain. The Castle grew out of the rock some thirty men above him, or so it seemed to him. It was probably slightly less, but not much.

The Lone Hart bobbed gently, moored against one of the three wooden jetties that thrust out into the sheltered inlet, which formed the harbour at Wrainhaff. From where he stood it looked as if the dock was on a small lake surrounded by high granite walls, but at closer inspection, on the northern side at the opposite end to the jetties, the waves beat in through a narrow opening to the sea, at right angles to the length of the main inlet, forming a natural harbour.

Between the jetties and the sea towered the Castle Deswrain. It stood on what would have been an island except for a narrow track at cliff top level, no more than two carts wide, with vertical cliff faces on each side that connected it to the mainland. In hundreds of years to come the waves would finish the job and make it an island, but until then it made an unassailable fortress, home to the Deswrain Royal family. To the west and north the sea pounded the cliffs around it. To the east ran the inlet that led into the sheltered harbour of Wrainhaff behind its bulk.

From the Castle gates, the track led inland for five fields before a turning ran back towards the sea, down a winding and sometimes quite steep wagon track to the harbour side. At the bottom of this track stood the three carts that had carried the Royal travellers down to the dockside. Queen Bertal and her party were returning to Nisceriel.

Bertal had bid her brother, King Kadrol, a fond farewell, and even now the Dowager King Mother Bertralac, waved from a tower window in her apartments. Bertal waved back and made the children wave to their grandmother too.

She walked confidently down the jetty and across the gangplank onto the Lone Hart. Princess Patrikal led her brother Prince Gudrick on board, almost dragging him behind her. Young Harlada, his best friend, followed confidently behind, unaided.

Harlada was a very confident four year old, almost as confident as Patrikal had been at that age but not quite so precocious. Gudrick and he were inseparable, but the shy Prince always pushed Harlada forward. In any new situation or in any new game, it was always Harlada that went first, encouraged by Gudrick, so Harlada became more and more confident and Gudrick more dependant on him. The only reason Gudrick was on the boat first was that Patrikal had dragged him aboard.

Rebgroth followed, leading Reassel, Allaner and Serculas onto the boat, to be welcomed by Captain Nordrall. Harlada and Gudrick had been told bedtime stories of his adventures and couldn't wait to see him again since the voyage down. The King's special Envoy Mendel was last to board. He had been charged by Kadrol to see his sister safely home and to remain with her for a few moons to ensure her safety, a clear signal to King Gudmon.

Twelve Nisceriel Castle Guard boarded a working lugger called Lady Wrain that was captained by Dombard, one of Nordrall's original crew who had prospered as a trading Captain too since their adventures together. The Lady Wrain was not as fast as the Lone Hart but was a very seaworthy triangular sailed boat.

Both craft sailed with reduced crews due to the number of passengers they carried, eight on the Hart and six on the Lady, so only three oars on each side of the Hart were manned as they pulled down the inlet and swung the vessel sharply to the left and out into the swell. They had to row out of the small bay before turning northeast and unfurling the large square rig that Nordrall had chosen for this trip.

The Lady had no rowing positions, and Dombard laughed and waved at Nordrall as he skilfully tacked out of the inlet with loud guffaws about real sailors.

There was a steady, perhaps strengthening, south westerly wind that suited the Lone Hart's square rig as it filled the sail from behind, pushing her rapidly on her course with the flood tide. Nordrall had wanted to leave half a watch earlier, with the dawn, but the Royal party would not hear of it. As it was, the last half watch of the trip would now be made against the ebbing tide and would be slower, just as darkness was falling, but with a strong following wind this would not be a problem.

They steadily outpaced the Lady Wrain and she slid farther astern as the day wore on. The children became bored but Serculas told them stories of Captain Nordrall, and as he was there with them, they had to be true. Nordrall, however, was feeling uneasy. All the signs were of stable wind and weather, but it didn't feel right to him. Years at sea had built an instinct in him that was seldom wrong. He couldn't say what it was that was amiss, the feel of the swell, the smell of the wind, he didn't know, but he was suddenly quite concerned.

He cornered Rebgroth and Mendel, pointing out some landmarks to seaward, a small island in the middle of the estuary, and the coast of Whorle far beyond. When he had their attention away from the ladies he spoke of his unease. The others felt that as they were more than halfway, and it was further back than to Ffonhaven, they should go on. It was difficult for Nordrall to argue on just a feeling, so they sailed on.

A quarter watch on it was too late. The wind increased noticeably and swung to the northwest, blowing almost straight onshore. Nordrall reduced sail, but they still made good headway for a while. As the sun set the spring tide that had carried them upstream on its flood reached its peak and began to ebb. The wind began to build further and the waves built too. The onshore wind was still good for the square rig, but the mast light of the Lady Wrain, far behind, grew slightly closer. Her heavier build and triangular rig were coping better with the conditions.

The clouds above grew darker very quickly and the rain began to fall, then to pour down. The crew could not rig a canvas shelter in the conditions and everyone of Royal blood or not was soon soaked to the skin and increasingly cold and miserable, the children crying in discomfort and fear. The adults too were not without concern.

Nordrall stood at the steering oar and peered into the darkness ahead. He knew exactly where they were, the outline of the low cliff to their right, so close but so black. This was the tricky bit, where the gap between the sandbank to their left and the cliffs was at its narrowest for twenty fields or so. The onshore wind pushed the swell against the cliffs and they could hear the waves crashing against the rocks even though they could no longer see them in the darkness. But for the wind change, they would have been safe in Ffonhaven by now.

The wind gusted higher, the boat pitching and fighting the current that now roared downstream. Nordrall wisely had four of the crew stand by in rowing positions, their oars lifted from along the sides of the boat, now resting in their rowlocks across the boat, hand grips on the decking, blades out over the sides, but this just made his passengers more nervous.

Nordrall looked down at his craft from the steering platform. Two of the crew fought to hold the steering oar steady on course, with his aid too at times; otherwise he was braced against the high stern, left foot locked in a rope loop on the gunnel and right hand in a rope grip on the stern beam, the tail of the Hart.

His passengers had all obeyed his orders instantly and without argument. They were all now sitting in the bottom of the vessel spread around the rear, leaning against the outer hull or against the steering platform. They were all so wet, the water they had shipped and in which they sat, didn't matter for the moment. The other two crewmen were in the centre of the boat bailing steadily with leather buckets. It was purely water shipped from waves that broke over the bow that filled the bottom of the boat, and two men bailing could cope easily with that.

The ladies and Patrikal sat with their backs to the steering platform, facing the bow. Rebgroth sat to their right, back to the hull, head against the rear rowlock on that side. He held Gudrick under one arm on his lap and Harlada under the other. Opposite him, Mendel smiled at the boys in what he hoped was a reassuring way, although he could have done with a bit of that himself.

Nordrall could just make out the end of the cliffs ahead. It was more a change from dead black to a deep dark grey that he saw, but he knew. Here the deep channel swung north, away from the shore, but they would turn southeast, around the headland and into the mouth of the Ffon and Ffonhaven, hidden behind the cliff from them now. Almost there.

Quite suddenly, the rain that had been driving into his left ear drove straight into his face. The wind swung round impossibly quickly to the northeast, head on to them and straight down stream. The Hart lost headway immediately, the sail flapping with loud cracks as the two crewmen beneath it fought to drop it to the deck before it caught in the wind and drove them backwards.

The Hart rocked wildly. Nordrall screamed for shoreward oars and the two crew on that side expertly grabbed their oars and pulled deep. On the seaward side the crewmen readied their oars and pushed back, tightening their turn. It was the most dangerous moment, sideways on in mid turn.

If they got the boat round they would make sail again and run down wind and tide to safety, however far that took them, but as they turned the current swung them wide on the slight bend of the channel and just as they were straight a breaking wave lifted them high before dropping them into the following deep trough. In the instant before the next wave lifted them clear they crashed down on the very edge of the sand bank, kicking the boat sideways onto her left side.

How she righted herself and didn't capsize Nordrall was never sure. It was probably something to do with the buoyancy of the oars that dipped deeply into the channel, lifting the side of the Hart back upwards before she could fill, but two of his crew had been lost over the side, one losing his grip on the steering oar as it kicked wildly, and one of the two crew amidships was bodily thrown from the boat by the main spar swinging wildly and catching him full in the chest. In that weather they were lost unless they could swim ashore, but they were beyond help from the Hart. All sorts of deck gear followed them over; three of the four unused oars, the water barrel, and almost everything that was not tied down.

What he saw below him however, in what almost seemed slow time, was totally devastating. As the Hart kicked violently onto her side, the ladies all slid sideways into a heap, grabbing anything they could for support, including each other. The side rails of the Lone Hart rose ornately behind the final rowlocks to meet the steering platform, and the pile of falling females hit this hard, but it saved them all, catching them roughly but securely.

Rebgroth however had a boy in each arm. He slid rapidly across the decking until his feet caught Mendel squarely in the chest, winding him. With no hands to grab onto anything his momentum carried him headfirst over the side, Gudrick in one arm, Harlada in the other. Almost instinctively Mendel grabbed Rebgroth's heavy fur linen cloak. He had wrapped it around the boys and himself in an attempt to stay warm. It pulled tight, the clasp at the neck snapping open rather than arresting their fall.

As the Hart righted herself they were gone. It took a few moments for everyone to come to their senses and realise what had happened. Bertal and Serculas were screaming, Allaner and Reassel trying to calm them, and Mendel was peering hopelessly over the side, the heavy cloak in his arms.

Nordrall knew his craft was safe now but at such a terrible cost, and at what consequence he had no idea.

Rebgroth hit the water with a loud smack. The momentary resistance to his fall of the cloak pulling at his neck had stopped him diving head first into the depths. Instead, it meant he hit the water flat on the top of a wave as it descended into a trough. He clung to the boys and kicked his legs wildly; trying not to panic or let them go whilst endeavouring to stay afloat. The waves lifted him and dropped him, dipping their heads underwater frequently.

Looking back Rebgroth realised that losing his cloak in that way was the first of a series of coincidences, or perhaps of divine interventions, that saved their lives, any of which missing would have meant their deaths. The weight of the cloak alone would have dragged them down.

Harlada clung to him grimly, Gudrick screamed and wailed until his mouth filled with water as they submerged again. As they broke the surface he was coughing and spluttering but at least had ceased screaming in Rebgroth's ear for a while.

Rebgroth felt a hard thump across his back and fought to turn around and face whatever it was. One of the oars from the Lone Hart rose in front of him, threatening to crash down on them but then settling beside them for a moment along a trough in the waves. He couldn't grab it with a child in each arm so with a feat of personal strength that many could not have achieved, he heaved Harlada over it, the oar under his arm.

Harlada let go of Rebgroth and looped his arms around the oar, his chin resting on it. Rebgroth let him go and did the same. A little more secure now he helped Gudrick attach himself firmly to it too. The oar was more than two men long, almost three, and was heavy but very buoyant. It hardly seemed to feel them clinging to it, and its length kept it parallel to the waves, making their ride on it possible.

On the top of each crest Rebgroth looked around them. The Lone Hart was agonisingly close but sailing away from them, running down the wind and tide that was pushing them along rapidly too, but much slower. He shouted twice, but even if they had heard him, they could not have turned to help them.

He realised how bitterly cold he was getting. The boys were hanging on to the oar but their smaller bodies must be terribly cold too. Another wave crest and the mast light of the Lone Hart was almost gone. Perversly, the rain had stopped. The wind continued to whip the tops off the waves and into their eyes though, so it was not really any more comfortable. The clouds parted for a few moments and in the moonlight, Rebgroth got a view around them.

The current, wind and tide had driven them down the length of the narrows incredibly quickly and they were almost at their end. The cliff fell away from a rocky point into a wide bay that cut a long way back inland to a large sandy beach that would take a man half a watch to walk along. The deep channel cut straight across to the far point on the other side of the bay.

Rebgroth began to kick his legs steadily in an attempt to guide the oar towards the shore. As they passed the near point he told the boys to kick too, not that he expected them to contribute much, but the effort might help keep them warm.

They all kicked and slowly the oar moved across the current, many lengths forward for every one across, but steadily so, until Rebgroth sensed they had left the main current and were caught in a giant eddy that swirled into the bay. There was almost no swell here and he kicked until he was so tired and cold that he really felt he could do no more. He heard himself apologise to the boys as his feet swung downwards again, no kick left in them, only for them to bump on the bottom.

The water here was not much more than waist high, although they were a long way from the beach. His feet pressed into the mud with a new strength that propelled them towards the shore. The tide was going out rapidly, against his progress, and at times it was all he could do to dig his toes into the mud and hold them against it, but soon he was on his knees, still a field length away from the sand and the marshes beyond.

Holding the oar he stood in the mud. His feet sank in and he had to keep moving so as not to sink too deep. As soon as they could, he told the boys to stand holding the oar and walk. He crawled with them until the mud became firmer sand where he could walk. He picked them up, stepped over the oar and staggered slowly on the wide sandy beach.

It was so hard to walk on the soft sand, his soaked calf leather boots sinking in with every step. Reaching the sand dunes that marked the border between the beach and the marshes behind, he flopped down exhausted. The boys were shivering uncontrollably. He wasn't sure that getting ashore had done them much good.

He thought he saw a light along the beach. He rubbed his eyes but just spread sand across his face. It was a light. He called out and tried to wave, seeing it the boys shouted too, and as he passed out, Rebgroth could just make out two strangely dressed men carrying a large burning torch, walking steadily towards them.

He awoke in a stone shelter built above the rocks on the south and west end of the beach. Normally it would be tucked out of the prevailing winds, but this north easterly beat against its ill-fitting door, driving draughts across the room and fanning the flames of a large fire, too large for the small fireplace, but needed to warm them quickly. It also provided the only light in the room.

The roof was a thatch of reeds similar to the ones strewn over the rock floor. It was very dry inside and the single room was warming rapidly. Rebgroth realised he was naked and wrapped in blanket of some sort. He didn't recognise the cloth but it was warming him successfully. The boys were sitting in front of the fire, each in a man's shirt that swamped them but again was warm.

One of their rescuers was sitting on a stool beside a small table watching the boys. He said something to them and laughed happily, but in a language Rebgroth did not understand. The boys didn't understand either but they laughed with him, feeling the goodwill in his voice. He was dressed in tight fitting linen garments, a dirty and washed out brown colour, with light soft leather boots, each sown together above the foot with no added sole and stopping just below his knees. Hanging behind the door was a darker brown lightweight waxed leather cape; a Marsh Dweller. Rebgroth had heard much about them but had never met one.

Their clothes were hanging from the beams of the low roof. They had stopped dripping but were still very wet. He hadn't been unconscious that long.

He shuddered suddenly in an uncontrollable shiver and struggled to sit up. The smile on the Marsh Dweller's face immediately disappeared and he seemed to grumble something under his breath. He reached for a large carved wooden mug on the table and getting to his feet, dipped it into a metal pot that stood beside the fire. He handed it dripping to Rebgroth, without a smile or words. He took it and thanked him. It was a broth of some sort, and it was warm and very welcome.

The boys realised he was awake and jumped up, tripping on the long shirts as they tried to run to him. He shouted at them to be careful but they still managed to slop the broth over themselves, not caring in their delight at seeing Rebgroth back with them.

They sat for a couple of hours with arms around each other as the warmth in them all grew, exchanging small talk about their adventure in the waves. At least the boys thought of it as an adventure, Rebgroth could not quite believe they were alive, but tired as they were, none of them slept. The Marsh Dweller said something and left the room.

"Where's the other one?" Rebgroth asked the boys.

"Don't know," offered Gudrick, typically.

"Gone to get his friends I think," said Harlada. "He left as soon as they had got you here. That one undressed you and put your clothes over there, and your knife and sword. He spent ages wiping them dry and polishing them for you."

Rebgroth looked up and saw his knife and sword hanging against the wall almost beside him. It looked perhaps as if they were guests rather than prisoners. The Marsh Dweller must just prefer children to adults.

The door opened and he entered the room with more logs for the fire. They were dry so there must be a store or another building nearby, a cave perhaps. He grunted something guttural and piled them by the fire. He added one to it and sat back at the table.

He pointed to himself.

"Glurk," he repeated, "Glurk." Then he pointed to the boys, "Aalada, Gudrike."

"I see you boys have made your introductions," commented Rebgroth in a whisper. He raised his voice and pointed at the Marsh Dweller, "Glurk," he said, then pointing at himself, "Rebgroth."

"Rebgloff," repeated Glurk.

"Rebgroth," he corrected.

"Rebgroff"

"Close enough I suppose," he laughed, but there wasn't a trace of amusement on Glurk's face.

"I don't think he likes me, boys," Rebgroth said as he rose carefully from the pallet bed. He reached sideways and took down the scabbard and belt from the wall. Glurk tensed and poised himself for sudden movement if required. Rebgroth drew the sword and examined it before replacing it and checking the long fighting knife also. They had both had the seawater rinsed from them and been thoroughly dried and polished.

"Thank you my strange friend, you have done an excellent job." He hung them back above the bed. Glurk relaxed a little. "What is it about me I wonder," he said to the boys as he tested his shirt and leggings. The thin leather of the leggings was dry and he pulled them on. The woollen shirt was still wet, and trying to dry it more quickly beside the fire would just mean it would shrink. His boots near the fire were dry too, and if he left them there longer would start to crack. He pulled them on; light riding boots. Luckily he had not been wearing heavy ceremonial boots; they would have dragged him under too.

He donned the sleeveless leather jacket that matched his leggings and was dry also, and went to leave the shelter. Glurk stood quickly between him and the door. He carried no obvious weapons, and Rebgroth's still hung from the beam above the bed. He looked into Glurk's eyes. There was no fear there, a slightly un-nerving calm actually. He moved purposefully around Rebgroth to stand between the boys at the fire and the door, his hands half raised sideways as a barrier to the boys, then he nodded to the door.

The meaning was clear enough, he could leave but not the boys, yet he wasn't frightened of him although unarmed. This would prove an interesting night. He moved to the door and went out into the wind. The tide was way out now, beyond where the eddy had swung them inshore. The deep channel was the only watercourse now, and in the moonlight, the mud banks beyond were visible too.

He turned and walked to the cliff face, opening the ties on his codpiece. He faced down wind and relieved himself, smiling at the truth of the old proverb about pissing into the wind. His mind was still racing however, despite a numbing tiredness he felt. He could stay here with a fire prepared and when a ship sailed by, he could light it to attract their attention. They could not scale the cliff at the far end of the beach, and from this position he could see over the dunes to the treacherous marshes beyond them. The moon's reflection glinted back at him from water hidden by marsh grass and rushes. There was no way home inshore without help.

There was plenty of water here; a number of springs ran from the cliff side. Food might prove a bit harder, but they shouldn't be here long. In fact, if Nordrall was not driven too far down the estuary, and did not put back into Deswrain, they could well appear back on the rising tide that morning. The wind was definitely dropping and was probably nearer northerly now. All he had to do now was prepare things, persuading Glurk, by force if necessary, to let him get on with it.

As he reached the door of the shelter, it was too small to call a house; he looked back out to sea in the darkness. Movement caught his eye to his right, and from the bushes at the foot of the cliffs, a column of Marsh Dwellers marched raggedly into sight. No less than forty. Force was no longer an option, and diplomacy would be difficult without a common language. It looked as if the Marsh Dwellers desires would prevail, and indeed they did.

He entered the shelter, the warmth hitting him now, and pointed outside to Glurk, moving to the bed and sitting down. Glurk went outside. He held a restraining hand out to the boys before they could get up and join him.

"Do not argue with these men, do you understand?" He didn't wait for confirmation. "You do exactly as they want, whatever happens."

He removed his jacket and donned his shirt, damp but wearable. He replaced his jacket and buckled his scabbard belt over it. The door opened and a large Marsh Dweller entered, followed by Glurk. He was sure more would have come in had there been room.

He looked at the boys in a way that Rebgroth could not quite read, but his expression was clear enough when he turned to him. He grunted something then thumped his chest.

"Klarss." He pointed at Rebgroth. "Rebgroff."

Rebgroth nodded slightly in acknowledgement. This man appeared unarmed too, but he was brimming with confidence. Rebgroth was tempted to give him a demonstration of why he should show some reverence to him, but he did not want to endanger the boys in this confined space. A bundle was passed through the door and thrown to the boys. It contained dry clothes the same as the Marsh Dwellers were wearing, just smaller. Rebgroth told them to get themselves dressed, and his eyes rolled as he watched Harlada sort himself quickly and easily, before helping Gudrick, who, in his short life, had probably never dressed himself yet.

Klarss clearly beckoned them to follow him outside and left. Rebgroth moved to the door and stood just outside the frame. The Marsh Dwellers were in a large semi-circle around the shelter. Klarss beckoned again and shouted something at him. When he did not move, Klarss moved towards him. Rebgroth's hand moved to his sword hilt. In a blur of sudden moment, every Marsh Dweller reached behind his head and half drew a short sword from sheaths that hung down their backs from their necks, inside their garments. In the marshes, a sword hung from the waist was dipped into water far too often, quickly ruining a good blade. The Marsh Dwellers had therefore developed this way of keeping their blades out of the water most of the time.

Rebgroth removed his hand. Pissing into the wind had crossed his mind again. Forty plus short swords were replaced in sheaves quietly and hands returned to sides. For all the land around it looked to Rebgroth as if nothing had happened, except that he now knew the Marsh Dwellers' will would prevail. As he called the boys out from the warmth of the shelter, he could not fathom why they left him armed at all. He could only assume it was some kind of diplomatic nicety; leave your prisoner armed but let him know to use them would mean death.

A boy holding each hand, Rebgroth entered the marshes, closely following Klarss' lead, so as not to step off the path and into the quagmires around them. Glurk followed them closely, a short rope in one hand in case they did. The column moved inland.

Chapter 15

Nordrall stood before the King in the great hall. The King's Councillors sat arrayed below the dais on which the throne almost dwarfed Gudmon. The King had listened to Nordrall's report, and then listened to the detailed evidence of Mendel and of Dombard, Captain of the Lady Wrain.

Mendel's evidence had to be taken seriously. He was an official envoy of King Kadrol of Deswrain, which meant his words were his King's. He was also not Niscerian and had no connection with Nordrall. Captain Dombard too was known as a man of honour, who would speak the truth under the eyes of Wey.

Both had told of the departure from Deswrain, and how there had been no hint of the turn in the weather to come. Indeed, quite the opposite. The weather sooths had all forecast a steady southwesterly for two days and more. There had been no risk taken with the lives of the Queen or the Royal children, Wey alone called for the change in the wind at the precise moment that would have meant the death of them all but for the skill of Captain Nordrall and his crew.

The King stared at Nordrall. He was desperate to blame someone for the loss of his son, heir to his throne. His mistress had been inconsolable at the loss of her son, and the Royal household and Royal Guard would miss the strength of Rebgroth. Sadly the Queen did not perish, for which he would have thanked Nordrall.

"It would appear Captain, that your legendary skills saved the rest of your passengers and that the loss of my son was not down to the negligence of any individual. Go then and leave us to our grief. I suggest another long voyage of adventure in case I should change my mind!"

Nordrall didn't know whether to smile or not, so taking the path of discretion, he bowed solemnly and backed down the hall, turning after six paces and walking as confidently as he could to the large double doors at the far end of the hall. He felt a huge wave of relief wash over him, as much for his crew as himself. He had always wondered about that land to the west they had seen on the voyage north so long ago. Now might be the time to go and have a look.

Eilana had watched and listened intently to the proceedings, a hollow still in her chest at the loss of her son. Her father had collapsed when he heard and was still very ill, her mother distraught. Harlmon offered to take revenge on whoever Eilana ordered, but she expressly forbade him to do any such thing.

As Nordrall backed away the child inside her kicked and moved. It was reminding her of its presence she thought, a boy she was sure. With Gudrick dead, and girls unable to succeed, illegitimate or not, he would be the only male child of the King and would be recognised by most as heir to the throne, and her as the future King Mother. It was almost worth the death of little Harlada. The terrible realisation hit her that it was worth it. Wey what had she become.

Queen Bertal sobbed pitifully, bent over on a smaller throne beside Gudmon. It irked Eilana to see Bertal there whilst she had to sit in the gallery, but Gudmon insisted she was Queen, even if he had grown to detest her, and she must be treated as such.

Princess Patrikal comforted her. At nine years old, she had come through the horror of the journey better than most. She insisted to her mother that Gudrick was alive. She said she would know if he was dead, and he wasn't. The whole court thought she was so brave and kind to comfort her mother that way, but of course they could not know that by a hereditary quirk she had a strong strain of elf in her from her great grandmother, and fed by the bumbleberry, it meant that she knew such things.

Eilana made her way back to her apartment, the Queen's old rooms. She grew tired quickly now with only a moon to the birth. The Queen's party had arrived only a few days before, after returning to Deswrain for half a moon before braving the voyage again, this time on an almost flat calm with a light breeze.

Serculas was still numb with the loss of her love. Unfortunately, with the boys gone and Patrikal grown so, there was little for her to do except sit around and cry. Eilana talked of all the help she would be when her child arrived, but that was a while away yet.

The Queen was strangely respectful of her. She had expected more spite, more venomous words, but they did not come. Gratax was always near the

Queen, and Eilana finally decided she was happy with her status and her love of Gratax. She decided not to go looking for trouble in that quarter, but to watch for it.

Reassel, however, was another matter. She had let the whole business go too far in a clumsy attempt to get close to the Queen's thoughts, and if she was honest, a stupid curiosity about sex with another woman. Reassel was furious to find Eilana pregnant and sleeping with the King. She was hurt and deeply scarred by Eilana's apparent lack of concern at her feelings.

After keeping her patience until bursting point, she was waiting in Eilana's room as she returned. She screamed her hurt at Eilana, who tried to calm her but would not say the things Reassel wanted to hear. Eventually Reassel began to threaten her with exposure of their affaire. Eilana tried to tell her that the King just wouldn't believe her, which was true, but others would, Gratax for one.

As Reassel left the room Eilana was not sure what she would do. She thought she had calmed her for a while, but she was becoming unstable, and hence unpredictable; dangerous.

She rang for a maid and ordered her cloak, leaving a message for the King that she was off to see her sick father. Making her way out of the Keep, her mind was racing, different courses of action flowing through it, their consequences and likely outcomes. There was only one way out of this mess.

She reached her parents' house to find her father had died moments before; in fact she had crossed her sister who had been dispatched to fetch her. Her mother sat by the fireplace, on the stool which she usually used at the table. It had slightly uneven legs and if anyone else used it, she was always telling them off for rocking on it and not sitting still, so she used it herself.

She looked up at Eilana as she entered the little house and stretched her arms out to her as she rose, hugging her silently.

"He was so proud of you, ashamed too, and you carrying the King's child! Oh, how you confused him so, but little Harlada's loss was just too much for him." She laughed a little. "He was a wonderful man, we must celebrate his life, then I will join him soon I feel."

"Oh mother, don't talk so," Eilana sobbed on her shoulder. It was hard to get close she was so big with child. "My son cannot lose both grandparents before his birth." She turned her head as she heard another stool scrape back beside her as Harlmon stood from the table.

"Hello pretty one," he said. She left her mother and hugged him, and seeing Harlfel beside him, now almost sixteen himself, she hugged him too.

"Look after mother Harlfel, I must speak with Harlmon."

She took his arm and led him from the house, walking slowly round to the stables where there was always a bale of hay or two to sit on.

"I need your help brother, your special help."

"It is done my pretty one. What is the problem?"

"You know Reassel, Lady in Waiting to the Queen." He nodded. "Well she has threatened me, and that means us all. I need you to remove that threat." He looked at her then smiled.

"There were rumours about her and her preference for the company of other ladies." He was smiling broadly now as Eilana's discomfort grew. She could hide nothing from him. "Oh Sister, why didn't you tell me? Girls doing it to together; if only I could have watched."

"Well you couldn't, now are you going to help me, it will need to be soon."

"Of course. Tell her it is too dangerous to see her in the Keep and arrange to meet her behind the stables a quarter watch before midnight, there will be no one around then. I will see to her."

"I knew I could depend on you, and I think I have a way then that we can be close again, like we used to be, but do this for me first."

"I will my pretty one, I will."

They walked back to the house where Eilana sat with her mother and Eival for a quarter watch before returning to the Royal apartments and seeking out Reassel. They had a curt exchange in the hallway before Eilana begged Reassel to forgive her. Now she had returned with the Queen she realised how much she had missed her. The King was just a reaction to her going which stupidly left her pregnant. Just meet her behind the stables a quarter watch before midnight and she would make it up to her, the straw would be comfortable. She hugged her and hurried away. Another triumph for her acting ability she thought as she reached her rooms. Now it was up to Harlmon.

He hid himself in the shadows just inside the stable doors and waited. Reassel arrived a little early, eager as she was to see Eilana. She looked up and down the alleyway and stepped backwards into the shadows of the stable doors. The dim light on her face told Harlmon it was her, and he stepped quietly forward.

His left hand clamped over her mouth and the knife in his right pressed on her throat, just penetrating the skin enough for a trickle of blood to run down the blade.

"One sound and you are dead bitch," he hissed and pulled her into the stable.

"I hear you like the company of women eh, well I think it is time a man did something about that."

She was petrified with fear. She wanted to scream, to fight him off, but her limbs were frozen in the belief that if she just did what he asked she would live.

"Do exactly as I say and I will not hurt you," he lied, "I'll just let you know what you're missing."

He bent her face down over a pony trap in the corner, the knife point on the back of her neck, making her grip the wheels each side.

"If your hands leave the wheels or you make a sound, you die." She took it as a statement of fact. Listening to him behind her, she shook with fear as he fumbled with the laces of his codpiece and freed himself. He pulled up her skirts to find no underclothes. She had come dressed for the occasion he thought, but not this one.

With the excitement in him, and with the thought of this woman and his sister lying together, he was already aroused, and he forced himself roughly into her from behind.

"Now that's what it's supposed to feel like bitch."

He seeded all too quickly, and as he did he brought the butt of the knife held tightly in his fist, crashing down onto the back of her head. She lay spread-eagled face down on the trap, unconscious if not dead. He didn't care which.

He wiped himself in her skirt and put himself away, lacing his leggings. He laid a horse blanket behind the trap then loosened Reassel's hands from the wheels. She slipped backwards off the trap and neatly onto the blanket. He wrapped her in it, heaved her up and over his shoulder, then carried her hurriedly down the alley and a fair distance around the wall, confident there would be no-one about to see him. He was right.

He tossed the bundle from his shoulder roughly onto the cobbles. She hit them with a dull thump. Pulling the blanket from her he drew his knife again.

"This is for my sister," he said as he drove the blade deep into her throat. From the blood that sprayed across the cobbles she had still been alive, but she was not now.

Harlmon walked back to the house and poured some water from the jug on the table. Everyone was still asleep; they had been when he went out. He sat by the fireplace and finished his drink. He enjoyed helping his sister.

The next day brought mayhem. The body was found with the dawn, which caused a commotion, but when it was discovered to be Reassel there was great consternation. There had not been a killing within the Castle walls for longer than most could remember, and certainly not of a Lady in Waiting. But what had she been doing out in the alleyways at that time of night? Speculation grew.

Gratax led the investigation personally. The death of one so close to the Queen could mean she was at risk too. His suspicion fell immediately on Eilana, but then he knew she had been friends with Reassel, close friends he believed, so that didn't make sense without a strong motive. The investigation got nowhere.

A rumour spread that Reassel had been killed by a spurned lover, one of the crew of The Lone Hart or the Lady Wrain, both of which had sailed on the pre-dawn tide. He had discovered her taste for lovers of her own sex and murdered her in a jealous rage. Harlmon congratulated himself on thinking of that one; it tied in nicely with the whispered rumours of her and the seamstress.

A few days later Eilana lay with the King. She persuaded him she should have protection. If Reassel could be murdered here, within the Castle walls, anything could happen, and she was carrying his son. He agreed and said he would ask Gratax to recommend a suitable officer to assign to the task, with perhaps two or three picked men.

Eilana ran her fingers through the hair on his chest. No, there was only one person except the King himself who she trusted enough to do the job, and that was her brother Harlmon. He would have to make him an officer in the Royal Guard, no, for absolute security, in her guard.

The King never could say no to her, and that very day, despite General Gratax's bitter opposition, Harlmon was commissioned an officer and given command of Eilana's personal guard, independent of the Royal Guard, and reporting directly to the King. Harlmon immediately recruited five of his closest friends, all strong working lads, into what was the birth of her private army, the Castle Bluecoats. The King even paid for the uniforms.

Half a moon later, after another relatively easy birth at which Serculas acted as midwife, although Ferlmun fussed around her giving unheeded advice, Eilana produced a healthy boy. She named him Prince Gudfel after the King's grandfather, and no one argued about the title Prince either. Better to get things established early she thought.

Chapter 16

Klarss walked confidently at the head of the long file of Marsh Dwellers and their captives as they wound their way through the marshland behind the beach. He was confident because he had risen to be War Chief of the West Marsh and it was in his nature; confident because he had walked these paths many times before; but mostly because Glurk, his best scout, was some distance in front of him checking that the path was still there.

Behind him Gudrick and Harlada travelled in the arms of two strong Marsh Fighters. The boys had started the trek holding Rebgroth's hands, but it became impossible to walk like that as the path narrowed and became very boggy and slippery. As Rebgroth struggled to lift them from the clammy mud, one in each arm, the two Marshmen stepped forward, unbidden, and took them from him. One said something that meant nothing to him, before setting off after Klarss.

They had walked like this for almost a watch now and Rebgroth's calves and ankles ached terribly from continually halting slips and slides as he trudged forward. He was determined not to show weakness to his captors so he struggled on, gritting his teeth on occasion.

He could see now that they were steadily approaching a line of low hills that formed a hog's back ridge leading inland at right angles to the shore, and as they came closer still, he could see a large village on the slopes above the marsh and stretching over the ridge. Half a watch later they were there.

The villagers lined the small streets to see them arrive. Many greeted Fighters in Klarss's Company, but all stared curiously at the boys and quite definitely suspiciously at him. No-one spoke to him, not that he would have understood, nor tried to communicate in any way. In fact he realised that if he deviated slightly to one side or the other, the onlookers moved back rapidly to avoid him.

As they reached a large central roundhouse, the boys were put back on their feet and Klarss led them inside. A small group of old men and women sat around an open fire on the opposite side of the large room from the door, about eight in all. Three of them each had a bowl of a liquid in their hands, which they drank from as they talked in their strange tongue.

They were dressed in the same dark and rough weaved garments as Klarss and his men, but without the long and belted waxed leather tabards. The elders went quiet as they approached and stopped beside their circle. The three with their backs to their captives rose slowly and moved around the circle before sitting again. The boys stepped forward into the gap, Rebgroth stood behind them with a hand on a shoulder each.

A woman of many years who had long wispy grey hair that hung almost to her waist, looked up deliberately slowly and spoke to them, and although her accent was strong they understood her well enough.

"Greetings children of the storm, our people have awaited your arrival for more than thirty life times; it is good that you are here." The boys looked at each other, then up at Rebgroth, before Harlada replied.

"Thank you Lady. We are very hungry." They all smiled at his directness and she replied.

"Then you shall eat before you travel on, and rest for the little light there is left of the day and for tonight. At dawn you will leave for the Hill of Grass and Berries where you will be guests of our Lord Priest Cralch and our Wise Ones, but while we have food brought you must sit with us and tell us of your young lives, you cannot be more than four or five summers yet you carry yourselves well." Her eyes hardened as she turned towards Rebgroth.

"You however are no friend to the Marsh People and are not welcomed by us. Nevertheless you will be treated as an honoured guest as we have been ordered, but not within our circle." Rebgroth was taken aback by the sharp tone of her voice. She spoke with genuine venom.

"It will of course be as you wish My Lady, but I have never done harm to your people, and I mean them no harm now. I am grateful for your aid and only wish to see my charges returned to their home and their families."

"You may wish us no harm now, but you will. It is not my place to talk of such things however. Klarss will take you to a warm house for the night, where you will be comfortable and be fed. As is our custom for an honoured guest you may chose a woman if you wish to be comforted, but you will not sleep under the same roof as any of our villagers this night. The children will remain with us, one of them is very important to us, and as we do not yet know which one, you may be sure they will both be kept very safe and guarded from all dangers. Go now, your presence offends us."

He was going to protest, and attempt to understand their problem with him, but he realised it would be useless. If it was not her place to tell him then it must be someone else's; probably this Lord Priest. He would just have to be patient.

"Despite your words I am grateful, My Lady. I will retire now and will require no comfort."

"That is as well. As the Death Bringer, no woman of the village would wish to lie with you and would do so only for the honour of the village, and for the Death Bringer's seed to leave life in one of our people would not be well for us, but I have said too much. Klarss, take him to his bed."

Death Bringer she had called him. He could not imagine the circumstances, unless they expected him to fight his way out, which would more likely lead to his death than to many of theirs.

He bowed slightly and turned towards Klarss, not backing away as he would have done for formal politeness, and followed him out of the roundhouse. They crossed the narrow street and wound their way up the slope to a typically small mud and straw one room house on the crest of the hill. People still stared at him as he walked, but at least he could understand their reaction now, if not the reason behind it. He thanked Klarss and entered the room.

In the fading light he had looked on the other side on the ridge. Flat marshland stretched for at least as many miles to the south as he knew lay to the north. To contemplate escape was a waste of time, as it was impossible to go north or south, useless to go west back to the sea, and with just the route east open to him, he could only imagine it to be well guarded.

There was a pallet bed and blankets near the good sized fire, with plenty of split logs piled beside it, and on a small table were laid bread, cheese, cold meat of some sort and berries. A jug of water and a wooden goblet stood beside them.

He sat on the bed and ate; all the comforts of home, except for Serculas. He was sure she was alive and well. The Lone Hart had run down wind so fast he was sure they would have got back to Deswrain safely. He thought of calling for a woman, just to ruffle these damn peoples' feathers, but it was pointless, and obviously would not be very kind to the poor woman that was despatched to satisfy his desires. No, sleep and rest for his poor legs was definitely best; they ached terribly now.

He had fallen asleep fully dressed against the cold that crept into the room as the fired died. He awoke to the sound of two village women in the room, one putting small wood chips onto the glowing embers of the fire which burst into flame and kindled the heavier split logs she laid on them, the other had placed a bowl of porridge and milk on the table, a fresh pitcher of water and some bread, replacing them on her tray with the empties from the night before.

They hurriedly finished their tasks and left the single room as he sat up and they realised he was awake. He shouted a thank you after them but they wouldn't have understood anyway. The grain porridge and bread told their own story though. He had seen some animals around the village, but there were no crop fields. That meant grain was brought into the village from afar, probably traded for fish and meat, which in turn suggested a developed society where resources were moved around to where people were, rather than people moving around as they used to do, to where the food was.

As he finished his breakfast, which was very good, the door opened without a knock and Klarss entered the room, the two boys running past him and hugging Rebgroth; not something they normally did, but then things were hardly normal for them. He guessed he had become their one link with home and security.

"Hello young men, have you had a good night?"

"They sang dreadful songs and laughed at things we could not understand for ages," complained Harlada, "but when we were so tired we could hardly stay awake, they brought us two straw mattresses and we slept by the fire."

"It stank in there this morning," added Gudrick, "we probably stink of it ourselves now."

They certainly didn't seem to have a system of emptying the waste buckets from behind the screens very often, certainly not as often as in the Royal quarters at Castle Nisceriel.

"You know what is funny? No-one has asked me my name, or tried to talk to me at all," said Harlada. Always the thinker that Harlada, thought Rebgroth, a bright boy. "They don't seem interested that Gudrick is a Prince."

"No they don't," agreed Rebgroth. "Now, have you all your clothes on ready to travel? I fear we have far to walk today." They nodded in unison, "and you have eaten?"

"Oh yes," confirmed Gudrick, "it was very good, and all we could eat."

Klarss spoke, pointing at the door, and Rebgroth steered the boys through it and outside, where a small crowd was gathered. Beyond them Klarss's company of Marsh Fighters were lined up, ready to leave, and all wearing their waxed cloaks. They obviously expected rain.

The old lady with the long wispy hair approached Rebgroth. He spoke before she could.

"Thank you, My Lady, for your hospitality."

"Thank me not Death Bringer; if not for the strict orders from our Lord Priest Cralch, you would be dead now. I do not pretend to understand the intricacies of the ancient prophesies, or why we cannot change what is fated, but let me warn you, Klarss would far rather see you dead now and perhaps save the lives of many of our people in the future, so give him no excuse to disobey his orders, he prays for just such."

"I do not understand either My Lady. I repeat that I bear you no ill will, but neither can I see the future. I can see no reason for my King or myself to ever bear you or your people ill will, unless you should cause harm to these children, my charges, so again I thank you on their behalf, and indeed, on mine."

"Were you not the Death Bringer I would consider you an honourable man, but you need not fear for the children. The Water Gods will turn the prophesies to actuality in due time. I may live till then, I may have gone to join them, but I will at least be able to tell my grandchildren that I met the Death Bringer and the Children. Your God walk with you and forgive you."

Rebgroth looked at her for a moment, on the edge of anger but with his curiosity aroused almost to bursting point.

"Live long then My Lady, perchance our paths will cross again."

"They will not Death Bringer. Go now. Klarss, away."

Klarss grabbed his elbow to lead him away. Rebgroth shook him off angrily and glared at him. The old lady snapped at Klarss who stormed away towards his men. Rebgroth looked again at her, and with half a smile and half a shrug, he took the boys' arms and led them after Klarss.

"What does she mean Rebgroth?" Harlada asked, "I don't understand."

"Neither do I my boy," he replied, "but I am sure we will find out when we meet this Lord Priest of theirs, so be brave and be strong, they have at least told us we will get home eventually. Come on Gudrick, you must both be the young men you are. Follow Klarss now. Go on."

The company of Marsh Fighters moved out of the village, eastwards along the ridge of hills towards the hill of Grass and Berries, the two boys walking behind Klarss, Rebgroth behind them.

Gudrick and Harlada walked for the best part of half a quarter before Klarss waved two of his men forward to pick them up. Rebgroth smiled at them, they had done well. Klarss had set a good pace that left the boys almost running at times, but that quarter watch had given Rebgroth plenty of time to look around and take in the landscape to either side and before them, between the breaks in the trees.

To the north, the marsh lay behind the long flat beach they had washed up on. There was a large hill that stuck out into the estuary at its southern end, before another similar beach ran behind the hog's back of hills along which they travelled. Rebgroth could see how their walk the day before had started inland, skirting the east of the hill then crossing the marsh almost due south to the village.

Beyond the marsh, a line of tall hills rose steeply from its edge, three or four times the height of the hog's back. From behind the northern end of the beach, they ran inland as far as one could see, curving steadily to the south. Just over them, Rebgroth knew, was a narrow stretch of marshes before the thin line of hills that divided them from the river Ffon. Over those hills lay Nisceriel, but it might as well have been ten times as far. There were scouts placed permanently in those hills, where they could see ships sailing up the estuary, almost a day's sail away in clear weather, but they were no help to him here.

To the south, the marsh stretched even further before the land rose into hills that ran east and west and formed the wild northern borders of Deswrain. To the east they curved slightly to the north, and much further inland, they met the hills to the north, ringing the marshes completely.

When they walked over the highest rises along the hog's back, Rebgroth could see that this long low ridge of hills ran inland, each lower than the previous, until it flattened completely as the marshes to the north and the south joined behind it. Across these wetlands to the east from there stood a single hill, not very tall and ringed by water. From where they were, the backdrop of hills was far beyond. It was clear from there why the land trip from Niseriel to Deswrain took so long. It was a very long trek inland around the marshes.

They stopped after a three quarter watch for a short rest, then pressed on. Klarss was obviously keen to cover the journey to a set timetable in his mind. Members of his company took it in turns to carry the boys, each for about quarter, and the boys were enjoying it, sitting high on shoulders and playing giants.

Soon after noon the light grew dimmer and looking over his shoulder, Rebgroth could see a bank of dark clouds rolling quickly towards them. The rain followed shortly and he was thankful for the waxed cloak the Marsh Fighters had given him. The boys were carried under cloaks now, their view much restricted but they remained mainly dry, despite the fact that it rained on them continually throughout the afternoon.

At dusk, earlier than normal with the dark skies, they reached the end of the hills where a few huts surrounded a roundhouse. It was much smaller than the one in the village, but then there were few permanent inhabitants of the small hamlet. This, however, was obviously Klarss' objective for the day, and the Company prepared to bed down for the night in the roundhouse as darkness closed in.

A large fire was lit in the centre of the room, filling it with smoke to start with, then drawing through the single hole in the centre of the roof and sucking out the smoke as the flames grew. Rebgroth sat close to it without waiting to be invited and drew the boys to him. Various cooking implements were assembled and with food supplied by the locals, a meal prepared.

They settled down for the night where they sat, wrapped in the woollen blankets they had been given. Gudrick and Harlada cuddled up to Rebgroth and slept relatively well, he however found sleep difficult as his mind rehearsed a hundred different scenarios for the meeting he expected the next evening with the Lord Priest. As he drifted in and out of sleep they became more bizarre and unreal, until he became angry with himself for not sleeping, but the angrier he got, the more awake he felt. As the first glimmers of light appeared he fell soundly asleep, to be woken what seemed, and indeed was, only moments later, by the sound of breakfast being prepared for the Company. It was the porridge again, and actually, it was quite good.

Shortly after the dawn the Company assembled outside the roundhouse. To Rebgroth's experienced eyes, camp had been struck professionally; even though they had all slept in the roundhouse, there had been no shortcuts. If he was to be the Death Bringer, he would have to be very good if these Marsh Dwellers were trained and disciplined to fight as well as this.

Glurk led off into the marsh, but this time two other scouts followed him, each about twenty paces back. Klarss led the Company in single file behind them. The boys were firmly in the arms of two strong Fighters from the start, as although the rain from the previous day and night had stopped, it had raised the water level enough to make this part of the journey particularly tricky.

They trekked all morning, slipping and sliding along a winding path through the marshes and mires. Only someone with an intricate knowledge of the hidden paths could have led them through. Chief Scout Glurk had the knowledge, but with the heightened water levels, even he was taking the precaution of three men testing the path.

Noon came and went before they stopped to rest and eat. They carried cold salted meat and cheese which Rebgroth enjoyed. The boys found it boring, but hungry as they were, they devoured what they were given quietly.

Rebgroth wanted to ask all sorts of things. At times he voiced questions but was ignored. He had assumed no one spoke their language yet felt it worth trying, but if anybody did understand him they did not respond. In fact no one did speak his language. The old lady in the village was a wise woman who had retired from the Grass and Berry Hill and returned to the village of her birth. She was a very educated woman and spoke Niscerien and Deswrainy, although they were almost the same.

They moved on as before, but after only a quarter or so they came to open water. One small wooden dwelling stood beside a wooden jetty that jutted out across the water for thirty paces at least. The high reeds and marsh bushes stopped at the waters edge, and from the jetty Rebgroth and the boys looked across the water to the Hill of Grass and Berries, which was exactly what it was. It rose as an island out of the lake, except it looked like the far side was marsh rather than water, it was hard to tell, but it was a long way to there from where they stood.

A wooden craft was tied to the jetty. It was about three tall men in length but quite narrow for its size, which made it seem a little unstable. A trained eye would appreciate the depth of its hull and heavy keel. There were two rowing cross-seats for four oarsmen with passenger seats fore and aft. A raised stern gave a seat to a steersman who could see over the length of the boat and guide them with a single oar lashed to the stern upright.

Klarss beckoned them forward and pointed to the boat, as five heavily built men came out of the hut where they had been waiting for them. One wore a leather field jacket, and it was he that approached Rebgroth.

"Welcum to me craaft Deff Bringerr," he said in a heavy accent. Rebgroth was surprised to hear his own language. He didn't seem the educated type. "Surrprized I cun speak to ee are ee?" He grinned.

"I am delighted you can, and thank you for your welcome. I do not seem too popular compared to the boys." The boatman laughed.

"Deff Bringerr ee may be, but at I's age I weren't a be travelling far to fight ee, so I'se a guess I'ld a not has no reason a dislike ee."

"Then please be so kind as to thank Klarss here for bringing us this far, and wish him and his men well."

The boatman looked at him and almost shrugged as he turned and spoke at some length to Klarss, who looked Rebgroth straight in the eyes and spoke to him. Rebgroth returned the stare as the boatman translated.

"Klarss says ee'd a rather ee were dead, nn ee uld gladly do it if ee could. As tis ee can't, ee'd a be ordered not ah, nn ee be sad bout it. Ee wish ee elf. Deff Bringerr ee may be, but ee say live till ee can fight ee, for tis said a Marsh Fighter will kill ee in time, nn he prays it'll be ee."

Rebgroth looked back at Klarss and shook his head. He stood straight and slapped his arm across his chest in a salute to the brave. Klarss eyed him warily, then did the same. Rebgroth nodded and led the boys onto the bow of the boat behind the oarsmen who were already in position.

The boatman stepped nimbly and confidently aboard, having untied the craft forward and astern, and took up his station at the tiller. The two oarsmen nearest the jetty used their oars to push them off at an order from the stern, returning them to their rowlocks and pulling away in unison with the others on the command. Harlada looked back at Klarss and his Company.

"Will we fight them one day?" he asked Rebgroth.

"They seem to believe I will my boy, but not you."

"Why would you fight them and not me? It doesn't make sense." Rebgroth held him close.

"No it doesn't Harlada, not now anyway, but who can tell why they think it? Perhaps the men on that island will tell us."

"Whatever they say, we are friends, we must fight together."

"Yes Harlada, you are quite right young man, we are friends. Let us hope nothing changes that." Gudrick nodded and hugged Rebgroth too.

"Let us hope we get many answers when we reach that island, I am becoming tired of this game they play."

They stood in the bow watching the island grow closer. The boys stood on the bow seat, Rebgroth behind it with a hand on their shoulders. They could see the island more clearly now and what had made its outline so strange from a distance.

It was a wooden island fortress; wooden but formidable none the less. A rampart over two men high ran around the very base of the island, and with the lake waters high from the rain, they lapped against the bottom of the thick upright logs that formed the wall.

Facing them were two small towers on each side of large studded gates that opened onto a decked wharf, built out from the island into the lake. Two boats similar to theirs were tied up unloading goods, but the wharf was long enough to accommodate another two.

The hill rose quite steeply from the ramparts on the water's edge. The grassy slopes were broken up by a host of thorny bushes that turned red with berries in the autumn, and at this time of year were adorned with white flowering buds that gave the hill the look of a recent snowstorm.

From the gates, a stone track wound up the hillside. It was slightly to one side of the gates where the slope was least, made up of a series of short straights and hairpin bends. It led the eye up to the wooden tower at the top. It could not be called a keep exactly, as it was really a single square tower some ten men high, with a collection of other wooden buildings that seemed to have been built piecemeal around it, but it was still impressive to the eye.

Rebgroth could just make out a group of figures in white robes looking across the water towards them from a rampart at the very top of the tower. He knew that would be their reception committee viewing their arrival. He wondered what was in their minds. He would soon find out but he still felt an enormous impatience.

The island was further away than it had seemed and was bigger than they had thought from a distance. Up close, the wooden walls were at least three men high, and the towers on each side of the gate were much taller than they had appeared from across the water. Rebgroth could not help but take in the effectiveness of the defences, and to admire the killing ground that these decked landing wharfs would be in a siege situation.

They were met at the dockside by a single white-robed official who bowed deeply to the boys. He summoned forward two large liveried servants who picked up the boys and placed them high on their shoulders. He turned slowly to Rebgroth and curtly gestured him to follow, turning away again and setting off at a steady pace up the winding slope.

The odd-looking group was closely observed by a small crowd that had gathered on the lower slopes of the hill. Rebgroth could not help but notice that they were nearly all liveried in some form or other. These were not curious citizens as they had met in the villages, but retained servants of those that ruled here.

After a tiring climb they reached the main gates of the tower on the summit. They stood open but with guards armed with short swords and a kind of short spear that was new to Rebgroth. It seemed short enough to use in close combat but probably just long enough to throw. Each guard held three, one in his right hand and two behind the shield in his left; something else for him to remember.

As the party entered the gates, the guards fell in around Rebgroth, boxing him in a square between them, but with no hint of disarming him of his sword or long knife. The large ground floor room they entered had tables around the edges, laid for a feast to come but empty of people.

A large wooden staircase rose from the centre of the floor and their guide walked straight up it to large double doors at its top. He hammered three times on the door, then twice more. There was an answering knock then silence. Moments later the doors swung back and they walked through onto a small landing that split left and right then turned back either side of the stairs into a large room that filled the tower at that level.

A small spiral staircase could be seen in the far left corner that led above, but the room was dominated by a high dais that ran across its far end. On this stood eight white-robed men, all reaching the end of their life spans at first glance, but one who stood slightly in front also sported a pale green sash across his chest. It was he who spoke in almost perfect Niscerien.

"Welcome my children. We have awaited your arrival for very many generations since the first Lord Priest Cralch told of your coming. It is a great honour to me to be his thirty-fourth successor and to be the chosen one to welcome you both, Boy Warlord and Doomed Companion. I know not yet which of you is which. You will remain with us in our care until I do, and then after an important ceremony, you may return home to your loved ones, leaving fate to play out its path." He turned to Rebgroth.

"As for you Death Bringer, you too are welcome only that without you the greater good of the prophecies would not come about. By letting you live we allow the death of many of our people at your army's hands, but should you die now, fate would lead to the death of all our people. So the prophesies of the first Lord Priest Cralch tell us, and so we believe. Thus you may remain armed while you are amongst us Death Bringer, but should you bring about your own death by taking up your arms against us now, you will have the satisfaction of knowing that you will indirectly bring about the end of all our people. Should you choose to live longer than this moment, you will still bring about the death of very many of our people, but we will go on to grow strong as a people and flourish under the leadership of the Great Boy Warrior. Choose wisely then Death Bringer, both your fate and ours."

Rebgroth stood silently for a few moments, thoughts spinning in his head. Before he could answer Harlada spoke, shocking him back to reality.

"Lord Priest, Rebgroth is our friend and has saved our lives, he is our friend, our mothers' friend. I do not understand how you can tell us that either Prince Gudrick or I could fight him. I am only a boy sire, but I cannot believe what you say."

"Well spoken child, you are the friend of a Prince, and of the Death Bringer, I know. Such is the conundrum of the ancient prophecies. They are difficult for a priest to understand, and impossible for a boy of five summers, although I can see you are bright and strong." Rebgroth broke in.

"Lord Priest, I will cause no problems to you here and now. I cannot foresee any circumstance to become your enemy unless you have any malice towards my wards, or unless you should refuse to let us return to our homeland."

"You will return therefore, with your wards, for so the prophesies say, but only after we discover which of these boys is the true one, and I cannot say when we will see the sign. You have to remain until then, whenever that may be."

"Then so be it Lord Priest, but hear this, should my patience with this nonsense become frayed, it will lead to my death and your doom, remember that."

"I cannot forget Death Bringer, for so the teachings have told me since my youth. You are a great warrior too, an honourable and brave soldier. It is not your fault that fate has given you a role we understand but you do not. In other circumstances I would be pleased to become your friend. Now we will go down and eat with a ceremony to new guests, for such you all are."

Chapter 17

Eilana awoke, lying beside the King who still slept, quite peacefully for once. She was very content. The day before had been Prince Gudfel's first bornbless party, and a very special day it had been.

A child's first bornbless was always celebrated more than most others, because so many infants did not reach their first bornbless, and most that did lived on for many years more. There were of course those that succumbed to tragic accidents, as had Gudrick and her Harlada a year before, and she still felt the loss when she let herself, but what had made Eilana so happy now was the feast held after the children were in bed.

For the first time, she had sat beside the King at the top table, at his left hand. The Queen had sat at his right, the guest side, with General Gratax next to her, recognition of their relationship. Yes, everything had settled down perfectly, and now amicably too. Bertal knew Princess Patrikal could not rule and eventually accepted Prince Gudfel as Heir to the throne, making Eilana the future King Mother. There was nothing else Bertal could have done, but it allowed Gudmon to live happily with Eilana and her with Gratax, and for her to remain Queen, everywhere but in the King's bed.

Eilana rolled sideways and kissed Gudmon's cheek then leant across him and kissed his neck until he awoke. She made love to him with a passion she had not felt for a while, and which completely delighted him. All he needed was to feel loved and wanted, and when she wanted to, she knew exactly how to do both.

They held each other contentedly. No matter how cynically she had entered the relationship, Eilana had grown genuinely fond of Gudmon. She really couldn't call it love, but it was the next best thing, she was happy with him, and she enjoyed pleasing him. It made her happy to see him so genuinely content.

King Gudmon had always had a theory of life however, a theory that hard experience had taught him. It was that when everything was perfect, when life was exactly as you wished it, enjoy it to the full, because something would surely come along to ruin it, and in this particular case, it was a rider from Bridgebury, a small village in the eastern corner of the realm, the lowest crossing point of the River Ffon.

The rider approached the gates of Castle Nisceriel and reigned in his sweating mount with a clatter of hooves on the drawbridge. He had ridden all night and now, half a watch after the dawn, his horse was spent, almost dead on its feet, but the news he carried was worth it.

He shouted for the Guard to open the gates, he was the bearer of great news for the King himself. His uniform, the red and black of the Royal Guard, was his automatic authority for the guards at the gates. They threw back the huge studded portals and the messenger spurred his exhausted mount through the gates and into the Castle, finally pulling him up outside the stable block. He leapt from the saddle and ran across the square, slightly awkwardly from the stiffness in his thighs after a night in the saddle.

The Officer of the Guard took his report and ran inside shouting for Greardel, who was readying the King's clothes for the day in his robe-room. He heard the calls and rushed out into the hallway to meet the Officer.

"Rouse the King," he cried, "there is momentous news from Bridgebury."

"What news? If you think I am going to disturb His Highness for some petty report from the borders you are..."

"Do it Greardel you fool," the Officer snapped, "do you really think I ran up all those stairs for nothing!"

Greardel stared at him for a moment, then turned to the King's bedroom door and hammered loudly upon it.

As Gudmon and Eilana were shocked from their cuddly doze, their bodies still slightly hot and clammy with sweat and juices from their lovemaking, Gudmon smiled ruefully then laughed.

"That Greardel's timing is becoming harder to bear each day."

"Then send him away my King, it is not that late."

The knocking became more urgent and then, almost without precedent, Greardel called out.

"Your Majesty, an urgent dispatch." Gudmon gave Eilana a resigned look.

"Wey, it must be urgent," he said, "come my love, make yourself decent, we will have to let him in."

Eilana rose naked from the bed and wrapped herself in a woollen blanket. The King pulled on some leather leggings and ordered Greardel's entry. He hurried in, the Officer of the watch beside him. The messenger had wearily reached the top of the stairs and stood outside the door. He was joined by most of the Royal Household who had gathered at the commotion.

"Well?" asked the King.

"A messenger from Bridgebury Sire, shall I bid him enter?"

"I think you'd better Greardel, after disturbing me so."

Greardel half turned and waved the messenger in. He bowed deeply before the King.

"Your Majesty, I am bidden to give you news by the.."

"Yes yes man, what news?"

"Sire, as dusk fell last night, a cart arrived at Bridgebury driven by the Second Officer of the Royal Guard Rebgroth, and carrying Prince Gudrick and his companion Harlada. They are well and are resting overnight before leaving for here this morning Sire."

There was a scream and a crash from the hallway as Serculas fainted, Prince Gudfel in her arms. Patrikal grabbed him from her as she fell heavily but safely against the banister rail.

Eilana was numb. So many emotions and feelings raced around in her mind. There was an immediate surge of emotional gratitude that Harlada was alive, but then a terrible regret that Prince Gudrick was. Gudfel was no longer heir, she no longer the future King Mother, that role was Bertal's again. How could she be so angry her Harlada was alive? She was washed over with guilt and self-loathing, but only for a moment, before her brain once more started to race. She would re-establish herself somehow; she just had to work out how.

The King just stared at the messenger for some moments before he found his voice.

"Thank you good sir, your name and rank?"

"I command a third Hundert Sire, a sergeant of arms Sire, Badraman by name and your loyal servant"

"Well you are Officer Badraman now, by my personal decree, and you will be attached to my personal guard. See to it Gratax, I can see you out there."

Officer Badraman was led from the room somewhat stunned before he could thank the King, but the King had forgotten him already. There was a

165

thump behind him. He swung round to see Eilana slumped back into a chair, the blanket dropped around her waist as she fell, her breasts on show to the world.

The King spun back shouting and herding everyone out into the hall where Serculas was just stirring. He slammed the doors shut and ran to Eilana, bending and hugging her.

"Oh my love. Such good news. It's all too perfect." He mistook her tears for emotional joy, but they were tears of frustration. So close and now this. How could she be so angry her own child still lived? She stood and hugged Gudmon, her blanket falling completely away. He carried her to the bed and lay beside her, holding her in his arms for nearly a quarter.

Eventually Eilana sat up and looked down at Gudmon. She kissed his forehead then spoke.

"My love I'm so sorry. I should be helping you to celebrate not lying here. I think it was just the shock. I was so certain Harlada was dead and had probably suppressed my grief too much, but now Gudrick and Harlada will be back by nightfall with luck, and Rebgroth of course. We must organise a celebration."

"You are right as always my dear," replied Gudmon. "Come, we will dress and eat then get things organised."

"One thing though my love; I don't really understand these things, but now that Gudrick is back, Gudfel is still a Prince is he?"

"Of course my dear, he is my son, but Gudrick is the Prince Heir, as is his right."

"Oh of course, I realise that. No this is wonderful. It will be just as if they hadn't been gone. I cannot wait to see Harlada." She kissed Gudmon and turned towards the connecting doors to her room. "I will get dressed."

She shut the door behind her and leant back against it. Her whole body was quivering, excitement pumping in her veins. She hadn't realised exactly how important Gudfel being heir to the throne of Nisceriel had been to her. She remembered her nakedness and called loudly for Eival.

She had taken on her sister Eival as her handmaiden when she had reached her Maiden's Day some moons before. Slowly she was surrounding herself with people she could trust. The experiment with Reassel had been a disaster, if an experience, but Harlmon and his Bluecoats were a huge success. Now a third of a Hundert in number, she knew it would not be too long before she could persuade the King to let her have her own Hundert. Eival arrived with her clothes.

"Oh Eilana what wonderful news, Harlada back tonight."

"Listen my sister, we are alone so I forgive you, but you must call me 'My Lady'. If you do not do it all the time you will one day call me by name in public and disgrace yourself."

"Of course My Lady," She bobbed a curtsey as she said it. Eilana laughed and hugged her.

When she was dressed she began to organise things for the evening, sending Eival to fetch Harlmon. She wanted an honour guard for the boys as they returned, and for Rebgroth to inspect her Bluecoats.

Harlmon had done a superb job. As the Bluecoats' duties were only Eilana's personal protection, there was plenty of spare duty time for them, and Harlmon had them training non-stop. Training with arms and training their bodies. As the Royal Guard were all cavalry based, Harlmon set out to train his men as the best light infantry there was, and he pretty well succeeded, but then again, he hadn't ever met Klarss' Marsh Fighters.

The celebration that night was one that would live in the memory of everyone who attended it as long as they lived. A Third of Royal Guards had been dispatched with spare horses to meet the party travelling from Bridgebury, but even speeded by fresh mounts; it was after dusk that Rebgroth led the party through the gates. Gudrick and Harlada rode proudly behind him in the torchlight. Gone was Rebgroth's fine red and black uniform; gone were the boys' fine weaves and light wool; instead all three wore dark green and brown shirts of a rough material that looked like a heavy linen, dark brown leather leggings with matching light leather knee boots, and heavier leather tabards, gathered by ornate leather belts. The boys were like little replicas of Rebgroth.

The procession was cheered through the streets by the entire Castle's population, the Royal Guards enjoying riding behind the centres of attention. As they reached the courtyard outside the Keep, the King stepped out to greet them, flanked by Eilana, the Queen, and General Gratax.

The riders pulled up in front of them and slid down from their saddles, the boys jumping. The King stepped forward as Rebgroth bowed.

"No no, stand before me Rebgroth and let me greet you." He stepped forward and hugged him like a long lost brother. "I am deeply indebted to you for returning my son and the Lady Eilana's to us both. You obviously saved them from the sea and goodness knows what else to get back to us."

"I am only grateful to have been of service, Sire. I have much to report when the time is right, but perhaps Sire, tomorrow."

"Tomorrow indeed Rebgroth, for tonight we celebrate."

The boys had stood back for a moment before running to their mothers, both of whom were crying tears of joy at their return. Patrikal stood by Serculas who was holding her half brother Gudfel. She remembered her homecoming, but then she hadn't been gone very long in comparison.

The party went on long into the night, Rebgroth could hardly remain awake after almost a moon of travel, and the boys slept on furs near the fire. He just needed some sleep, and Serculas, and probably in that order, but somehow he was certain it would be the other way around. Indeed, when the party broke up, Serculas led him up to her room and they made love a little hurredly and a little clumsily, then slept. The next morning however they rediscovered each other slowly and with a passion that left them both physically and emotionally drained.

Queen Bertal however woke in a cold sweat, lying on her back and staring at the ceiling. Gratax was still asleep beside her, but she had awoken from a strange dream. It was like a memory of something that hadn't happened to her. She had been looking down at two babies in a cot, one a weak boy who would only ever sleep with men, and one who would be a heroic war leader and rule a vast Kingdom, but her child was the weak one.

Whenever she drank too much wine, these sorts of strange dream memories came to her afterwards and she ignored and forgot them quickly, but this one was so vivid. Gudrick and Harlada, it could not be, it was a dream damn it, the result of fading drunkenness and imagination. She was not too sure though.

No one rose very early the next morning. Serculas left Rebgroth dozing after their early morning love making and went to tend to Gudfel, finding Prince Gudrick and Harlada happily playing with him and getting to know the new young man in the nursery. Gudrick was so happy to have a brother. He didn't like girls, especially Patrikal, who he found too bossy, but then all older sisters are. He couldn't quite work out why they had different mothers, but that didn't matter to him.

Ferlmun was fussing around the boys trying to establish their level of well-being, which anyone could tell was excellent, but he was getting very old now and slightly less lucid.

The boys started to tell Serculas of some of their adventures, adding to the little she had heard already from Rebgroth. She was delighted to listen, understanding the five year olds' perspective that tended to warp events a little. She would be one of the few who would miss Rebgroth's report to the King at noon, as she had to look after the children. This reminded Ferlmun to head for the Great Hall in good time if he was to hear.

With everyone so slow rising, noon seemed to be upon them very quickly, and the hall filled rapidly. The King sat on his throne, Queen Bertal beside him. Eilana sat in a chair on the step below Gudmon, as did Gratax next to Bertal. The Council all stood in a semi-circle around the foot of the steps, with many senior household members behind them. Mendel watched attentively.

There was a loud ceremonial knock on the Hall's main doors and everyone fell silent. An Inner Guard opened the double doors to Rebgroth. He asked his name, although of course he knew it perfectly well, then turned towards the throne at the other end of the Great Hall and called loudly.

"The Officer Rebgroth Your Majesty, Second in Command of the Royal Guard, to make his report Sire." He bowed very formally.

"Come forward to us Officer Rebgroth. You are very welcome in our presence." The semi-circle of people parted enough to give him a clear passage to the throne, and then closed again behind him as he walked forward. He bowed before the King then knelt with one knee on the bottom step.

"No no Rebgroth, feel free to stand in honour before us and tell us of the many moons you have taken to get back to us. Bring some wine and water for my brave Officer; he will have much to tell."

"Your Majesty is very kind," said Rebgroth, "but after last night I am sure just the water will be fine." The crowd laughed at his confident informality, but only as the King did, and not before.

The drinks arrived on a tray and a small table was placed at the foot of the throne steps to hold it. Rebgroth began his report.

He told them of the sea, the divine intervention that had saved their lives, diminishing his part in it. He told of the beach, the strange scout, the Company of Marsh Fighters, and the first long walk to the Hog's Back village. He told of the aged wise woman who spoke Niscerien, but he did not go into detail.

Rebgroth had given the report much thought as they travelled back to Niseriel. He would have to say something about the Marsh Dweller's prophesies, but thought it best not to tell them of all the detail he had discovered over the eleven moons he had spent amongst them. No matter what he made them promise, the boys would say something about it, so part of the truth was essential. All however, would be foolish.

He told of Klarss, the Warlord, and their trip to Grass and Berry Hill together. He described the long walks, the boat trip over the lake, and their arrival and greeting by the Lord Priest Cralch and the other Wise Ones in their White Robes.

He explained they had been treated very well because there was an old prophesy among the Marsh Dwellers that the sea would bring forth a man and two boys. The man would be the Death Bringer. If he were killed by them whilst he was amongst them, the Marsh People would die out as a tribe completely; if he lived he would bring many deaths on them later, but they would survive as a people, and hence his safety was assured whilst with them. He was allowed to keep his arms and come and go as he pleased, but of course he would not go without the boys.

He claimed to have difficulty in understanding the prophecy regarding the boys. He told them that it appeared one would be a friend to the Marsh Dwellers and one an enemy. He could not discover more with the difficulty of language. They would not tell him more, but they were keen to try to find out which one was which.

The truth, which he did not tell, was that one of them would lead them to glory, death and survival, the other would die young, but not for many years yet.

There began a long period of tests that they put the boys through which continued throughout their stay. Most were mental, reasoning, thought games of many sorts. Some were riddles that they had to work together to solve, one of which took nearly one moon alone.

Rebgroth was bored to distraction, but set about learning all he could about the Marsh Dwellers. If they were to be his enemy one day, he would learn all he could about them. Knowing your enemy could be of great advantage.

A few of the tests were physical, and some in Rebgroth's eyes, quite dangerous. The Wise Ones told him not to worry, the prophecies were clear, neither would die here. Rebgroth was not so sure, and was particularly worried at what turned out to be the final test.

A boat had been anchored some four men's length from the shore. A thick rope ran from the top of the wooden rampart around the island to the top of the boat's mast. The boys were to climb along the rope to the boat, then down the mast. The drop to the water was at least three men.

As always, Harlada went first. He lay along the rope and edged himself out.

His chin was on the rope which ran under his chest and stomach to his crotch. His left leg hung down on one side, but he kept his right foot hooked onto the rope. He pulled himself with his arms and pushed with one leg, bending his knee and bringing his foot up to his backside, then straightening it as his arms did their job.

The rope swayed increasingly as he reached the middle, but his hanging leg acted as a balance and kept him fairly stable. If he fell now he could at least swim; Gudrick could not.

Harlada was getting tired, and more frightened as he did. He pulled himself on, but now he was pulling uphill; ever more steeply the closer he got to the mast. There was a gasp from the watchers as his balance went and he slipped sideways from the rope, hanging by his hands.

Everyone could see the grim determination on his face as he moved his hands along the rope until he could hook his legs around the mast. Tears streamed down his face as he slid down it to the deck. A man in a small leather lined frame boat rowed him back to the slip. He jumped ashore and ran back through the gates and up the ladder to Gudrick. Claps and noises of approval came from all the watchers, almost all in white robes.

Rebgroth could feel disaster coming. Gudrick was not up to this, and if he fell, could not swim. However, after eleven moons here, he also knew that it was useless to protest. Protesting just seemed to prove him weak in their eyes.

Gudrick was crying before he tried to mount the rope. As he did so, Harlada pulled him back and turned to Cralch who stood behind him on the rampart. He looked up at him.

"Gudrick cannot do this, he will hurt himself," he said simply.

"He must go Harlada. The test is clear; the rope must be crossed two times by you boys."

"Then I will go again." A huge look of relief showed on Gudrick's face as he stood back from the rope.

"You are very tired Harlada, you nearly fell last time. You could well fall this time."

"I might, but Gudrick will."

"So be it," declared Cralch and stepped back.

Harlada looked up at him and turned slowly to the rope. He hesitated for just a moment before taking the rope in his hands and edging his way out again. Lord Priest Cralch stepped quickly forward and grabbed Harlada's waist as he crossed the wall and dragged him back.

"It is enough that you would do this for your friend in order to finish the test. The test was really how you might achieve the end when all knew Gudrick could not do it. Now come and eat, then you must rest, you begin a long journey tomorrow."

A short while later, they stood in the Hall, eating from a large spread of cold food laid on a long table. Rebgroth sought out Cralch.

"You said the boys have a long journey tomorrow Lord Priest, may I ask to where?"

"Home," said Cralch and turned away. Rebgroth had so many questions suddenly, but they would not be answered now.

Cralch looked back over his shoulder and spoke.

"There will be a farewell ceremony at dawn you will need to attend, and then you will be taken by boat to the end of our lands in the east. From there you make your own way, but believe me, you will get home safely." He turned his back again.

After they had eaten, Rebgroth took the boys to the room they all shared. He spoke to them of the ceremony the next morning, of behaving correctly. Correct behaviour had already lost these boys a year of their childhood, of playing, of fun with their families, but they had learnt so much if they only took heed of it all.

They settled down on their pallet beds, Rebgroth too, and sleep came to them all quickly. Although early for Rebgroth, he slept all night and woke refreshed when there was a persistent knocking on their door a quarter watch before dawn. He rolled upright, sitting on the edge of his bed and shouting. Pulling on his leggings as the boys stirred, he moved to the door and opened it.

Two ladies stood outside, one holding a tray with three bowls of porridge and one with a small folding table. They entered without a word, placed the table in the centre of the room with the tray on top, and departed without looking at him. He was more than tired of this attitude but had learned to live with it, so he just grimaced to himself and began to encourage the boys from their beds.

They dressed and ate, readying themselves for the dawn ceremony, and as the sky began to lighten in the east, there came a second knocking at the door. Rebgroth finished buckling his belt and scabbard around the leather tabard which he now wore. They had no other possessions except the clothes they stood up in. He smiled at the boys and opened the door.

A single priest in his white robes stood outside and beckoned them to follow him. He led them to the Hall where the other priests stood arrayed on the dais. Rebgroth stood before them, Gudrick and Harlada on each side of him. Cralch raised his arms and the priests began to chant monotonously. Ceasing the chant, Cralch raised his head skywards and seemed to evoke their gods in prayer, all the priests joining him at times. He finally ceased his prayers and looked down at Rebgroth.

"Please attend me Rebgroth," he requested, although his manner was that of one whose requests were normally taken as orders. Rebgroth squeezed the boy's shoulders and stepped up onto the dais, facing the Lord Priest but showing no deference.

"On your departure Death Bringer, we have for you this gift." A priest stepped forward, a cushion in his hands, on which laid a ceremonial knife. The blade was polished and bright, the hilt of dark and ornately carved wood. "This will protect you from hidden enemies until the time when your destiny and ours again come together, but it will never bring death to one from the Marshes. Although you have a terrible part to play in the fate of our people, you have chosen to live and have given us a future; for which we thank you, our wise ones and our people. I am sure you will understand that many Marsh Dwellers cannot comprehend this and hence remain hostile to you. It is for you now to take these children home."

Rebgroth had rehersed many things to say at this moment, whatever was to happen, but he just took the knife and slid it into his belt. He bowed silently and turned away, rejoining the boys. Cralch summoned Gudrick next, who climbed onto the dais and stood before him.

"To you Prince Gudrick we give this." Another cushion appeared beside him, it held a woven necklace with a very finely carved wooded medallion. Cralch placed it around Gudrick's neck as he spoke.

"When your time comes to leave this life, this will tell the Water Gods that you are a friend of the Marsh People and you will be treated accordingly, joining our heroes in the afterlife. You are honoured to have a friend such as Harlada, and we are honoured to have met you. Go now and meet your doom young Prince." Gudrick didn't understand, so he smiled and climbed back down beside Rebgroth.

"And now you Harlada." Harlada hesitated at Rebgroth's side, but his protector placed a hand between his shoulder blades and pushed him gently forward. He wasn't scared, just trying to understand what was being said. When he stood in front of the Lord Priest he looked up confidently.

"You Harlada are the Boy Warlord who will one day lead our people to glory, so we give you but one small gift." This time Cralch drew a small silver coin from within his robes. It hung on a fine silver chain. "This coin was blessed by the first Lord Priest Cralch, to be given to the Boy Warlord when he came. By this coin, recognised by all the People of the Marshes, the Boy Warlord will be known. Wear it always Harlada, for when you return to us in your need all will know you and come to your aid, and you will lead us, many to death, but our people to victory."

The Lord Priest Cralch knelt in front of Harlada, and there was a muffled gasp from around the Hall.

"You honour me by coming in my lifetime, the chosen Boy Warlord, and making me, the thirty fourth Lord Priest Cralch, also the last. The prophecies are reality, fate will guide you now. We will meet again Harlada. Your Gods walk with you."

He stood and bowed to Harlada, then turned and led the priests from the room. Rebgroth stared up at Harlada on the stage as Gudrick jumped up beside him and hugged him.

"Oh Harlada, he likes you!" Gudrick cried, "Maybe you are a Prince now too." Harlada put an arm around him, leading him back to Rebgroth, and they all hugged.

"What does all this mean Rebgroth? I don't understand and I don't think I like it."

"Don't worry about it now my boy, now we go home."

Of course Rebgroth did not give all the details to his enthralled audience as he spoke, but he did go into detail on the last part of the story, for he had come very close to death.

He had led Gudrick and Harlada down to the gates on the Hill of Grass and Berries and onto the wharf. A boat stood there. Rebgroth smiled as he recognised the boatman and crew that had brought them to the island.

"Good Morning Captain, are you here for us?"

"Marn Deff Bringerr, I'd a be, but ee permotes I abuv I's place, I'd a no be a Capn, jus a boaten."

"Well you should be my friend, I'm glad to see you. Where have you been told to take us?"

"Tuh theys hills werr sun ups. I'd a put ee ashore werr a cart nn orse waits ee, but thad a no be ferr some time."

"Then let's leave Captain, we have no luggage and no escort it appears."

"De Gods a be a lookin Deff Bringerr, nn I'd a be supprised if no uver."

They sailed most of the day, the boys more relaxed than he had seen them for many moons. To the east of the Hill there was still a long but quite narrow lake that was bordered with wide marshes north and south, and they sailed down wind along it.

He laughed with the boatman, who he had genuinely grown to like, and played guessing games with Gudrick, but now only for fun. Harlada sat for a while in the bow and looked steadily ahead across the water. Rebgroth moved forward and sat behind him as the boatman let Gudrick hold the steering oar in the stern.

"Do you think I will come back one day?" Harlada asked. Rebgroth gripped his shoulder affectionately. This had all been a lot for a boy of just five summers.

"I don't know my boy, but if you ever do, it will be for their help, and they will give it."

"But will it be help to fight you Rebgroth? I don't see that I could do that." Tears were suddenly streaming down his face. Rebgroth smiled and held him close. At last he was being the child he was again.

"I promise you this Harlada; you will never be my enemy, always my friend, but if I should ever do anything that offends your honour, I may become your enemy, but that choice will be yours. I also promise to do all I can to protect Prince Gudrick from any danger, with my life in fact. Now is that not enough to make you smile."

Harlada continued to hug him for a while then sat upright again in the bow.

"Thank you; I will always remember what you have done for us." He turned again and stared at the hills, which seemed suddenly much closer.

Half a watch later they were ashore. They waved a smiling goodbye to the Boatman and his crew as they rowed out against the wind to create enough of an angle to tack.

It was not far off dusk as they examined the small lightweight four-wheeled cart and horse that stood near the bank. It was filled with provisions, so they ate some of the cheese and salted beef they had found, whilst sitting on the bank and watching the boat zigzag its way back up the lake.

As darkness fell, they wrapped themselves in the blankets from the cart and slept beneath it, starting their journey north the next morning.

Rebgroth wanted an early start so they again ate cold food to save time. He ate his own as he hitched the horse to the cart. It seemed quite a normal horse, not too docile but no real trouble. He smiled to himself, just like the perfect woman, and Serculas jumped back into his mind, his crotch stirred at just the thought.

"Come on boys, climb up; time to start the long trip home."

The track led steadily uphill away from the lake. The slope was gentle but persistent, and still fresh, their horse pulled with a measured pace that he seemed used to. They climbed for over a quarter through scattered trees and brush. The trees were many but one couldn't call them a forest. They spread in every direction, but thinly.

They reached a brow on the hillside where the slope flattened for half a field before climbing again towards the top. As they pulled over the brow three Marsh Dwellers came into view, standing across the trail some ten or twelve cart lengths ahead. Rebgroth pulled up the cart as the men faced them.

The men were Priest Guards, not Marsh Fighters. They were dressed in the green of the Hill not the dark brown of the marshes. More importantly to Rebgroth, they each had their short stabbing sword, shorter in fact than his fighting knife, sheathed in their belts. Each, however, held a short spear in their right hand, and a small circular shield in their left, with two spears clasped in the grip. Of their line across the track, the one on his right stood a good pace nearer him.

"Stay here and do not, I repeat, do not get off this cart." He almost hissed his instruction to the boys. "You will not help me if you do. You will distract me and may well get me killed." They got the message.

He never took his eyes from the Guards as he jumped lithely down from the cart and deliberately slowly, walked in front of the horse, idly patting his nose as he passed.

"Well gentlemen, this is a surprise, I had assumed we were away, now I wonder if you are official or free enterprise. The latter I feel sure." He moved a little towards them and felt as much as saw them tense.

"Now of course you will all die if you stay, and I would be only too pleased if you left, however I am the Death Bringer, so the choice is yours." He smiled at them. Inwardly it was a smile of irony. His habit was to talk calmly in the hope of cracking the confidence of an enemy just enough to plant that seed of self-doubt, but he realised they wouldn't be able to understand a word of Niscerien. Still he hoped the calm tone of his voice and easy confidence would suffice.

He stood quite still, looking at them, then in one swift flowing movement crossed his hands and ornately drew his weapons, sword and fighting knife. He was in tactical difficulties enough against three men, but armed with throwing

176

spears as they were, all they had to do was corner him with little room to move and launch a spear each at him together. Without a shield that could block more than one spear at a time he could only parry them off in flight, and he would be lucky to manage three.

He laughed and put on his most contemptuously mocking voice. He had to tempt one out.

"Come on then gentlemen, don't tell me I worry you now you've come all this way!" He grinned at the one nearest him on the right, he was the crazy one. "Come on you pig's arse." He spat towards him and saw his eyes flash with anger as he braced to throw his spear.

The guard's arm flashed forward hurling the spear. He leapt after it, pulling another free from his shield. He now had one in his right, and the other in his left, held by the middle across the back of the shield. This gave the shield an attacking role to.

Rebgroth leaned sideways a little and let the spear fly past his shoulder. The Guard charged at him, thrusting the spear over arm at his chest. Rebgroth dropped on his left knee, parrying the thrust upwards. With his sword horizontal above his head, he drove his fighting knife into the unprotected ribs below the guard's upraised arm. The guard's momentum carried his already dead body past Rebgroth, helping to wrench free the deeply imbedded knife.

That had been too easy. The proud one had been rash and easily separated, the other two would be more cautious now. As Rebgroth regained his feet they started to move apart.

"So, we are starting to fight clever are we gentlemen. Now then, how are we going to handle this one?"

He didn't have to answer himself. He heard a sudden multiple crack and hissing filled the air, instantly recognisable to Rebgroth as arrows in flight. He had dropped to his knees the moment he heard the arrows fly, but there had been no need, they were not aimed at him. The two Guards staggered in their step, one sagged to his knees then fell backwards, the other collapsed flat on his face, but both had three arrows through the chest.

Rebgroth stood slowly and looked to his right. A dozen Marsh Fighters moved out of cover, six carrying long bows the height of a man. Rebgroth had not seen their bows before. He hadn't seen all their secrets then. Klarss was quickly recognisable as they approached. Except for him they stopped some distance away. Klarss stormed past Rebgroth with a grunt towards the first Guard. Much to the boys' fascinated astonishment; he grabbed the body by the hair and hacked off the head with the sword he whipped out from behind his back.

As the boys jumped from the cart and ran to join Rebgroth, Klarss did the same to the other two. He sheathed his sword, and carrying the three heads by their hair in his left hand, he strode towards them, stopping in front of them. He held the heads at shoulder height and spoke forcefully, shaking them, then held himself upright and slapped his right forearm across his chest, repeating the salute to the brave Rebgroth had given him at the lakeside. As Rebgroth returned it, Klarss turned and led his men away, still clutching the heads.

Rebgroth did not engage his audience in any debate as to the motives of his attackers, nor why Klarss was shadowing them.

His personal view was that the Priest Guards were working independently or for some minor priest that believed if the Death Bringer was killed away from the marshes it would negate the prophesies. As to why Klarss was there, he believed it was at Cralch's orders, although he would have liked to believe it was because Klarss himself had decided to be around to protect them. He kept to facts though and continued the tale, which was now fairly event free.

They continued to climb steadily from the scene of the fight. Gudrick asked how long they would be travelling. Rebgroth told him not quite a moon. Gudrick groaned. Harlada asked how he knew which way to travel. Now that was an intelligent question.

He explained that he had a very general knowledge of the lay-out of the lands around Nisceriel, as all good commanders should. He knew that if he headed roughly northeast, that meant half left from where the sun rose, they would be taking the shortest route over the hills.

Next he showed Harlada the streams they passed and followed. All of them were flowing back behind them. Some flowed across their path, but if you looked down the slopes they all eventually turned towards the direction from which they had come. As they reached the watershed of the hills, all the streams flowed away from them.

Rebgroth explained that these streams now all flowed down to a river called the Ffrom. This river flowed across their path from right to left, and large as it seemed, it was a tributary of the Ffon. When the streams led them to the Ffrom, all they had to do was follow it downstream to the Ffon, then follow the Ffon downstream to Nisceriel. The main problem they would have was crossing the bigger streams that joined both rivers as they moved downstream, but he was hoping, as was the case, that as they got nearer the rivers, tracks and roads would guide them.

They avoided people and settlements while they could. They were in ungoverned land that belonged to the southern and western edges of Merlbray, but they had no real control there. It was wiser therefore to rely on the abundant supplies they had been provided with and sleep beneath the cart at night.

The weather was mixed but not too unkind to them and progress was steady. After eighteen days they were travelling west on a well-defined track along the south bank of the Ffon. They were alone on the track, but a number of travellers were moving downstream parallel to them on the north bank, and the odd shouted exchange across the river lightened the day.

Gudrick was bored but stood up to the rigours well. Harlada was always asking questions about things he saw, to the point sometimes where Rebgroth got angry with him for no other reason that he needed a break from it. He explained to Harlada that they were trapped on the south bank now until they reached the crossing at Bridgebury. The Ffon was too deep to ford, and although it seemed quite narrow at times, it was there that it was deepest.

Bridgebury had grown up around the lowest point downstream where Niscerien bridge building technology allowed them to succeed. The river was slightly tidal here, which seemed to slow the river's flow at times and make it race at others.

They reached Bridgebury just after dusk on the twentieth day. The three guards on the bridge challenged them. Rebgroth knew there was a small garrison of Royal Guards there, but these were local Hundert men.

"Who are you and where is your business?" challenged the one guard who bothered to stand from sitting on the bridge wall. The others looked up at the cart idly.

"I am Officer Rebgroth of the Royal Guard escorting Prince Gudrick and Harlada back to the Castle Niserien."

The guards all laughed and the one standing grabbed the horse's bridle.

"Now we are not fond of funny men at the start of a long night's watch, so state your business or we will turn you back to spend another night in the open."

Rebgroth stood and vaulted down easily from the cart, bringing the other two guards to their feet. He walked calmly up to the guard holding the horse and stopped directly in front of him. His voice was authoritative with a cold menace when he spoke.

"A year ago I crawled ashore in the southern marshes, with Prince Gudrick and his friend. We have spent eleven moons escaping the Marsh Dwellers and most of one travelling to here. I have fought and killed to get this far so removing one more obstacle is not something I will shrink from. Go now and raise the detachment of Royal Guard whilst my patience lasts, because if you don't, and if I haven't killed you myself first, you will hang for disobeying my orders and delaying the Prince's return. The King himself will order it, now go."

The man stared at the cold anger in his eyes for a moment before turning and running up the road towards the Guards' billet. The Third Hundert stationed there turned out almost immediately and double marched to the bridge.

The thirty-three men were led by Sergeant Badraman, a good professional soldier promoted by Rebgroth himself. As they reached the river he halted the men and crossed the bridge in the gloom. He recognised Rebgroth immediately and almost broke into a run, stopping in front of him and slapping his right arm across his chest.

"Sire, this is too good to be possible. We have thought you all dead for a year." The mouthy militia guard slid away into the shadows.

"Well as you can see Sergeant, we are quite definitely alive. Now we just need an inn with hot water, but you Sergeant, take the fastest mount here and ride overnight to Castle Nisceriel and announce our return. We will leave with the dawn and should get there around dusk if we have decent weather."

"As you command," snapped Badraman, saluting again and running back over the bridge shouting orders. Rebgroth climbed back aboard the cart, a little wearily. He was so nearly back, to home and to Serculas.

"Come on lads," he said, "let's get ourselves cleaned up."

"And so Sire, we travelled hard all day to reach you last night. That is really all there is to tell."

A spontaneous ripple of applause sprang up that suddenly grew into loud clapping and cheering, until the King held up a hand for silence.

"I owe you a great debt Second Officer Rebgroth, as does the Queen and the Lady Eilana. You are honoured among Niscerians, and now sit on my Council as of right, not by Military rank. You have permanent residence in the Royal quarters as long as you live, and if I could think of any other meaningful honour to bestow on you that you do not already hold, I would gladly give it."

"There is only one request that I would make Sire, if you could see fit to grant it?"

"If it is within my power, it shall be so. Name it."

"I realise it is not normally permitted within the Royal Household, but I would ask your blessing to marry Nanny Serculas, Sire, if you could see your way to allowing it."

"That is easily done within the rules. Serculas, you are now relieved of your duties as Nanny and I hereby raise you Lady Serculas, Lady in Waiting to The Lady Eilana. You may of course continue to help look after the children by way of a personal diversion if you wish. Now that should make everyone happy." He smiled a self-satisfied smile.

Rebgroth dropped to one knee and spoke, looking at the King's feet.

"Sire, you are too kind, I only did my duty. The children were astonishingly brave, I could have done it with none other."

"Stand up Rebgroth and look at me. If you ever kneel before me again I will begin to get cross with you. As a personal Councillor to the King you should never do that again, is that clear?"

"Yes sire, it is just such an honour you bestow on me, it will take me a while to believe it is so."

"Well believe it Rebgroth, it is so. Now luncheon calls, come and dine with me, we have a wedding to plan."

Chapter 18

Serculas had enjoyed the happiest year of her life; for her it had been a dream. Within a moon of his return she was married to Rebgroth and they were settled in fine apartments in the West Tower of the Keep.

The wedding had been a magnificent affair, completely at the King's expense. He had insisted on the best of everything. Rebgroth's family, none of whom she had met before, had made the very short trip from Brocklow, but it made it all the sadder for her that her family had all died in the Great Sickness twelve summers ago. It had only been the lowly position she then held at the Castle that had saved her. Almost the whole of her village had died.

The celebration had gone on all night, culminating in a huge wedding breakfast, eaten in the walled garden as the dawn broke on a glorious spring morning. Everyone of any stature in the realm was there, and dressed in her magnificent gown, a present from the Queen, Serculas felt like a Princess. Patrikal acted as her Lady Maid and Gudrick and Harlada as Pages.

Within two moons she was pregnant and her joy complete. In the preceding years she had feared pregnancy and the complications it would bring. She had even determined to visit the healwitches to end her pregnancy rather than risk Rebgroth's position if needed. Although if she was honest, there was also a selfish desire to protect her own. She never had become pregnant though, to the point where she had begun to doubt if she could, but it was as if the marriage had released her body to function normally, and she had conceived almost immediately.

Their daughter Rebetha was born within a moon of the shortest day the following winter, to the great delight of the Court. Rebgroth had rushed back for the appointed time and had been with her, rare amongst Niscerien men. Rebetha was healthy and strong, and Serculas insisted on feeding her herself. The birth, however, was just one of the hugely significant events of that year.

When he had been thought lost two years before, a much-heralded officer named Tamorther had been promoted to Second Officer of the Royal Guard. Rebgroth's return had of course caused an embarrassment, as Tamorther had carried out his duties to perfection and it would have been difficult to demote him and reinstate Rebgroth.

General Gratax resolved the problem by creating a rank of Commander, senior to Second Officer but not in the command chain. Tamorther reported directly to him still, and Rebgroth was given the tasks of completely reviewing the fortified defences of the walled villages throughout Nisceriel, and of streamlining the call to arms procedures for raising the Hunderts. By coincidence, future events would show this to be a decision that held Nisceriel in very good stead.

Rebgroth had spent the intervening moons travelling and mapping the villages, designing defences and working with builders to create them. He also developed an intimate knowledge of the country, its strengths within the Hunders and the training levels of the Hunderts they could raise.

It had always been assumed that a war would begin with an exchange of envoys and formal declaration, as the rules of conduct between states demanded, but Rebgroth felt the threat of war had changed.

The alliances through marriage and family had secured a level of peace now for over two generations between the more powerful civilised Kingdoms. Rebgroth felt the main threat in their age was from unheralded attacks. Some of the wilder rogue tribes were perfectly capable of doing so, or even a minor Kingdom, trying to establish itself. If they could not be measured as major invasion threats, they were at least capable of launching substantial raids. A village lost this way could be very costly to win back, far better it not be lost in the first place.

A formal declaration of war would give time to mobilise all the Hunderts and gather an army, but an unannounced incursion would mean a village defending itself with its own Hundert, and possibly the help of one or two nearby Hunderts if there was warning enough for them to gather and reach the threatened village in time. If they could not get inside the walls before an attack came, they were better to fall back and wait for the main force.

Each outlying village would need to be fortified to hold against high odds long enough for the rest of the country to mobilise their Hunderts and come to their aid, and this was the task Rebgroth set himself. It took two summers to complete, one past and one to come, but it was a wise insight on his behalf.

Bertal had a worrying year. Politically she was feeling far more secure. She was re-established as the future King Mother which made her feel better about the future after Gudmon's death, and with Gratax heading the army, she felt sure she would be secure. Gudmon was thirty-six years past his Bornbless day now, as long as and more than many men lived, and for him to reach forty would be rare. She was four years his junior and women tended to outlive their husbands. She had to plan ahead.

It was her dreams that worried her. More and more she woke up in a cold sweat, not just in the mornings, but in the middle of the night. The dream would be on the edge of her consciousness, half remembered, a mixture of faces she recognised and fantasy. Occasionally though she saw and recognised something that jolted her awake, shocked or scared.

She awoke from a dream of Gudmon and Eilana making love in front of the fire in his room. For a while, half conscious, she had watched them, almost aroused by it. Gudmon was doing things to Eilana he had never done to her, and Eilana was participating in ways she would never have thought of. She thought her love life had been revived with Gratax, but it was tame and staid compared to this.

Most importantly, she knew she had seen all this before, before she had left for Deswrain, many years before, just after Gudrick's birth. She only then realised that if she had but remembered, she had known Eilana would replace herself in the King's bed long before it happened.

Just before the birth of Rebetha, she had woken with Serculas' beaten body in her mind. Raped and bleeding she lay on the nursery floor, Gudfel and Rebetha in their cots in the corner. She had not seen who had done this, or if she had, she could not remember. Was this something that was going to happen? She could not believe it.

She started trying to dream about people, Gratax, Gudmon, Gudrick, but it never worked. She lay on the edge of sleep with a person in mind but woke in the morning none the wiser.

She woke on the longest night of the year with Moreton in her mind. He was standing on a tiny balcony of a room, high in a Castle tower overlooking the sea. She thought of Castle Deswrain, but that had no such balconies. He was thinking of her, but he was surrounded with a shimmering aura, a disturbance in the air around his body. She seemed to drift up and away from him, seeing the island just off shore on which the castle stood, the rough seas beating against it, then he was gone and she was fully awake.

This was a situation she had to face alone. There was no one she could think of she could talk to about it. Allaner perhaps; since Reassel's death she had become more and more like a sister.

Eilana had begun an acquaintance that would also have far reaching effects. Her interest in governance was where she had channelled her frustrated energies since Prince Gudrick's return. She had thought of many ways to change things, but all were impractical or beyond thought. She could see no way apart from his death that Gudrick would not succeed, and she would not contemplate that.

Her attendance at the King's Council was now official. She sat at the table and very slowly, began to contribute, mainly on social issues, and very diplomatically. She steered well clear of things Military. It was a growing friendship with Chancellor Bradett that was to become significant. He eventually saw beyond a woman, through the reluctant sexual attraction he felt, and into an intelligent sharp-witted mind.

He began to respect her views, and by the end of the year would sometimes seek her out before meetings to ask her opinions on some matters, particularly ones where he felt he would find it difficult to gain the King's support. If she would speak for him, the King was far more likely to decide in his favour. It became an alliance of mutual benefit, based on mutual respect with just the mearest hint of sexual chemistry, as much as Eilana allowed.

Harlmon had made the most immediately significant progress that year. His Bluecoats had now attained Hundert status. The King had given Eilana his permission in the midst of the wedding celebrations at a time cleverly chosen by her to ask.

He had done it over six moons however. He had not dashed off recruiting anyone who wanted to join. He had gone around the country carefully seeking out, choosing and persuading particular young men to sign up. They were all of a type, young, strong and of an almost loutish manner, but controllable. They were easily moulded into an elite team that felt itself the best there was, the best trained and the fittest soldiers ever known to Nisceriel.

Discipline was very strict. A breach of code meant instant removal from the ranks and apparent banishment. The very few that were stripped of their blue uniforms were never seen again after they left the Castle Nisceriel.

Harlmon's biggest problem was barrack space. Quarters for another Hundert within the Castle walls was impossible, so a Third, those on guard duties, were billeted in converted store rooms within the Castle, below Eilana's rooms, the other two were built new barracks on the edge of Castlebury, where their training was based.

It was in the mess hall at the barracks that Harlada sat in judgement on a Bluecoat charged with fighting and theft. The facts were quite straightforward and not in dispute. He had got into an argument with two off-duty Royal Guards over a bet made the day before. He was right but the Red and Blacks would not have it.

Standing Orders were quite specific, fighting with other soldiers was absolutely forbidden. The very existence of the Bluecoats was anathema to General Gratax and Harlmon was determined to give him no opportunity to claim his men were not under strict control. The Red and Blacks soon realised this and went out of their way to goad Harlmon's men into trouble. They often had to back down ignominiously from enormous provocation, but many a Royal Guard had met with a mysterious accident in the dark after such an incident.

In this case though, the soldier had cracked and given the two Royal Guards a beating. His far superior training in unarmed combat, compared to cavalry troops, had won the fight. The defeated Royal Guards had slunk away but not reported the incident, too embarrassed at having lost to one man, but it had been witnessed by a Bluecoat Sergeant and so the soldier stood before Harlmon now.

Harlmon ordered him drummed out of the Hundert and strongly suggested the man go back north from whence he had been recruited. He made his usual speech about how absolute obedience was vital within an elite unit, his unit. The only reason he did not have the man thrown into jail was that he had won the fight.

The soldier was literally drummed out under escort to the northern edge of the village and dispatched on his way. Some half watch later, Harlmon and two Sergeants left the barracks and set off on horseback in his wake.

Just over half a watch's walk north the road wound through some heavy woodland, and here the soldier had been met by six Bluecoats, previously members of his own Eleven. They surprised and bound him, dragging him to a clearing set well back off the road that had been used for this purpose before.

The soldier had feared it would happen, he had heard of it within the Bluecoats. He had decided that if it was true he would not escape it so it was better to face it. He believed he had just made the task easier for the Bluecoats, for they would indeed have got him eventually, and being of the mind he was, he almost believed he deserved what was coming. He had let his Hundert down, his comrades and Harlmon.

Harlmon arrived and wasted little time. The soldier was tied standing with his back to a tree, his arms stretched around the trunk behind him. Harlmon walked straight up to him, drawing his long fighting knife from his belt. He drove it into the soldier belly and ripped it upwards, blood spraying over his uniform and spattering those around him. The soldier slid down the tree as far as his binding allowed, his strangled scream dying with him.

Harlmon turned to his men and spoke.

"He was your comrade in arms, but he let you down. He let us all down, let the Hundert down. He deserved to die because if he let you down in a fight he could cause your death, and we look after our own. We are Bluecoats, the very best, and you do not leave the very best, you die for them. Am I right?"

The men cheered him. He had chosen them well. They were proud to be part of a unit so tough they killed their own when necessary.

He strode back to his horse where his Sergeants had remained mounted, and shouting at his men to bury the body, rode away. He smiled to himself, he had enjoyed that.

Chapter 19

This dream was the worst she had experienced. She had lain making love to an attractive young man when suddenly she was drowning. She opened her eyes to see his head bent right back, his throat cut from ear to ear and gaping, his blood pumping into her face, her mouth and nose.

She caught a glimpse of the killer before blood filled her eyes, he was young; she knew him but could not remember who he was as she awoke.

"That's for my sister," he had said as he let the head flop down into her face while she screamed.

She sat up with a start, waking Gratax beside her.

"A bad dream again?" he asked. It was a stupid question really; she was shaking and soaked with sweat. Tears ran down her face as she turned and flung her arms around him.

"Wey it was so real!" She buried her face in his neck.

"Then tell me about it my Queen, perhaps it will help." He always called her that in his tenderest moments.

She told him what she had seen as she had woken.

"Try to remember where you were, were you in a castle with stone walls? A wooden house? Try to see for me." Bertal sat up slowly beside him.

"I can't really be sure, I can't see, but it felt like it was my room, a wooden hut, but I only feel that now, I can't say I saw it. Wey I could feel him inside me then…" She burst into tears again. He sat up and hugged her close.

"Alright my Queen, what you describe has reminded me of something that happened some years ago. I investigated a murder in Castlebury, as you describe."

"I remember it. Somehow I was the girl, actually her. Wey what is happening to me? I was her. That poor boy was killed making love to me, I could feel him, I really could feel him."

"You couldn't see the killer's face?" He couldn't help but ask, and it began just the sort of tirade from Bertal he would have expected, but she calmed herself and apologised, as did he.

"You have a gift my Queen; it lies within you; if only you could harness it we could achieve so much."

"I am not sure I want such a gift my love. I cannot help but think it is something to do with that elvish medicine I had after Gudrick was born. I seem to half remember seeing things about people then. Perhaps the elvish blood in my Grandmother is coming through, that and that damned Bumbleberry. I think I will have to stop drinking it."

"I think, my Queen, perhaps you should drink more!"

"Yes, I suppose you would." She looked around the room, lit only by the glowing embers from the fire. "Why don't you put another log or two on the fire as we are awake, then come back here and hold me."

Gratax grumbled something and rolled upright from the bed. She was right of course; it would be much warmer in the morning if he did. These autumn mornings recently had been very cold indeed.

Bertal watched his naked body as he moved across the room. He was in wonderful shape for his years. She felt ashamed to admit it, no disgusted at herself was not too strong, but she was feeling extremely aroused, and as Gratax climbed back onto the bed and lay beside her she rolled on top of him.

Her skin was hot and clammy against him, but he was not complaining as she kissed his neck and slid down his chest, kissing as she went, kissing his stomach. Surely she wasn't going to, she never had before.

He was aroused and astonished as she took him in her mouth. Her thoughts had drifted back to her dream of Eilana and Gudmon. She pushed them aside.

Gratax sighed loudly as he filled her mouth. He had tried to stop her, to disengage and make love to her, but she was determined to complete the task.

"What did I do to deserve that?" he asked jokingly. She wiped her mouth on the blanket.

"That's just my thank you for putting up with me, and I fear for what you might have to put up with." He kissed her and lay her back on the bed.

"My turn now," he laughed.

"That's for my sister." The phrase haunted him. It filled his mind, every quarter of the day he thought of it, every day of every moon that passed. He knew it was significant, but he couldn't attach it to anything specific. That is he couldn't until Bertal's next very bad dream the following spring.

Time seemed to have drifted steadily by. Gudmon was still ecstatically happy with Eilana, and to a great extent, she with him. It led to a great stability that everyone felt. It was totally accepted that Eilana was Queen in all but title, and Bertal, whilst only Queen by name, held her rank as the future King Mother and was effectively accepted as wife to Gratax.

Patrikal turned eleven and the boys, totally recovered from their long ordeal two years before, became young men at seven. Theirs was the most significant Bornbless celebration. At seven they became young soldiers and began their training at arms. It was something Harlada took to as a natural. Gudrick found the skills harder but mastered them all with plenty of practice with Harlada. Their coach was Officer Badraman, a fine swordsman and delighted to have a role so close to the King himself.

Eilana had developed into a senior Councillor, the King often leaving her to chair the Council, giving her his absolute power of decision; her word was his. She ruled wisely, even the King's greatest critics for giving her such power had to admit it.

She ruled particularly astutely in the continuing arguments between General Gratax and Chancellor Bradett. Although her sympathies were more at home with Bradett, he could not be sure she would rule for him unless his case was sound, and although Gratax felt at an immediate disadvantage, he had to admit that it wasn't so. Bradett however felt a growing intoxication for Eilana. She was like a drug to him, the more he was near her the more he needed to be, but he knew it was totally useless even to dream.

Harlmon's Hundert of Bluecoats continued to train for every eventuality, and added an unauthorised fourth Third; a mounted section, the excuse being that they needed a trained cavalry unit to escort the Lady Eilana and the King's children on any trips away from the Castle. The King said nothing and so no one else complained.

Harlmon himself had moved into Allaner's old room above what were now Eilana's rooms. Eival was above him in Reassel's old room. Serculas of course lived with Rebgroth so the Nannys' rooms above the nursery would have been empty, but Eilana moved her aging mother there from the old house. This meant Harlfel, now almost of military age himself, took Eilana's old room until he joined the Bluecoats on his Sire's Day as ordained.

190

Bertal had had some of her dreams, some disturbing about those close to her but nothing frightening. She dreamt that she had looked right into Gudmon and been saddened by what she saw. She understood now how she had hurt him and determined never to let it happen between Gratax and herself, but she felt no desire to put things right between them.

When the next bad one came though it was truly horrifying, and shook her badly. She had a quiet afternoon with the children in the walled garden and had supper with them; bread and pink honey washed down with bumbleberry juice, lots of it.

That evening, Gratax had brought an old friend who was visiting from Merlbray, back to their apartments for dinner. They ate well and downed far more wine than they intended. When they went to bed Gratax was feeling rampant, except his body was weak with drink. He pulled Bertal to him and began kissing her breasts, none to gently. He snuggled his face into her cleavage and relaxed to enjoy the moment, but before he knew it he was asleep, and she lay there on the way to arousal but too tired to be upset. In fact she was probably pleased he had gone to sleep, he could be quite unsubtle when he was drunk.

She slept with her arms around him until the dream came. A man grabbed her from behind. She was in a stable she knew. She was terrified he would hurt her. He was saying something about her preferring women and how he was going to show her what it was really about. He threw her forwards across a cart and made her hold the wheels. He would not hurt her if she just did what he told her.

He lifted her dress and forced himself into her. She had no underwear on, she remembered she was expecting to have met someone else, but who? She was dry and he hurt her as he thrust himself deeper into her. She was so scared she felt nothing until he seeded inside her, his juices lubricating her for a moment and making it a little less painful, only for a moment as suddenly everything went black.

The next thing she felt was a huge painful thump as she hit cobbles. As her eyes struggled to open she heard the words, "This is for my sister." An agonising pain split her throat. Her eyes opened wide in agony and she saw that face again, her blood gushing from her body. She couldn't make it out, except that it was the same face.

She leapt upright in bed screaming, determined she was not going to die with the girl of her dreams. Three times she screamed until Gratax, suddenly wide awake beside her held her to him.

"Alright my Queen, alright. I'm here you're alright." He squeezed her to him. "It's alright now, I am with you."

"It was him, he killed me. It was him, him, him!"

"Now then, try and calm down my Queen and tell me quietly, who was it?"

"Him. The one who killed that boy, now he's killed me, for his sister he said, for his sister."

Gratax felt she had slapped him, but it was his mind that felt stung, not his face. He stood Bertal up and walked her to the table, sitting her down and pouring some water for her. She drank a sip or two then looked up at him. Sweat was pouring down her face, her naked body wet and shimmering in the firelight.

"It was him. The same man killed that boy, I saw him. I know it was the same man but I can't see him. Wey I can feel his seed inside me but I can't see him."

"What happened? Try to tell me." Her breathing grew steadier.

"He caught me from behind in a barn. I could smell the horses and the hay. Then he bent me over a cart and raped me. I can still feel him now. He was saying something about this was what it was supposed to be like, then he seeded and he must have hit me, because the next thing I knew I hit some cobblestones. He said "This is for my sister, and...." She dissolved into tears.

"Alright my love, it doesn't matter now, I am here."

"But it does matter, he killed me, he drove a knife into my throat. Don't you see? I felt the death wound but I am alive." Gratax held her close for a while. She stopped shaking and he led her back to the bed, laying her down gently. Unbelievably she was asleep.

He returned to the table and drank some water himself, looking into the fire. He was sure Bertal had dreamt Reassel's death, just as she had dreamt of Grendal at Keffnon's murder, except this time she had been the victim. He didn't know how close she had come to her own death that night and it scared him, but now he knew he had to connect an itinerant tumbler and a Lady in Waiting to a murderer's sister.

Chapter 20

It was the Festival of the Gathering when everybody across the land celebrated the completed harvest. It was a time of plenty, of excesses, and the Castle Nisceriel led the festivities as always. This night in particular would set off a chain of events with terrible consequences.

Eilana was not herself. Her mind was definitely off balance and she was not thinking straight, although it could be argued she was at her best when she stopped thinking and acted purely on instinct.

It wasn't the wine, although she had downed a few, more than a few in fact. No, it was the death of her mother three days before. She was just short of thirty-nine years past her Bornbless, about an average life span, but she had been quite fit still, until she stepped on a large wooden splinter in soft sandals and it had pierced her foot.

Dear old Ferlmun had finally passed away in the late spring, and with the very little ill health anyone suffered in the Royal Household, they had been very lax in replacing him with a new proven healer.

The poison set to work in her foot and she was soon very ill. She died alone in her sleep in the mist of a terrible fever. Eilana wasn't upset that she was dead, in fact she felt guilty that she didn't feel grieved enough. She wasn't upset because she hadn't said goodbye, or because she hadn't thanked her for her life, she had given her a fairy tale existence the last two years for goodness sake. She had lived in the Royal Quarters, mixing with Royalty, and with a Prince for a grandson.

Eilana was upset that she had been dead for over a day before anyone noticed, including herself. Eival had finally discovered her when she went up to see her to talk about arrangements for the Festival. That was two days ago now, and they had buried her quietly the next day in a very private ceremony.

Tonight Eilana was going to enjoy herself. She looked around the Great Hall, at all the gentry of the land. They had travelled from all over Nisceriel to be there, and they were mostly all having a good time. She could see that Bradett wasn't. His wife was displaying herself beside him, enjoying being the Chancellor's wife, a Lady of standing. She was putting on some terribly superior airs. She spoke in her most aristocratic accent to the Ladies around her as Bradett moved away.

Gratax and the Queen were at the far end of the hall, but every time she glanced that way he was looking at her. She spotted Harlmon and moved towards him.

"Is all well brother? Your boys are being very discreet tonight."

"Yes My Lady, we'll let the Red and Blacks do the formal stuff, look pretty and get their toes stood on, while we get on with the work. One or two are getting a little noisy but we'll slip them out if they get too boisterous. It's the cheap wine you know. Can't you persuade the King to put on something decent?" He laughed and moved away.

It was no good; she would have to head for the toilets. They were all situated on the west side of the Keep where the holes in the walls dropped to the foot of the building into the diverted stream that ran in a culvert under the moat, into the main stream and down to the river. It worked well, except sometimes in the height of summer when lack of water and heat combined to make it a little unpleasant.

From the Hall the quickest route was along a narrow corridor that twisted its way to the far corner of the Keep. Eilana was just over halfway along it when she met a slightly worse for wear Bradett on his way back. He stood back against the wall for her to squeeze past.

"My Lady, I am so sorry. Do please pass."

Eilana looked at the gap. He was playing with her, seeing if she would push past him or make him move back down the corridor to a doorway. She moved towards him and turned sideways, facing him, and began to squeeze by.

"You smell divine My Lady," he whispered, in what Eilana took to be an attempt at a desirable voice. She looked up into his eyes, and when she had his full attention on her face she grabbed his codpiece hard and pushed him against the wall.

"Now listen my dear Chancellor," she said, "I have your balls in my hand now.

I am not afraid to touch them or to bring you pain." She closed her fist and he choked back a squeal.

"If ever I choose to use my hands to bring you pleasure, which I might do one day, on a whim perhaps to see if you are half the man you think you are, I will let you know in good time. Until then, go back to your arsey wife and keep your thoughts to yourself."

She clenched her hand again then let go and stormed down the corridor, aware of him still leaning with his back to the wall. She laughed to herself, men were so easy to handle.

As she returned however and was about to enter the Great Hall again, the doorway was filled by the large form of Gratax. He pulled the door shut behind him. His mind had been going over and over everything Bertal had told him, and everything he had gathered on Keffnon's and Reassel's murders. He had always felt Eilana was involved with Reassel's death, but it was only a feeling. There was no evidence whatsoever.

He had heard more and more of the rumours about Reassel and a seamstress. He didn't know which one initially, but it wasn't hard to find out. A lot of questioning and a promise of discretion, led the seamstress to confess to her affair with Reassel, and to tell of a mystery lover she was sure she had; another woman. Eilana was her best friend.

Then his mind went to Keffnon, and pure inspiration made him wonder about Harlada's father.

The brother clinched it for him. That evil bastard Harlmon was capable of anything. Rumours from his men were rife, but they all worshipped him, and he Eilana.

There was not the least shred of evidence. His only hope was to trap her into giving something away that could lead to him proving a connection, and right now her defences were down and Harlmon was out of reach.

"Are you enjoying your evening My Lady?"

"Thank you General, I am, or at least I was. Have you closed the door for a reason? I was just going back in."

"I just wished to offer my condolences on the death of your mother."

"Thank you General, it is not like you to be so considerate on my behalf."

"Well it is just that you have suffered so many deaths of people close to you, and your one bit of good news, young Harlada's return from the dead, also stripped your little Gudfel of the throne. Such bad luck!"

Eilana's blood was surging around her body, her mind was racing but the wine fuddled her thoughts. Instinct took over. Her eyes were hard and piercing as she looked into his face.

"And what deaths were you thinking of exactly General?"

"Well, there's your best friend Reassel, more than a friend some say, a very special friend." She fought to keep any expression from her face. Luckily it came across to Gratax as seething and barely controlled anger. He couldn't possibly know anything for certain. "And then of course there was young Harlada's father, such a shame for one so young. How's your brother by the way, still playing soldiers is he? You're so lucky to have someone so close that would do anything for you." He's fishing; he's trying to trap me. Her instincts were at their peak.

"Reassel's awful death was a terrible blow to me, but it was not bad luck General. It was a despicable act by a cold-blooded killer from all accounts. As for Harlada's father, I have never claimed him dead. If Harlada thinks that now, then all the better, but I have never told him so, he has never asked. When he does I shall decide what to tell him. Only three people in this land know who his father was; myself, and my closest friends, Serculas and Reassel, so now there are only two. Even the father does not know who he is."

She looked away as if suddenly overwhelmed with emotion and then stared back into his puzzled eyes.

"Serculas is sworn to secrecy, and as my friend I believe she will keep her promise, but if you must General, I suggest you talk to her, she may at least confirm that the father is still alive. And now General perhaps you would remove yourself from my way and let me return to the hall before I get really upset and go straight to the King. I am not sure what game you are trying to play with me General, but I know the King will be determined to find out from you should I choose to tell him. Now get out of my way."

She stormed at him and almost struck him as he moved quickly back through the door, bursting into the hall with quite a noise. The guests around the door swung round to see what had happened.

"Oh I'm so sorry General," she apologised, "I stumbled. Are you alright?" The amused onlookers turned back to their conversations.

"I am quite well My Lady, thank you." She leant towards him and almost hissed in his ear.

"Then let's hope you stay that way General. If I understand your insinuations correctly, those around me would seem to be, uh, somewhat unlucky."

She flounced away theatrically, looking far more relaxed than she felt.

Bradett and Gratax in one evening! Her problem with Bradett was almost amusing and well under control, and also very likely to be useful in the future. Gratax however was proving more than just a headache. She would need to think about this one, very hard.

Gratax watched her move away. She really was astonishing. Was that a threat or a sarcastic jibe? He could take it as either, and what was more, he was certain she had meant it exactly that way. He had gained nothing from the exchange, except perhaps to worry her enough into making an attempt at his life. That at least would draw her out.

He would need to discuss this with someone he could trust. Rebgroth was the obvious choice, but he was too close to Eilana, husband of her best friend; her best living friend he added in his mind with a mental chuckle. One thing was certain to him, now more than ever. Evidence or not, Eilana was at the centre of it all, but proving it to the King's satisfaction was going to be next to impossible.

He looked around for Tamorther. He would arrange a meeting in a few days to run through his suspicions, just in case something should happen to him. He could not imagine Eilana was really threatening him, but that Harlmon was capable of anything.

Strangely enough that very same thought was in Eilana's mind at that very same moment, but it was much later that evening when Harlmon came to her room before she spoke to him. The King was very drunk and still drinking. She had excused herself and gone to her room. Harlmon followed her at a discreet distance. He checked around her outer rooms and the Bluecoat guards on duty there, before joining her.

"Well that seemed an exciting evening for you my pretty one!" She looked at him and smiled.

"Bradett is a fool sometimes. Mostly he is a wise Councillor, one of the best, but like many men, a few glasses of wine and his brain drops to his crotch."

"And the General?"

"Now there we have a serious problem, but don't you dare do anything until I have thought this one out. Promise me brother."

"As you wish My Lady." He bowed elaborately.

"I mean it Harlmon. He will have to go; he has got too close to the truth. He is only guessing, he has no proof at all, I am certain, but he is too great a threat to us now."

"Whenever you are ready My Lady."

"And not until, understand? It will have to look like an accident. There must be no mystery, no hint of foul play. Think of something brother, then talk to me about it and we'll decide together."

He smiled at her in his deceptively innocent way. He kissed her cheek and turned for the door.

"As My Lady wishes," he said as he opened the door to the back stairs. "I will be in my room if you need me."

"Just get out brother," she shouted after him. She was so happy he was with her; he made her feel very secure.

She went to bed tired but with a warm glow about her. She lay looking at the ceiling for a while, remembering being in bed beside him, watching him. It was almost an automatic response. She imagined him looking down at her, watching her, he always knew girls did it too.

For the next two moons Harlmon had General Gratax followed for every moment of every day. He told his men it was an exercise. As a security unit they must be able to carry out surveillance covertly, and if they could do it with the General, they could succeed with anyone.

Harlmon developed a picture of the General's life, his every habit, his vulnerable moments, everything. What interested him most was the twice a quarter moon he visited the Inns of Castlebury with his Officers. He told Bertal he was out inspecting the guard and that he had a drink in the barracks before he returned to the Keep, when he finally left his horse in the Keep stables before retiring to the dowager wing where he lived with the Queen.

What he actually did was to saddle his mount and ride to the barrack stables where he would meet the Officers of the Royal Guard who were not on duty. Uniformed none the less, they rode to Castlebury where they would frequent one of the three inns and where they would perform some ritual male bonding, team building he called it, before riding a little erratically back to the Castle.

Gratax would bid his subordinates farewell at their stables and ride alone across the square to the Keep stables. He would unsaddle his horse, usually holding an intelligent conversation with it, or so it always seemed to him, before turning to the well in the corner of the stable's covered yard. Here he would lower the pail and draw some cool water. He would drink some from the bucket then splash water over his face, placing the bucket on the edge of the well. He would lean over the low wall and peer downwards into the crystal clear water. He could see the well shaft narrow to the water level some two men below, from the full arm and a half width at the top to the two forearms wide at water level.

On two occasions most recently, a stable hand had been on duty to see the ritual. Each time he had been on duty later than usual because there were reports of royal messengers who could arrive late and would automatically go to the Keep stables. Harlmon had ordered it. None arrived either night, but each time the stable boy, a different one each time, saw Gratax at the well, and observed his rolling gait.

The following quarter moon Gratax arrived back as usual. He was feeling particularly pleased with himself because he had won at cards. They didn't often play, and he won less often, but that night he had. He was at peace with the world and the Queen would be there when he went to bed. Their love life had settled into more of a routine now, less urgent passion, and it all had to start with him. The days of Bertal initiating their lovemaking had waned, as it had with his previous marriage before his wife's death in childbirth, and as his fellow Officers joked, it had in their lives too, although actually they were quite serious about it.

He unsaddled his horse and threw the heavy leather unit over a wooden rest. The stable lad would brush the horse in the morning. He walked the few paces to the well. No-one around tonight, back to normal. He tossed the pail down the well and drew it back up on the thin rope, balancing it beside him on the low rim. He knelt and bent over the edge, peering down into the clear water.

His legs suddenly lifted under him as someone grabbed his feet and wrenched them upwards. He plummeted head first down the well. A thousand things raced through his mind from fear to clever bitch.

He jammed his arms outwards but the speed of his decent and his weight pushed him on until his head and shoulders entered the water, his shoulders jamming against the edges. His hips and legs were above the water, but he couldn't breathe through his legs. He was stuck solidly. He held his breath, his thoughts blind with panic until he finally accepted he was doomed. His mind suddenly calmed as his lungs reached bursting point. A mixture of anger and acute sadness filled his mind at the moment his lungs emptied of air and he gulped in water and faded into unconsciousness and death. Drowning was not the painless death people often said it was.

Harlmon watched the legs that had thrashed madly cease to move and smiled. Perfect. He had hidden behind the hay pile and crept out as Gratax had leant over the well. The stable lads would testify as to the General's habit of leaning over the well, and of his inebriated state. This time he had just leant a bit too far, a terrible tragic accident.

Quietly entering Eilana's rooms Harlmon reported his success. No one had been about and they would not find Gratax until they went to water the horses at dawn the next morning. It was unlikely the Queen would send guards to look for him. She would embarrass them both if she called Gratax back from some late night card game like an errant child.

Eilana hugged Harlmon and kissed him.

"Thank you brother, but you see what a little patience and planning can achieve."

"Yes my pretty, you are right as always. That's why we make such a good team."

"Good. Then just do as I say and don't go trying anything clever without talking to me first, agreed?"

"But of course my pretty. One day you will tell everyone what to do you know, I can tell." She smiled at him.

"Perhaps brother, perhaps. Who knows? But now get off to your bed and cover your tracks, you had your Sergeant bring you supper in your room as we planned?"

"Yes sister, just before I left. He will be able to testify I was in my bed unwell if required, but I'm sure he won't be."

"Good, then get off to bed and eat it. Goodnight my brother, sleep well." She laughed at her unfortunate choice of words, the pun was completely unintentional.

As the dawn broke the alarm bell sounded. Rebgroth jumped from his bed, pulling on his uniform as quickly as he could. Tamorther too tumbled from his bed, and they both arrived where a crowd of guards and officials were gathering at the Keep stables.

"It's the General we think Sir, in the well." The Officer of the watch reported, but wasn't sure who to report to.

"Second Officer Tamorther is your line Officer, report to him," commanded

Rebgroth. He was totally confident in his position and didn't feel the need to stamp his seniority on Tamorther. He left the Officer reporting to Tamorther and walked straight to the well, where a Sergeant looked respectfully and sad eyed at him.

"Tricky one this Sir. It looks like the General's boots and scabbard, but we're just figuring how to get him out. We've sent for ropes Sir." Rebgroth nodded. The General's legs were wide apart against the edge of the well shaft.

"Get me a long spear, or a lance Sergeant," ordered Rebgroth as Tamorther approached. "It looks like him I'm afraid. Must have fallen in last night. We'd better find out who he was with and where."

"Me for one," sighed Tamorther. "We did drink a lot, particularly him. He was winning at cards and spending all his winnings, our money, on drinks for us all. Typical of him. He left us at the main stables and rode up here. I saw him dismount across the courtyard. That must have been only a few moments before he fell because he unsaddled his horse first."

"Right, see if anyone else saw anything while I try and get him out."

The Sergeant returned with a light cavalry lance as the ropes arrived. Rebgroth had them make a noose in the end of each rope. He placed the lance through one loop then lowered it, point first, into the well, the noose held just short of the point. He placed the point on one of Gratax's feet and manoeuvred it away from the edge, then he shook the rope free and the loop dropped over Gratax's foot. He pulled the noose tight around the ankle. He repeated the process on the other leg. It took a lot longer the second time, getting the noose over the other foot, but it worked in the end.

They threw the ropes over the beam in the stable roof above the well and teams of guards pulled hard. The body would not budge. After a number of efforts they harnessed two workhorses and had them pull. For a horrible couple of moments Rebgroth thought they were going to tear the legs from the body, and they certainly couldn't have done it this way on a live person, but suddenly the torso tore free with a tearing and scraping of cloth, leather and skin on stone.

They swung the body up and out of the well and respectfully laid it on the ground. It was strange the way the head and shoulders were soaked and the rest was dry. Rebgroth was trying to make out whether it was fear or anger on the frozen features as he closed the eyes, just before a screaming cry came from the doors to the Royal quarters and the Queen rushed out, Allaner at her side.

"Rebgroth, tell me it's not him," she cried as she ran towards him. He caught her by he shoulders before she could see the body behind him.

"I'm afraid it is Ma'am." What else could he say? She tore herself from his grasp and screamed again as she saw Gratax's body, and wailing she threw herself across his chest. Rebgroth turned to Tamorther.

"When she's ready, take the body to their rooms. I will report to the King."

"Yes Sir," replied Tamorther. Rebgroth was amused that this was one time Tamorther was obviously perfectly happy not to be in command. He walked towards the Keep.

The King took his report in the Great Hall, where Bradett and two other Councillors who were currently resident in the Castle had gathered. Eilana stood beside him next to the throne.

"Is it true Rebgroth?" asked the King before he could speak.

"Yes Sire, I am afraid it is. He would appear to have fallen headfirst into the well in the Royal stables last night Sire, on his return from Castlebury." Gudmon paused only for a moment before he spoke again.

"You are hereby appointed General to my armies Rebgroth. I want you to investigate this thoroughly; I want to be certain what happened, you hear, certain."

"Yes Sire, and thank you Sire." Rebgroth was a little unsure what to say in the circumstances. He had always dreamed of being the General.

"You deserve it my boy. I am only sorry it has come about in this way. I am not sure a celebration would be appropriate."

"No indeed Sire, nor I. If you will excuse me?"

"Of course General, be about your duties."

Rebgroth bowed and backed away for six steps then turned and strode away. He enjoyed being called General. It was an ill wind!

Tamorther, with a lot of support from Allaner, had finally persuaded the Queen to rise from Gratax's body and allow his men to carry him up to their chambers where they laid him on the bed.

Bertal dismissed them all and sent Allaner for warm water as she began to undress his body. Her mind was numb to the reality one moment then racked with pain the next; one moment coldly calculating all the possibilities of what had happened, the next in almost blind panic as to how she would live without him.

She had removed his outer clothes by the time Allaner returned with the water in a large pitcher. She placed it on the table, and guessing Bertal's intentions, she fetched a large bowl from the table behind the screen and two cloths that hung there too. She placed them beside the bowl.

Bertal was struggling. Gratax's dead weight was too much for her to handle easily, but she shunned Allaner's help, ordering her from the room, and when she tried to object the Queen screamed at her to go until called. She reluctantly left the room and found Tamorther waiting outside. They spoke briefly then left the apartments together in search of Rebgroth.

Bertal continued her struggle until Gratax was naked on the bed and then fetched the water. She began to wash the body gently. Almost two watches underwater had not been kind to his face and she wiped the pale skin softly, her tears often dropping again where she had just washed them away.

. The room was dark although it was now well into the day. The heavy curtains were pulled across the windows and the daylight only showed around their edges. The fire was lit as it was only a moon to the shortest day, and the fire's warm glow gave some colour to his skin.

When she finished she looked down at him from the end of the bed. He looked asleep and she almost felt that if she shook him he would awake. She seriously considered joining him in death, and only the thought of leaving her children in that Eilana's care stopped her.

She moved to the side of the bed and lay down beside him, her head on his shoulder, her arm across his chest. He was so cold to touch, so lifeless, but she lay there for nearly a quarter, talking to him, asking him how he could have been so stupid, asking him to come back and see her in her dreams.

She ran her hands over his body, even the parts that had brought her so much pleasure and then she sat upright beside him. She had come to terms with the fact the man she loved was gone, the body she sat beside was now no more than a cold lump of meat, his spirit gone.

"I will wait for you to come back and tell me what happened my General, in fact that's an order, you hear me? You come back and tell me."

She went to his robe room and fetched his dress uniform. He had looked so fine in it at the Festival of the Gathering where he wore it last, and when she had finished dressing him she headed for the dining rooms. She was hungry now, although food would not fill the emptiness inside her. She needed some lunch however, but she discovered she had arrived just in time for dinner. She hadn't noticed the dark.

Second Officer Tamorther sat at dinner with his new General, Rebgroth. He wasn't the least bit resentful. He had held hopes of Generalship, but as soon as Rebgroth had returned a hero, having saved both the King's son and the King's mistress's son, he had bowed to the inevitable. Of course he hadn't expected there to be any movement in that area quite yet.

He talked politely but with a troubled mind. Rebgroth was a man of great insight when it came to his men and could see he was somewhat distracted.

"You have not been under my command for a few years now Tam, but I have not forgotten that look of yours when you want to say something yet fear to. You should remember, I hope, that I would always rather hear the bad news and deal with it than have you bottling things up."

"I do General, of course I do, it's just that sometimes things are hard to say without sounding stupid oneself, when telling of something that you cannot credit could be right."

"I know you are not a stupid man Tam, so tell me."

"Yes Sir, well, it's something General Gratax told me a couple of moons ago. I couldn't believe what he was telling me then, and I don't now, but he made me promise to act on it if anything happened to him, so I must tell you of it."

"Indeed you must, so do so now." Tamorther took a deep breath, looking at the middle of the table as he spoke.

"At the Festival of the Gathering, General Gratax came to me towards the end of the evening. He told me there was a matter of great import and delicacy he needed to discus with me, and to report to him after first daylight watch change the day after next." He shifted uneasily in his seat before continuing.

"It seemed a bit odd that if it was so important it was not of more urgency so I was intrigued. I duly reported to him and he sat me down to a private breakfast with him, in his room in the main barracks. What he told me was to be kept a secret, and only divulged to anyone if anything untoward happened to him. I was also to gather any supporting evidence, no matter how seemingly unimportant, and report back to him regularly." He looked up at Rebgroth and registered the controlled impatience in his eyes.

"I'm sorry Sir, this is a little difficult." Rebgroth nodded slightly and smiled.

"I can see it is, carry on Tam."

"Well Sir, he would not say where from, but he said he had strong circumstantial evidence that the Lady Eilana's brother, Officer Harlmon of the Bluecoats, was implicated in the killings of that itinerant tumbler murdered in Castlebury some years ago, and of the Lady Reassel also. He would not expand on his reasons, but he said both had threatened the Lady Eilana in some way and they had been killed to protect her. He also said that he had put this to the Lady Eilana and that she had threatened his life also, but that he didn't take it seriously."

Rebgroth grunted acknowledgement as his mind absorbed what he was being told.

"You see Sir, with his death so recently afterwards, whilst I cannot believe there can be any connection, I had to tell you."

"Why on earth did he not say anything to me?" Rebgroth was thinking out loud but Tamorther answered him.

"He said because you are married to the Lady Serculas who is the Lady Eilana's best friend. It wasn't that he didn't have implicit trust in you, but in a matter of such delicacy, and you being so close to the King, he thought you might have felt obliged to say something. I assumed that meant whatever evidence he thought he had could not be substantiated if it was put to the test."

Rebgroth was both very angry and somewhat shocked, but he forced himself to remember these were not Tamorther's accusations.

"Thank you Tam. I understand your reticence in telling me this, but now that you have, I suggest you forget it completely unless I raise it again. It is far too dangerous to be even thinking such things about the King's Mistress, unless of course you are officially sleeping with the Queen."

"Yes Sir, I mean no Sir I'm not, I mean......" Rebgroth interrupted him.

"I know what you mean Tam, I'm sorry, it wasn't a question. Now then, I will certainly bear what you have said in mind in completing my investigations into the General's death, but I have to say that so far there is nothing at all to suggest anything but a tragic accident. There were no discernable tracks around the well but his, and we all know the state he was in. Stable lads have seen him leaning over the well on other nights, and it would appear he just leant too far the once."

"Thank you Sir. I have to say I agree with you."

"I will research Officer Harlmon's whereabouts that evening out of respect for the General and let you know the result. Right, thank you Tam, I should have a drink, you look like you need one." They both laughed.

"That is an order I am delighted to obey Sir. Perhaps you will join me?"

"I think perhaps I will."

Rebgroth made the enquiries the next day, disguised as a blanket enquiry of all Officers' whereabouts. Harlmon was reported as retired early not feeling too well, evidenced by his Sergeant aide who had taken a little food and drink to his room just before the accident.

The Sergeant reported the enquiry to Harlmon, who later told Eilana. It was of interest to her that the enquiry had been made, and she congratulated herself on covering her brother's back so well. She decided she was very good sometimes.

The funeral was held two days later, a burial with full Military Honours of a faithful servant to the Crown. The Queen sobbed throughout, comforted by Allaner, who protected her from courtiers who really just wanted to be seen at a Royal occasion. Bertal's tears were of anger and frustration as much as grief. She had gone to sleep each night since determined to dream of her lover's death and had failed each time. 'If only she could control her gift' had been his words, and he had been so right.

Chapter 21

It was almost midsummer's day, the longest day of the year, but in this particular year, this nondescript day was the most important by far. The people of Nisceriel had been talking of nothing else for a moon before, and as the day arrived excitement reached fever pitch. It was King Gudmon's thirty-ninth Bornbless Day, the most significant birthday a man could reach, for on that day he moved from just a man to a venerable and revered citizen, acclaimed by all as someone to be lauded and respected. Of course if you were already King, you moved almost into the realms of deity.

Thirty-nine was an age most did not achieve in any land, even in the most advanced Kingdoms. It took wealth and power to eat and live well enough to survive beyond it, but often even those could not protect a man from the fevers and infections that claimed the lives of most citizens before that age. Thirty-nine onwards was borrowed time to be enjoyed actively as most men never got the chance.

The main celebration was in the square in front of the Keep's gates, where all the citizens of Nisceriel who wished to could attend. As the day wore on and the evening approached, it appeared that most of the Kingdom had descended upon the Castle to join the occasion.

Darkness fell and a huge fire was kindled in the centre of the square, its flames roaring skywards. Fireworks made in the far West lit the sky to the roars of the crowd in the square, and in the streets around, for the square had filled a watch before.

Even Queen Bertal appeared, looking drained and tired, but she was surprisingly active for all that. She had been almost a total recluse for over a year and a half since Gratax had died, seeing only Allaner, who was at her side now as always, and her grandchildren when they visited.

Rumour told how she lay awake most nights, desperately trying to dream of her deceased lover, so that the effort actually did the opposite and kept her awake. When she did fall into a dreamless sleep, the slightest disturbance would awaken her and she would repeat the process so as not to waste the opportunity to dream the next time her eyes shut. She had grown old before her time.

As the King appeared the music stopped and was replaced by tumultuous cheers from the crowd. He waved back enthusiastically, as did Eilana at his side, and the four children, Patrikal, Gudrick, Harlada and Gudfel, all of whom were totally absorbed by the occasion.

Patrikal had just become a young woman at thirteen, with all the emotions it triggered in her. She had grown close to Eilana, although she still loved her mother dearly, but her mother had turned strange since Gratax had died.

At nine Gudrick and Harlada had become young soldiers, accomplished with sword and lance. Badraman had taught them well, as coach and mentor. Strength was building in their immature physiques that would stand them in good stead in later life; Harlada at least.

Gudfel was a spoilt five year old that wanted for nothing, spoilt by doting parents and amused by elder siblings. Even on this night he managed to command special attention from everyone.

The party in the square reached a crescendo well before midnight, when most of the youngest children were whisked away by parents reluctant to leave the revelries, but many returned later when their little ones were asleep.

It was almost midnight however when there was a disturbance on the far side of the square on the approach from the main gates. There was a strangely muted cheer from the crowd as they parted to let a rider through their number. Patrikal used her sharp eyes to see through the gloom, using every bit of light from the fire.

She saw a rider who wore a deep maroon cloak over the same colour habit. His long black hair was loosely tied back, but it was grey white around the edge of his forehead and over his temples, which seemed to set his face in a halo of white. As he looked across at the Royal party, Patrikal ran towards him and screamed his name in pure joy.

"Moreton! It is you."

He leant foreward in the saddle and grasped her arm, swinging her up onto his lap.

"Well now, surely this young lady cannot be the little girl Patrikal I left behind me," he laughed as she threw her arms around his neck and hugged him tightly, tears on her cheeks. He raised a hand in greeting to Gudmon.

"Greetings my King, and a happy Bornbless to you."

"Get off that horse and attend me my friend whilst my joy overwhelms me, and before I remember how angry I was when you left without a proper goodbye."

He lowered Patrikal back to the ground and slid stiffly from the saddle. Hardly able to straighten his back he struggled to walk to the King and flung his arms around him in the embrace of a long missed friend. The King returned it, at least equally.

"Where have you been, apart from away too long?"

"I needed to return to my monastery in the far north, but all that is not for now. Can a man get a drink in this Castle? In less than a quarter it will be my thirty-ninth too you know?"

Drinks arrived speedily as everyone tried to speak at once and the music started again in earnest. Moreton looked at Eilana and smiled. He leant towards her and whispered conspiratorially in her ear.

"I see you have risen above Nanny status young lady, as I knew you would."

"Indeed Sir, although it was down to the confidence you gave me."

"Nonsense young lady, you were destined to rule the King's heart from the moment you entered the Castle."

"Leave my Eilana alone and drink to our health Moreton my friend, to your return, and to our reunion. If I could have chosen the best Bornbless present Wey could provide a man, it would have been for your return, and here you stand. To us my friend, to us."

They struck their pewter goblets together and drank deeply, wine spilling down their fronts, before they both laughed and threw an arm around each other's shoulders.

Bertal watched them laugh, and in her mind she saw Gratax standing slightly aside from them, a commanding figure but never quite as close to the King as he had wished, but then Moreton was an exception to every rule.

She looked to her right to see Eilana looking at her. Her instinct was to quickly look away but she didn't. Neither of them looked away so their eyes met and held for a few moments. Bertal could read nothing in Eilana's eyes. They were expressionless but not cold, just a passive stare that eventually seemed to radiate a confident lack of interest in her.

Eilana however felt the hatred and personal malice in Bertal's eyes. It hadn't been there before Gratax's death. She had been quite comfortable to live with the mutually convenient peace between them then; each living their lives in parallel, with their men and without either friendship or hate. Now the hatred was there and Eilana was certain in herself that Bertal knew that she was responsible for her lover's death.

Her thoughts were interrupted by Bradett, Wey he was always around her these days.

"Well what a surprise My Lady. Seven years away having left without a word and he just wanders back in as if he had never been gone, to be treated like a returning hero. I really don't understand it My Lady."

"Perhaps if you had any close friends, Chancellor, you would."

"Oh! I'm sorry; I didn't mean to offend you, or the King, My Lady"

"What makes you think you have Chancellor?"

"I could not help but feel a sharpness in your remark My Lady, about my not having any friends."

"Well do you Bradett? I am not aware of any." He knew when he wasn't wanted, or he did now anyway.

"I am sorry My Lady, I have few true friends, and would be honoured to count you among them, but that would appear not to be your wish." He started to turn away.

"Bradett, listen to me. You have not offended me. I am delighted to know you and respect your work enormously; you know that from the King's Council. Just now Moreton's return is more of a shock to me than most. I know what he means to the King and things were very different before he left, if you understand me, so I am merely a little on edge. One day perhaps our friendship will blossom."

"I look forward to that My Lady." He bowed and moved away. She smiled after him, she was growing to quite like the poor man, a very clever brain but not really a ladies' man, or a man's man either she thought.

As the early watch came the Royal party drifted into the Royal Quarters, many excusing themselves and retiring. As Eilana was about to do the same, Moreton caught her arm.

"Is that your brother in that smart blue uniform my dear? I have seen a few of them around."

"It is indeed Sir. He commands my personal guard, the Castle Bluecoats. Gudmon set them up after Reassel's murder, he was frightened for me."

"And how many of these guards of yours are there young lady?"

"A Hundert of Guards, light infantry, a third of Horse and a third of Special Security troops."

"I see you have been busy, independent of the Royal Guard no doubt?" She nodded. "And Reassel murdered you say? I have much to catch up on. I have only just heard of the General's death."

"A terrible accident Sir, tragic." He looked her hard in the eye and grunted. He turned back towards the King and slapped a hand on his shoulder.

"We are neither as young as we were my King. I am going to retire if there is a bed for me somewhere, then in the morning we must breakfast and you can begin to catch me up on all that has happened since I left."

"Of course my friend. Your old rooms are as you left them, except I have ordered them put ready for you since you arrived. I was certain you would return one day." Moreton laughed and smiled warmly.

"Thank you my King, and a good night to you all."

Eilana slept with the King that night, she was determined to remind him she was there and take his mind off Moreton's return. They made love passionately, the wine delaying Gudmon's completion of the act, but that was perfect for Eilana. She was not interested in her enjoyment, she just intended making it a night to remember for Gudmon, but as he was taking so long her body reacted naturally, and eventually everything else left her mind as she concentrated on herself. She climaxed with a series of deep groans, gripping the King's hips with her thighs as the contractions pulsed through her, her nails digging into his back.

Her moment of ecstasy was just what the King needed to bring him to a conclusion and he too groaned loudly before collapsing on her, crushing her beneath him. She laughed and pushed him off her onto his back, rolling half way with him and leaning on his chest.

"You make me very happy my King."

"As you do me Eilana." She kissed his cheek and laid her head on his chest.

"I am so happy for you that Moreton has returned, but I confess to feeling a little jealous of there being someone else in the Castle you love so much."

He pushed himself up onto his elbows, and lifting her from him he looked into her eyes, there noses almost touching.

"Moreton is my dearest old friend, as close as a man can be to another, but you are my lover, as close as a man can be to a woman, mother of my son Prince Gudfel, and closer than any man could ever be." He wasn't sure that was true but he knew it was what she wanted to hear. He lay back down and hugged her to him. The next thing they knew there was light at the windows.

Breakfast that morning was a strange affair. With so many people staying overnight in the Castle, numbers were high. Conversation seemed to be a tone higher and considerably louder than normal as everyone tried to be jolly and bright, when actually the majority sported the most dreadful hangovers, and those that didn't were still drunk.

Gudmon and Eilana were no different, although the food and bumbleberry juice had them both feeling quite human before too long, so they both smiled genuinely when Moreton entered the dining hall after an early morning ride with Patrikal. She had told him a great deal of what had happened from the uncomplicated view of a child, but he said nothing of that and soon he sat with the King in his rooms with Eilana, Bradett and Rebgroth. Patrikal sat by the empty fireplace as Greardel refreshed the pitcher of water on the table. He glared at Moreton, unable to restrain his resentment entering his expression.

The morning went quickly; there was so much to tell. Moreton was especially interested in Rebgroth and the boys' adventures with the Marsh Dwellers, of whom he seemed to know a great deal but kept hidden. The tales ended with the death of Gratax, a stupid end to a great man.

Greardel was summoned to bring wine and cheese. He brought some fresh bread too, and a rich butter. They all ate, genuinely hungry now after only forcing a little food into their systems at breakfast.

"I must take some air," said Moreton. "I thought I might ride to the hills north east of here and have a look out over the old country."

"A good idea Moreton, but I fear I am not up to much today," replied the King. "You go ahead."

"General Rebgroth, I thought perhaps you might ride with me and tell me of all the fine work you have done on the village defences these last couple of years, will you join me?" Rebgroth knew a command from Moreton when he heard one.

"I would be only too delighted. I could do with some exercise. Generalship can tie you down far too easily."

They left as soon as horses were saddled and rode slowly side-by-side for a three quarter watch, Rebgroth telling Moreton of his thoughts on the likely threats to Nisceriel and how he had planned to counter them.

They arrived at the hill on top of which the King and Eilana had first made love, although Rebgroth did not know it of course. Moreton however could feel it as they climbed the hill and rode into the open clearing on the summit, that and many other pieces of history that had been enacted up there.

Moreton swung down from the saddle and unslung a water skin from its leathers.

"Come General, sit with me awhile. You must tell me more of your time with the Marsh Dwellers."

"There is not much more to tell that I didn't speak of this morning I'm afraid."

"Oh but there is General. It is me you are speaking to now, and you know there is no-one more concerned with the future of Nisceriel. How about what they called each of you for one?"

Rebgroth looked him straight in the eyes and realised it was pointless to play games with Moreton. He looked away, out over the Castle in the distance, across the River of Number to the shores of Whorle, and began the whole story of his time with the boys. It took a quarter or so to tell.

"So Death Bringer, what did you make of it all?"

"There is no doubt that they believe Prince Gudrick is for an early grave, how early I cannot say, and that I will lead the Army of Nisceriel against them, but most strangely, that they will be led by Harlada. It is their belief that despite great losses to their people, they will win and I will be killed in the battle. It must also be that it happens fairly soon because they call Harlada the Boy Warlord and the like, so he must still be young when he does so."

"That is indeed what they believe. In my times away from Nisceriel, both recently and as a child, I have studied many other peoples, their past and even their future dealings with Nisceriel. They all seem to believe that one day Nisceriel will bring forth a King that will unite all the Kingdoms of the lands around, and that all will fight a common foe who would be unstoppable were they not so united."

"Do you believe it so Moreton, that all these prophesies will come about?"

"Prophecy is a strange art General. If I prophesy that you will die, there is no doubt that my prophecy will come true. If I was to prophesy when and how though, now that would be more difficult."

"But that I will die is a certainty."

"Exactly the point Rebgroth. You are a soldier, for me to prophesy that you will die in battle would be a better guess than for many people, it is your profession to fight. If you do, people would say I was a great seer. If I were to pick easier things in the near future and more difficult things decades ahead, as long as the short term ones come true people will believe the long term ones and pass them on to their children, for neither I nor they will be alive to know any different, and if they do not come true, who will really care.

"Others argue that if you prophesy something reasonably vague in the future, if you wait long enough it will happen somewhere eventually."

"I see what you are saying, but the Marsh Dwellers believed that a man and two boys would be washed up on that very beach, and have done so for thirty-four generations, and then when we did, we even fitted in with the prophesies in that I could at least theoretically lead an army against them."

"There is no doubt that sometimes someone comes along that has some sort of great gift, but then the philosophising comes into the argument as to what gift. Cralch, the first of that name and Lord Priest of the Marsh Dwellers was certainly such a person. Some will say he had the gift of foretelling the future, a true seer, but just think General, if the future was laid out that clearly, if our lives were fated that exactly, why should any of us struggle to achieve anything, it would just happen anyway. If you had not trained as a child in arms, if you had not dreamt of being a General one day, or just an Officer even, would you have been standing here with me today? I venture to suggest not."

"That is indeed true; there were many choices in my life that led me to this, many choices that either I or my parents could have made that would have led me to a very different life. So what talent do these real seers have, how do they do it?"

"No-one can tell you that General, for no-one knows. Others from my Order, far more academic than I, have studied these things for hundreds of years with no real result. The best theory is that they have a gift for seeing their way through the myriad of choices the future holds in a way neither they nor us understand, but I cannot believe the future cannot be changed by man. Were I to kill you now, Cralch's prophesy would not come true."

"Indeed not, but you are not going to are you, so it may?" Moreton laughed, "And if Gratax had not fallen down the well I would not be a General now, and far less likely to lead an army against the Marsh Dwellers. Apart from which, no-one can even hint at why Nisceriel would start a war with them, or them with us."

"Except perhaps to fulfil a prophecy? Who knows?"

"But then why in Wey's name would Harlada be fighting for them?"

Moreton couldn't help but laugh out loud. He turned and walked a few paces away before turning back. He threw an arm around Rebgroth and looked down towards the Castle.

"I should not tease you my dear General. Your questions and their like have been studied by my order for centuries and we are no nearer the answers. Theories abound but fact is very rare. I do know however that these things have a momentum of their own that we may not be able to stop because we just cannot know the factors that are critical to doing so, but I ask your help General. Something threatens Prince Gudrick if Cralch's prophesy about him is to become reality. Help me to protect him."

"With my life Moreton, for he and his like are our future. I so swear."

"Thank you General, but now there are two other things on my mind I must ask you."

"Then tell me Sir, I will help if I can." Moreton took his arm away and walked towards the horses. As he led them back to where Rebgroth stood he spoke.

"What are these Castle Bluecoats all about?" He looked straight at Rebgroth.

"They are the Lady Eilana's personal guard, set up by the King himself."

"Hmmm, so I heard, so why so many, and why Harlmon?"

"Well Sir, apparently, except for the King himself, the Lady Eilana would trust no-one but her brother to command such a unit. General Gratax argued hard that they should come under his command. The King insisted they remained independent; not that he did not trust Gratax, it was the principle."

"Indeed, I can hear the Lady Eilana's voice in that statement, and the number?"

"Again Sir, the King let them grow, against the General's advice. They started as a Third, but always the King had reasons for them to expand; increased risk, bigger areas to cover if Eilana and the children were not to be prisoners in the keep, and before anyone was really conscious of it, they were a Hundert. Next there was a Third of Horse to accompany them outside the Castle, but now this Special Security Third is a mystery to everyone I think. They are just an elite troop of highly trained thugs in my view."

"Perhaps they are there to protect her from the other Bluecoats."

"I'm sorry Sir?" Moreton laughed again.

"I jest General, and in very poor taste too." Rebgroth smiled and nodded.

"Yes Sir. I see your point. You said two things Sir?"

"Yes, a straight question. Was the General's death an accident?" He watched Rebgroth turn slowly toward him.

"The honest answer is that I cannot prove it was and I cannot prove it wasn't. All the circumstantial evidence says an accident, and that is what everyone believes. With the complete lack of any motive or evidence to the contrary, an accident it was."

"And now the whole truth General." Rebgroth really was shocked this time, but he should have understood by now that Moreton would know he was hiding something. So he told him of what Gratax had told Tamorther, and what he had passed on to him; all of it. Moreton mounted and looked down at him.

"So Bertal dreams. Have you considered that it might be the truth General, for Wey forbid, I think it might be? Remember your promise General, with your life, but then that would scupper Cralch's prophesy." Laughing he kicked his horse down the slope, leaving Rebgroth to mount and catch him.

They spoke little on the return ride, Rebgroth coming to terms with all that had been said, but as they approached the Castle Moreton turned to him.

"It is important that what we discussed today remains between ourselves General, I have given you that trust. Say nothing to the King and most importantly, nothing to Serculas. It would appear that anyone with information that might harm the Lady Eilana could be under threat. Do you agree General?"

"I do Sir."

"Good. Just keep a careful eye on things and tell me anything of interest, particularly about that young tumbler or Reassel."

"Those are almost exactly the words Gratax used to Tamorther Sir. Please be careful not to fall into any wells." Moreton looked at him and smiled with genuine warmth.

"If Gratax was killed General, it was because he threatened Eilana or let her know of his suspicions. I will do no such thing, and nor I suggest should you. I work for the future of Nisceriel and for my dear friend King Gudmon, in the sincere hope that both are the same thing. I put great faith in you Rebgroth, more than many would suggest is wise, but I see in you great strength and loyalty to the King and to Nisceriel, I know I can trust you."

"You can Sir, implicitly."

Moreton nodded and kicked his horse into a trot through the Castle gates.

Chapter 22

Moreton felt a great lump in his chest, a tight ball of pure emotion as he hugged Patrikal. It was a mixture of love, deep affection and pure pride.

It was the morning of her Maiden's Day, fifteen years after her Bornbless, and she had matured into a beautiful young lady, in body and in mind. Moreton was proud of her both as her father's childhood friend, and as the mentor that had helped mould her attitudes in her early life. They had helped her become the sensitive and extremely intelligent young lady she was.

He had continued to guide her over the two years since his return, to debate with her, challenge her mind about the life she led, help her appreciate the lives led by those in the Kingdom not as privileged as herself, and to realise the rigours of a life in the countryside of Nisceriel.

This was as far as he could go in preparing her for the future. He knew only too well the fate of the royal family of Nisceriel, his greatest friend and family, but it was fundamental to the vows of his order of Weymonks that he should do nothing that could affect the course of the future.

From the study of the prophesies of seers from lands spread around the island on which they all lived, prophesies studied for more generations by his order than most people could comprehend, he knew the most likely fate of them all. The smallest hint of what was to come based on his knowledge could radically alter the future, could change choices made without that knowledge.

He had watched the developments over the last two years move inevitably towards the most likely future for them all, and he was deeply affected by his vows not to do anything to influence it.

In a positive vein he had developed a close working relationship with

General Rebgroth. It was built on a mutual respect and trust that underpinned all they discussed. Rebgroth had continued his task of enhancing Nisceriel's defences, fine-tuning immediate defence plans and speedy mobilisation measures.

On the negative side, and very sadly for him, he had seen his friend King Gudmon descend once more into despair and depression. The Lady Eilana had become pregnant again shortly after his return, and Gudmon could not have been happier, but he wasn't as sure of Eilana's feelings.

In fact she was quite happy about it. A second child would further re-enforce their relationship in the eyes of the court, if that was possible, in the sense that everyone knew she was Queen in every thing but name, but this of course was a happiness based on political advantage rather than purely personal feelings.

Eilana's real desire was to see her son with Gudmon, Prince Gudfel, become the next King instead of Prince Gudrick, his elder son with that ever stranger recluse, Queen Bertal.

As her pregnancy advanced, satisfying Gudmon's needs became more difficult, and somehow the effort involved this time just seemed too great. As Gudmon's frustrations grew, so did his temper, and thus raised voices started to be heard outside the King's apartments. Then tragically, and very unexpectedly, at six moons Eilana miscarried, losing the baby and nearly her own life too.

The tragedy altered something in her head as well though. Somehow it was all Gudmon's fault, and whilst even she realised it was ridiculous, her mind rejected him, making her feel awkward around him and deadening any sexual desires in his direction.

King Gudmon had experienced this before as his relationship with Bertal had crumbled, but this was even worse. He had loved Bertal in his way, and had been deeply hurt by her rejection, but Eilana was the love of his life, his soul mate, and now the same was happening again. It turned his mind to bitterness, to the rejection of women in general, they were all the same.

Why was this happening to him again, the same feelings of rejection, wondering what he had done that someone who had fulfilled his every desire and need, suddenly couldn't stand to touch him, and flinched at his touch. His anger and frustrations grew, and Moreton knew they must explode outwardly or they would implode again as they had done with Bertal, causing him to breakdown and once more plummet to the depths of depression. This time however, they were to explode in a horrific way.

It was at least a quarter after midnight when Gudmon entered his chambers. He was drunk, not to the point of falling over but not too far away either. Patrikal's Maiden Day had been a huge success, her party a great celebration, and now he just wanted to go to bed with his mistress, or so she was supposed to be. His anger rose, and fuelled by the wine; he burst through the adjoining doors into Eilana's bedroom.

She was not there; she was asleep in the protection of her brother's arms in his room above hers. All Gudmon knew was that her bed was empty, and torn between rage and tears, Gudmon turned back into his bedroom. His mind went to more wine and the oblivion to his pain it would bring. As his eyes looked towards the fireplace and the rope he needed to pull to summon a footman, his eyes found the bottle on the mantelpiece that had sat there for more years than he could remember, a present from Greardel.

He reached up and slid it from the mantelpiece. Turning to the table where two empty bottles stood that he had drunk with Moreton and Rebgroth before the party, he fumbled with a corkscrew. He finally opened the bottle, a bottle of now mature bumbleberry wine, not that he knew that.

All he knew was that it tasted superb, the best wine he had ever drunk. Luckily, after the second goblet his emotions overtook him again, and leaving the partly drunk bottle on the table, he stormed back into Eilana's room. Seeing no-one he opened the first door separating the room from the nursery, and as he did the most overpowering surge of despair overwhelmed him. He remembered standing between the doors as he witnessed Eilana in her bath all those years before.

The despair quickly turned to a deep anger, a fierce desire for sexual gratification, and the need for revenge on womankind for making him feel this way. His emotions spiralled ever higher, his anger turning to an uncontrollable rage, and his leggings bulging with his desire. He threw back the second door and blundered into the nursery.

Serculas jumped round in surprise as the door burst open. She had been called to settle Gudfel back to sleep, which she had just managed. He would be seven in a few moons and would graduate out of the nursery, but until then he was still under her supervision.

She smiled to greet the King, but suddenly saw how drunk he was and the glazed look of hatred in his eyes. She stepped back and half curtseyed, edging towards the main doors, panic rising in her as she could not help but notice the bulge behind his codpiece.

"Come here you bitch," he said as he jumped forward and grabbed her wrist, "Can't you stand me either?" He slapped her hard with his other hand. She tried to break free, crying out, but her scream was cut short by a punch to her face that broke her nose.

Her head swam and reality left her as blow after blow stuck her, even after she had fallen to the floor. She felt as if she was floating above her body, watching it happen to someone else. He ripped her thin linen blouse off her shoulders and downwards, exposing her breasts, grabbing them and squeezing hard. She struck at him but it just began another flurry of punches to her face.

The King wrenched at the laces of his codpiece and pulled himself free, erect and pulsing with uncontrolled desire. She tried to roll away but he hit her solidly again before raising her skirts above her waist and ripping off her underclothes.

He entered her roughly to her complete horror, pumping his hips in a cold and animal like fervour. She screamed again, only to receive another skin splitting punch. This monster of a man was inside her and she could do nothing about it.

"You're all the same you bitches," he growled. "You all deserve to get hurt, you're all my subjects, my women, so you'd better get used to it."

He thrust into her over and over, again and again. The large quantities of alcohol in his body meant he would never seed no matter how long he tried, but that just fuelled his anger more.

Serculas had stopped struggling; switching her mind off to the pain, but her screams had not gone unheeded, although the footman who had heard them dare not enter the room. He ran for help, and as luck would have it, met Moreton on the way to his bed. Thus it was Moreton that rushed into the nursery, taking in the scene at a glance. He pulled the King off the semi-conscious Serculas.

Gudmon spun with a wild curse and swung a blow at Moreton, who swayed back and hit the King solidly on the point of the chin with a right uppercut that projected him backwards and left him senseless in a heap on the rugs by the fire.

Moreton turned his attention to Serculas, helping her slowly to her feet. Her face was covered in blood that had run into her hair while she had been on her back, but now ran down her face and dripped onto her breasts that hung over the remains of her blouse.

"Go and fetch the Healer Nedlowe from the hall and send him to his rooms, tell him I sent you. Speak to no-one else. Go, now!" The horrified footman hesitated, then fled from the room to carry out his orders.

"Come My Lady, we will take you to the healer's rooms," he said in his most comforting tones. Serculas was shaking in shock, her blood and tears mingling on her face, which was swollen and disfigured.

Leaving her in the care of the healer, who had been given a brief description of events and sworn to secrecy, Moreton returned to the nursery. Greardel stood looking down at the King, trying to make sense of what he saw, the footman beside him. Moreton explained events and had them help to carry the King back to his rooms.

As they entered them he saw the open bottle of wine on the table. Having laid the unconscious Gudmon on his bed with both their help, he turned to the table and picked up the bottle, his suspicions growing. He smelt it then wiped his finger around the goblet beside the bottle, touching it to his tongue.

"Oh dear Wey! Where did this come from Greardel?"

"The goblet Sir, I have no idea."

"The wine you bloody fool, the wine," demanded Moreton. Greardel had never heard Moreton swear before.

"I really have no idea Sir; it has been on the mantelpiece there for years." Moreton turned to the footman.

"What is your name?"

"Brenham Sire,"

"Sir, I'm not a Royal. Now you know of my reputation, the things I can do to people's minds?"

"Yes Sire, uh Sir," he quaked, correcting himself. Moreton had a reputation, totally unfounded, of being some sort of wizard who could control people's minds, for good or evil.

"Then you know what I can do to you if you breathe a word of what you have seen tonight to anybody." Brenham nodded nervously. "Good, then get Officer Tamorther here immediately, go, go." The footman ran from the room.

"Now Greardel, get the nursery cleared up before anyone else sees the mess in there, and not a word of this to anyone."

Greardel nodded and moved away, faster than Moreton could ever remember him moving to a command. Wey, what a mess! It was going to be a long night and a longer morning, and he was going to have to find a way of explaining this to Rebgroth.

Tamorther arrived and was immediately questioned by Moreton.

"I need a trustworthy man Tamorther. I will explain shortly, but I need someone loyal to the Crown and trustworthy. I need him to carry a message to the Elves in the eastern forest, and hopefully to bring back whatever help they will be. I will also need you here, so who should it be?" Tamorther did not hesitate.

"Officer Badraman is the obvious choice Sir. He has the King and his family close to his heart. I will fetch him."

"As quickly as you can, I need him away before the explanations have to begin." Tamorther rushed from the room.

He turned to the bed and looked down sadly at the King. It was not really his fault. Made into alcoholic wine, the bumbleberry, the sacred Elvish fruit that brought such health and benefit to all as a juice or in food, brought out all the evil from within a person, releasing all the constraints of society and conscience, turning a man or woman into an animal. Moreton did not ponder for long on the common contradictions of life, so many things that contained both good and evil, such as every person that existed.

Greardel straightened the furniture, his mind confused. He had finally got his petty revenge on Gudmon and Moreton, but he had not had any idea that his stupid flouting of Moreton's decree that no wine should ever be made from bumbleberry would have such awful consequences. He would never have wished this to have happened to Serculas, who of all people in the Royal Household treated him with the most respect.

He looked at the dried blood on the wooden floorboards and decided he had better fetch a mop and water. His eyes found the cot in the corner and he wondered that little Gudfel had slept through it all. Leaving the nursery by the main doors he saw Badraman follow Tamorther into the King's rooms.

Moreton greeted them and began to explain to them both exactly what had happened. If at all possible no-one but those who were already aware would ever know what had happened there that night, except of course for Rebgroth, who he would have to find a way to tell. He explained to Badraman what was required of him and sent him on his way.

He then told Tamorther of their next task, who looked incredulously at Moreton for a moment before silently leaving to fetch some rope. On his return they spread-eagled the sleeping King face down on his bed, and then tying rope to both of his ankles and both of his wrists, they bound him to the four bed posts. Tamorther could not help but speculate that this could prove a difficult day.

Next Moreton went to Rebgroth and Serculas' rooms and knocked on the doors. This was going to be one of the most difficult conversations of his life.

Rebgroth opened the doors and was immediately alarmed at the sight of him.

"What has happened?" he asked before Moreton could speak. He was used to Serculas not being with him sometimes at night if Gudfel was playing up, but she had been gone a while longer than was normal.

"I need to come in and speak with you General."

"Oh Wey, that bad!"

"She is alive General, but she has had a terrible experience, I need to tell you of it."

"Where is she? I must go to her."

"Not yet my friend, not yet. Now please sit down and listen to me." He pushed past him into the main living room and sat himself by the table. Rebgroth joined him.

"Don't treat me like a child monk," he said, "I need to know quickly before I beat it out of you." Moreton smiled inwardly, it was just the General's way of coping until he knew the worst.

"There is no easy way to explain this General. The King, already drunk, was drugged, poisoned if he had drunk more of the corrupted wine. He really did not know what he was doing, but he did the most terrible thing." He looked up from the floor into Rebgroth's frightened eyes. "He beat and raped Serculas; I can put it no more gently."

Rebgroth rose slowly to his feet, shock quickly turning to blind fury in his eyes, his immediate desire to kill the King no less because he was the King.

"Take me to her monk, before I do you harm, I am finding it very difficult to control myself, I may do you harm."

"Of course, but you must realise she is hurt and in deep shock, she may not wish any male company." Rebgroth grabbed the front of Moreton's habit in a clenched fist and lifted until his hand was in front of Moreton's nose, raising him onto his toes as his garment caught under his arms.

"Where monk?"

"I will take you to her when you put me down, and when you will listen to me." Rebgroth held him a moment longer then lowered him to the ground. "I will take you to her now, but you must promise me to listen further to me before you try to see the King, and I promise to take you to him too."

"Lead on monk, and I will try to do as you ask, but I cannot promise."

Moreton led him to Nedlowe's quarters. He paused by the entrance, turning to say something to Rebgroth, but Rebgroth pushed him hard from his path, flinging back the door and bursting into the room.

Serculas was sitting in a large wicker chair by the fire. She was curled up in it, almost in a foetal position, her knees under her chin, and she did not look around to see who had entered the room with such violence.

Rebgroth stood and looked at her for a few moments, not really believing what he saw. Tears appeared in his eyes, running down his cheeks. It was not a sight many would ever have witnessed. He moved slowly across the room and knelt on the floor beside her chair. He went to take her hand but she flinched away, so he sat beside her on the floor until she was ready to speak with him.

Moreton looked at Nedlowe who just returned his look with a hopeless shrug and smile, before sitting at his apothecary's mixing table. Moreton sat for a while by the window.

In her mind Serculas was slowly sorting her feelings into bits she could understand, could cope with. Her thoughts were a mixture so jumbled and confused she needed time to come to terms with them all. Rebgroth's presence was a comfort in one way, but just now a man that close was not comfortable.

The fear had gone. She knew she was safe now; Rebgroth had brought that at least. Why the King had done it was beyond her, but he had, a man she would have trusted her life to. Then there was the pain, although that was almost secondary. Her breasts hurt. He had kneaded them like dough, slobbering on them and biting her nipples, but her crotch ached appallingly. Not only was there the pain, but she could still feel him inside her when she shut her eyes, remembering her thoughts, begging Wey that he did not seed inside her and make her pregnant. She felt dirty, corrupted, spoiled, and totally humiliated.

She desperately looked for fault in herself. Had she done anything to encourage him? Not in the nursery, it had all been too quick, but earlier in the evening? Her mind dwelt over the events of the night. No, there was nothing she could recall.

Next came a thought that racked her with guilt. As she had lain there whilst he thrust into her, she had tried everything to avert the horror of what was happening, and she remembered that for a few moments only she tried to enjoy it. It was impossible of course, her revulsion at what was happening was far too great, but she felt so ashamed that she had even thought it.

Deep inside was a terrible fear at the heart of her trauma. How could an act

224

that had brought her such heights of pleasure over her years with Rebgroth, now seem so hideous? Could she ever feel the same again with him? Would he understand, and if not, would he leave her?

She let out a terrible wail of anguish which seemed to come from her very soul. Rebgroth got back on his knees in an instant, but didn't know what to do.

"I am here my love," he said, "I will look after you." Then with an unconscious insight into her mind he added, "None of this is your fault my angel, I will always love you, and always be with you."

She closed her eyes that had been staring sightlessly into the fire and slowly reached out a hand towards him. He took it and squeezed it gently. She felt a raw surge of energy pulse down her arm, or so it seemed, a warm glow of love and comfort. She drifted into sleep.

Rebgroth gently placed her hand on her leg and looked towards Nedlowe. "How badly is she hurt Healer?"

"Physically, I don't think she is seriously hurt. She is badly bruised. I have reset her nose which is broken, and I fear there may be a rib gone too, but it is hard to tell. She will certainly need a few days of complete rest and a moon to recover totally. Her face will be swollen and discoloured for a while, and certainly won't look too pretty for half a moon or so, but she will recover completely in time. Her mind however is a different matter, and one in which you will be very important. You will need to be very patient and understanding, and totally undemanding, until she is ready to return to normal, if, I hesitate to suggest, she ever really does."

Rebgroth nodded slightly. The King would pay for this.

Moreton rose and put a hand gently on his shoulder, reading his thoughts. "Come with me."

"I must stay with her." Rebgroth replied.

"She is sleeping and Nedlowe will summon us if she stirs. Now come."

He walked out into the main hallway where Brenham stood wondering what he should be doing. Moreton held out an arm to stop Rebgroth and spoke to Brenham.

"You are party to a secret that you may never tell, so from this day on, whatever your duties were, you are now the personal servant of General Rebgroth and the Lady Serculas. Do you understand?"

"Oh yes Sire, uh Sir." It was actually a promotion for him beyond anything he could ever have aspired to normally.

"Good. Now get in there and help the Healer, get anything he requires for

225

the Lady Serculas. It is all done on my authority." Brenham bowed and was gone in an instant.

"Now General, I will take you to the King."

"I am not sure that is wise monk."

"I know what I am doing General, and if you keep referring to me like that with such disrespect in you voice, we are going to fall out." He didn't wait for a reply; he walked quickly away towards the King's rooms.

The deep-seated anger held in check within Rebgroth flashed for a moment, then he set off in pursuit of Moreton, a smile almost on his face. He had not been spoken to like that since he had been a cadet, and he probably deserved it, yet no-one but Moreton could have got away with it.

He followed Moreton through the anteroom and main doors into the King's quarters. He had tried to prepare himself to face the King and keep his self control, so he was surprised to see him face down on his bed, fully dressed with his ankles and wrists tied firmly to the bedposts.

It was nearly a three quarter watch past midnight and only the light from the fire, and one candle on the large table, lit the room. Moreton waved a hand towards the bed.

"The King is in a deep sleep, unconscious almost. I punched him when I found him with Serculas and he probably won't wake up for quite a while, not from the blow but from the drug induced sleep I helped him into." Rebgroth looked incredulously at Moreton.

"You punched the King?"

"Laid him out cold. I was quite proud of myself, but it was easy really in his condition. Anyway he took a swing at me."

"I'm not surprised you tied him up then, he'll have you hung when he wakes."

"No General, he will wake with a terrible hangover and will not remember anything that has happened this night. He will have no idea what he did to Serculas but he will not be the man you knew. He will be foul-tempered and quite simply evil."

"Better I open his throat now then, before he hurts anybody else."

"And then you will lose your head for his murder." Rebgroth laughed at Moreton's comment.

"Not with the Royal Guard at my back. They will follow me when they hear what he has done. We will crown Prince Gudrick at dawn." Moreton looked sadly at him, and shook his head.

226

"And what if the Lady Eilana decides differently, General? She has a Third of her Bluecoats at hand and a Hundert close by, highly trained for just such an opportunity. I would be very surprised if she does not already know exactly what has happened this night, her intelligence gathering is better than this Kingdom has ever known. So next we would have civil war, and given your two Hunderts of cavalry against the Bluecoats I would not be at all confident of your victory."

Rebgroth sighed and sat heavily on a chair by the table. Moreton was right of course. He could not let his personal anger at what had happened effect his better judgement. Moreton was right about those damned Bluecoats too. He stretched out a hand towards a half drunk bottle of wine on the table. He needed a drink.

"Don't touch that!" commanded Moreton. This was too much, but before he could get to his feet Moreton spoke.

"Please General, remain seated. I will join you and explain." He too sat by the table. "I apologise Rebgroth my friend, so much has happened that needs explaining. Only a man as strong as you would have trusted me this far."

"I know you have Nisceriel in your heart Moreton, and the King too, but just now I find loyalty to the King a little difficult!"

"The King has been poisoned in a sense, what he has done is not something he would have done otherwise. Such evil thoughts can enter the mind of the most honourable men, you will admit that yourself or be a liar, but they would never dream of carrying them out. Every man is capable of such behaviour, but we suppress it within ourselves, choosing to live by the laws of our society for the good of all. The King however has drunk two goblets of that wine and it has released in him every bit of evil his soul contains."

"Don't try to tell me he did it because he was drunk!" Moreton pointed at the bottle on the table and raised his voice.

"Because he drunk that General. That is not ordinary wine, that is wine fermented from bumbleberries. I gave very strict instruction that none must ever be produced, but some fool has done so and brought all this about."

"I don't understand Moreton. What is so special about bumbleberry wine?"

"The bumbleberry is the sacred bush of the Elves. As you have seen, it has almost magical powers of health giving and curing illness. I don't believe it is magic. If we did but understand the processes of healing I believe it is a totally natural result. A thousand generations of Elves have been brought up and lived their lives using bumbleberries as part of their diet, and I believe they are responsible for making Elves what they are today.

"They honoured us and took a huge risk in letting man have even a few bushes. They are normally only grown in sacred clearings in the forest. It was only Patrikal's specific request, in return for the great service she had done them, that persuaded them.

"Elves, you see, have never used wines of any sort, nor mead, ale or cider. Their legends tell of the terrible evil brought about by drinking any such thing, but if you study their history as many have in my order, it is the terrible consequences of producing bumbleberry wine that led to their belief. It would seem General, that as with many things in our life, things which can create such great benefit, if misused can also create terrible evil.

"The King will awake the same monster that raped Serculas but won't know he did it. If we let him free he will create mayhem, an evil and wicked King who will bring death and tyranny to Nisceriel. I cannot let that happen."

"So are you going to open his throat then? I will lend you my knife." Moreton laughed and clapped a hand on Rebgroth's shoulder.

"No General, no. I have sent Badraman to the Elves for help. Elven healing has been based around the bumbleberry for a hundred times the years that Nisceriel has existed. I am sure they will help us, but he will not return until at least mid-day tomorrow."

"And if they won't?"

"I am sure they will." He smiled. "Until then General, we must keep the King restrained and this whole incident a secret."

"You ask too much Moreton. Do you really expect Serculas and I to carry on in the King's service as if nothing had ever happened?"

"I was confident you would my friend. The King will not know what has happened, or why you should not, and I was hoping that understanding why he had done it would help you to do so."

"It is Serculas that is the one you need to ask, not me."

"I think you will find that why he did it will be one of the biggest problems in her mind. She will fear all men now, in case anyone she trusted as much as the King should suddenly do the same. Understanding why will help her enormously, and you must explain it to her. After that we will see."

Rebgroth slumped backwards in his chair and threw his head back, clasping his hands behind it and looking up at the ceiling. He needed time to consider all this, and sleep, he needed sleep.

"Go to her General, and send Nedlowe and Brenham to me here. I will need their help. Sleep beside her and when she asks, tell her the truth." Rebgroth rose slowly and stood looking down at Moreton.

"You look like you need rest yourself."

"I have to explain all this to Eilana before she jumps to the wrong conclusions." His eyes rolled as he said it. Rebgroth moved to leave the room then stopped at the door and looked back at Moreton.

"Good luck monk, you'll need it." His voice was full of respect.

Broad smiles crossed both their faces.

"Thank you General, I think you are probably right."

Chapter 23

Badraman had been a cavalryman all his adult life. He knew exactly how hard he could push his mount to make the best time. He understood that the frustratingly slow progress made when he was walking and leading his horse was as important as the times he cantered. Whilst he had to head east as quickly as he could, he had to get back just as quickly.

The dawn had risen more than a three quarter watch ago and mid-day was not much more than a quarter away. He had made good time, not stopping since he had left Castle Nisceriel almost a watch after midnight.

He had been awake all the previous day of course, and he had drunk a fair amount of wine at Patrikal's celebration party, being off duty as he would have been from dusk until mid-day that day. He had been in bed for a quarter when Tamorther had woken him. A quarter after that he had been in the saddle, and it would be almost dusk before he reached the forest to the east. He would need his wits about him then, and if he could persuade the Elves to help, he would then take as long to return. It looked like it would be late afternoon the next day before he would see his bed again.

He swung back up into the saddle and set off at a steady walk, dozing as the gentle rhythm of the ride let sleep wash over him.

King Gudmon however was now wide-awake. He had screamed curses at Moreton, threatening him with the most terrible death if he did not let him free, until to his fury, Moreton gagged him tightly.

He himself was not in the best of moods. He had left Nedlowe and Brenham to watch over the sleeping King and gone in search of Eilana. He knew where she was, or rather he had guessed where, and he headed for her brother's rooms. He had decided there was something unhealthy about their relationship.

As he left her chambers by the back entrance he met her coming down the spiral stairs, Harlmon and two Bluecoats at her back.

"You were looking for me I assume, coming from my bedroom?" she said, and without waiting for an answer added, "I assume also you have come to tell me what has happened?"

"Indeed I have My Lady, but I will need to do so in privacy."

"Harlmon has my total confidence; his men will wait outside the door. Pray re-enter my rooms Moreton, I am keen to hear what you have to tell me."

"I really feel it should be for your ears only My Lady."

"Then I will waste a lot of time telling Harlmon what you have just told me after you have gone, so he may as well hear it from you had he not." Moreton said nothing and turned his back, entering her rooms.

Eilana and Harlmon followed him in, Eilana seating herself near the fire and Harlmon standing behind her.

"Well Moreton, you had better explain why the King is tied to his bed. I have assumed that you have a good reason other than open rebellion, which is my only reason for not having the Castle under the martial control of my Bluecoats in his defence."

Moreton looked straight at her, into her. He had been certain she would know already and he was right. She had come a long way this ostler's daughter.

He told her of the night's events and all he knew of the reasons for it. She knew where the wine had come from. She remembered the King telling her and her refusing to drink anything that was a gift from him, but she wasn't going to tell Moreton, it was far too useful a piece of information. Moreton told her that Badraman was on his way to the Elves and would hopefully return with help.

"Thank you Moreton. As always you have Gudmon's well-being at heart. I agree this must remain a secret, but do you really believe it can? I am not sure what Serculas will feel about it, let alone Rebgroth."

"Rebgroth understands I think. Tamorther, Badraman, Nedlowe, Brenham, and Greardel are the only others who know, and all are sworn to secrecy. I believe they will keep their oaths."

"I would prefer they were unable to tell anyone but I suppose that is impractical." Moreton was staggered she had the confidence to even hint at what he thought she had just suggested. He looked coldly into her eyes.

"If anything should happen to any one of them My Lady, I will lay it squarely at your brother's door, do you understand me? He may have got away with such things so far, but I know the truth My Lady, as I am sure you suspect. My vows are such however that it is my secret, but you should also know that neither can you harm me. I am beyond your reach."

Harlmon braced at his words and went to move past her, but Eilana hurriedly held up the back of a hand to his chest.

"I understand you Moreton; no harm will come to them, but after what has happened this night the King will never touch me again. You must tell him that, and if he tries to remove me from my quarters, or from his council, or if he threatens my sons in any way, I will shout his deeds across the land and my Bluecoats will hound him from this Castle. Do you understand me?"

Moreton stared at her for a moment. She really had become quite some woman. He grudgingly admired her strength. Finally he nodded slowly.

"Good, then we understand each other. I have been reading about your order Moreton, fascinating, all of it. Is it true that some of your order study the future?" He nodded again. "And do you know my future?" This time he smiled.

"All I will say My Lady, is that the higher one climbs, the further there is to fall."

"Which is why you rope yourself to the tree as you climb."

"Then be sure your ropes are not rotten My Lady." She stared after him as he swept from the room, a blur of deep maroon.

"A very dangerous man, pretty one."

"Then heed what he said brother. You cannot sneak up on him, so leave him well alone. His vows stop him doing anything to change the future that he knows of; I read about it in that book Nedlowe gave me. An interesting man himself that one. So Moreton is no threat to us brother, leave him well alone. In fact if I am correct in reading him, he can do nothing to hinder us."

"As you wish pretty one."

"And now I am going to get some sleep." She pointed at the door to the King's bedroom. "Tomorrow you will put a bed across that door and sleep in here with me for my protection. Tonight you can sleep here and comfort me."

The other side of the doors, Moreton spoke to Nedlowe and Brenham.

"I will sleep here until the King awakes. You two had better try and get some sleep. Look after Serculas Nedlowe, and Brenham, you are to see to her every wish." They nodded almost in unison and left for Nedlowe's rooms.

Moreton looked at the King and thought of Badraman, wishing him a speedy journey. He did so again, when listening to the King's complaining grunts at mid-day.

Whilst he slept in the saddle, Badraman's mount paced his way eastwards, mainly because that was the direction the small track he walked was heading, but when a wolf broke cover some distance to his right he shied and snorted which jerked Badraman into wakefulness.

He too saw the wolf, only one, but a lone wolf was rare. He settled his mount and trotted on towards a patch of more open ground ahead where he would see any threat at a distance. He was confident wolves would not attack a man on a horse unless they were desperate for food, and there should be plenty of small game about. He was right.

As the first sign of the dying light the tree line at the forest edge became a clear barrier across a very shallow valley that rose steeply up on the far side, the drop of a high escarpment. The track entered the trees and could then be seen running diagonally up the steep slope and into the trees again at the top. It was almost as if the trees at the bottom had spilt over the edge of the forest above. In a sense they had.

He stopped for a moment and looked for movement. He could see none bar the gentle waving of branches. He kicked his mount on across the valley at a canter, but as he approached the trees two Elves appeared out of nowhere in his path. He reigned in and stepped down from his horse, so as to be on their level and to show he did not intend to fight from its back.

"I am Balida, Tree Warden and scout to Retalla, what business does a man of the Nisceriel Royal Guard have with Elves?"

Badraman bowed formally to them both.

"I am Officer Badraman; I carry an urgent message for Retalla from Moreton of the Far Island. I carry it in great haste and need."

Moreton had told him exactly what to say and he was sure he had got it right.

"And I am Ranor, also a Warden of the Trees. Moreton is well known and loved by us; he is an Elf-Friend. What could be so important that you have ridden so far so quickly? Both you and your horse look exhausted."

"It concerns King Gudmon, father of the Princess Patrikal. Moreton pledged me to speak of him to Retalla only, and that as his message concerned the father of another Elf-Friend, he felt sure you would escort me to Retalla with all the urgency of his need." Ranor smiled.

"You speak all of the right words Officer Badraman, you were truly sent by

Moreton. I will take you to Retalla. Leave your horse here with Balida. He will protect it from the wolves that follow you while it rests, and we will climb the path more quickly without it. Follow."

Badraman followed him into the trees to the foot of the steep path up. As they entered the trees the light faded to nothing and he found it difficult to see Ranor at all. There was a little more light as they began the climb and he did his best to keep up with the Elf, but his relentless pace left Badraman with his heart pounding and his lungs bursting to the point where he just had to rest. As he stopped he realised he was at the top and night had fallen.

Ranor offered him a drink from a small flask, only a quarter the size of the water bottle at his hip. It was bumbleberry. Refreshed, he passed it back to Ranor and thanked him. Half a quarter later, he stood before Retalla in a small clearing that was lit by a ring of torches, suspended in the trees around it.

He was dressed as all the other Elves Badraman had seen, in light leather leggings, dark green linen shirt and long dark leather tabard, belted at the waist. He could see no distinguishing marks of his rank. The fact was that amongst Elves Retalla did not need any badges of rank. Every Elf felt his authority just being in his presence; a hangover from the telepathy of their youth.

"I hear you have travelled swiftly at the Elf-Friend Moreton's request. What does he bid you tell me?"

Badraman bowed and walked forward, dropping to one knee before Retalla.

"It is not necessary that you kneel before me, Officer, such displays of subservience are not custom amongst Elves."

"Indeed not my Lord," replied Badraman, "but that is all the more reason for me to show deference to the Lord of all Elves as I would such a man in my own Kingdom." Retalla laughed in genuine amusement.

"Moreton has obviously schooled you well in the ways of Elves my friend. Now tell me why you are here."

Badraman told him the whole story as he knew it. Moreton had specifically told him to hold nothing back; Retalla would tell if he did, not what, just that he had. Finally he spoke of the honour with which the people of Niseriel had accepted the great gift of the sacred bushes, and how they greatly regretted the deed of some single foolish man who had corrupted the fruit by making wine from it. They would find out who and punish him in time.

Retalla looked saddened and turned to an attendant. He spoke quietly to him and he walked quickly into the trees.

"We realised the great risk we took in letting man have even the three seeds we gave you, but when Patrikal asked as she did, having saved the life of an Elven child, honour would allow us to do no less. As always though, man has managed to despoil that which is perfect, turn good into evil. We will help your people this once, but you must tell our friend Moreton that he must assess the good bumbleberry can do your people against the harm that could be done if such happens again. He may return the bushes with honour at any time. You must tell him this."

"I will my Lord, I so swear."

"Good, then also listen well to what I tell you now. Your King can only be cleansed by that which fouled him. You must give him bumbleberry juice and that only for fourteen days, then he may have a little bread with pink honey for two more days. By then his body and mind will be cleansed. He will sleep a great deal after the first few days, and he will need to be force fed the juice until then, at least eight goblets a day, and he will not thank you for doing so. He will however remember nothing of it all after sleep and bumbleberry has cleansed his mind.

"As for Serculas, juice with every meal, and mix in the herbs I give you now each evening. Do this, and with love and patience she will understand the realities of what has happened to her with a clear mind. It cannot be undone, but it can be understood and lived with almost as before. Remember all I have said Officer Badraman, we will not help you again."

He turned as he heard the attendant return and took two pouches from him, passing them to Badraman.

"Give our greetings of affection to our Elf-Friends Moreton and Patrikal. Go now"

Before Badraman could begin to bid him farewell, Retalla had turned and walked away. He had not seemed to hurry but he was gone in a moment. Ranor held his elbow from behind and steered him around and back towards the track down the escarpment.

"Your horse will be rested. My brother Ranamo and I will run with you and guide your horse. You can rest in the saddle for a while before we leave you and return."

"Thank you Ranor, I appreciate all you are doing for us."

"We do it in honour of our Elf-friends and for no other reason. We gave up trying to help man centuries ago."

They reached his horse that grazed beside Ranamo who passed him the reins as he spoke.

"Balida has gone ahead to divert the wolves away. We will take you a safe distance to where you know your own way. Mount"

Badraman did so without a word. He did not feel the Elves were being rude, just themselves, and he was glad of the help. He was desperately tired and was asleep in his saddle within moments.

He awoke just half a watch from the Castle, alone on his horse. He recognised where he was and could not believe he had slept so long. Looking around he could see no sign of the Elves, but he felt sure they could see him, so he waved a farewell and kicked his mount on.

Chapter 24

For once Patrikal felt the Princess she truly was. She was dressed in her finest dress, a soft linen that clung and showed off her youthful yet mature figure to its best. At sixteen she was a young woman with her mother Queen Bertal's figure; slightly overlarge breasts and slim hips, and this day she was the centre of attention again and felt truly a woman.

A Prince was visiting the Kingdom of Nisceriel in search of a wife. He was nineteen and a formidable soldier, but of an uncouth race. He was Prince Bocknostri of Whorle. His father, King Draknast, had heard of the young Princess of Nisceriel and he had always wanted to gain a foothold across the river.

He ruled from his walled capital of Moonmarl, which lay a day's ride through a winding deep-sided valley up a beautiful river tributary of the River of Number. Its mouth was almost opposite Castle Nisceriel and could be seen from the towers. It flowed through a gorge, almost like the Ffon but not quite so spectacular, but the forested valley inland was breathtaking, especially in autumn.

Unfortunately the people of Whorle were nothing like the land in which they lived. They were rough and uncultured. All they had above the wild tribes to the north was that they had united under one ruler two centuries before and had developed an almost fanatical nationalism. Had they developed learning and a disciplined society they would have challenged even Nisceriel. Instead, their sense of belonging held together an unruly country governed by brute force and fear, but a tyranny all accepted as the norm. To complain or give voice to strong opinions was to play with death.

Prince Bocknostri, whilst Royal and with a natural arrogance, was out of his depth in the far more cultured land of Nisceriel. He realised it when his party reached Gloff on their trip to the Castle. They had taken the shorter direct route over the wooded Hills of Drean. Taking this route was one side of a triangle compared to the longer route of down river to the Number then along its banks upstream to Gloff, but it was such a hard trek that it could take at least as long.

To the proud young men of Whorle there was no decision to make. The tougher shorter route was the obvious choice and they pushed themselves hard to stay ahead of time for the long trip. Reaching Gloff though was a blessing. They were tired and wet through.

The stone and wood bridge that spanned the narrowing and powerfully flowing River of Number reached the bank at the foot of two towers. Between them stood the massive metal-barred and studded double gate of the village of Gloff. He was impressed. It was set back two wagon widths from the waters edge, and a track led each way right and left, down stream and up, sandwiched between the walls and the river bank.

It was an interesting defensive strategy to him. Most bridges would have carried a road straight into the village, whose walls would have been built along the river's edge. An attacking force would be cramped for space on the bridge and would have to take the village to get across. Whilst harder for the attackers, it would condemn the village to its eventual destruction before an invader could enter Nisceriel.

As it was, an invader here could get across and past the village, but only by moving along the banks over narrow killing grounds that would cost a large number of lives. Whilst an invasion force would lose many men, they could get around the village and into the countryside beyond without having to take the village. Their leader would then have to make the decision whether to take the village at great cost, or leave them surrounded by a small siege force and move on.

It was a strategy that gave the village a longer survival opportunity, probably relying on help arriving before too long. He tucked the memory away, but under a heading of weak Nisceriel thinking. They were not people to fight like men, it would appear. He couldn't have been more wrong of course; it was a very well planned strategy on Rebgroth's part.

A messenger was dispatched immediately to warn the Castle. Bocknostri was travelling with an honour guard of fifty men, large enough to impress but not too large so as to threaten. Threatening they were however to the people of Gloff, who felt very uncomfortable in their presence. They were loud and raucous. The soldiers of Whorle drank, sang all night, and couldn't understand why the girls of the village were so unaccommodating. If their officers had not been under strict orders to keep them under tight control, there would have been more than the two rapes there were that night. Singing loudly in their ugly guttural language, they just frightened the villagers more.

It was all to be to their detriment however, for it gave the villagers an insight as to what it would be like if Soldiers of Whorle were ever to enter their village by force.

Prince Bocknostri and his second in command, Cregenda, were invited to dine by the Hundert of Gloff, Gerlaff, at his home. He was a strong-minded but slightly built man, and Bocknostri could not understand how someone so weak in body could possibly have risen to power. Nisceriel was definitely a weak kingdom. His manner held even more distain than normal towards Gerlaff, but his wife Laranna, an attractive lady, found herself the centre of his crude attentions, his crude gestures, and wandering hands, that did not need interpreting.

The evening was a disaster, and Bocknostri left drunk, not really understanding why he hadn't been offered Laranna's company for the night. The interpreter thanked them on behalf of them both. Gerlaff could not believe he had got them out without violence. He had an Eleven of Guards standing by next door for his call, but thank Wey he had not needed to summon them. That really could have started something. A quarter later a second messenger set out for Castle Nisceriel to warn them of the habits of their future guests.

The next morning, but not very early by the time they were all assembled, Bocknostri led his men south towards Castle Nisceriel, flanked by outriders of the Royal Guard. The soldiers of Whorle had never been close to Cavalry before, and couldn't understand why a man in his right mind would want to fight on horseback.

Bocknostri looked at their lances held upright as they rode, and the cavalry sabres at their sides. It would be an interesting fight against these soldiers on horses if it ever came to it. His own men carried large heavy swords in the main, with round painted leather on wood shields. A few preferred to fight with axes and no shield, but it was an individual's own choice. His men would slaughter these lightweights on their trained animals.

All Patrikal knew however was that a Prince was coming courting. She tingled with girlish excitement, but she had no-one to share it with. Her body was reacting in ways she could not really understand. Her sheltered upbringing and lack of girlfriends of her own age meant that her experience of boys and lovemaking was virtually nil. Her mother, Queen Bertal had said a few things to her on the technicalities just before her Maiden's Day, the year before, but she hardly saw her now, and she had left her with more questions than answers.

Her mother spent most of her time in darkened rooms trying to sleep. She had once told her that when she was asleep she was closer to Gratax, and one day he would visit her and tell her how he died. Of course what she didn't realise was that it was the mixture of bumbleberry juice and wine that opened her mind to her dreams, and she drank little of the first and none now of the other. What she did do, however, was to frighten Patrikal so that she didn't visit her very often.

Allaner too had become withdrawn, paranoid that she would die like Reassel, convinced as she was that there was more to Reassel's murder than some slighted lover. She had convinced herself she was next if she was not very careful. She kept doors locked and always had a palace guard with her as she moved around the Castle. Between them both, the dowager's quarters were a strange and un-nerving part of the Castle for a lively sixteen year old.

The Queen would join them soon, she knew. Her father had insisted that she must attend him as Queen for the formal reception of Prince Bocknostri.

Her father smiled his rather uncertain smile at her from his throne. He had recovered from his illness after her Maiden's Day celebrations, the year before, but he had not really been himself since. She was not certain what had been wrong with him. He had been in isolation for almost a moon and was very frail when he re-entered court life. He had left the running of the kingdom to Eilana and the Council, knowing full well of course, the influence Moreton held over them, and even now, he took no part in the day to day running of his Realm.

He had in fact no memory of that time at all or of the end of the evening when he had become ill. He knew something terrible had happened, he could sense it, but he could not remember and no-one would tell him.

Moreton was his usual self, telling him nothing had happened and that he had just taken bad. General Rebgroth had become more distant and very formal, but he put that down to the weight of his position. Serculas he never saw, except on formal occasions like this, and then she came at the last moment, and went as soon as it was not rude to do so. Perhaps that was Rebgroth's trouble, his woman: Gudmon understood that problem allright.

He blamed himself but didn't know what he had done. Eilana had ceased all physical contact with him. He loved her deeply and was distraught on recovering his health to find Eilana polite but cold towards him. She said she could not help it; it was as if a flame had been blown out within her. She told him she blamed it on a reaction to the loss of their second child, when she came so close to bleeding to death herself. She said the fear of becoming pregnant again was so great she could not possibly enjoy lovemaking again. She had called it love making, but she had not meant it, he knew. It had stuck in his memory.

He tried to understand and live with it. She was after all, the leader of his Council and the mother of Prince Gudfel, such a strong young boy, much more like Harlada than Prince Gudrick. Bertal's father, the late King Gabral, had been a strong man, and her brother King Kadrol was a renowned warrior too. It must be blood from her side of the family that flowed in Gudrick. Perhaps he should have been a girl like Patrikal, he and Bertal were obviously good at girls.

Moreton stood a step down from the throne to Gudmon's right, and General Rebgroth a step below him. The other Councillors were gathered at the foot of the steps, looking important and making falsely loud casual conversation, laughing confidently in the King's presence.

Moreton saw Greardel in the doorway to the left of the throne where he awaited any order from the King. His eyes met Moreton's and he smiled uneasily. He had been sworn to secrecy on pain of death by Moreton, as had Badraman, Nedlowe and Brenham. Moreton was confident of Badraman and Nedlowe's word, but he had threatened Greardel and Brenham, that he would know if they told a soul, his powers would tell him, and he would use those powers to punish them with death if they broke their promise of silence.

Brenham was scared witless, believing the rumours of Moreton's greatly exaggerated powers. Greardel however was not so sure, but was certainly not going to take the risk unless he was. Moreton had been up to something in the fourteen years he had been away from Nisceriel, and there was certainly a different look about his eyes, and a far more easy confidence about him since his return this time.

Greardel looked away from Moreton with an acknowledging nod, his eyes stopping on Bradett at the foot of the steps, and he noticed the Chancellor's eyes light up as Eilana pushed past him. Greardel apologised, backing out of the doorway. Harlmon gave him a sideways look, before joining Eilana a few steps down to the King's left. He registered his Bluecoats at strategic points around the room, unobtrusive but in position. The Royal Guard was of course formally on duty that day.

The Great Hall fell into an embarrassing silence as Queen Bertal entered through the same doorway. She was dressed very formally, her Queen's tiara making a strong statement. She politely greeted Gudmon and sat on the smaller throne beside him. She glanced down at Eilana, and to those watching it was hard to tell whose eyes held the most malice.

Patrikal moved across and stood to the left behind her mother's throne, putting her right hand on the Queen's left shoulder. She smiled down at Eilana who returned it with some genuine warmth. She had always liked Patrikal, her mother was the problem.

Everyone was in place and a muted excitement hummed amongst the courtiers that filled the Great Hall, although they had left a clear passage through their midst, from the main doors, along its length, to the Throne. It was almost noon.

King Gudmon breathed deeply and prepared himself for whatever was to come. He was keen to ally himself to Whorle. It would complete a circle of allies around Nisceriel, except to the north where there were no kingdoms known to them, just wild tribes, but he was concerned at the news he had received from Gloff. He had told no-one except Moreton, who just advised him to let events take their course, but to have the entire guard standing in readiness for trouble, just in case.

Moreton had gone straight to Eilana and told her the situation, and inevitably Harlmon too, of the events in Gloff the night before. Harlmon agreed, in fact suggested, that he should support the Palace Guard with a Third of his regular Bluecoats and his Third of Special Security Guards. His full Hundert of Bluecoats should be stationed in Castlebury to protect the population there. His Third of Bluecoat Cavalry would circle around behind Bocknostri's column as they approached and let them know that a hasty retreat was not an option if it came to trouble.

That was all the day before. Bocknostri and his men had arrived at the Castle as dusk closed in and were offered a campsite just north of the Castle. Moreton acted as envoy to the King and rode out to greet him. He explained through Bocknostri's interpreter, that a formal welcome was being prepared for him and his senior aides the next morning at noon. He would be presented to the King and his family, including the Princess Patrikal, but both he and his men should camp outside the Castle that night, as they could not be accommodated within. Moreton was not sure the subtlety of his words was being reflected by the interpreter from Whorle, but given no-one he knew spoke Whorlean he had no choice.

Prince Bocknostri was not sure whether to feel insulted or not, but Moreton assured him it was custom that he could not enter the Castle before his formal reception the next day. So now Bocknostri stood in the anteroom off the entrance hall and beside the main doors to the Great Hall. He brought only Cregenda and his interpreter with him. He needed his other two officers to control his men and keep them away from the village south of the Castle for a second night. This was a strange Kingdom that did not allow the Guard of a visiting Prince to enjoy their Taverns and their women. It was not civilised.

Second Officer Tamorther entered the anteroom without knocking and stood before Prince Bocknostri. He had grown in self-confidence over the last two years under Rebgroth's command. Not that he had lacked much in the first place, but Rebgroth treated him with a total trust that generated it itself. He knew the General had sworn the others that knew the truth of the King's illness to secrecy, but he had never said a word to him, trusting him as Second Officer of the Royal Guard to be above the need.

He was dressed in his best uniform. The black basics with red trim on his shirt, leggings and tabard were perfect, and his black cloak with a wide red band around the edges and red crown on the back marked him as Palace Guard. Crossed thin red sashes heralded him as Second Officer.

Prince Bocknostri, Cregenda and their interpreter however were dressed in the fighting dress of Whorle. Dark grey leggings entered black knee length leather boots. The same dark grey material made the shirts they wore, and black leather sleeveless jackets, decorated with sheepskin and tied with black leather thongs, covered those. Their heavy fighting swords hung weightily from leather belted scabbards on their left hips. Their long unkempt black hair tangled at the sides of their faces with untrimmed beards. To Tamorther they looked a mess, but then Bocknostri was a Prince in his land and must be given due respect, however difficult.

"Prince Bocknostri, Sire, my King Gudmon welcomes you and your Officers to Castle Nisceriel and awaits your presence. Pray follow me Sire." Tamorther bowed formally and turned towards the door.

"About damned time," complained the Prince, "Tell me, what's this Princess like eh? Worth filling is she?" Of course Tamorther did not understand a word that he said, which was just as well, and his interpreter said nothing as they left the room. They stopped outside the main doors.

Bocknostri went to walk past him but Tamorther held an arm across his chest.

"I am sorry Sire, it is custom for me to announce you." The interpreter spoke rapidly before Bocknostri's anger flared, so that he only glared at Tamorther, his sword hand returning to his side.

Tamorther asked the interpreter for their names. He told him Cregenda but not his own.

"I here to speak for my Prince, I not real here." Tamorther nodded, drawing his sword slowly so as not to alarm his guests. He banged the end of the hilt three times on the right hand door, and then he held it vertically before him. The doors swung back into the room and he marched forward two paces.

The inner guard asked his name then turned towards the throne. His voice boomed out.

"Second Officer Tamorther Your Majesty, with guests."

"Name your Guests Second Officer," commanded the King, as ceremony demanded.

"I present to Your Majesty, and to your court Sire, Prince Bocknostri of Whorle and Officer Cregenda." He stepped aside and beckoned them forward.

Bored and baffled by the whole procedure, Prince Bocknostri stepped into the Hall, and with Cregenda and his interpreter at his heel, he stormed his way through the Courtiers to the foot of the throne.

King Gudmon watched them approach and almost found himself raising his eyebrows. Their dark hair and black leather were in stark contrast to the display of colour of the Niscerien Courtiers.

"Welcome to Nisceriel my Prince, your good self and your companions are most welcome."

Without waiting for a translation, Bocknostri flung out an arm in Patrikal's direction and spoke in his guttural tones. It did not take a speaker of his tongue to interpret his body language, and when his interpreter spoke, not many believed it was a genuine translation of his words.

"My Prince thanks you your Majesty, and asks if this lovely maiden is the Princess on which his dreams of the future are based, and to whom marriage would cement everlasting friendship between our Realms?"

Before the King could reply, Bocknostri spoke again. His thumbs in his sword belt, he harangued his interpreter, who looked ashen as he turned back towards the throne.

"My Prince also asks when a guest in this land may expect a drink and some comforts?"

There was a deathly silence in the hall. Bocknostri looked around him and Cregenda turned to face the Courtiers behind them, his hand almost moving towards his sword hilt, but he saw no threat, just a sea of stunned faces. It was Moreton who broke the silence.

"I think, my King, that our guests are hungry. May I suggest we move to the gardens for luncheon a little early. I feel the subtly of State is wasted on our visitors."

The King looked at him then laughed, and the tension eased. He looked at the interpreter.

"Please tell your Prince that a luncheon is prepared in the walled garden where we can talk and he can meet my daughter less formally. Pray follow my Officer."

The interpreter spoke rapidly and they followed Tamorther through the side doors towards the gardens. The Royal family all looked at each other, bewildered looks on all their faces. Patrikal leant towards the King.

"Father, you cannot possibly suggest…"

"Quiet girl. You will do the King's bidding, now go and talk with our guest."

Tears welled in her eyes as she turned away. Her mother put a hand in hers and stood, leading her away.

"Your father is not stupid daughter, do your duty as he says." She squeezed her hand reassuringly. Eilana was intrigued by this motherly display, the family that was no more, acting suddenly as if they were still functioning as one. Prince Gudrick, who had been hidden behind Moreton, followed his sister and spoke as they walked. Harlada walked with them.

Serculas left in the opposite direction, she was returning to the nursery to supervise Prince Gudfel and Rebetha. Eilana whispered in Harlmon's ear.

"Stay close brother, and have your men alert. I feel anything could happen from here."

"Have no fear pretty one, this could all prove quite amusing." He grinned broadly and hurried after the main party from the Hall.

Cregenda watched his Prince cross the lawns towards a long table set with wine and goblets. He took in the walled garden. It was a perfect trap in there, walls three men high on three sides and the Keep wall behind them, with only one doorway into it. It made a warrior uneasy, but he told himself not to be stupid. They were guests of the King and in no danger.

He continued to note his surroundings however, it was pure habit. Royal Guards stood around the garden's edge, perfectly placed ten paces apart with their backs to the walls. His interest, however, was caught by the more casually interspersed soldiers in pale blue uniforms. There were not as many, but to the trained eye, they looked far more formidable than those in red and black, and they were congregated much more along the Keep wall. Why guard unclimbable walls with no doors? If anything went wrong he and his Prince were not in a strong position. In fact they would be next to helpless if it came to it.

Of course there was no need for anything to happen, but he knew Bocknostri was capable of anything when he was this angry, angry at himself for feeling so inadequate amongst such obvious culture. Why should he feel inferior? He was a Prince, a proven warrior who had sired eight children to his knowledge. He would not be made to feel inferior to these weak bodied Niscerians, with their finery and correct manners. He was a man of Whorle and proud of it. Cregenda could read these thoughts on his Prince's face. Better be ready for anything. He turned to Gragonor the Interpreter.

"Find out who are the soldiers in blue. There were mounted soldiers in that blue north of us from the camp this morning. They look as if they know their business. See to it"

"Yes Lord, will you tell the Prince though, only he could become angry if I am not near him when he needs me?" Cregenda smiled and nodded, turning just in time to take the goblet of wine Bocknostri thrust into his hand. From the runs of wine in his beard he had obviously already got a taste for it.

They stood together and drank. It was plain to all that their interpreter was not with them so everyone smiled politely and nodded at them. Bocknostri's scowl grew more intense as time passed by and wine passed his lips. Gragonor returned and began to speak to Cregenda.

"The troops in blue are the personal guard of the Lady Eilana, the King's mistress, or so she once was. It is astonishing what these people will tell a stranger over wine. They are commanded by her brother Officer Harlmon, standing there beside the General. Apparently it is her brother who shares her bedroom these days, not the King."

"Hmm, good man, now attend the Prince, King Gudmon and his party approach." The round of conversation groups rotated steadily and the King waved a hand in acknowledgement to Prince Bocknostri. Cregenda watched his hackles rise, and moved close behind him.

"Ah Prince Bocknostri, there are so many important people here to honour you today, it is so hard to speak to them all." Gragonor translated as Gudmon spoke, and a strangely disjointed conversation began as he translated as quickly and tactfully as he could while they spoke.

"All more important than your guests it would seem, where is the Princess?" Cregenda wondered if Gragonor had translated with quite the bite that Bocknostri had meant. He had.

The King's party all had wine goblets and all seemed to be looking into them, taking a drink at the same time, hiding their shock. Gudmon coloured a little but smiled politely.

"She is here, good Prince," and he beckoned her forward from where she was hidden behind her mother. Bertal was angry too, and was drinking wine at a rate because of it. Patrikal moved forward between General Rebgroth and her Father, then curtseyed to the Prince of Whorle. Eilana's eyes met Harlmon's and she nodded slightly. He slid into position.

Bocknostri flung his left arm around Patrikal's shoulders and pulled her to him, his right hand fondling her breasts in turn.

"She certainly has the feel of an exciting bride," he laughed, as his left hand slipped down and grabbed her buttocks. She leapt forward, slipping from his grasp and slapping him firmly across the face as she span away,

"Damned bitch!" he cried as his hand flew to the knife in his belt, "I'll carve her face for that!" but before it was free from its sheath Rebgroth's sword rang free and was at his chest. A glance over his shoulder showed Harlmon's knife at Cregenda's throat, again before he could draw his weapon.

"What of Drew is wrong with these people?" he asked. Gragonor had not translated any of what had been said, it hadn't needed it, but for a reason unknown to himself he translated that.

"Tell your Prince that we do not behave that way with our women, we treat them with respect and dignity. It is clear to all that for me to allow her marriage to you, my Prince, would be for me to condemn her to a life of misery. No my Prince of Whorle, you must first leave my Castle and then my Kingdom, with all speed."

Bocknostri spewed a torrent of guttural words and stormed towards the doors, out of the garden and back into the Keep. Harlmon pushed Cregenda after him. Gragonor stood trembling and spoke to Gudmon. He obviously feared to incur his wrath for what he had to say, if not even bring about his own death, but not to say it would bring about the same result from Bocknostri. He dropped on one knee before the King.

"Your Majesty, my Prince say this day you make sworn enemy, him and

Kingdom of Whorle. He swear you will live to regret this day, but no for long after. He will come one more but no with just guard, but with big army." He looked up at Gudmon, fear clearly in his eyes.

"Have no fear from me man of Whorle. You do your duty, no more. Return now to your Prince and tell him I hear his words but do not fear his return, which would be a foolish mistake for him."

Gragonor rose and bowed but said no more. He almost ran from the Garden. Rebgroth was first to speak.

"Second Officer Tamorther, take a Hundert of Royal Guards and escort our guests to our northern borders, past Gloff. They can return the long way home. Perhaps they will have cooled off a bit by the time they have got there. Perhaps, Officer Harlmon, you could reinforce my men with your Third of Cavalry to guide them north?"

"He would be delighted," replied Eilana, "and they will follow them north to the far crossing at Teekford Vale to ensure they cross and do not try any clever doubling back to Gloff."

"Excellent My Lady," said Rebgroth, "please Officers, be about your duties."

Tamorther and Harlmon moved away as the King turned and hugged the tearful Patrikal.

"I am so sorry father, but he.."

"I know my pet, he is an ignorant native of a backward land. He doesn't even know what he has done wrong, it is just the way they behave."

"But if he comes back and there is war it will be my fault!"

"No my darling, I would not have let you leave with that monster, even if he had turned your head, no no, it has only brought forward what my father feared years ago. The wild men of Whorle with ambitions of conquest, it was always inevitable, and thanks to our General here, we are ready for them, and what is more, we know far more about what to expect. Is that not so, General?"

"Yes Sire, and their visit has convinced me of something else which I will explain at your Majesty's leisure, but first Sire, can I suggest we all adjourn and let the excitement die down?"

"Very wise General, come all, let us all rest inside and perhaps snooze away the effects of some of this wine, in fact perhaps a little more and I might sleep better." There was a cackle of polite laughter as they made their way back inside. Eilana alone hung back in the garden, looking up unconsciously at the little window of what once had been her room. This needed thinking about, definitely a bath night. She walked purposefully after the others.

When Bertal reached the Hall where people were talking in huddles, she realised she was quite drunk. She walked to a table laid with bread, cold meat and drinks. She took a wedge of fresh bread in one hand and a goblet of bumbleberry in the other. She added some cheese as she ate the bread and felt much better. A second goblet of Bumbleberry and she was almost back to normal. She circulated for a short while, saying farewell to Patrikal and making her promise to come and see her the next day. Suddenly feeling very sleepy, she left for her rooms.

She looked back as she left the room. Gudmon, Moreton and Rebgroth were in deep conversation near the throne steps, she wondered what about for a moment, then shut the door behind her.

The two young Noblemen of Whorle, junior officers of the Prince's Guard, had spent the last watch chivvying their men along as they broke camp. The Prince had ordered it personally. He had insisted that after the formal reception they were bound to be given the run of Castlebury, it would be grossly discourteous for King Gudmon not to allow it. They all agreed he was right, but as their eyes met, their thoughts were of trouble to come, and they looked back towards the gates of Castle Nisceriel.

Prince Bocknostri marched arrogantly across the drawbridge and turned towards the campsite where his junior officers stood. Taking one side of the triangle, he crossed the grass between the bushes, rather than the longer but easier two sides on the road.

His whole demeanour was of anger. His walk matched his mood and they realised something was terribly wrong. Cregenda was at his heels and looking equally disturbed. Poor Gragonor was a few paces behind, still trying to catch up. By the time they reached the campsite the Guard had been assembled, and they were ready to move or to stay, although the betting amongst the men was on moving.

Bocknostri stopped in front of his Guard and faced them.

"Soldiers of Whorle," he shouted, "Never has a Prince of Whorle been so badly treated, and never have the people of Whorle been so insulted. These weak men of Nisceriel will feel the revenge of our Kingdom; they will learn to give us the respect we deserve."

A cheer grew in the ranks of men he addressed.

"We will leave this unworthy place, but be ready for trouble. They may try to kill us all and expect to avoid the wrath of Whorle. I say to you now, if we die fighting our way home we will die heroes of our people, but even a number as small as ourselves, fighting men of Whorle, can defeat a large force of these weak minded people." The acknowledging cheer was heard within the Castle.

"We will march for home insulted, but we will return an army. Every man of us has a duty to get home; to tell of what has happened, and to lead an army back, are we as one?"

A sharp shout of agreement snapped back at him. He turned to Gragonor.

"Did you tell Gudmon what I said?"

"I did my Prince."

"And what did he say?" Gragonor took on the look of a cornered animal, his eyes filled with fear. He swallowed audibly and replied.

"He said, my Prince, that he hears your words but does not fear your return. He said it would be a foolish mistake for you to do so."

Gragonor was right to be afraid. Bocknostri visibly shook with rage, an anger which he had to release, and he did so by pulling a knife from his belt and plunging it into Gragonor's chest before he could move. He staggered back, astonishment and fear in his eyes, his hands clutching his chest hopelessly trying to stem the rush of blood, before sinking to his knees and pitching forward onto the stoned road.

"Such is the fate of any man whose words so insult Whorle."

His men looked approvingly at their leader's display of power and anger. It was only right, but the moment was broken by a thundering noise towards the Castle. They all looked to see Tamorther lead a full Hundert of Royal Guard Cavalry, at the gallop, across the drawbridge and down the road from the Castle. They formed up along the road in a battle line, their red and black uniforms making them seem almost a single living being.

As Bocknostri was about to shout an order a Third of Cavalry in light blue uniforms burst from the trees to their north east and charged towards them, veering away just out of spear range and turning north up the road. They turned and looked back, almost inviting Bocknostri to lead his men at their rear.

He realised they were inviting him to, to march northwards escorted from their lands, and his anger grew. It was anger built on frustration and inadequacy. These damned men on horses were too mobile. He could not attack them; all he could do was wait for them to attack him. A thought crossed his mind, if he marched at the Castle they would surely move to cut him off, but almost as if they had read his thoughts, rather than predict them as Rebgroth had, the drawbridge began to rise.

Castlebury then. If they marched towards the village it would surely make them react. He waved his men forward. They had no formal training. Their fighting was instinctive and individualistic, their battles a melee of one to one combats, so they moved forward as a bunch, vaguely spread into a loose line, two deep.

The line of cavalry they faced split in the middle, turning outwards left and right. Both halves wheeled away from them, riding for two fields before turning inwards and reforming their line, but that much further away. Bocknostri led his men on; their spirits rising as their enemy apparently retreated before them. Eleven men on each end of the line of Royal Guards spurred their horses forward. Bocknostri's men stopped as the cavalrymen lowered their lances to the horizontal and charged towards them, closing into a single line behind each other and heading at their right.

As they closed the sound of hooves behind him made Bocknostri swing round to see the Bluecoats about to hit them from behind. He shouted orders but it was over in moments. The riders clipped the flanks of his force, out of easy reach of his men's weapons, but as any man moved out to try and engage them, he was isolated and took a lance in the chest.

The Royal Guards swung back to their lines and the Bluecoats back to the north. Three of his men lay dead where the Bluecoats had passed and two on the Guards' side. He would never reach Castlebury like this. They would pick his men off a few at a time and he had no defence. These men were cowards to fight this way, and he roared this to his men. They would march home with dignity, and when they returned with an army, they would lie with these cowards' women, their mothers and their daughters, but he did not feel terribly dignified as he led his men northward, in the dust of the Bluecoat horses that guided them at a safe distance ahead, and followed by the Hundert of Royal Guard.

That evening they stopped short of Gloff. The Royal Guard had swung west of them to cut off the road towards it, and the Bluecoats had taken the right fork, northwards again. He discussed with his officers making camp and trying a night move towards Gloff, but the cavalry units showed no sign of camping, and they decided to push on into the night.

As they moved beyond Gloff the Royal Guard fell into place behind them

251

again and they all processed through the night, stopping at dawn to eat and for a short rest.

They moved on, tired and dispirited as their immediate anger died, but all it needed was to look ahead and behind for the ignominy of their escorted retreat north to fan the flames again.

The Bluecoats disappeared into a narrow avenue that wound between the trees which formed a large wood ahead. Bocknostri watched the last horses turn out of sight.

"I don't like the look of that my boys," he said as they trudged towards the tree line. "It's the ideal spot for an ambush."

"I think not my Prince." It was Cregenda who dared to contradict his leader.

"Why so my friend?"

"Firstly, my Prince I think if they had wanted to kill us they would have done so without coming this far north. They could have done so outside their castle walls and put on a great show for those on the battlements. Secondly the woodland is foot soldier terrain. They cannot fight on their damned beasts amongst the trees; there is no room to manoeuvre. They would have to dismount and fight us man to man on foot."

Bocknostri stopped, halting the column of his men behind him as he did so, and slapped a hand on Cregenda's shoulder.

"That's why I need you my friend; you have a good mind for fight ground."

"And it tells me my Prince that now is the time to show these bastards they cannot treat us this way without a cost." Bocknostri laughed and shook Cregenda's shoulder, turning him to face him.

"Give me your thoughts Cregenda, and speak up so the lads can all hear." He grinned. "Speak up."

"These trees would seem to run east to those hills off to our right, and along the hills northwards. We can ambush those following us as they move through the trees. Hit them hard, just once from one side, the east. We should kill at least one man each, maybe half of them, but then quickly retreat through the trees eastwards to the hills and northwards again. They cannot follow us through the trees mounted and dare not on foot. The Guards will be panicked and trying to control their horses driven into the woods to the west, and we will be away before those Bluecoats realise what has happened and can come back to reinforce them. I doubt they will try to follow us. They could head north and wait for us to come out of the trees, but we can do that at night, anywhere at any time. I think they will go home."

Bocknostri looked at him for a moment, almost in admiration.

"You see my boys, this is a true man of Whorle, but stay quiet, no cheers, they will come later. Walk on now, well into the woods." He set off with a new spring in his step, a huge smile on his ugly features. He spoke to Cregenda.

"Give your orders as we march." Then he called over his shoulder. "Listen well my boys." Cregenda raised his voice and spoke powerfully over his shoulder.

"When the last man rounds the corner in the trees, call out. The nearer this side we do this the further we are from the Bluecoats ahead. Spread yourselves along the track then move to the right, well into the trees. If they are not completely stupid they may well send scouts through, or even just out of habit. Stay back until they return then move up nearer the edge on me. Stay hidden until the last man passes me at the back then hit them hard on my shout. Most importantly, listen for my shout to pull back into the woods again. No heroics. When I give the order, break off and we will all live to hit them again later."

A muted rumble of approval rose behind Bocknostri, and he again slapped Cregenda's shoulder.

"That's what you're here for my boy."

They entered the trees and did exactly as Cregenda had ordered.

When they had finally had moved north from the Castle, Tamorther had led his cavalry after them, but only as far as the body of poor Gragonor, a victim of Bocknostri's wrath. He halted and swung down from his saddle, walking to the body. As he knelt down and rolled it over a groan and a twitch told him Gragonor was not dead as he had thought. From the wound in his chest, he should have been, but sometimes people survived the cruellest wounds, whilst others died from the smallest of cuts. Tamorther looked up at the young officer that had been riding beside him. He was inexperienced, but intelligent and able.

"Officer Cranalie, this will be your first active command. You know the plan, carry it out. Wey guide you all." Cranalie smiled proudly.

"You can depend on us Sir." Tamorther nodded, and the young man led the Hundert after Bocknostri's rabble. Tamorther waved at the Castle walls where watching guards read the situation and sent out a cart, to where he still knelt beside Gragonor. His horse stood reluctantly beside them, keen to follow the others.

Now however, Cranalie approached the tree line. He reigned in and waved his Sergeant forward.

"Well Sergeant, your thoughts?" He had always been told to trust your Sergeant. They were old hands, experienced soldiers.

"Perhaps an eleven Sir, straight through and back would be the norm, six wait the far side, five back."

"Agreed Sergeant. Do it."

With a few curt shouts and a flurry of dust, an eleven galloped forward into the woods. Even if they had walked as the rulebook said, they would not have seen Bocknostri's men, but at a gallop they had no chance of doing so. Their mistake was when they reached the end of the woods and the track emerged into the open and they reigned in.

The Levener looked northward. The track ran up a slight incline for about two fields then disappeared over the brow of a low rise. Cregenda was lucky. He had not thought that scouts would surely wonder why they could not see them on the far side. The Levener however, just assumed they were out of sight beyond the brow and waved five back without a word.

Knowing exactly what was expected of them, the rear five peeled away and again galloped through the wood. If they had walked it would have saved most that died, for the Levener and one trooper rode their mounts slowly up the track, but by the time they reached the brow his five were waving the Hundert forward on the far side of the wood.

For a moment they stared ahead. The Bluecoat Third was way to the north, but stationary, as if waiting. It was the trooper who asked the obvious question.

"Where are they?"

"Great Wey's shit! They're in the wood." The Levener was talking to himself rather than answering, as he swung his horse and spurred it down the slope, shouting ahead to the four troopers at the tree line.

"Stop them, ambush!" he screamed, but he was almost on them before they understood him and could turn themselves. Already at the gallop he thundered past them, all they could do was kick their mounts and chase after him, back into the woods.

Bocknostri was at the end of the line deepest into the wood, so it was Cregenda who watched the returned five wave the column of twos forward and join the end as they re-entered the trees. Cranalie had led about half the column past him when something happened inside the wood. In fact Cranalie had not nearly reached Bocknostri's position when the Levener scout came screaming at the gallop down the track.

Bocknostri read the situation immediately and rushed forward out of the wood, swinging his double-handed sword with perfect timing, catching the Levener just below the breastplate and cutting him almost in half as he rushed past. He pitched back from his saddle and rolled, breaking into two bits as he hit the ground in front of Cranalie. His mount crashed into the trooper's horse behind and bounced sideways into the woods, impaling itself horribly on a branch. It saved Cranalie though, for its weight killed the soldier of Whorle who was rising to hack him from his mount.

At Bocknostri's move, his fighting line jumped from the woods in a wave that brought death to nineteen Guardsmen before they could react. They were unready, their lances vertical and hooked in their stirrup cups. Before they could drop them and draw their sabres they were hacked down, their shields helpless on their left sides. Cregenda hadn't planned that, it was luck supporting the brave.

The Levener had died for his mistake, but he had saved more lives than died. Had the Hundert fully entered the wood, fifty long and two deep, and been fully surprised, they certainly would have lost at least half their number.

The lucky ones, on the left of the column, struggled to control their horses as they were forced sideways off the track. Their comrades to their right were hacked from their horses, but their empty mounts prevented Bocknostri's men from reaching beyond them.

At the front of the column, Cranalie was faced with over twenty others who had leapt from the woods but had not been reached. Not carrying a lance, he had drawn his sabre, despite the shock of the upper torso and head of the Levener being one side of him, and the hips and legs the other. Retching and without thinking he rode at the soldiers of Whorle.

The momentum of the Levener and horse had spun Bocknostri back the other way, despite having almost cut right through him. His heavy sword spun him further and he ended in a heap at the edge of the trees, but it saved his life, because attracted by Cranalie's futile gesture of defiance against odds that should have killed him, Bocknostri's men did not hear the five other scouts gallop around the bend behind them.

The first four were crammed abreast across the track, and their levelled lances pierced five of Cranalie's assailants from behind, one of the middle lances cutting through one man and deep into a second. Releasing their lances the moment they struck, the troopers and their mounts crashed into the crush of men. They fought to wheel their mounts away as the fifth trooper rounded the bend. He swung his lance towards the rising form of Bocknostri but was just too slow so that it raked his side, ripping leather, cloth and flesh, painfully but not seriously.

The trooper was reigning in as he thrust, so as not to collide with the others, and they all turned away, back up the track, the wounded Cranalie's horse bursting through the carnage after the others.

Cranalie was hurt but not badly either, more down to luck than anything else. He called to the troopers and turned to charge back into the fight.

At the other end, Cregenda leapt from the trees with a cry and downed a helpless trooper with the first sweep of his blade. He turned to the trooper behind, but this one had now dropped his lance and ran his mount at Cregenda as he drew his sabre. Cregenda blocked the downward sweep of the light cavalry weapon and swung his sword sideways into the trooper's chest. The Guardsman grunted as the blow struck, his metal breastplate stopping the cut, but a rib breaking beneath it from the impact.

He looked back down the column. As they had planned, there wasn't enough room for Guards to do much effectively, quickly at least, but his men had done all they could; to stay now would achieve little and cost lives. He cried out loudly.

"Away Whorle, away."

The cry was echoed up the line, and the men of Whorle disengaged and ran deep into the eastern woods. They slowly came together as they ran, eight less than had entered the woods, and now thirteen less than had entered Nisceriel, but over twenty Royal Guards lay dead along the woodland track, and a few others were wounded.

They laughed as their run slowed to a walk. They clutched wounds and slapped each other on the back. The day was one of honour for the men of Whorle. They continued east for half a watch then swung north, forcing a path through the trees.

The elves watched them go and had seen it all. They shook their heads in wonderment at what man was capable of doing to man, then moved south to report what they had seen. Two remained however, and followed the warriors of Whorle north through the trees.

Chapter 25

Eilana lay back in her bath beside the fireplace, just as she always did. She was more relaxed now, her tensions fading as the water cooled.

She had been quivering as she stepped into the metal tub, shaking almost. Her mind had been shooting off down many paths, her thoughts alive but jumbled. Now however, a good soak later, they were ordered and clear.

Her time was approaching, almost upon her, but it was not yet all under her control. She had known that an opportunity would arise if she was patient, if she bided her time and built circumstance around her so that when one did come she was ready.

Greardel was easy. She had known he had given Gudmon the bumbleberry wine, Gudmon had told her, and she had wisely kept it to herself. The King had forgotten after his illness, but she knew, and she had used it to her advantage, that and the knowledge of his hidden bitterness. She had learnt that from Reassel, who had been told with Allaner by Queen Bertal one winter's evening: sworn to secrecy of course, but then lovers tell each other all their secrets. For a moment she almost felt a pang of regret over Reassel, almost.

She had cornered Greardel one afternoon when the King was out hunting and Greardel was preparing his evening wardrobe, for him to change into on his return. With Harlmon and two of his Bluecoats at her back, she had confronted Greardel with her knowledge. First he denied it vehemently; next he roared at her that she had no proof, and finally when she had told him of her investigations, he broke down and admitted it.

It had not been difficult to cut down the possibilities of who could have produced the wine, and after half a watch of questioning by Harlmon in a room deep under the Castle, Fenlon confessed all. He had actually confessed after half a quarter, but Harlmon needed to leave him in no doubt who was in charge of his life from now on. Unmarked, he had been sworn to secrecy at pain of a slow death, sworn to Harlmon as a spy, and released a hugely relieved if sore young man.

Greardel too thought his time was up, but Eilana had told him that soon she would need his help to gain her ends and that she would give him his chance to avenge himself on Gudmon for a life of service. Until then however, he must continue as normal and do her bidding, reporting all events he witnessed to Harlmon or the Officer of his Special Third.

Serculas had got over her horrific rape, the bumbleberry easing the memory and allowing her to live with it, but inside she hated Gudmon with a passion. As her best friend, Eilana had spent watches talking with her, helping her come to terms with it all, and again promising her that one day she could help Eilana revenge themselves on the King.

That help would be in steering Rebgroth along the right path. He was a man of honour, of simple right, and he would never contemplate any form of rebellion, in fact he was more likely to take firm action against even talk of any such thing. Even though he hated Gudmon for what he had done, Gudmon was his King.

She had to use Rebgroth's strengths, to put him in the position where supporting her was the right thing to do, which meant that her son Prince Gudfel would need to be the rightful heir to the throne. With Gudmon out of the way, Prince Gudrick would be the next problem, but if she could bring about what was in her mind now, within a year, maybe two, Gudfel would be King of Nisceriel and she, King Mother.

There was one other she would need firmly on her side, and that was Chancellor Bradett. If Rebgroth supported her with the Royal Guard, and Bradett with the administration, she would be doubly secure. Yes, now was the time to give Bradett the treat of his life. He would be too easy. He already drooled over her and with a little success in that area, he would eat out of her hand.

She would need to explain it all to Harlmon. She was missing him already. He had gone off playing soldiers to see Bocknostri safely home, but a Bocknostri that was still smarting and angry. It was a dangerous task if not handled carefully, but very necessary to her plan. She hadn't explained it all to him in the rush to get him away, only what he had to do and to trust her until his return.

As always, instinct had led her. She had not really thought through the rest of the plan herself then, but she was relying on Bocknostri returning with an army as he had promised. Next spring was possible but probably the one after was more likely. If he was angry enough, he might ideally be back next spring with an underprepared army, making her plan easier.

It was her plans for Bradett that she would need to explain, so Harlmon didn't get jealous. If he realised relations with Bradett was just a means to an end, he would be perfectly happy. It would only be if he thought Eilana was actually fond of Bradett that things might be a little more difficult.

Her relationship with her brother had developed rapidly after he had moved into her rooms. She hadn't intended it that way; it had been the almost inevitable outcome of the situation though.

The fact was she enjoyed lovemaking enormously, and orgasms were addictive to her. Once she had discovered them she had to have more. Since her love life with Gudmon had ended they had been far more infrequent of course, although even then, despite the fact he had been a thoughtful lover, she had often had to rely on herself to achieve them.

Serculas had told her that many women never experienced one. She found that hard to believe as they came so readily to her, given the right stimuli, but she could only feel sorry for those women. To her there was little better in life. When an orgasm had washed over her, her body faded back slowly from the heights of feeling until she was totally relaxed, the only time she ever really was, and it freed her mind to think clearly and to wander where it would.

She could happily go half a moon without the desire, but slowly it would grow within her, and she would find a quiet time, in the afternoon, at bath time, or in bed when Harlmon was not there, to relieve the tension. She never needed to fantasise about a man, or a woman for that matter, when the time was right it was right.

Harlmon had moved into her room to protect her from the King's unwanted advances. They had slept in the same room for years as children and young adults. She had discovered all his secrets and he all of hers, and it had made them much closer. It had affected Harlmon far more than her though. Eilana was his only real relationship with a woman. He had raped and killed women; and to release his carnal desires, he frequently paid the whores in Castlebury, who lived on the needs of the soldiers from the Castle. He had never loved any woman however except his mother, who was now dead, and his sister; with whom he had shared far more intimate moments.

259

He felt no embarrassment with her, and when he climbed into bed at night, if the desire took him he would relieve it without a thought of his sister across the room from him. Actually that was not true; his thoughts were all about her.

It had been after a couple of moons that he had entered the rooms tired and dirty after a day exercising with his Bluecoats. He had burst into their rooms without a thought to find Eilana sitting in her bath. He began removing his clothes. She had sat upright as he entered; covering herself until she saw it was him, when she relaxed back in the water.

"You gave me a fright."

"I'll get in that water when you get out. Get rid of some of this dust."

"You had better be quick then. This water is not too hot now."

He walked naked across the room to the tub. She was struggling with the soap behind her back. He took it quite naturally from her hand and soaped her shoulders. He had done it so many times before, but this time he felt his desire grow. He became very erect.

Eilana lay back to rinse off her back, sat back up and climbed out of the tub, reaching for the towel on the chair. She looked around to see Harlmon still kneeling behind the bath in his excited state. She laughed as he stood up.

"You better relieve yourself brother," she said as he rose, gripping himself with one hand as he did so. He stepped into the bath and lay back, still gripping himself. He looked straight at her.

"You could always help." His eyes were mischievous, but there was a pleading there too. Wrapped in the towel she felt herself move towards the tub before she was really conscious of doing so. She knelt beside it and reached out a hand.

He seemed to seed almost before she started. She rinsed it from her hand and stood up, smiling with genuine warmth.

"Don't say I never do anything for you." He looked up at her.

"Thank you pretty one. You know you will never come to any harm while I am alive."

She knew it was his way of telling her he loved her.

"I know brother. Now wash yourself, we have things to discuss."

Two nights later they were both in their beds. Eilana had listened to Harlmon, pretending she was asleep as usual, until she heard him get up and walk across the room. She felt him sit on the edge of her bed.

"Teach me how to do it for you pretty one," he said, looking at her in the half-light of the fire. She tried to explain that women couldn't just turn it on and off like men, they had to feel like it, be in the mood.

"You're not in the mood now then?" he had asked. She smiled resignedly. "I'll show you anyway," she replied.

From then on they fell into a routine of pleasuring each other, Eilana for Harlmon far more often than he for her, but they had never made love with each other in the two summers that had followed. She had always thought that would have been unhealthy, and neither of them seemed to feel the desire to anyway.

Harlmon was a complicated man however, sick in the mind many would have said, and he became jealous for Eilana, not for physical reasons, but for her affection. Her children were the only ones he could stand showing any affection for her without feeling blindly jealous, almost uncontrollably so.

She stood up and stepped out of the tub. She would dress and go down for dinner. Bradett would be there she was sure, and she smiled to herself. She would flirt with him tonight and warm him up a bit. She would do that for a few days she decided, until he was ready to burst, then she would let him, and the final piece in that half of the jigsaw would be in place.

Tomorrow's bath she would dedicate to how she was to get Moreton out of the way. An idea was in her mind already, and if she was really clever, it could have other benefits too. She dressed and pulled the cord for a footman to have the bath removed. Normally in the mornings, her sister and handmaiden Eival, or her friend and handmaiden Ereyna, helped her to dress, but she always dismissed them in the early evening to give herself peace in the tub.

As she was about to leave the room there was a most terrible screaming and commotion outside her door, either in the anteroom or in the hallway beyond. She hurried to see what was happening. As she opened the doors to the anteroom she could see Queen Bertal beating the chest of one of the two Bluecoats that guarded the main doors to her rooms.

The poor guard did not know how to restrain the mad woman that rained blows on him, she was the Queen after all, and the other Bluecoat kept putting out a hand to pull the Queen away then withdrawing it, afraid to actually touch her. It was almost amusing until Eilana began to understand Bertal's rantings.

Bertal had left the hall and walked steadily back to her rooms, meeting Allaner on the stairs. She hadn't drunk wine for over a year but the food and bumbleberry juice had helped enormously.

Allaner was carrying a tray of biscuits and juice. She laid it on the Queen's table as they entered her apartments. The Queen sat in her cushioned chair and slowly consumed both as they discussed Prince Bocknostri and expressed their concerns for poor Patrikal, who had been so excited about the visit, only to

261

discover her suitor was an ill mannered animal. They agreed she would get over it soon enough, especially when the next Prince came along.

Bertal drifted into sleep. Allaner covered her in the chair with a light woollen blanket and retired to her own room, until she too was woken by a crash and banging of doors. She jumped up to find Bertal gone from her room, the blanket cast across the floor and the small table that had stood beside the chair overturned; the goblet and wooden platter it had born on the blanket. She ran for the doors after Bertal.

The wine and bumbleberry together had awoken the Queen's latent gift. While she slept she saw her dear Gratax dismount from his horse, unsaddle it and wobble towards the well. He retrieved the pail on its rope and placed it on the low wall that ran around the edge, drinking from the ladle it held. He leant forward and looked down the well, and as he did so, a shadowy figure in a light blue uniform crept from behind a nearby stack of straw and stalked towards the General. He crouched behind her love, grabbing his ankles and lifting them from beneath him, so that he pitched forwards and down the well shaft.

She watched the Bluecoat look down into the well and creep quietly away from the stables. She too moved forward and looked down the shaft. She watched her lover's legs kick above the water, and his trapped torso struggle until they ceased, twitching as his lungs filled with water and his life slipped away.

She awoke with a cry of anguish. It was that same man, she knew it was, Wey, why could she not see him clearly, know him? She leapt out of the chair, the blanket falling from her. She knocked the table from her path with her knee but didn't feel the pain. Opening the doors she ran down the mezzanine hallway in a blind rage. She didn't care where, but suddenly the two Bluecoat Guards outside Eilana's rooms, her old rooms, came into view, and her rage had a focus.

She flew at the nearest one, punching, scratching, kicking and screaming at him wildly.

"You bastard! Was it you, you bastard? You'll know who killed my love. Tell me who killed him, who killed my Gratax? It was one of you bastards." She kept on flailing and shouting until the inner doors opened and Eilana strode across the anteroom to the open hallway doors and came into her sight.

"Tell me you bastard, tell me. Did that pig Harlmon order it? Was it him? Who......"

Quite suddenly she calmed completely and stepped back a pace, staring at Eilana. The red of her flushed cheeks turned a cold white. Allaner rushed up behind her, holding her shoulders and looking over her right one at Eilana.

"Or did you order it you little viper? Did you order your evil tick of a brother to kill my Gratax? It was you, wasn't it? It must have been. That twisted brother of yours wouldn't do it himself. He knew something about you, didn't he? Something you had him killed for."

"Allaner, get her back to her rooms, she's obviously ill. I don't know what she's ranting about, but I'll not have her saying such things. I'll have Nedlowe sent to her."

"You are evil Eilana. It is you and your brother who are sick, you're unnatural, the pair of you." The Queen did not say any more. She turned and led Allaner away.

Eilana walked quickly away too. Bradett would have to wait; it was Rebgroth and Moreton she needed to see now.

She found them in the main dining room, sitting with Bradett as it happened and discussing the King, who had retired very early and very much the worse for wear. They had all had plenty of wine that day, even Moreton, but the King had not stopped since Bocknostri and his men had moved off north. They had watched events from the Keep's tower battlements as they evolved just as Rebgroth had predicted they would.

Tamorther had ridden back in alongside the cart that carried the wounded Gragonor. He had desperately wanted to carry out Rebgroth's plan, escorting Bocknostri out of Nisceriel, but Rebgroth had insisted that Officer Cranalie was perfectly capable of accomplishing the task and needed the experience of command.

"Gentlemen, good evening." Eilana greeted them all. They acknowledged her graciously.

"Gentlemen, I need a few moments of your time. The Queen is unwell."

They looked at each other as Moreton answered.

"I think the Library might be the place," he said as he got to his feet. "Lead on My Lady." She smiled weakly and led them out of the dining room, across the entrance hall and through the large oak doors into the wood panelled library. The large room was empty of people, but its walls were crammed with old books and manuscripts. It looked a jumble but it was all scrupulously catalogued.

"What ails the Queen, My Lady?" asked Moreton as they all gathered by the huge fireplace, in which the small fire looked a little lost.

"I am not really sure gentlemen, she was certainly a little drunk, well very actually, and she was apparently sleeping it off when she awoke claiming she had dreamt that a Bluecoat had murdered General Gratax. She saw it all in this dream she says, and she attacked two of my guards. When I arrived to see what all the noise was, she had concluded that if it was a Bluecoat, then my brother must have ordered it, and hence it was done on my command."

They all looked at her with puzzled looks.

"I can assure you gentleman that she is of course talking complete nonsense, and hence I thought it best to call you together to tell you about it. I am really so upset by it." She looked almost ready to burst into tears, but she cleverly played the role of the tough lady who would not cry in front of fellow King's Councillors.

"I see," said Moreton. "She has certainly not been well since poor Gratax's death. She seems determined that he will return to her in spirit and tell her what happened. I can only imagine that so much wine, after as long a period without, has turned her mind."

They all nodded sadly. She really had gone past sanity this time.

"I sent Nedlowe to her; he will be with her now," Eilana informed them.

"I will tell the King in the morning," said Moreton, "I think we can say no more for now. I will also go to the Queen after speaking to Nedlowe. I will inform her that she just cannot say such terrible things. Now, perhaps Chancellor, you would be so kind as to escort My Lady Eilana back to her rooms. I need some time with the General here on other matters."

"It would be my pleasure," replied Bradett, the funny thing was he meant it too.

"Thank you gentlemen, until tomorrow then, goodnight."

They all acknowledged her farewell and she took Bradett's arm. He led her from the library, closing the door behind them. Rebgroth looked at Moreton but said nothing. Moreton sighed and poured some water from a jug that stood on the central table into one of the goblets that stood beside it. He drank a mouthful and sat down, looking up at Rebgroth who leant on the mantelpiece, his left hand gripping its edge at full stretch, slightly above head height.

"Well General, what do you think?"

"You are the one that understands these things, not I, but if I understand our last conversation on such matters, we must believe that a Bluecoat did kill the General."

"I am afraid you are right my friend, and I am afraid the Queen may also be right that it was Harlmon who did it, and that if so, Eilana who ordered it. Gratax gave Tamorther no idea what evidence he had tying Harlmon to that acrobat's and Reassel's deaths?"

"None Sir, none at all. It was you who told me the Queen had dreamt it. Gratax said circumstantial evidence. I imagine he thought if he told Tamorther it was the Queen's dreams he would have thought him crazy."

"Indeed General, and no more can we take any action on it than could Gratax. We too must wait and watch and be very careful for the Queen. She has made a bad enemy this night, an enemy that cannot let her live if she is believed. I do not think they dare take the Queen's life, but then I never thought they would actually dare kill Gratax."

"I will have the Queen closely guarded, on the grounds of her illness, that she is weak of mind and needs close attention for her own safety."

"Excellent General, and we must watch Harlmon and his men closely too. I am sure there is more to them than just that woman's guards, in her mind anyway." He stood and moved towards Rebgroth.

"I tell you my friend, I am certain the King is in more danger than the Queen. I should not say even this much, but not only am I as sure as you are of Prince Gudrick's early death, but also that our King has not too much longer to live either, although how his death may come about I know not. Now enough, I speak of things I am avowed to keep hidden. Just do your duty General, you are the rock on which this Kingdom will stand, remember it, and do all you must to protect it."

Moreton looked quickly away, almost embarrassed by what he had said, and guilty that he had said too much.

"You can have faith in me Moreton, I have already sworn it."

"I know my good General, I know. Now I must go to the Queen. She has to understand that she cannot make such accusations in public, but she needs to know that some of us do not disbelieve her." He slapped a hand on Rebgroth's shoulder and turned, leaving the General with his thoughts.

Eilana's thoughts were very different. She looked at the ceiling and decided that as a means to an end, this was really quite pleasurable: in fact she was thoroughly enjoying herself.

As Bradett had escorted her to her rooms they talked casually, and with a whisper in his ear, her lips a little too close, a squeeze or two of his arm, a brush or two of their hips, Bradett was almost drooling over her by the time they reached her ante-room.

It was empty after the dramas earlier. Eilana looked him in the eyes, only slightly above hers, and smiled.

"Thank you Chancellor, that was kind of you." She was standing too close to him and she was amused at his discomfort. He didn't know whether to step back or stay put. He stood his ground.

"It was my pleasure, My Lady."

"Talking of pleasure," her hand moved forward and pressed on his codpiece. He flinched at her touch then straightened confidently, matching the pressure of her hand. "The last time my hand was there, I told you that if I chose to give you pleasure I would tell you. Well now is that time Chancellor, follow me if you wish."

She turned and opened the doors to her rooms, entering without looking back and striding to the fireplace. She heard the doors close and turned to see him standing in her room. She smiled at him.

"Come Chancellor and loosen the ties at the back of my dress." Again she turned her back as he crossed the room. He pulled the small bows open, starting at the top. Her bare back appeared to him as the dress opened. She wore nothing beneath it. He pushed her hair aside and kissed her neck, slipping the dress off her shoulders. She shook her arms free as it fell, hanging from her waist. His hands slid around her, gently caressing her breasts.

After a few moments she turned in his arms, pushing him away.

"Get out of those clothes," she ordered simply, and walked to her bed, untying the ties at her waist. As she reached the bed her dress fell to the floor, and she pushed her underskirts off her hips. Naked she turned towards him.

He couldn't get undressed quickly enough, fumbling with the ties and clasps. Except for the blue silk sash of office, which he had placed carefully on the table, he let the rest of his clothes fall in a heap where he stood.

Finally his leather leggings fell from his hips, and he kicked them away. Unembarrassedly naked and half aroused, he walked towards the bed. Eilana was genuinely intrigued. He was quite small in stature, but from her experience of men, he was far better endowed than any she had known.

He turned out to be a very considerate lover. He really was very good. Her eyes glazed and the ceiling went out of focus. She shut her eyes and concentrated on her body's sensations, on him above her and inside her. He really was very good.

He lasted well for a first time, and although she knew she would climax if they continued, she began to fake it to save his embarrassment. She needed this to be perfect for him, and seed he did, collapsing on her as her little cry of ecstasy signalled his perfect timing.

They lay beside each other unspeaking for a few moments before Eilana rolled swinging her legs from the bed.

"I enjoyed that Chancellor, very much in fact. Now get dressed and go. This is our secret, so keep it and we will do it again soon."

"I don't really know what to say." He fumbled for the right words.

"There is nothing to say Bradett. I am a grown woman who knows exactly what she is doing, so just enjoy the situation, and do as good a job next time." She swept up her clothes and walked to the door of her dressing room. She paused in the doorway, turning back to look at him sitting on the edge of the bed, his nakedness now looking a little inelegant.

"Don't be late for the Council tomorrow Chancellor, there are important matters to discuss and I may need your support." His eyes looked up at her.

"Is that what this was all about?"

"If you think that, you are a fool."

She shut the door behind her.

Chapter 26

The Council convened at the usual time, a quarter before midday. The King had left early after a hearty breakfast, with two of his drinking friends, both ambitious Hunderts, one of Castlebury and the other from Ffonhaven. Moreton had informed him during breakfast of the events of the previous evening. He had laughed, saying it all just confirmed his view that Bertal had gone completely crazy.

He then asked Moreton about Eilana, how she was, and did she still control the Council as well as ever. Moreton told him she was well and that she was strong as always in Council. Although the King tried to listen with indifference, Moreton could see the hurt in his eyes, and could sense his deep sense of loss.

The Ministers from the Countings had all enjoyed breakfast as they normally tried to do; arriving early so they were relaxed and rested from their journeys before the meeting. For this meeting however they had all arrived the day before for Prince Bocknostri's reception. By the time they entered the Great Hall together, Moreton was already there, in his usual maroon habit, talking with General Rebgroth, who wore his red and black uniform of the Royal Guard.

The Ministers were all in their usual finery of woollen leggings and linen shirts, their narrow pale blue sashes of thin wool crossed their chests beneath their jackets of heavy linen or coloured light leather.

Chancellor Bradett breezed into the hall with a friendly smile to all. He was obviously feeling in top form, dressed almost for a ball rather than a meeting of the King's Council. His wide light blue sash distinguished him as a senior man.

Having all greeted one another in their usual overly polite and slightly loud way, they sat around the table, rising to their feet as the Lady Eilana entered from the passage to the Royal Quarters. She chaired the meetings and spoke for the King, on his precise orders, pronounced years ago now and never rescinded, despite their growing apart.

"Do sit Gentlemen," she said, and they all made themselves comfortable.

She sat at the head of the large table, her back to the throne steps. Rebgroth sat to her immediate left, Tamorther beyond him. Moreton was to her right and Bradett in his usual seat, at the far end of that side. He had arranged his chair so as to be almost on the corner of the table, facing her but not quite sitting at the opposite end. The Ministers of the Countings filled the other chairs.

"Gentlemen," Eilana began. "This meeting was due to be held today but I am postponing our normal business to discuss the recent visit of Prince Bocknostri. Following that, General Rebgroth has something to put to us of the highest import which involves decisions we must make, both Military and concerning the consequential financial and organisational implications."

They all agreed that what had happened the day before was unfortunate, but given the behaviour and culture of these visitors from Whorle, almost inevitable. There was no way that Princess Patrikal could possibly be married into their Royal Family. They were uncouth, uncultured and ignorant, and such a marriage would have condemned her to a life of misery.

They also all agreed that war was the inevitable outcome of the visit. Prince Bocknostri clearly felt humiliated by events, and the skirmish outside the Castle confirmed this for most of them. At the time they were meeting of course, Bocknostri was inflicting casualties on the Royal Guard cavalry in the woods north of Gloff, but as yet they were unaware of it. It would be the next day before they heard, and it would confirm to them all that they had reached the right decisions this day.

They reached agreement relatively quickly. Nisceriel would certainly not start hostilities. There was a slim hope that King Draknast would restrain his young hotheaded fighting men, but knowing Whorle, it was a slim one. They must assume they would be attacked, but when and where was the question.

A wise invader would not invade in haste next spring. To gather an army, properly equipped, trained and with adequate supply logistics, would take longer than the winter to achieve. Bocknostri however was impetuous and supremely confident, arrogant even. He could raise an army of almost two thousand men of Whorle if the little intelligence they had was accurate. They would be untrained hills men, but strongly motivated by the hugely inflated patriotism they felt, driven by the stories they told of ancient deeds and the songs they sang passionately, again and again.

The consensus was that they would come the next spring, relying on victory and conquest for the supplies they would need. It would not seem a risk to Bocknostri.

Rebgroth felt Nisceriel was ready. Its state system meant it was always ready, and the Hunderts could be raised quickly, a trained and fully equipped army. His latter work had planned for invasion from the north, south or east: no Kingdom had enough ships to land an invasion force from the River. He was convinced Bocknostri would invade from the north, simply marching on Gloff. It sounded simplistic, but he knew the way. By the time he got home he would also know that to move around to the north beyond Gloff was too far to move an ill supplied army.

Crossing the river at Gloff would be costly but he would be confident of taking the village he had stayed in, given the weak willed people he thought he had met there. To ensure victory against this invader though, General Rebgroth had some ideas to put to the council. Eilana called on him to present his proposals. She had spoken of them with him a watch before and was fully in favour. Her plans required a battle that they won, and Rebgroth's thoughts were sound to her. Moreton too knew of them and supported them fully, but only of course because they were sense.

Rebgroth stood and moved to a table at the bottom of the throne steps that was covered in a woollen blanket. He pulled it aside and turned to address the Council.

"My Lady, Gentlemen, as you know I have travelled far and studied fighting men and their tactics in many realms. I have come to a view, particularly relevant to fighting soldiers of Whorle, but one I would advocate even were we not under threat from there. It concerns the weaponry our infantry should carry, and how we should fight. Let me explain."

He paused and half turned away, his head bowed, a hand on his chin, as if choosing his words carefully before turning back, straightening up and speaking again.

"This is the current sword used by our infantry." He picked up a large single-handed sword from the table beside him and swung it expertly around his head and shoulders in his right hand. "It is a good weapon; strong but not too heavy, yet it still takes a strong arm to wield it for long."

He slipped his left arm through the two leather straps on the back of the shield which lay face down on the table, gripping the leather handle near its edge. He lifted it to his side. It was red and adorned with the white thorn bush of Nisceriel.

"And this, Council, is our standard issue shield. As you see it is round, wider than my fist to my elbow by two hands. In metal, it is stronger and more effective than the leather and wood carried by many soldiers, but it is heavier. One is also liable, however, to try to fend off heavier blows, from a battleaxe for instance, when avoiding the blow would be a better strategy. A very heavy blow tends to transmit itself through the metal and can break an arm. Still, it is the best I have seen."

He moved away from the table and from the nearest Councillors, swinging the sword in wide aggressive arcs around him as if striking at an enemy.

"This is a weapon that needs to be swung to create cutting power. Stabbing with it is clumsy and lacks real effect. In a battle you have to stand at least two weapon lengths each side from the men next to you, otherwise you risk striking your own side with swings, follow-throughs or parried blows.

"Fighting this way means your battle lines are wide and spread, easily breached and flanked. A battle will turn into an uncontrollable melee of single combats. Inevitably, the side with biggest numbers is likely to win. To avoid just this, the last battles our armies fought, over forty years ago now, were fought by infantry standing shoulder to shoulder. Of course now there is a problem; there is no room to swing a sword. A shield wall forms; weapons and arms are trapped above your head or by your side. Few blows are struck by either side, but you cannot do much to defend your head and your legs are very vulnerable, although again, no-one can really strike at them. A battle becomes a pushing match in the main, and in this case too, the side with the greatest numbers is likely to win.

"This pushing contest is very tiring; not as tiring as wielding heavy weapons, but exhausting none the less. The side that tires first loses, and which ever way the battle is fought, a quarter or so of either and one side will give way."

He moved back to the table and laid the weapons on it.

"We have seen that Whorle fights as a hoard of individuals who use heavy weapons; two handed swords and battleaxes. They are skilled fighters, and I am sure, strong and fit hills men. They will not tire as quickly as many Niscerians."

There was a mutter around the table. The Councillors did not like that, but in their heads they knew it was so.

"We need therefore, to keep them at a distance as long as possible, using our archers to whittle their numbers, and they obviously don't like cavalry, but I am sure they will have learnt from their experiences here yesterday. They will also probably number nearly two thousand. At worst that means four of them to three of us." He walked to the table and leant on the back of his chair, looking around the Councillors.

"In summary, if we get involved in a loose fight, or in a traditional shield wall pushing match, we are likely to lose. I have of course battle plans and tactics to avert such an end, which I will not go into now, but with this in mind, I would like to show you some things I have developed with the help of our blacksmiths and armourers."

He walked back to his table and turned to face them.

"In my time with the Marsh Dwellers I studied the way they fight, watching them train daily. They use short throwing spears, which can be used in close as stabbing weapons, either underarm or overarm. They carry three each, two to throw and one to fight close with. They have small leather and wood shields on their left arms. The point is I could not help but notice that close in, in a shield wall, they were able to thrust their short spears at waist height. They were able to inflict wounds when a normal shield wall can only push.

"Even these short spears were too long, but Councillors, I believe a weapon such as this is the answer."

He turned to the table and lifted a short stocky sword. It looked more like a long but heavy knife. The blade was only as long as a forearm and fist, with a small hand guard and a strong leather bound wooden handle. There was another murmur round the Council table.

Rebgroth cut and thrust with the weapon, demonstrating its matched weight and balance.

"It is heavy enough to cut with, but mainly it is designed to thrust and stab. With a shield in the left hand a man can stand shoulder to shoulder with his comrades, form a shield wall, and still fight. Each soldier can carry his long sword on his back, should it be needed against mounted troops for instance. If an enemy like Whorle attack in loose formation with heavy weapons, our tight line will set three men against one."

They were all staring at him and his short sword, unsure what to say. Before anyone could say anything, he strode back to the table and lifted a large rectangular shield.

"Finally Councillors, I believe our first two ranks at least, should be equipped with these."

The shield reached from chin to ground, a rectangle curved slightly inwards lengthways.

"These protect the whole body, and a shield wall of these is impervious to arrows and spears. The front rank holds their shields upright, the second rank holds theirs flat above their heads, and above those of the front rank. When all soldiers have them, a Hundert battle line will be safe until it meets the enemy at close quarters."

There was silence. It was obvious and simple, but the General was not finished. He spun the shield around. There were two short wooden spears with iron points slotted into leather straps on the back.

"Finally, these spears can be thrown when the enemy is within range. Their killing range is fairly short, but two can easily be thrown while the enemy is charging at us and within range. Two hundred spears per Hundert in thirty paces will slow any charge. The dead and wounded will block a charge's impetus. The attackers will have to step over their casualties, their own men. Similarly an attack of ours can only benefit from two volleys of spears in the final thirty paces."

Bradett looked at Tamorther.

"Did you know about this, do you agree with it?"

"I did Chancellor. The General discussed it with me throughout its development. I think it is a brilliant and inspired insight into fighting a battle, and it has my unequivocal support."

"And you Chancellor?" asked Eilana, "Does it have yours?"

"My Lady, it is a bit of a surprise to be presented with this so suddenly, but I must say, there is a clear logic in the thought process that seems so basically simple I cannot understand why no-one has ever thought of it before. If our fighting men support it, and Tamorther here certainly does, then I certainly support it."

Nods of agreement came from around the table.

"I take it then the Council supports the production of these weapons and for training to commence in their use?" She was ahead of Rebgroth now. Bradett continued.

"There is just, My Lady, the matter of finance, how fast they can be produced, and how soon can Hunderts be trained in their use?" Rebgroth spoke in reply. He had returned to his chair.

"If armourers and blacksmiths are committed to produce nothing else throughout the winter from now, we will have enough for five to six Hunderts. We can train each Hundert for a moon, passing on only one set of equipment if necessary. If Bocknostri comes next spring, that at least will give me many improved options in battle tactics. If he comes the following spring, we can equip the whole army."

"But what of ploughs and other such repairs and replacements, surely we need some work done in those areas if we are to tend the fields and feed ourselves?" It was the Minister for the Eastern Counting who had spoken, a Counting that produced most of the grown crops for Nisceriel. Eilana answered him before Rebgroth could.

"I am afraid, Minister, that should we not do this, you will have no fields to attend in the east, and any food they produce will be feeding soldiers of Whorle, not Nisceriens."

"And the cost, My Lady?" persisted Bradett.

"Must be found if we are to survive." She made it sound a statement of fact rather than an opinion.

"I am sure," she continued, "We all thank the General for the work and the planning that has gone into this, and I take it we are unanimous in our support for his plans to be put into immediate effect." She paused for a moment, in which she caught Moreton's wry smile. He was thinking what a clever young lady she was.

"Good, that is agreed then. Now that concludes the business of the Council for today, except to add that General Rebgroth now has the King's personal authority to demand any help or support from any subject of Nisceriel. He has the King's purse, and any payment agreed or promised by him will be paid without question. I will give him papers of authority directly. Council is dismissed Gentlemen, but Chancellor, I would be grateful if you would join me in my quarters as soon as is convenient. I think we should dwell on some of the financial implications further." Bradett's eyes were sparkling.

"Most certainly, My Lady."

"Good day Gentlemen." She rose and quickly left by the door through which she had entered. Moreton leant across the table as he stood.

"Well done General, excellent. Now make it happen hey!"

Rebgroth nodded and smiled.

"Yes, there is that." He laughed silently to himself. "There is that."

Chapter 27

In the late afternoon, Eilana lay back on her bed, studying the wooden planking of her bedchamber's ceiling, the floor of the room above, Serculas' room. It brought a smile to her face. She realised she was looking for knotholes. That would be an irony, Serculas watching her after all she had learnt from watching Serculas. That was so long ago now.

She had not intended to entertain Bradett again so soon, or so she had convinced herself. When she had ordered him to join her in her rooms it was to work, and she had spent half a watch going over figures of how much Rebgroth's proposals would cost in new weapons, raw materials and labour, was there enough ore available? How quickly could they really expect to equip a Hundert?

When she felt they had come to some useful conclusions that both made sense and made it all achievable, she reached across the table for the wine jug and goblets she had ordered left there earlier. She poured two goblets and handed one to Bradett before settling back in her chair.

"A good afternoon's work Chancellor; I look forward to Rebgroth putting that uncouth Prince firmly in his place."

"Indeed My Lady, I'm more than sure he will."

"Are you really Chancellor? Is there no chance of Whorle winning a battle against us?"

"Anything could happen, My Lady, but with the General's planning and skills I feel it very unlikely there could be any other result, very unlikely. Whorle have to do everything by bravery, bravado, individual heroism. They will fight bravely and with fervour we could never match, but they are a realm of individuals. We will win because we are disciplined and will fight cohesively, and we have Rebgroth, Tamorther, and indeed Harlmon, to engineer victory."

"Harlmon will not fight in the battle." She almost said it too quickly, as if already planned, as of course it was. She recovered hastily. "He will be here guarding me and all the rest of the family here in the Castle; that is the role of my Bluecoats." Bradett raised an eyebrow slightly.

"I fear your brother may have other ideas. He has trained his men relentlessly; surely he will want to blood them."

"He will do as I order Chancellor, as I see fit." She snapped her reply with a flare of temper. Bradett sipped his wine and looked away, by chance towards the bedroom door.

Eilana was angry with herself. Nothing to do with their conversation, she was just conscious, now they were not working, of the ache in her stomach, a flutter in her breasts, she was desperate for this man. He had been very good the day before. She was intrigued by his size, and Wey help her, she could feel him inside her as they talked.

She had simply stood up, taken his hand and led him to the bed. They hadn't undressed this time, and her own passion had meant the whole thing was over far quicker than the day before, but it was so good.

She had sent him away immediately it was over. Slightly bewildered, he had left. In fact it took him a couple of moons to realise she was using him in exactly the way he might use some serving girl in his household, as he had done on occasion. By then however, he didn't care. By then he realised that if he played this right, real power could come his way.

For now however, Eilana could still feel him inside her, even completely satisfied as she was. She stood up and shook out the creases in her dress where it had been bundled up around her waist and grimaced to herself, she was leaking, his seed on her thighs. What would Harlmon think of her on his return? He would understand her plan, approve of it. She wondered what he was doing as she thought of him.

Harlmon was having a wonderful day. His blood was pumping. He had killed two men, a plan he had gambled on had worked perfectly, and his Bluecoats had been successful on a day when the Royal Guard had more than embarrassed themselves, and it was not even dusk yet.

He had led his Third of Bluecoat cavalry out of the woods to the brow of the slope and looked over the landscape ahead. Between the river to his far left and the forested hills to his right, the land undulated gently northwards, the rough track winding through patches of trees as far as one could see. Half a day's ride upriver lay Teekford Vale and the next river crossing. Beyond there the trees thickened and the northern tribes lived their harsh existence.

Not wanting to pressure the following Whorlean soldiers, he led his men on to the top of the next rise some three fields beyond, where they paused and looked back towards the wood.

They could only see the first rise with the tops of the trees just visible above it.

Harlmon was just starting to feel uneasy when two Royal Guards appeared on its crest. They stopped then swung their mounts and disappeared. Now he knew something was wrong. He kicked his horse and shouted for his men to follow, not stopping until he had reached the rise where he slowed to a walk, not sure what would come into view.

There was nothing to see, just the track leading into a gap in the trees, but then he just caught the sound of fighting in the woods and the situation was suddenly clear to him. He shouted orders.

"Second Eleven, fan out towards the river, drive them back into the woods if they try to leave them. Third Eleven, the same to the forest edge, Sergeant and Firsts with me."

The Second and Third Leveners led their men away left and right as Harlmon kicked on into the woods, flanked by his Sergeant and followed by the First Eleven. He was not at a full gallop. He didn't want to ride recklessly into trouble.

They rode past a Guard's severed body followed by a number of other bodies, including some Whorleans, though not many. The body of a horribly impaled horse hung grotesquely from a tree, not a pretty sight. Riding out of the forest he saw the ragged formation of Guards ringed around the wounded Cranalie, who had just called Sergeants and Leveners to him to decide what to do. The ring parted to let Harlmon ride into their mist.

"Well Officer Cranalie, how did you manage to let that happen?"

"They let the scouts through and back then ambushed us as we rode through."

"Well they would, wouldn't they?" Harlmon rolled his eyes. "Now send a rider back with word of what has happened immediately, then send an eleven back with the wounded and the bodies of our dead. You'll need to make litters for the wounded and strap the dead over their saddles. With me so far?" Cranalie nodded.

"Good, then fan the rest of your men from river to the forest and as far along the forest edge southwards as you can, with the last Levener and a five to patrol beyond that. You are to ensure Bocknostri does not swing back and head for Gloff, do you understand me?"

"Yes Sire," replied Cranalie. He seemed to have accepted Harlmon's authority without question.

"Good. Now ensure your messenger tells the Lady Eilana and General Rebgroth what you are doing, and that I am taking my men to harry Bocknostri to Teekford and beyond if necessary."

Cranalie was suddenly angry. He was angry at himself for getting his men killed, and suddenly he was angry with himself for taking orders from this trumped up Bluecoat without protest. He shouted at Harlmon.

"I will do as you say because it is wisest, but not because you order me. You are not my superior. You are not even a Guardsman!"

"Indeed I am not Officer, I am Harlmon, brother of the Lady Eilana, and I speak with her voice here. She, as you well know, speaks with the voice of the King, by his personal decree, so my word is the King's. Argue therefore at your peril Officer, for you have caused enough damage here today." He wheeled his horse and rode back to his admiring Bluecoats, who as one, turned and rode after him back through the woods, watchfully.

They burst out of the trees on the far side. Harlmon called to his Hornman.

"Report."

The Hornman blew a staccato pattern on his curved horn. Immediately the Bluecoats within view and those hidden from them, turned their mounts and headed towards him, reforming their Elevens and they drew closer. The Second arrived first.

"Levener of the Second reporting Sire, no signs whatsoever."

"Thank you, well done, and the Third?" Their Levener had just reined in beside him.

"Definite movement in the woods Sire. We couldn't see anyone; they are deep into the trees, but there are undoubtedly men on the move, and moving north."

"Good man. Now listen my boys. We are going to make their lives as difficult as possible, between here and Teekford. Firstly we need to keep them in the trees, so Second Eleven, you are to spread yourselves half a field from the tree line and move slowly north at foot pace, remembering they are forcing their way through some pretty tough undergrowth at times. I need them to see you and to believe we are patrolling the forest edge along its length. That should mean they keep moving north just inside the tree line. They will hope to get as far up as Teekford then break for the ford tonight, if they reach it in time. Do you understand me Levener?"

"Yes Sire, absolutely."

"If they break cover before that, fall back and sound three short blasts. We will be back with you at the gallop. Don't engage them, wait for us. The rest of us will set a trap for them half a watch or so north of here, where the Chell valley cuts back into the forest. Be sure your men are well in view as you get there, the Second. I want them looking at you."

His men were all grinning at him. They could read his mind. They had exercised around here often in recent moons, away from inquisitive eyes, and all knew the terrain.

"Now let me reiterate one thing above all. Kill anyone, any number, but Bocknostri must live. He is not to be hurt. We need him to get home angry and humiliated, and for that he must be alive! Alright my boys, good hunting."

He rode away at a canter with the First and Third Elevens. The Second slowly spread themselves along the forest edge as a screen, clearly visible to anyone looking from the trees.

Harlmon led his men along the tree line for half a watch before the Chell's bubbling waters were visible, running across their path from the centre of a shallow valley. A field wide, the valley sloped gently back up into the hills, clear of trees for two fields and more, before they again formed the forest edge at its top. Harlmon held up a hand, halting his men.

"We will ride on to the stream then walk up its bed to the trees. I don't want tracks visible to anyone crossing the valley. If they see tracks in the stream it will already be too late for them."

His men let out an involuntary cheer, they were right, and they were ready to take revenge for the death of the Guardsmen. They followed him eagerly into the valley and up the stream. They entered the forest and dismounted, watering their horses, then tying them to trees just out of sight inside the forest.

Harlmon set a watch with strict instructions to concentrate on the southern side of the valley. Next he posted two men in the trees with a horn at the head of the valley, again on its southern side. In the unlikely event that Bocknostri did move around the valley rather than across it, he didn't want to be surprised on his flank, dismounted and vulnerable.

He was relying on Bocknostri arriving at the valley's edge, unaware that it was there. He would have to decide whether to cross it in the open or to move inland, up the valley, across the top where Harlmon was hidden, and back down the other side. He would be in a hurry as he needed to get far enough north by nightfall to be able to break for the ford at Teekford in the dark. He would lose a lot of time going around, and he would see a loose screen of Bluecoats well spaced to the west watching for them to break cover, but by the time they could react and gather in any numbers they would be across. Being seen was not a problem; they were known to be in the forest and obviously heading north.

The wait became unbearable. Harlmon told himself that the longer it was before Bocknostri led his men to the valley, the more likely he was to cross in the open. He was right. One of the look-outs rushed to his side.

"Movement in the trees Sire, I'm sure it's them." Harlmon clapped him on the shoulder, then he thrust his hand into the air. With clenched fist he pumped it up and down. The signal was silently passed on, and his Third mounted within the forest and moved to its edge, but still within the trees.

Harlmon moved as far towards the edge as he dare, his Sergeant at his side.

"It's them Sire, they're about to go."

"Hold back; let them move into the middle of the valley, half way, as far forward as back."

"Perhaps not quite halfway, Sire. They're bound to break for the far side. They won't go back." Harlmon laughed and nodded.

"Quite right, Sergeant, and we'll make some of the distance before they see our tracks, or us maybe."

"Aye Sire. About now I'ld say."

Harlmon spurred his mount forward, his men charging out of the trees on either side of him. As quiet as they tried to be the Whorleans saw them almost immediately, and after a moment's hesitation and a shout from Cregenda, they splashed through the stream and ran for the trees.

Harlmon let out a wild yell as soon as he saw they had been seen, and his men echoed his cry as they charged down the slope.

Bocknostri realised they were not going to reach the trees before they were ridden down and called his men hurriedly into a ragged fighting line, but the Bluecoats hit them at a full gallop, their lances spearing fourteen Whorleans as they shattered their line and rode through them.

Harlada had buried his lance in the chest of a large hills man. It punctured his leather tabard as easily as his chest and burst from his back, wrenching it from Harlmon's grasp. He reined in sharply and turned to see their affect on the Whorleans.

Two Bluecoats were down. Cregenda had waited for the last possible moment as his enemy rode at him with levelled spear, steady on his right side. Almost as the horse was upon him, Cregenda dived to his right, away from the line of the lance and towards the horse's left flank.

The horse shied to its right and spilled its rider over its left shoulder and over his target's head. Cregenda recovered his footing, spun round and sank his two handed sword into the Bluecoat who lay winded at his feet, killing him instantly.

As he drew his sabre, Harlmon watched the second Bluecoat dance his horse away from Bocknostri. He had pulled up swerving away as he realised who he was about to spear. It cost him his life. The horse backed into three other Whorleans who stuck at its rider mercilessly. He fell, dead before he hit the ground.

A third Bluecoat spun his horse, lashing about him with his sabre as the Whorleans tried to get close enough strike him. A large hills man moved forward bearing a huge battleaxe. Harlmon could see he was going to use it on the horse. He rode hard at the axe man from behind, swinging his sabre down hard on his shoulder as he turned to face him, but too late. The sabre sank deep into his shoulder, snapping his collarbone and severing arteries. Harlmon and his Bluecoat crashed their horses out of the surrounding Whorleans and galloped down the slope to where their Third cheered them back.

"Just the two Sergeant?"

"Aye Sire, just the two, but we must have got twenty of them."

"Nearer fifteen I think, but that'll do. Good work men."

"Are we going back at them Sire?" One of the Bluecoats cried. A cheer of approval accompanied the question.

"No, my boys. That'll do for now, we'll have more of them later, fear not. Recall Hornman, sound the recall."

The horn blew loudly and the men of the Second Eleven returned to the main body, joining them as they headed north again.

"What next Sire?" His Sergeant knew he would have something else in mind.

"We'll head for the copses between the forest and Teekford. We'll rest the horses and ourselves until nightfall when Bocknostri will have to break for the ford. I am sure he will make a break as soon as he gets up there. Moving in small groups I would think, rushing from copse to copse. That's what I would do. But

281

he won't get there until at least midnight, so we'll get plenty of rest then split into fives. We'll snipe at them as we can, harry them, kill and wound a few, hit them and run. I don't want any more casualties so pressurising them is as important as kills."

"Sounds like a good night to me Sire."

"It should be Sergeant, it certainly should be."

All this went through his mind as he remembered the events of the day, sitting on the edge of a small copse, and looking to his right, he watched the sun go down behind the wooded hills of Whorle on the far side of the river.

Chapter 28

To Harlada and Prince Gudrick, it was almost like Mid-winters Eve, although at twelve years old they were almost too grown up to feel that way. Everyone seemed to be gathered in the library, some standing, others in the comfortable cushioned chairs, but all with their eyes fixed on Harlmon as he told his story.

The Watch Officer had rushed into the Keep to bring the news that a small column of Bluecoats had been sighted by the tower watch, in the far distance, approaching from the north. He had found Moreton first, in the Great Hall. He was studying an old manuscript, which he had taken from the library. He wanted to compare its contents with the large old parchment map that was framed on the wall near the doors.

The news had spread fast from there, and the boys had run to the gates to greet them. They liked to think of themselves as young men now, but boyish ways still excited them at times. Badraman had taught them well in all matters Military, and they yearned to ride with the Guard, or more especially, the Bluecoats; they were tougher. Harlada was a born swordsman, even now of considerable skill. Gudrick was competent, but he would never have the natural ability of his friend, nor his aggression.

They waved and shouted as Harlmon led his men into the Castle. He saw them immediately in the crowd that had gathered and beckoned them to him. He pulled Gudrick up in front of him and swung Harlada up behind him.

A Royal Guard messenger had returned to the Castle four days before with news of the ambush. He had also told them that Harlmon was pursuing the Whorleans and intended to harry their crossing at Teekford; still outnumbered as he was by Bocknostri's diminished guards.

"Did you kill them all Harlmon?" asked the Prince as they rode up the street towards the Keep.

"Enough of them," he laughed, "but I will not tell the story twice. You will have to wait for my report to your Father and the Lady Eilana."

Harlada grasped the handle of his uncle's sabre and loosed it in the scabbard.

"Did you kill any with this Uncle?" Harlmon pushed it back, lifting his hand away.

"A couple, my boy. Now, sit quiet till we reach the keep whilst I wave to the crowd." He didn't want to miss the opportunity to revel in their success and growing notoriety, especially when the Guards had embarrassed themselves so. His men too were enjoying the recognition as they rode two abreast behind him.

The boys jumped down easily when they reached the Keep, where most of its occupants were gathered at the doors. Harlmon swung a leg across his horse's neck and slid down from the saddle, landing lightly on stiff legs.

"Welcome back, my boy," greeted the King, clasping his hand to Harlmon's forearm in a formal Military greeting, as Harlmon did likewise.

"Thank you, Sire. I am pleased to report that Prince Bocknostri and a few of his guards are skulking their way home, through the woodlands of Drean."

"That is indeed welcome news. Now, greet your sister and then all will gather in the library in a quarter to hear your full report." The King turned away moving back into the Keep. He glanced back to see Eilana giving Harlmon a hug. He still loved her desperately, and despite what some people whispered, he was certain they did not sleep together.

He was one of the few that knew there were two beds in her rooms. Hers was the old four-poster, the Queen's bed that had been specially strengthened when he had been so very heavy and fat, before all this began, before Gudrick was born, before Eilana. The other was a pallet bed that was placed across the adjoining door to his rooms, making access directly from them impossible. That one was Harlmon's bed.

He still got that hollow empty feeling in his stomach whenever he thought of her. He knew she didn't love him anymore, but he could not hate her for it, in fact he could not stop loving her despite it. He sighed and headed for his rooms. A drink before the meeting was what he needed.

Harlmon washed quickly and donned his other uniform. It was of lighter weight material and better around the Castle, so he looked his best as he entered the library, almost exactly a quarter watch later. His secret was an old and extremely accurate sand timer of his father's that he had made sure to purloin on his death.

The library was full of people. He looked around taking them all in as best he could see. Serculas was almost hidden at the back, behind the King, but Rebgroth stood close to the empty fireplace, beside Gudmon. Tamorther was behind his General.

Eilana sat in a cushioned chair opposite the King, as did Bertal to his surprise. Badraman stood behind the boys, a hand on a shoulder of each of them to ensure they acted as adults in adult company. Bradett and two Councillors completed the ring of faces staring at him as began his story.

As he told of the events of that first day, he looked for Moreton, surely he was there, then he saw him. He was sitting on a lounger in the near corner with Patrikal sitting attentively beside him. There was another group of people he couldn't make out at first in the far corner, but finally he caught a glimpse of Nedlowe, and later Greardel and Brenham. Quite what brought them to hear his report he could not imagine, other than pure curiosity.

He told of that night, how Bocknostri had broken his men up into groups, each of which tried to find their way independently to the crossing at Teekford. Harlmon was proud of his correct assumption, but in fact he owed it to Rebgroth's way of thinking, imagining he was Bocknostri and what he would do, and it had worked.

They had split up into fives themselves, sixes in fact with Harlmon, his Sergeant, and three Leveners each taking a five. They hid in copses and in hollows, hitting Bocknostri's men and running whenever they could. Sometimes they would kill a Whorlean, or just wound a couple, sometimes not, but throughout the night they were active, making Bocknostri's men stay vigilant every moment of darkness.

When dawn broke they rode as pre-arranged to gather just north of the ford. There was nothing at Teekford except two deserted wooden houses on the Niscerien side and one on the Whorlean. No-one knew who had built them, or who had once lived there, so now they were used for shelter by anyone who had reason to cross the ford and had to wait for the weather or the tide. It was virtually non-tidal there, perhaps a forearm or two, but when the river was in flood, it could make a difference. For Bocknostri that day however, the water was as low as ever across the half field of the river's width.

Bocknostri was already there with two men he had led in, but Cregenda had arrived first, with just one. The remaining men straggled in, slowly joining the fighting line he had formed for protection between the two wooden buildings. They had arrived in six groups, in twos and threes. Every group had lost a man or two, and each claimed to have killed one or two Bluecoats. Only one had actually died that night, and none others injured. Again, sadly, the man who had died did so because he hesitated to kill Bocknostri, and what was worse, it turned out that it wasn't Bocknostri but Cregenda he had fought.

With every group in and daylight well established, Bocknostri led his nineteen remaining men into the river. The fifty-three Whorleans that had crossed the bridge at Gloff now numbered only twenty, and Bocknostri swore he would return to avenge those he left behind as he entered the water.

It was only just above his knees, but as Harlmon watched, he knew it was deep enough to prevent a horse from galloping or turning quickly. They would not be able to attack the Whorleans as they crossed.

Instead he made a great display of riding his men along the riverbank to the crossing, jeering and booing the retreating soldiers, laughing and making rude signs. Although the Whorleans did not understand the words and gestures, they certainly grasped their general meaning.

They made a great pretence of riding back south as Bocknostri and his men entered the trees on the other side, and they rode south for over a quarter before turning inland and swinging back around behind the many copses and reaching the ford again about three quarters later.

They crossed quickly and searched for a rear guard, but Bocknostri had not left one. It allowed them to follow slowly for over a day before they hit Bocknostri's men one final time, just when he had felt safe on home ground.

They waited to catch him in the open, and still thirty-one strong, they charged at the gallop straight through them, downing another six, dead or badly wounded. Though he could not manage it then, Cregenda had decided that the only way to fight cavalry was to bring down the horses, then fight as infantry. He could already picture the long spears they would need to keep the horses away, or kill them if they charged directly into them, but it had cost them so many lives to learn.

One Bluecoat had a deep wound to his leg, and one a sliced forearm. Both were sown up, and if they avoided a fever, they would both survive.

Harlmon led them back to the river, then after a night's rest, they headed south west along its Whorlean bank. They rode as swiftly as their mounts could sustain until they surprised the look-outs at Gloff as they rode into sight and across the bridge to the village.

After a night as guests of Gerlaff, Hundert of Gloff, they rode out of the village at dawn, a depleted but proud Third. As his listeners knew, they arrived at Castle Nisceriel late in the afternoon.

The library burst into loud applause as Harlmon reached the end of his report.

"Well done my boy, well done indeed."

"Thank you, Sire," bowed Harlmon.

"An excellent piece of soldiering Harlmon," it was General Rebgroth that spoke, "but I can think of nothing more certain to guarantee Bocknostri's return, next spring, or more likely the one after."

"That was not my intention Sir," replied Harlmon. Eilana smiled to herself, it certainly was. "I merely felt they should not be allowed to return unhindered after their ambush of the Royal Guard in the woods; a totally avoidable engagement."

"He did the right thing General," the King interrupted before Rebgroth could rise to the bait. "An unfortunate mistake by an inexperienced Officer; he has most certainly learned by it. So, everyone, I have arranged drinks and some food in the Great Hall. We must celebrate the Bluecoats' first action, and so successful a one too. Come Harlmon, I have a thirst."

Later that night Eilana lay in the dark looking at the canopy above her four-poster. She had the maids put it back the day before. Somehow she was feeling much more feminine since her affair had begun with Bradett.

Harlmon had taken it very well. She had explained the reasons for its necessity, and he had accepted them readily, after all, it wasn't as if she was fond of Bradett or anything. In fact she found him almost impossible to do it with, or so she had lied to her brother.

She had pressed him on Bocknostri. Would he come back, was he humiliated and angry enough? Harlmon had assured her he was; particularly after they had pursued him into Whorle itself, and killed Whorleans on home soil.

She smiled inwardly, she was almost there. Everything was in place now, she just had to tie all the pieces together, make it happen the way she had planned it.

Having that poor wounded Whorlean interpreter fall into her lap was just the piece of luck she needed. It made the trickiest part of her plan so much easier, the part that had been concerning her most. Gragonor, that was it, she had such trouble with the Whorleans' ugly names.

He was healing so well, despite the discomfort of the west dungeons, but being there put him under Harlmon's control. They were under her rooms, four levels below. The bumbleberry had helped so much of course, and within a couple of moons, just when she would need him, he would be perfectly fit. She must make sure he is kept out of mind so no-one realises he is so well and moves him before she is ready. Yes she thought, she must have Harlmon deal with that.

She glanced at Harlmon's sleeping figure. He had fallen asleep almost before he had lain down, exhausted after his soldiering over the last quarter moon or so, but she had never seen him happier. Killing was certainly in his heart, and very much on her mind.

She fell asleep too.

It was a moon after midwinter's eve. Eilana had watched all the children receive their presents as she always did. Patrikal was past the age now where she got a present but she was there, enjoying helping the young ones almost as much as getting one herself.

At twelve, Gudrick and Harlada had a couple more to go. They would both be having their thirteenth bornbless shortly, and the presents would cease after their Sire's days at fifteen. Patrikal would enjoy her seventeenth bornbless soon after their thirteenth, quite the young woman now Eilana thought. So much had happened in those years since the boys' births.

Eilana thought back to her own seventeenth bornbless. Had that been the one she had spent with Serculas, or Reassel? She could not remember. Harlada would have been two a few days before. Was that right? Wey, the wait was driving her crazy!

Now however, a moon further on, she felt relaxed and composed. Now she was putting the final parts of her plan into action, and as always she felt alive and confident once her instincts were leading her again.

Greardel stood in front of her chair in her room. Harlmon leant against the edge of the fireplace watching them both, Greardel was trying to look arrogant and impatient but was failing to mask his underlying nerves. His beautiful sister was making mincemeat of him. Serve him right for trying to be clever. He had learnt years before it was no good trying to outwit his sister verbally; she was far too bright, and too quick tongued.

"Now you are certain your Fenlon knows exactly what is expected of him tonight?" she asked Greardel.

"Yes, My Lady."

"Then tell me again Greardel." He almost sighed in exasperation but thought better of it, so dutifully repeated it all.

"He is to sneak into the walled garden exactly half a quarter after midnight, armed and with a spade. He must go to the bumbleberry bushes and start to dig one up. He will be caught in the act and arrested by three Bluecoat guards who will bring him to your brother for questioning. There may well be others there, but he will be a prisoner of the Bluecoat Special Security Third so he will be under your brother's control.

"He will admit to trying to steal a bush for wine making. He is to say that he had heard legends of the quality of wine bumbleberry makes, and that he was sure the Royal Family had some made secretly for themselves. A wine merchant from Merlbray had offered him a huge sum for a bush when questioning him on the other wines Nisceriel produces, and he had stupidly decided it was time to cash in on this offer and start a rich life elsewhere. He will be placed in the dungeons until his sentence is decided, and will be put in a cell with Gragonor of Whorle, who speaks Niscerien and who he is to befriend."

"Very good Greardel, what next?"

"Two nights later, My Lady, a Bluecoat guard will collect him to bring him for sentencing. He is to attack the guard who he will apparently knock out when they have left the cell. He will let Gragonor out and they will leave the dungeons through the wine cellars that Fenlon knows from his work.

"They will leave the Castle by the tunnel that brings the stream through the walls into the cellars, and where the iron grilles have rusted through and have already been broken. It has long been forgotten that this weakness in the Castle exists.

"They are to run to the river where a fishing boat will be tied up at the jetty. They will steal it, and on the rising tide will be able to row and sail across the river to Whorle. He is then to persuade Gragonor to take him on into Whorle to give the information to Prince Bocknostri as instructed. This information will........."

"Alright, alright, that's enough. Are you sure he is capable of doing all this?"

"Yes, My Lady, certain. The reward you offer on his return is more than he could ever dream of possessing, and he also knows that if he were to fail you, your brother's men would hunt him down and kill him, wherever he tried to run. He will not fail you."

"Good. This is the start of your revenge too Greardel. Don't you let me down." He smiled a somewhat pained smile.

"I will not My Lady. Partly because it is my chance to revenge myself on the King for all these years of servitude, partly for your promised reward, but quite honestly, mainly because I dare not."

Eilana glared at Harlmon as he laughed out loud.

"I'm sorry sister, I never thought of Greardel as such an honest man." This time it was Greardel that glared at him, but fear was in his eyes too.

"Enough! Greardel, go now and ensure Fenlon is ready, and be sure to remind him what awaits if he succeeds, and what to expect of us if he fails."

"Oh he knows, My Lady, but I will remind him." He bowed, backed away and then turned, walking smartly to the door and out of the room.

Eilana looked at Harlmon, a slight frown on her face.

"Are you sure we are not expecting too much of this Fenlon? We are relying on a wine maker."

"He will do it all perfectly, at least until he gets to Whorle. He will have told Gragonor by then what he has in mind. Gragonor has to win favour back with Bocknostri, so whether he takes Fenlon or kills him and tells Bocknostri himself, I cannot see that Whorlean animal not taking the bait."

"I'm sure you are right, brother. I am counting on it."

"Oh I am right, pretty one, I am right," and indeed he was.

At that very moment, Bocknostri was sitting on a ragged outcrop of rock that rose out of the trees on the side of a steep valley wall, just east of his home. Below him the river Drei flowed steadily westwards, and as he looked downstream over the wooded valley, its steep sides opened onto a small flat plain surrounded by hills where lay the large wooden village of Moonmarl. The river threaded its way down the valley, at this time of year a brown slash through the trees, until it horseshoed around the village and turned south, flowing through another, perhaps even more beautiful forested valley, before reaching the River of Number.

Here at its last, over time it had cut its way through a high rock sided gorge. Now its waters foamed out into the Number, causing eddies and swirls that were terribly dangerous to an unaware boatman. It was not as deep or spectacular a gorge as the Ffon had cut itself on the opposite side, but it was awe inspiring enough when sailed through.

From Moonmarl to the Number it was increasingly tidal, but here where Bocknostri sat it flowed calmly and deep. Not far upstream many shallow rapids made it impossible to travel any further by boat.

He often sat up here to look over the heart of his realm, for he was King Bocknostri now, absolute ruler of the Tribes of Whorle.

His depleted force had arrived back in Moonmarl half a moon after his last encounter with Harlmon's cavalry, delayed by the terrain and the wounded they carried. He had personally driven his sword through the throats of two of his men. Both had received killing belly wounds and were dying slowly and in agony. He would not have his men carry hopeless cases made worse by the journey.

He told their story to his father King Draknast and his close advisors the first night back, by the light of the central fire in the Royal Roundhouse. It had a fortified wall and ramparts around it and stood at the centre of the wooden walled capital, a fort within a fort. He told all, but greatly embellished the fights and the Niscerien losses, turning each Whorlean fighter lost into a hero.

Cregenda smiled to himself at the tale, had he really been there? He supported his Prince at every moment however, nodding, looking serious at their losses and proud at their achievements. It was not exactly the ignominious rout he had experienced. They had at least recovered some self-respect at the ambush in the woods, but even there, Bocknostri's tale greatly enhanced the reality. He featured well in the telling however and was not going to spoil the illusion.

Bocknostri finished by vowing to take a Whorlean army back to Nisceriel the next spring and to revenge the insults inflicted on the Kingdom of Whorle. The tribes must be raised, the fighting men summoned from the hills. They could gather after early lambing and be back for a late harvest if they were warned now.

Weapons could be prepared and repaired through the winter, meat killed, dried and salted, grain put aside for the march, but they must start now.

Draknast was not so hasty though. He decided to sleep on it and meet the next evening, so after a day of cornering and cajoling Draknast's advisors, Bocknostri stood before them again, tired and frustrated. He could not understand how men of Whorle did not immediately agree with him and retaliate against such provocation.

The debate lasted almost a quarter; going round in circles as far as Bocknostri was concerned. He grew slowly more and more angry. He sensed the decision coming, these old men calling for caution. They were Whorlean, and not against such a war. Bocknostri had been deeply insulted over the Princess and then hounded from Nisceriel against all the rules of safe travel.

They were concerned that the few moons through the winter would not be enough time to prepare. The Prince himself had described how they would need to fight against these soldiers on horses, and that would take time for the hill tribes to learn. The very thought of proud Whorleans being taught to fight was insulting in itself. They would never persuade them of the necessity and train them by the spring.

Bocknostri insisted all that was needed was the long wooden steel-tipped spears to be made. They would not need training to use them, they were Whorlean!

The decision was made though; they would march on Nisceriel the spring after next.

Prince Bocknostri stormed from the meetinghouse, Cregenda in his wake.

"It is not decided yet, my friend, I will lead our army into Nisceriel this spring as King of Whorle. No-one will argue with the King."

"Be careful what you plan my Prince, I fear it may be too extreme!"

"Then do not follow me Cregenda, but if you do, no man other than I will have more power in this realm."

"I did not say I would not follow you my Prince, I only suggest we plan ahead a little, even if just to tomorrow."

"Then be in the Royal House at dawn with my men. We will need at least fifty. Place thirty around the walls and have twenty, including those who were with us in Nisceriel, in the meeting hall. I will meet you there."

"We will be there, my Prince." Cregenda left the gates of the Royal Fortress and Bocknostri returned to his room in the Royal House.

He stayed there for the rest of the evening, until all in the village was quiet. It was a long while after midnight.

He rose from the chair in which he had waited. He hadn't lain on the bed in case he had fallen asleep, so he had sat on the chair and stared from the small window at the late comings and goings, coming to terms with what he was going to do.

It was not for his own sake, not a quest for personal power. He was going to bring new invigoured leadership to Whorle; see the end of old over cautious minds that held back its development. They couldn't see that when he had taken Nisceriel, he would move south into Deswrain, then east into Merlbrey. Whorle would rule all the known Kingdoms of this land, and then he would spread north and tame the wild tribes up there.

Bocknostri had no real love for his father. He had bullied all his sons, killed some even, when he felt them a threat. He had always strongly and unquestioningly supported his father's rule as he intended to live long enough to become King. He was recognised as his eldest living bastard, heir to the throne, but he would only become King if he was strong enough to grab it and make it his own, and now was the time.

He closed his door behind him and moved around the darkened corridor that circled the entire building, the meeting room at its heart, until he reached the King's rooms. There were no guards, no one else moved in the house at all. That would change; complacency was going to kill Draknast but Bocknostri would have to stay on his guard after this night.

He quietly opened the door to Draknast's bedroom. He lay on his stomach, his arms above his head, under the pillow. He was alone under a large fur that covered him to his shoulders. Bocknostri had feared Draknast might choose this to be one of the ever fewer nights he took a woman to his bed. It would have ruined his plan. He would have had to kill them both, making Draknast's death a definite assassination. At least now there would be some doubt. He would claim natural causes, and there would be no marks on the body. Most people would guess the truth; it was all too convenient for Bocknostri.

He crept across the room and stood by the bed, looking down on his father, his King, but he felt no compassion for the old man, it had to be done. He jumped astride the body under the fur, his knees either side of it. His right hand clamped over the King's mouth, pulling his head back hard from the pillow. With his left hand he pinched the King's nose shut.

Immediately awake, the King struggled beneath him, but Bocknostri's weight across his back and shoulders restricted his arms beneath the pillow, and by the time his hands were free his strength was failing. He ceased to struggle, quivering then becoming still as his life slipped away.

Bocknostri held his hands over the King's mouth and nose for at least as long again; he was going to be sure. When he finally let go and climbed off the bed he stepped back and let out a shuddering breath, the tension in him easing. He leant back over the bed, rearranging the fur cover and pillow, putting Draknast's arms back as they had been. He closed the wide-open and bulging eyes that stared lifelessly from the King's face, and finally, turned it into the pillow.

It would appear at a first glance that the King had died in his sleep. He couldn't see any marks on the King's face, so it was even probable that is how it would remain officially, but suspicion would remain, and when Cregenda arrived with his men in the morning, many would take that as an admission of guilt.

He returned to his room and lay down on the bed, on his back and looking at the ceiling. He had a feeling of elation in him. His whole body was tingling as he relaxed. There was no doubt that killing a man with your bare hands was an exhilarating experience, as good as a woman, almost; no better in some ways, but then they were both about power for him.

He slept until a loud shout awoke him at dawn. Draknast's manservant had entered his rooms and tried to wake him, finding him dead. Bocknostri leapt from his bed, still dressed in the clothes he had killed in. He ran to the King's room, where the servant wailed and shouted for help.

Servants and slaves ran from all directions. Bocknostri shouted for quiet. He instructed various servants to fetch all the elders of the village; all, not just Draknast's close advisors. Another he sent to bring the Drewbard Priests; he would need them to give him the blessing of Drew and the other Hill Gods.

There was more noise from the meeting room and from outside. The few armed guards that the King kept around him were arriving and being rounded up by Cregenda's men. He walked into the King's bedroom and saw the body of his father, naked and on his back, the fur on the floor. His manservant had rolled him over and pulled the fur from the bed in his rush for the door. He looked almost grotesque to Bocknostri. Draknast had been almost fifty, very old for Whorle. His body was still that of a strong man, but age had caused it to deteriorate. His eyes settled for a moment on the parts that had sired him. He turned and left the room. He must eat.

Some short time later, everyone he had sent for was in the meeting room as he entered. On a table near the central fire lay the naked body of Draknast; naked so that all could see there were no wounds on the body, no signs of anything but a natural death. There was an un-natural silence in the roundhouse however, before Bocknostri spoke.

"My Father Draknast is dead. I now claim the throne of Whorle as his eldest living son. If there are any here who challenge that right, speak your challenge now."

Drokhart, Bocknostri's uncle, stepped forward.

"Last night you argued with my brother King Draknast. Today he is dead. It is very convenient for you my nephew, as convenient as your lapdog Cregenda being here with your men before anyone else knew of his death."

"What are you suggesting Drokhart, or are you just musing on the situation?"

"I am suggesting nothing, just voicing what everybody here is thinking."

"My father died in his sleep, Drokhart. He had seen nearly fifty winters. Perhaps the argument last night and the strain of coming to the decision of an old man, and not a man of Whorle, were too much for him."

"Or too much for you!" There was an audible gasp from those in the roundhouse as Crondak stepped forward; Draknast's best friend and trusted advisor. He spoke again. "I suggest you killed the King in his sleep, or poisoned him. I challenge you and name Drokhart as King of Whorle."

There was almost a murmur of approval. Bocknostri swung towards him.

"You and Drokhart were with him long after me last night, perhaps you poisoned him?"

"Don't be absurd, boy. I am no poisoner."

"Nor I Crondak, and nor did I kill him. There is not a mark on his body."

"There need be no mark my boy; his death has your foul stench attached to it." There was a rising noise in the Roundhouse. Now was the time.

With a speed and agility that belied his size, Bocknostri drew the two handed sword that hung from his belt and swung it in one movement, arcing it savagely at Crondak. It clove through his shoulder deep into his chest. As he sank to his knees, Bocknostri wrenched the sword free and swung it again, hacking it down and splitting Crondak's skull, almost to his nose. He was already dead as the second blow struck but his knees were locked, and he now seemed to be kneeling in front of Bocknostri, who placed a foot on his chest and kicked him away and backwards as his sword came free.

"Now that is how a body is marked if I kill someone. Does anyone else challenge my right to the throne? You Drokhart?"

"Not I My King, I can see you have all the skills necessary to rule for many years to come. Take my advice though and pick your friends carefully. Trust no-one you did not trust before this day." He knelt on one knee in front of Bocknostri, took his hand and kissed it. "I am your servant, My King."

He rose and stepped away, and one by one, everybody in the room did the same, except for the three white clad Drewbards who were the last to come forward. They stood before him and each placed a hand on his head, chanting a prayer and a blessing. Finally one of them spoke.

"The mighty Drew blesses and recognises you, Bocknostri, King of Whorle."

A dutiful cheer followed the blessing. Most believed Bocknostri had killed Draknast, but he had shown himself strong and unyielding; a worthy King.

Now he sat on the solid rock, above the trees, King of Whorle. He had ordered everything prepared for war. He had almost a moon before he needed to send out the order for the tribes to gather. He had found himself questioning the wisdom of his rush to arms this spring. Drew help him, he was sounding like his father. He had consulted the Drewbards, who had spoken amongst themselves and to Drew of course. They had advised he wait to the last moment to issue the final command. They were sure something would happen to answer his question; an omen; a sign from Drew himself.

So here he was waiting, where he had often sat as boy and man.

He looked to the east, upstream, where the river entered the valley from a plain larger than the one Moonmarl occupied. It was where the tribes would gather. They would all come, their overdeveloped sense of belonging overcoming arguments and feuds between them to answer their new King's call to arms.

He smiled to himself.

He, Bocknostri, son of Draknast, was King of Whorle.

Chapter 29

Eleven days later the mighty Drew, Lord of the Hill Gods of Whorle, answered the prayers of his priests, the Drewbards.

A small sailing boat, its progress upstream augmented by an oarsman, one of its two occupants, came into sight around the sweeping bend in the Drei below Moonmarl. It was not a Whorlean boat. They made no such craft, only leather-covered round boats, the light waxed outer stretched over a light wooden frame. They made a good seat for salmon fishing but little else.

This was a Niscerien boat; a small but solid craft with a single mast and sail. It was no more than two men in length, but it was made of thin overlapping and shaped wooden beams, strengthened by a thicker skeleton. It looked old but sound, which indeed it was.

The oarsman pulled for the shore as the other occupant untied and dropped the sail into the bottom of the boat. A small group of curious villagers began to gather. Who could this be?

"That's Gragonor!" cried one, pointing at the oarsman who's back had been towards them until they reached the little wooden jetty, if you could call it such. The two men stepped ashore, Gragonor receiving much backslapping before his fellow villagers realised his companion was Niscerian.

The murmurs grew to shouts and jeers. King Bocknostri's stories of their insulting mistreatment and the deaths of his companions were fresh in their minds. Gragonor tried to calm them, and was struggling, when a commanding shout cut above the clamour.

Cregenda pushed his way through the throng, his ten guards forming a wedge that left an open path between them.

"Well, well, Gragonor. We thought you were dead."

"So did I." he grimaced, "So did I. They have talented healers in Nisceriel."

"Indeed so, and who is this you bring to Whorle, a Niscerian?"

"Yes Cregenda, and one who brings secrets that our Prince will wish to hear, and I hope be pleased enough to spare this life he has all but taken once already." Cregenda laughed.

"Your Prince is King Bocknostri now, and I am sure he has already forgotten why he harmed you, besides he will need you now if this whoreson is to tell us anything." He drew his sword and held it to Fenlon's throat, whose eyes were wide with fear as he looked pleadingly toward Gragonor.

"My Lord Cregenda, please do not harm him. If not for him I would never have escaped. He is a condemned man in Nisceriel. He killed a guard to get us out, and he has information that can help our King revenge himself on all in Nisceriel, as I am sure he wishes."

Cregenda flicked the point of his sword upwards, tapping Fenlon under his chin with the flat of the blade.

"I will inform our King. Bring them." He turned on his heel and replaced his sword as he strode quickly towards the central roundhouse, the Royal inner fortress, which was now manned by Bocknostri's guard, a hastily raised force of companions and young men local to Bocknostri's birthplace. There was no stronger tie than to be from the same village, it commanded total loyalty in Whorle.

Bocknostri saw them immediately, questioned them on their escape, then through Gragonor, questioned Fenlon on the armies of Nisceriel, their numbers, their tactics. Fenlon told all he knew, as he had been instructed to, for of course he knew nothing of General Rebgroth's new ideas for weaponry and fighting style, and anything else he knew was already common knowledge.

Eventually King Bocknostri asked why he should not take a small part of his revenge out on Fenlon, and indeed on Gragonor for bringing him to Moonmarl. Gragonor nearly fell over his words in the rush to tell him that Fenlon could lead them into the Castle Nisceriel, into the heart of the Royal quarters before they were discovered. He told him that when the Castle was fully manned it would be impossible. Patrols outside the walls and shear numbers within would mean an early discovery of a force large enough to have any hope of taking the Castle.

He explained however that if there were to be an invasion, if all their armies were in the north, preparing to give battle with the Armies of Whorle, the Castle would have a minimal guard, no patrols outside and few men within.

Fenlon could lead a small party, thirty men or so, into the Castle through an unguarded entrance. Once inside, the royal women and children would be at his mercy.

In the coming moon, Fenlon would lead a small raiding party to Gloff and steal a fishing boat, river worthy and capable of carrying thirty men. They would sail it back to Moonmarl, up the Drei as they had just come. When the invasion of Nisceriel began, they would sail back down the Drei, across the River of Number and go ashore close to the Castle. On the eve of the battle in the North, probably near Gloff, they would enter the Castle and kill anyone they could find.

"And what do you want, Niscerian, riches, power?" Gragonor knew the answer.

"He just wishes to have the bushes that grow in the Castle gardens My King, to make wine from, which is his trade." Bocknostri stared at him for a moment, then burst out laughing.

"They come cheap these Niscerians," he roared, turning to his companions to acknowledge their laughing faces. "Tell him when this succeeds; I'll let him rut with the old Queen."

Laughter reverberated within the Roundhouse. Fenlon smiled embarrassedly, just in case they were laughing at him. He caught a glance and a wink from Gragonor and felt a little more confident. All he had to do now was stay alive till the spring. Bocknostri was speaking again, addressing all in the roundhouse.

"My friends! The Drewbards promised me a sign, an omen that our war and my plans had the blessing of Drew himself. Well here it is my friends. Drew has delivered just such in his greatness; he has sent us this Niscerien traitor, one who will sell his loyalty for his own gain. Well so be it, if anyone ever doubted the success of this war, we have been given the means to tear the heart out of Nisceriel before the real battle begins." His voice grew louder, rallying his audience. He drew his sword and thrust it above his head, point to the sky.

"Drew has blessed us, we go this spring! Raise the Tribes! Whorle goes to war!"

The Roundhouse filled with cheers, before inevitably, they changed into a rousing rendition of Whorle's battle song. The whole village could hear it, and joined in. War against another Kingdom, all Whorle united against a common foe, it was very rare, but it would be glorious.

Another four days passed before Eilana sat at the head of the table as she chaired the meeting of the King's Council. Gudmon was hunting as usual, but all the other members were there, with one addition. Harlmon sat on Eilana's right, called as a Councillor by the King's decree. In essence, Eilana had placed the paper in front of Gudmon and he had signed it without any discussion.

Rebgroth sat in his usual seat to her left with Tamorther beside him this day, and the five Ministers of the Countings sat in their normal chairs, Moreton amongst them, except that to her right they were all one seat further away. Bradett however, had taken advantage of Harlmon's addition to move around the corner to sit fully at the opposite end of the table, facing Eilana. She was sure his newfound confidence stemmed from his sharing her bed every few days. Her stomach fluttered at the thought.

She welcomed Harlmon to the Council and asked him to report on security matters within the Castle. He reported that Fenlon had been executed at the King's direct orders following his trial for attempted theft of Royal property. It was a harsh punishment, but not unusual for the very rare crime of theft from the Crown. He had been dispatched and buried quietly and without fuss. Moreton stirred uneasily, he hadn't felt a death in the Castle. Eilana addressed the Council.

"I am very concerned that someone should attempt to steal a Bumbleberry bush. Whilst they bring great benefit to us, some of us are aware that mishandled or misused, they can bring great harm. We also have a responsibility to the Elves that gave us three of their sacred bushes. I ask your advice Moreton, but I believe we should consider returning the bushes to the Elves care and perhaps transporting the berries to the Castle as required, if they were agreeable."

Her statement came as a complete surprise to Moreton. He never dreamt that she would ever contemplate relinquishing control of the bushes. Did she not feel they were important to them? Did she actually think the Elves would let her have bumbleberries in the future if she took action of some sort against the King, which must mean a hostile stance to Patrikal? He was amazed.

"I appreciate the concern you have My Lady, and I am sure the Elves would agree. They have often regretted that their code of honour meant they had to grant Patrikal her wish in this way. It would be a huge disadvantage to us should they not agree of course, do you not think?"

"Bumbleberry is wonderful to have, but we have survived generations without it. It would be a loss, but not the end of the world. I am more concerned of the possible consequences of them falling into the wrong hands at any stage. Can you imagine what might happen if we had a setback against Whorle, and the Castle was taken. Unlikely I know, but imagine."

"You are right of course, My Lady." He was worried now. The Castle taken by Whorle, unlikely indeed, but the very thought! What was in her mind?

"Any other comments?" she asked. Dramburld, Minister of the South Counting signalled and spoke.

"My Lady, I wonder about security of the berries in transit." Harlmon went to reply but Eilana got in first.

"Understandably Minister, a sound concern. My view is simply that we risk only a load at any time, a finite risk, rather than losing control of the bushes. Secondly, of course, Harlmon will supply a more than adequate escort for each trip. Does that satisfy your worries?"

"Indeed My Lady, I just feel with my age and their healing powers so great, I would hate to be without them!" There was a general murmur of agreement and mirth, but Harlmon interjected.

"Not great enough to save that poor Whorlean interpreter, he died half a moon ago after a long fight against his wound, despite bumbleberry." Moreton looked sharply at him. He hadn't felt that death either; one missed was unlikely, two almost impossible.

"Thank you brother, the comment was addressed to me." Harlmon grunted an apology.

"My Lady," Moreton began, "I feel sure this is the wisest course of action, but if we wish to secure the Elves agreement to continued supply, we will need to handle them subtly. Can I suggest that Princess Patrikal and I return the bushes to them? We can dig them up and place them in pots. A small goods wagon, covered and normally adorned, would be ideal to transport them. The Princess and I can travel disguised. I feel secrecy and guile safer than a large guard, but more importantly, less noticeable and disturbing to the Elves than a large escort."

Eilana looked at him hard for a moment, their eyes locked. She had felt the same sensation before, as if he was looking into the soul, but she would not look away. Instead she spoke.

"I support that absolutely. Are we all agreed then?" and before anyone could respond, "Good, that's settled then. For total security, Moreton and I will discuss when exactly, later."

She sat back and paused for effect, then turned towards Rebgroth.

"General, perhaps you would like to fill us in on your progress with weapons and training the Hunderts?"

"It would be my pleasure, My Lady."

He told them of the short sword, short spear and shield production. It was on target, producing enough to equip a Hundert per moon. Those produced were used to train one Hundert the first moon after production, two the second moon, three the third. The last three Hunderts kept the weapons they trained with and the first three were being re-equipped and retrained as weapons were produced.

He had taken one other decision too, that was not liked immediately, but was now accepted as necessary. The Ministers all mumbled their knowledge of what was to come. They had all received the initial complaints of the Hunderts.

Each Hunder had to ensure that twenty of its Hundert were trained archers. Put simply, Rebgroth had stripped the twenty archers from each of the six Hunderts of the South and South East Countings and placed them with the third Eastern Counting Hundert, and the third Hundert of the Castle Counting. He had transferred twenty men back to each to replace them. The Castlebury Hundert and the Second Eastern Counting Hundert lost their archers too.

The end result was that the six Hunderts in the south were now all infantry and were trained with the new weaponry. Two Hunderts, one of Castle Counting and one of the East Counting were now all archers. Many men were away from home for the winter, and it did cause problems at first, but training had renewed their pride in their Hunderts and everyone settled to their tasks.

In the North, he transferred the archers of the Second Hundert to the Third, and assigned the First and Third to defend Gloff when the time came. It meant the two hundred defenders would have sixty archers on their walls.

As a final detail, the Eastern Counting's First Hundert gained archers from, and swapped infantry with, the Castle Counting's Third Hundert.

If the Whorleans came that spring Nisceriel would have six well trained infantry Hunderts within a moon or so, supported by archers and cavalry, with reserves.

"Will that be enough?" she asked.

"I will make it enough, My Lady. We will fight on my ground, and I am sure the Whorleans aggression will work for us. I will say no more, but with Wey's help and Niscerien discipline, we will win."

"I am delighted to hear it," she smiled. Looking around the table she felt like

302

asking was all clear. There were a few buried in the detail. "Now, Officer Harlmon, tell us of your plans."

"Yes, uh, My Lady, I have dispatched two elevens of my Special Security Third into Whorle." There was a general shuffling of discomfort.

"On whose authority?" It was Bradett who asked the question they were all thinking. He would never have been that confident a few moons ago, Eilana thought to herself, and the thought delayed her reply just enough for Harlmon to do so first.

"The Lady Eilana's, Chancellor, who I understand to be the voice of the King, by his specific decree." There was silence around the table.

"Continue," Eilana ordered before any more was said.

"The First Eleven will penetrate deep into Whorle, even to Moonmarl itself. With their Levener, they are split into four groups of three. Each group carries two pigeons. On the first sign of the tribes of Whorle gathering, they are to send back their first pigeon. They will study the situation closer before dispatching the second. They will then return. They are there to observe and have strict orders not to engage in any action unless discovered and attacked.

"The Second Eleven are mounted and will split into pairs. They will form a screen a day's ride into Whorle from Gloff. On first sight of the enemy army by any pair, one will ride back at the gallop to Gloff and report. We should have at least two clear day's warning by the time an army walks that far. The second will stay in contact for another half day and then ride for Gloff, in case of any change in direction or numbers."

"That is excellent." It was Rebgroth that spoke. He had long decided it was wisest to make the best of Harlmon's talents whilst remaining on guard. "We will know, if it be, of Whorle's intention to come this spring in good time, which means we can get two Hunderts into Gloff, gather the others and be ready to face them as I wish. I thank you Harlmon, it was a problem I needed to address." Harlmon was surprised at the praise, but delighted.

"Pleased to be of service," he grinned.

"My Lady?"

"Yes General."

"Might I suggest that if Prince Bocknostri is to come this spring, it will be in a moon or so? This might be the time to suspend this Council and form the War Council. The Ministers will be needed in their Countings, so I would suggest The King, should he wish, Yourself, Myself, the Chancellor, Tamorther and Harlmon."

Eilana was delighted at the last suggestion, she had expected an argument.

The Ministers were annoyed at losing their voices temporarily, but could not really argue.

"Very sensible and agreed, but there is one other bit of information Officer Harlmon has just received from a travelling weapons sharpener, an itinerant who has just come from Whorle."

They all looked at her, except Harlmon, who was grinning at his hands. "It is now King Bocknostri. Apparently his father died shortly after his son's return from his adventures with us." There was a silence for a few moments whilst the significance of the news sank in.

"They will come this spring then," stated Rebgroth.

"Yes General, I am certain they will. Until the King commands otherwise, this Council is suspended."

They all rose in a general hum of conversation. Moreton was still digesting all that had been said. Fenlon and Gragonor were not dead, he was sure. What was she up to? And moving the bumbleberry bushes? He had tried to see into her mind, but although she did not know it, her will was so strong she made it almost impossible. He had only sensed a genuine desire to protect the bushes if her plans went wrong. Could that be a hint of self-doubt he detected?

His conscience had only allowed him to ensure the bushes got back to the Elves, and despite his determination and oath not to interfere, he had suggested taking Patrikal to get her away from whatever was to happen, but in truth, he had only done so because it was sensible for her to accompany her bushes and be there to talk to the Elves.

Rebgroth found himself with Harlmon.

"You have a remarkable talent for the clandestine, Officer Harlmon. War has a habit of raising the importance of such a gift."

"Thank you General, if that was a compliment!"

"In its way, Officer, in its way."

"What are you two gossiping about? Tactics no doubt, or strategy?" Eilana interrupted before the conversation could develop.

"Spying, My Lady, and clandestine activities, but of course you would know nothing about such things." He smiled broadly and excused himself.

"A strange sense of humour that man," Harlmon commented.

"He is the finest man you will ever meet, Brother. He is intelligent, caring and very dangerous to have as an enemy. You do not need to like him, brother, but respect him."

She turned and walked from the room.

Chapter 30

For Eilana, the next ten days seemed to take forever to pass, but then things began to happen at a pace.

Harlmon's screen picked up a small party of Whorleans moving through the Drean Forest towards Gloff. They were moving stealthily and almost got past without being detected. One of the Bluecoat scouts rode for Gloff whilst the other shadowed the raiders, staying well out of sight. The rider reported to his Sergeant at Gloff, who commanded the Bluecoats' Special Security Third.

The Sergeant sent the scout back to rejoin his companion and return to the screen, but with high praise and strict instructions not to be seen. He sent a rider with the news to Harlmon before deploying his Third Eleven, or at least eight of them, in a semi-circular watching screen, across the bridge, about half a quarter into Whorle. Again, not being seen was crucial.

It was not too long before the raiding party was picked up. There were seven of them, moving carefully towards the river and the bridge at Gloff. The report that reached Sergeant Drenton was of five Whorleans, who seemed to be led by two Niscerians. This was intriguing, but his instructions were clear; observe and report, allow them to achieve their end. He had complete faith in Harlmon, and whatever was happening must be a small part of a bigger picture.

The party reached the tree line a little south west of the bridge. Here, the two Niscerians left the others and moved towards the bridge, but still in the trees. The five Whorleans headed downstream, just beyond the first horseshoe bend in the river, where the inside of the bend was hidden from Gloff and a small mud and sand beach began as the trees ended.

The two Niscerians were in fact Fenlon and Gragonor, dressed in the nearest

Niscerien looking garments he could find in Moonmarl. He could at least speak the language and understand what was being said at any time, although his accent was not good if challenged.

They waited until dusk and walked across the bridge, carrying two rabbits they had trapped specifically for this walk. They reached the Gloff Hundert Guards at their post on the Gloff side. As Fenlon had hoped, they really were not interested in two Niscerians returning with their evening meal, and hardly looked up from their dice game.

They turned downstream, the two man high stone wall of Gloff on their left, the river edge to their right. The bank was lined with a mixture of fishing boats and river-going goods carriers that moved grain and meat mainly, between Ffonhaven, Castle Nisceriel and Gloff.

One such freighter was tied to the outside of a fishing boat, about halfway along the row of boats. It was single masted and about four and more men long. It had three pairs of rowlocks set by three rowing seats across its beam, one forward of the mast, two aft. It was perfect, and no one was visible aboard.

They climbed across the fishing boat and into their prize. The triangular sail was tied around the boom, but all the ropes were in place. Fenlon untied the ropes that bound the sail, except one central one. They cast off from the fishing boat and pushed out into the river, taking an oar each on the forward bench. The oars were too heavy for one man to handle two, so they pulled out into the centre of the flow, letting the current help them swiftly away downstream. It had been so easy; all you needed was nerve enough. Unknown to them of course, Sergeant Drenton had ensured the waterside was clear, and the two Hundert Guards were actually Bluecoats. It was amazing to Drenton how Harlmon's name and a Bluecoat on your back commanded unquestioning obeyance these days.

The boat rounded the bend in the river below Gloff and Fenlon and Gragonor pulled hard for the little beach, now moving the large craft into and across the current. As they beached, the other five Whorleans left the trees and boarded the craft, pushing them off back into the flow. With four oars now manned they made steady progress downstream. The rising tide began to surge against the current as they rounded the famous curves in the river.

The darkness was becoming deeper but the half moon and clear sky made it possible to navigate the river comfortably. They should reach the bend where the river broadened into the wide estuary of the River of Number before its tidal surge formed the wave that would sweep upstream and around the bends they were now on. Twice a day to varying levels, it pushed upstream beyond Gloff. Bow-on, it was an uncomfortable experience, but caught beam-on, it was often disastrous.

Fenlon hauled the sail up the mast and set the beam to make the most of the light but steady wind. Now they were in the open estuary they made good time, staying close to the Whorlean side where the deeper channel ran to the mouth of the Drei. There the channel swung across to the Niscerien side off Ffonhaven before running close to that shore on its way south.

As a sailor, Fenlon was no more than a gifted beginner, but to the men of Whorle, boats were a mystery. He lowered the sail as they approached the Drei. The channel kicked left, partly redirected by a rocky point that protruded at an angle into the Number. The Drei flowed out on its other side. Fenlon decided the sail was just another thing to go wrong. He would keep it simple.

The tide was flooding in now, and the waters were deepening fast, slowing the downstream current almost to a stop. As they passed the point the Drei's waters were also fighting the tide and the water around them seemed to boil. He shouted to stop rowing on his right and to row for their lives on his left. He swung the steering oar and the boat lumbered around. It was almost as if it couldn't make up its mind whether to follow the current downstream, the tide upstream, or the wind across the river. It bucked on the white water before he ordered rowing to recommence.

The tide was winning there, and they rowed into the mouth of the Drei. They entered the short gorge through which it flowed, the sail still in the bottom of the boat. There was no easy wind between the rock cliffs, and with the tide in flood it was safer to row. The rock walls began to lean away, moving back from the river and becoming beautifully wooded hillsides, rising high above them on both sides. Fenlon could not help but feel that whilst the Ffon's gorge was larger and more spectacular, the Drei valley was very special.

Harlmon burst into Eilana's room. She was half dressed and Eival and Ereyna both jumped at his entrance. Before she could admonish him he spoke.

"A message from Gloff, My Lady."

"Leave us ladies," she commanded. Her handmaidens scurried from the room. "This had better be good, brother; else I might well be a little upset with you."

"Two messages really, one a watch or so ago, but a second just now that is significant."

"You mean you have had news for a watch and not told me? I do not believe you sometimes!"

"Calm, my pretty one. On its own, the first message meant nothing, just that a small raiding party from Whorle was moving towards Gloff, apparently led by two Niscerians, but the second is that these two, Fenlon and the other, who is probably a disguised Whorlean, stole a freight boat and sailed downstream, picking up the other five Whorleans. It begins sister, they have taken the bait."

Eilana's chest tightened and her stomach fluttered. They must have, it could only be that they needed a boat to get across the Number.

"So it seems Harlmon. Now for Wey's sake, tell me the moment anything is reported, anything."

Harlmon grinned and left the room, Eival and Ereyna entering before the door shut.

"Eival, go and find Chancellor Bradett, tell him I have urgent need of his advice." She rushed away. "Ereyna, let's get me dressed."

"Are you sure it's worth the bother, My Lady?" Eilana was shocked for a moment by the bluntness of the comment, but it was said with humour, and she had not been able to disguise the truth from them.

"You are my best friend Ereyna, but you are also a Lady in Waiting, my handmaiden, if I hadn't known you for so long that might have been taken the wrong way."

"Indeed, My Lady, but is it?"

Eilana laughed. Ereyna did know her too well. Her body was tingling with excitement and anticipation. She had thought of Bradett and realised she was desperate for him. To greet him in her undergarments might just dispense with some of the silly formalities, and she needed to feel him inside her.

"You are right actually. Leave me now, but wait in the ante room; I don't want anyone else bursting in for at least a quarter."

"Yes, My Lady."

Three days later, three pigeons arrived between dawn and dusk. The first came from near Moonmarl. The message attached to its leg was clear. The tribes of Whorle were gathering north east of there.

Harlmon had trained his men well, to fight, to spy, not to be seen, but he could not teach them all to read and write. He had taught them therefore a simple code of stick pictures, a system for direction based on the rising sun, the east. It worked and it was simple.

The second message came from a hillside that overlooked the Drei, just south of Moonmarl. It was a mixture of prearranged signs and a little initiative on behalf of the Bluecoat that drew it. Its message was fairly clear. A boat had passed them heading for Moonmarl.

The third pigeon had arrived from a spot somewhere near the first, from a second pair of scouts who had also penetrated Whorle as far as Moonmarl and had found the tribes gathering.

The Council of War met that evening. Rebgroth had decided to raise the Hunderts the next day. They would gather individually, near their homes, and then travel to join the other Hunderts, building the army, just south of Gloff. All except the First and Third Hunderts of the northern Counting, the Third joining the First in its home of Gloff.

It would take a quarter moon to gather, and it would take at least three quarters for the army of Whorle to march to Gloff if they left now, but Rebgroth wanted to be fully ready and prepared, his plan clear to all his officers and sergeants. To this end he had gathered provisions enough to sustain his army whilst they readied themselves, and they would be carrying a quarter moon's food with them as they arrived. He was sure it would not be too long before Whorle's army marched, for they had to feed around two thousand men, carrying food or foraging on the march. At least Rebgroth had provisions to hand.

All was agreed in the Council, but that evening Eilana had a furious row with the King. Gudmon had drunkenly promised Prince Gudrick and Harlada they could march with him to war, and fight beside him in battle. They were only thirteen and should not fight until after their Sire's days. Strangely, it was Moreton who swung the argument. He had arrived to discus his departure with Patrikal and the bumbleberry bushes to find the heated debate in full swing.

Eilana was starting to panic. If Gudrick was not in the Castle, all her plans would have to change, to the point where it could all fall apart. She appealed to Moreton for support. The boys were too young to go to war.

Moreton was caught in a dilemma; he did not want to interfere. He felt certain Gudmon would die on the day of the battle, but of Prince Gudrick he was not certain. He thought Gudrick more likely to meet his early death alongside Gudmon rather than here at the Castle, but he could not be sure. He gave the advice he would have given if he were looking at the situation without any of his patchy knowledge of what was to come. The boys should not go.

The King took it from his friend, particularly through the haze the wine made in his brain, and agreed to tell the boys they could not go. Eilana insisted he do it then and there, so led by Moreton, he set off for the boys' room.

Moreton returned shortly and told Eilana he would leave with Patrikal the day after next for the Elven Forest. Tomorrow he would dig up the bushes and pot them, load the wagon he had chosen, and leave at dawn the following morning.

"Thank you for doing this Moreton, I am sure it is for the best. Those bushes are a loss to Nisceriel, but should anything go wrong, we both know the consequences to the lands around if they should be used unwisely. We have both seen what they did to Gudmon."

"It is for the best." He paused for a moment before looking straight into her eyes. "You are a complicated women Eilana."

"I do not understand you Moreton." He smiled wryly.

"You will do what you must do Eilana, yet you are concerned with the well being of mankind. You would confuse most men who looked for logic in your actions."

"And you Moreton, do I confuse you?"

"I think not, My Lady, but many will die because of you. Thousands from all the realms of this land will die in battle, all from the consequences of your actions. It is not for me to judge you however, for it is destined. Were it not you it would be someone else, but eventually the greater good of all will be served, so I mind my own business and try to make things a little less painful for a few. Sometimes however, I am not sure that the end justifies the means."

She was confused now. Did he know what she was planning; surely he couldn't and let it happen? And what was he saying about thousands of deaths? She was not responsible for the war with Whorle, it would have happened anyway; she was just using it to her advantage, she hadn't caused it. As for deaths across all the realms of the land, he was fantasising. She decided to remain very formal.

"Goodbye then Weymonk, may Wey walk with you until we meet again."

"I do not think we will speak again in friendship after I leave this Castle, My Lady, but Wey guide you in his wisdom, and may he forgive you when you meet him." Eilana grinned mischievously at him for such a solemn moment.

"Why should Wey forgive me if I do his will?"

"Because Eilana, you will go far beyond what he asks of you, because your ambition and your intellect will take your actions far beyond what is needed to achieve his ends, and because deep inside, you are as mad as your brother, all of whose evil I place at your door." He turned his back to make his exit.

Eilana quivered with anger. She was angry because in her heart she knew he was right. She called after him.

"If we both live through all this Moreton, do not return to this Castle or to this realm. You will not be welcome." He didn't look back or acknowledge her words. She felt suddenly foolish for saying them. No, in the name of Wey, she meant it.

She searched for Harlmon, and found him with a woman in his workroom, a kitchen maid. She was spread on her back across his table, crumpling maps and papers. Harlmon stood between her thighs, her skirts lifted, his arms hooked under her knees which bent over his elbows, his hands gripping her hips. She looked wide-eyed at Eilana as she saw her enter the room, but Harlmon held on to her as he glanced at his sister. He continued to pump himself into her as he spoke.

"What do you want sister?"

"Come to my room when you have finished."

"No wait," he insisted. He thrust his hips a little harder and grunted as he climaxed into the girl. He stepped back dropping her legs and breathing a little heavily. "Away," he ordered, and the girl fled from the room. He turned to Eilana, carelessly wiping himself with the edge of the tablecloth and replacing his parts back inside his codpiece. Eilana couldn't help but think he might as well have done it himself for all that girl meant to him.

"So what brings you to me pretty one?"

"I need you to keep a very close eye on Moreton until he leaves with Patrikal the day after tomorrow. He must not spend time alone with Rebgroth or Bradett. Ensure he is interrupted if he comes into contact with either of them. Do not harm him Harlmon, do not even think of it."

"Yes, yes, yes, I will not even think of it, but sister, do you think it wise for Patrikal to leave the Castle at this time?" She knew what he meant. It had bothered her for a while.

"There has never been a blood line through a woman in Nisceriel, never a female ruler. I believe she will stay with the Elves."

"I did not mean she would challenge for the throne, merely that sometimes women can be determined and vengeful." He had a wry grin on his face as he said it. "I would hate for her to come back and haunt us."

"No, let her go brother. I want them both away from here before it starts.

311

If Moreton leaves the Elves before Bocknostri comes he will go to Gudmon and the army. I just want them away."

"As you wish, pretty one."

Eilana returned to her rooms. Wey! She wasn't going soft was she? No, her plans were coming to fruition. She was sure she had thought of everything, she was sure. She had to stop thinking about it all, just for a quarter or two. Where was Bradett?

Chapter 31

Bocknostri stood up stiffly, as if his back was slowly unlocking, but in fact it was his legs that were stiff. He had been sitting too long on his favourite rock outcrop, eating a whole cold chicken as the dawn sky brightened, pink and dramatically purple in places.

It was a cool bright morning and the damp cold of the granite rock had penetrated the leather leggings he wore. He felt as if they had chilled his bones, but he would not have been anywhere else at that moment, the last dawn before he would lead his army to war.

He tossed the chicken bones out over the treetops. They would land on the forest floor far below and some hungry woodland animal would be only too happy to gnaw on them.

He gazed up the valley towards the rising sun. The breakfast fires of the gathered tribes of Whorle numbered hundreds as they warmed their last meal before the march began. He turned as a noise behind him reminded him he was no longer alone.

"Are you ready my King?" asked Cregenda.

"I am my friend," he replied, "but I wonder if I will look out from here again, and what will have happened if ever I do?"

"You will be King of all the known realms, ruling the lands far beyond a man's sight in all directions; that is what will have happened. The tribes are all with you my King; not just because you order them to be, but because they wish to be. Whorle is ready for its great destiny. We have been too quiet for too long, Whorle is ready for war."

"Are all the tribes here yet?"

"No my King, but they come. Two of the northern tribes of Breecombe and beyond are pledged to come and will arrive. At the pace an army can move, and trampling a way through the forest as you will, they will catch you in days; well before you reach Nisceriel."

"I still say I should lead the raid on the Castle Nisceriel, that is where the key to this lies."

"My lord, we have debated this too often now. The tribes will follow you, not me. I will do what is necessary. You must win a great battle; lead your armies to victory. I will see to the Castle, and I will keep their women alive so we can bed them all as we swore we would."

"I could trust no-one more Cregenda, but I wish your wise council was with me on the march."

"If all goes to plan, I may still be at your side when the battle commences, perhaps with a trophy or two from the Castle. Perhaps you should stride into battle with his Queen's tits tied to your belt, her scalp on your shield."

"Drew has given you a tongue to make any man feel good Cregenda. You are right as always, come, off this rock. We must join our army then say our farewells."

They were not halfway back down the hillside to the valley below when a runner approached, slowing as he saw them.

"My King, I bring news of a small action, on the hill just south of the camp."

"What action?" It was Cregenda who asked first.

"A patrol stumbled across three of those Bluecoat bastards my Lord. On foot they were, and spying on our camp. They fought hard my Lord, they killed eight men before they were all felled, but my Lord, they had two small cages, and at first contact they released a bird. The other cage was empty."

"Thank you soldier, be gone." The runner bowed and moved rapidly away down the slope. Bocknostri looked at Cregenda.

"Aye my King, they know we are ready, and all the better. If there are three there will be more, so let us make a big show of departing. Send two tribes to take Teekford. They will report a split in the army, however small. It will focus their minds north whilst I take the Castle. They may even split their force and send men north to defend Teekford, or just to keep our force apart, either way, they will be looking elsewhere."

Bocknostri threw an arm round his friend and thumped his shoulder, his ultimate sign of affection and friendship.

"That's why I need you with me my friend, and you are right of course. We will defeat these wimps, crush them. They are no competition for the men of Whorle, whether they fight on horseback or on foot."

"You know how to handle the horsemen now my King; do not let the men forget. They must have their long spears to hand when they are needed."

"Yes, yes, Cregenda, don't nag your King."

They laughed and walked on to join the army.

The pigeon was well on its way back to Castle Nisceriel. It was not that far, down the Drei and across the estuary, not flying at least, and less than a watch later Harlmon was handed the small piece of paper the pigeon had carried back. It bore the number two and a large black cross.

Each bird had this piece of paper attached to it at all times. If a message was to be sent, the cross was removed and the new message attached. In this way, if the group were discovered as in this case, they just had to release a bird to let Harlmon know they were discovered without having to write a message.

Group two was the group that should have been in the hills almost exactly above Moonmarl. Group one was above the Drei, slightly to the west, and had reported the boat. Three was slightly east of two and had also reported the gathering. Four should have been further east again.

Harlmon told Eilana shortly after he received the message.

"They know we will be ready then, they know we will be waiting."

"They do, pretty one, but it will not worry them. They want to fight. They are that sort of people. They are certain they will win and the sooner they fight us the better."

"I'm sure you're right brother. Make sure the General knows though."

"I will tell him the moment he returns. He is out with Tamorther, riding the battle ground I believe."

"He is a very thorough man. He could teach you a lot brother, if he does not kill you first."

"He won't do that pretty one, he's on our side, and you will see that he stays that way."

"I pray so, brother, I pray so."

315

General Rebgroth turned upstream as he reached the Stroue. He was not sure if it was a small river or a large stream. It would be inconvenient but not impossible to cope with. He paused until Tamorther drew up along side him, and they both studied the hills before them.

At Gloff, the Kingdom of Nisceriel was at its narrowest. Its widest was at its southern border, along the Ffon, but from its mouth, the bank of the Number's estuary ran slightly east of north to Gloff. The line of hills that ran from Nisceriel's south eastern corner ran north for a while before gently veering west of north, again as far as Gloff.

Here, as if they realised they were too close, the river turned west of north and the hills east of it. Nisceriel widened steadily until Teekford, where its influence ran out across the ragged and undefined border.

At Gloff it was a little over a watch's walk from river to hills, but where Rebgroth and Tamorther were now at the Stroue valley, about half way between Gloff and Castle Nisceriel, it was almost a good watch and a half's march wide, certainly for an army.

The forested hills to their left were slightly nearer than the ones to their right. The southern hills drew a straight line until they seemed to run behind the hills to their left. As they rode on, the mouth of a valley came into view, tucked just around the corner of the northern hill line.

The trees grew down the valley slopes on both sides but stopped as the land flattened at its base. Trees and hills together conspired to form a natural funnel along the Stroue's course.

"We will need to draw them this far Sir," observed Tamorther.

"We will indeed. That will be the job of the Third of Bluecoats that will fight with us, and the Castle First Hundert. They won't like it, but they will be issued with Bluecoat uniforms as soon as they get here. I am certain after Officer Harlmon's antics, the sight of pale blue uniforms will blind Bocknostri to everything else. Once he sights a small army in this valley, I am equally certain he will fight. To march south and leave a sizeable army in his rear that could attack from behind, trap him between it and another army to the south, or at least cut off a retreat north, would be too foolish, even for him. Apart from that, he will want to fight because he is from Whorle, and because he will see an army a third of his number and an easy victory."

"I'm sure you are right General."

They rode slowly into the valley. The trees spilled slightly each side onto the flat valley floor, which was remarkably uniform in its width, the river running almost straight along its middle. Rebgroth explained his strategy to Tamorther as they moved.

"Across the valley, the South East Counting's First and Third will be on the far side of the river, the South East Second and South First on this side. These are four of our Short Sword Hunders. They will let the enemy attack and fall back steadily and as quickly as order allows, back down the valley in their fighting line.

"On the north valley side, along the tree line, will be the Eastern Second, and behind them the archers of the Eastern Third. On this south side will be the Castle Second, and the archers of the Castle Third Hundert. They will remain hidden in the trees until we draw the enemy into the valley. On this side though, they will be split, by this."

Completely hidden by the trees, another valley suddenly came into sight, cutting sharply away to their right. It was clear of trees for only half the width of the main valley, and it was only a field or so deep. A small stream flowed down it.

"Across this side valley will be the other two Short Sword Hunders, the South Second and Third. Behind them will be the infantry of the Northern Second in support."

As they reached the far edge of the side valley, the Stroue valley continued for only another eighty paces or so before it opened into three smaller valleys.

"Here is where our fighting line must hold Tam. If they get pushed back from here they will lose the protection of the hills and woods on their flanks. They will be surrounded and slaughtered. Hold here however, and we will have two thousand Whorleans boxed in the valley. They can only fight around their edges, wasting their numerical advantage, and our archers can put volley after volley into their centre. The slaughter will be theirs, but our line must hold here. The Eastern First will be in reserve behind them, with forty archers and sixty infantry to plug any gaps. The Castle First will be here too, recovered from their run, and no doubt, out of their blue coats! Will it work, Tam?"

"In all probability General, but we will make sure it does."

"Good man. If all is understood between us then, let us brief the Officers and Sergeants. Key will be first the tactical retreat down the valley, and secondly, holding here. Every one of the four hundred soldiers in that line must understand that."

"They will Sir, and they will succeed because they will know why."

Moreton left with Patrikal exactly as he had scheduled. They were in an old covered wagon with a large water butt strapped firmly to the rear backboard. This was mainly to ensure they could keep the three bumbleberry bushes well watered that they carried in three large pots in the back of the wagon.

They had dug up the bushes the day before, and they had each come from the ground so very easily. Both Moreton and Patrikal had the feeling they knew what was happening, that they were going home.

The wagon was pulled by a fit, heavy horse, mature but not old. It too seemed to feel an importance in what it was doing, but that was more to do with the way Moreton had of communicating with animals.

It pulled them steadily southeast for almost a day. The only way due east from Castle Nisceriel by wagon was to travel the road south east, almost to Bridgebury, before taking the track eastward to the hills, some day's travel beyond in a heavy wagon, at the borders of the realm.

They stopped and camped over night not far from Bridgebury, but they kept to themselves and away from other travellers. The next morning they moved steadily east on the road just north of the Ffon, until they met the forested hills at the eastern borders of Nisceriel. Here they turned north, following a track along the tree line at the bottom of the wooded slopes that climbed high above them.

Another day later, given their slow, bumpy progress on the rough-tracked road, they were almost due east of Castle Nisceriel, where Patrikal had first entered the Elven forest. They had seen no sign of Elves, but Moreton told her they had been watched since they had begun the trek north. When they felt comfortable, the Elves would show themselves and greet them.

On the first stretch of the journey, as they bounced south to Bridgebury, Moreton had looked sideways at Patrikal, to see her pale and shaking slightly.

"What troubles you Princess?" he asked. He knew she would tell him. She had always told him everything. She trusted him implicitly.

"It is strange, I have never really remembered before, but I remember riding in a cart with mother and Serculas all those years ago. The day Gudrick was born, the day all this began."

Moreton felt a shudder run through himself. He was still trying to convince his conscience that he was not breaking the most solemn vows of his order; that he was not deliberately attempting to alter the future, by taking Patrikal away from the Castle. He had convinced himself that if he was of that time, and that if he had no idea of what was to come, from the prophesies of so many tribes and peoples that his order had studied over centuries, he would have suggested what they were doing now anyway. No, he had almost convinced himself.

"And what do you remember my child?"

"I am not really sure. I remember the horse farting." She smiled despite her feelings of concern. "I remember mother screaming, seeing wolves, dear Rowl and Rawl. It was so sad when they died."

"That is the sad thing about such large dogs. They always have such short lives. Six summers is old for them."

"Yes indeed. I suppose it was just that they were the same age as me, we grew together, and all the dogs in the world, their sons or not, never really replaced them."

"So tell me Princess, why did you take the elfchild home?"

"I don't really know, even now. Because it told me to, I suppose, I just knew what I had to do, and the dogs knew too. It was not brave or anything. I just did it. Wey, I was only four!"

"And just look at you now!" laughed Moreton, "Just look at you now!" She thumped Moreton's arm, then leant sideways and cuddled him.

"What is going to happen, Moreton? Do you know?" He took the reins in his right hand and put his left arm around her shoulders.

"I cannot say Princess, but this land will be very different in a few days time. When the horror of war passes, when the dead are buried and some of them grieved over, I feel we will have many years of uncertainty. I think you may grow used to a life in the forest."

He held her to him, and he felt her sobbing quietly as they rode slowly away from everything she had known, her home, her family, her life.

A movement in the trees ahead brought Patrikal back to the present. Ranamo and Ranor stepped into the track before them. To the untrained eye they looked more like twins than just the brothers they were.

"Greetings Princess, elf-friend, and Weymonk Moreton, also an elf-friend; we are honoured by the visit of two such welcome guests together. Retalla sends greetings and commands us to lead you to him. Pray guide your wagon and follow."

Before they could say anything in reply they had turned and walked into the trees, but along a path the wagon could negotiate. Patrikal smiled. Retalla had seemed very old to her fourteen years before, but still he ruled the forests. He was a wonderful person, she seemed to remember. She liked Elves.

Chapter 32

The next half moon passed in a blur of activity in the Castle Nisceriel. The tension took its toll, with Eilana in particular, becoming bad tempered and on edge. Everything she had planned for was about to happen, or even fail to happen, but she refused to consider that. She also refused to consider the evil in what she planned.

She suddenly realised what had really angered her, what was actually at the heart of her foul mood. Moreton had said she was mad, like her brother, called her evil, even if indirectly. His words had been eating into her like a worm ever since. Well she was not evil, she was only doing what was necessary to achieve her ends, which would rid Nisceriel of a weak King and replace him with strong rule. Nisceriel needed it, and she would make it happen.

Harlmon had reported to the War Council. Three pigeons had arrived. The first was from the Third Group, their last one. It told of the tribes of Whorle marching to war. It was followed by two from Group Four, one giving the same news, a second telling of a force of some one hundred and fifty men, splitting from the main body and moving due east.

"I would suggest he is sending two tribes to Teekford," Harlmon advised.

"I am sure you are right," Rebgroth observed. "They will cross uncontested there and swing south. They may arrive in time to rejoin the main body, but I doubt it, and if not, they are too small in number to be a real problem. It will however give me the opportunity to make a show of sending the Royal Guard Cavalry north. Bocknostri will assume it will be in response to an attack on Teekford. He is not used to Cavalry and how fast they can move. He will not expect their return."

The Hunderts had gathered thirty fields south of Gloff, just north of the Stroue valley. Strategy had been explained and detailed plans made. The two Hunderts of archers and two of infantry that would line the valley sides were sent there. The Southern Second and Third Hunderts with their short swords, short spears and long shields, and the Northern Second infantry Hundert, were sent to their positions in the side valley. The Eastern First was dispatched to their place at the far end of the valley. Rebgroth wanted them hidden and the apparent size of his force to look much smaller than it was.

Five hundred and thirty infantry and two hundred Royal Guard cavalry remained camped in the open that early afternoon as the Tribes of Whorle reached the forest edge opposite Gloff. The inner screen of Bluecoats had done their job well and all was prepared for their arrival. They moved out of the forest and lined the banks of the Number, almost one thousand eight hundred of them, singing their battle songs and waving their weapons in the air. Eventually they began to set up a temporary camp.

Castle Nisceriel had been warned too. A rider from Gloff galloped his horse most of the way south, arriving as quickly as he could with his horse still standing. Harlmon brought Eilana another message however, and only to her. It was from the second pigeon of Group One. It reported the boat that had sailed up river over half a moon ago now, returning downstream, but this time carrying about thirty-five soldiers.

Eilana hugged her brother. It had to be Fenlon. It was working.

"Did you see Greardel before he left?" asked Harlmon.

"Of course I did. He will do his part, of that I have no doubt, but whether he gets caught or not I couldn't be sure, nor really do I care. If he doesn't, of course, we will need to deal with him when he returns."

"That will be my pleasure pretty one. I have never liked that man."

"Good. Now I do not think Fenlon can possibly get here by tonight, but we had better be ready in case."

"We will be standing ready. Our scouts will give us plenty of warning if they come tonight, but I don't think they will."

"Tonight and tomorrow is going to seem a very long time, I'm not sure I can bear it."

"But tomorrow night will come my sister, and the next day you will be Queen Eilana, the King Mother, and I, uncle to a King." He hugged her, pecked her on the cheek and left to recheck his guards.

For Cregenda there was no decision to make. They had sailed down the Drei more quickly than they could have hoped and having been amazed at the beauty of its valley seen from the water, they marvelled at the high cliff walls they rowed through, their sail in the bottom of the boat.

They pulled ashore as the cliffs diminished and a small jetty came into sight. They tied up and left two guards, more to let rope out as the tide dropped than for security. He couldn't remember the name of the village, Shepst he thought, but the villagers welcomed them and fed them in their roundhouse.

There was the briefest discussion of their situation. It was almost dusk. If they left on the falling tide they could move across the Number and approach the shore as it flooded. They would need to beach below the small line of jetties that formed the Castle Nisceriel's trading post, where many of its provisions arrived. The small stream that ran through the Castle cut a deep channel in the mud flats that allowed quite large vessels to dock there. They, however, would need a full tide to land just south of there unseen.

It was quite clear to Cregenda. They had left time for problems and there had been none. They were a day early and had to wait until the next night. This also had the benefit that they were Whorlean soldiers going to war. The villagers were obliged by tradition to supply a woman for each soldier that night.

It was not a duty they shirked; quite the opposite in fact. The women of the village looked on it as an honour, and a pleasure if they were lucky. Their young men had marched to war themselves a moon before with their tribe, leaving only those men too old or too young. It was an excuse for a depraved party. There were only eighteen women in the village and thirty-seven on the boat, so most of the women looked after the needs of two soldiers. In fact many did their duty with three or four that night, and they made sure the two guarding the boat were not ignored. They gave pleasure to those about to die for Whorle, which in this case meant all but two of them.

Bocknostri too had decisions to make, but his were not so clear-cut. He called the tribal leaders to his tent late in the afternoon, and a healthy debate about tactics ensued. Some of the younger tribal leaders begged for the opportunity to attack Gloff that evening. There was plenty of light left, and from the vantage points of the tallest treetops around, the diminutive army of Nisceriel could be seen camped south of the walled town. It should be taken before their army could move behind its walls and boost its defence.

Bocknostri was aware they were a day early also. The march had gone well. The promise of food, plunder and women had urged the tribes on, their stomachs putting up with light rations on the march in anticipation of gorging themselves when they arrived and were victorious.

Bocknostri had trouble restraining their enthusiasm without being able to divulge the whole plan or his concerns. He did not want his men taking Gloff that night and gorging themselves on the spoils too soon. They had to hold the army of Nisceriel's attention tomorrow and tomorrow night especially, to keep their minds from the Castle. They must seek to fight the final battle the day after tomorrow.

Bocknostri was just beginning to miss Cregenda's reason and was about to assert himself violently on the meeting if needs be, when Drokhart shouted above the noise.

"Our King has spoken. His words are blessed by Drew himself, and whatever our personal desires and views, our duty is to obey. Drew and our King will guide us to victory, and today is not the day for such. Tomorrow we will burn Gloff and have their women, the next day we will slaughter their army, if we can catch them!"

A raucous cheer, which was clearly audible within the village, filled the tent. Gerlaff, Hundert of Gloff, turned to his First Sergeant as they stood on the stone walls above the bridge gates.

"Will they come tonight Sergeant?"

"I cannot see why not Sir, but they do not seem to be deploying for any action. Perhaps we have until the morning."

"Well we had better stand ready in case they come in the night. The men must sleep at their posts, so if we raise the alarm they will at least be in the right place."

"I will see to it Sir." He moved away to instruct the other Sergeants of both his own First Hundert, all men of Gloff, and of the Third. The Third had an extra twenty archers, transferred from the Second, and all forty were deployed along the wall south of the gate. The twenty from the First were positioned along the shorter northern stretch. They were supported by half their number of infantry from their Hunderts, the rest being deployed somewhat thinly, around the remainder of the walls.

Gerlaff murmured a quiet prayer to Wey and left the walls for his home. He wanted to be with Laranna for a while. It seemed proper to make love for what might be the last time, but when he got home, and they lay naked in each other's arms, he could not do it. They lay for a while together, and though she fondled him gently, which would normally have excited him immediately, he just gazed at the ceiling and could not even raise a smile.

As it began to get dark he kissed her and with a final hug, he rose and dressed in heavy leathers. They might turn a blunt sword. He pulled a leg off the chicken that was ready for their dinner, and tore a chunk of bread from the loaf. He smiled at Laranna, still lying on the bed, and walked back to the wall, eating whilst he did so.

About midnight, he called a meeting of Officers and Sergeants. Grenfeld was there too, Hundert of the Northern Third, but as this was Gerlaff's home they were defending, Gerlaff was traditionally in command.

They went over their strategy for what it was worth. Don't let them over the walls was about all it amounted to, but with refinements. The archers would be key, they had to keep the enemy away from the walls, and if the walls were scaled, they would fight then as infantry where required.

"Let us get some rest then, if we can. Sleep with your swords and bows in your hands. We will stand ready half a quarter before dawn. General Rebgroth says we will only have to defend one or two concerted attacks before they decide to bypass us. We must do at least that, and inflict as many casualties upon them as we can. Wey guard you all."

He left the walls and went to his position in the centre of the village, in front of the Meeting Hall and just across from his house. He sat talking amongst his men for a while, mainly about things they had done together over the years. They all thought this could be the last time they would share such stories.

He lay back against the wooden steps that led up to the Meeting Hall and closed his eyes. To his amazement, the next thing he knew was his First Sergeant shaking him awake just before dawn.

"They are moving Sir; it will not be long after dawn when they come."

"Thank you Sergeant. Go back to the wall, I'll rouse this lot."

He moved through the rows of sleeping men, shaking and cajoling them.

"On your feet you dozy lot, you'll be fighting on empty stomachs else. Wake up and get some food in you, and plenty of water. Not too much though, we don't want no-one pissing themselves and those animals from Whorle thinking any of us afraid."

A general murmur of laughter signalled most were awake, and it roused those who weren't. They took Gerlaff's advice.

Chapter 33

Bocknostri stood before the men of the Lernbalck tribe. He had given his old friend Balkmern, their tribal chieftain, the honour of starting the war; crossing the bridge to take Gloff. They had no scaling equipment. A few men had cut down some small trees the day before to use as ladders, but most thought them too heavy to be carrying into a fight.

Two other tribes were in their rear. They would follow them across the bridge and over the walls. Bocknostri ordered them to war, and with a loud cheer they turned and ran for the bridge. It was a good bowshot across, with three men's length of road before the gates.

They charged over the bridge. It would only allow them to run a tight six or seven abreast. With weapons drawn and shields in front of them, those that used them that is, it slowed their charge. It did not quell their voices, however. A continuous cheer heralded their coming to those defenders who could not see them.

Gerlaff was one of those, as were his men. He stood in front of some thirty in number, all villagers of Gloff now too old to serve in the Hundert. They had all been through the Hundert once though, and trained to arms, it was just that they were all just short of forty and slower than they once were, but they gripped their swords just as tightly as they ever had, their round shields held in readiness.

Gerlaff was not a brave man, nor a very big one. He could use a sword but was not strong. He was convinced that he would come across a huge Whorlean whose brute strength would defeat him. Like all Niscerians though, his sense of duty kept him there. He would fight and who knows, he might live through it all.

His job was to watch for any breach in the defences, any point around the wall where the Whorleans got onto it, and to lead his men to repel them. If he was really lucky, that would not happen. His eyes caught the archers along both sides of the gates drawing their bows, and with a shout from their Sergeant, the first flight of arrows tore through the air and into the front ranks of the tribesmen.

They were only halfway across the bridge as many died and more were wounded. Shields caught some arrows but far too many struck home. The dead and wounded fell and were trampled over by those behind them, slowed by having to scramble over them. Another eight paces and a second volley hit them. They faltered but pressed on, those with shields had fared better and formed the leading numbers now, holding them over their heads and shoulders as they saw the cloud of arrows approach.

Pushed from behind by the chasing tribes, they burst over the bridge and forged outwards to both sides as the restricting walls of the bridge released them. They reached the foot of the village wall. Two tribesmen held a shield flat, a third jumped onto it and they thrust him upwards, the shield above their heads and the third tribesman waist height to the top of the wall. He parried one blow before the sweep of a defender's sword caught him above the right ear and split his skull. He fell back to the earth as the shield was lowered for the next man.

This was repeated along the wall either side of the gate, but it took two men for a third to fight, and then on an unsure platform. The archers continued to loose arrows at the shield-holders, although it was hard to shoot downwards without leaning over the walls and exposing oneself to the attackers.

The fight was fairly brief. Of the seventy-four tribesmen of Lernbalck, less than forty had survived the archers' aim and crossed the bridge. Many of the following hundred and fifty or so of the other two tribes fell to a continued hail of arrows. The assault on the walls cost the lives of many more before a shout to fall back sounded above the other noise of battle. The tribes retreated, some running, others backing away across the bridge, shields to their front. They had discovered the men of Nisceriel could fight, or at least defend a wall.

Over ninety tribesmen lay dead or grievously wounded below the stone walls or on the bridge, and as the survivors reached the far bank, they looked back to see the gates of Gloff swing open and a least twenty men run out carrying just long knives. A roar rose from the tribesmen as they saw them pulling arrows from the bodies of their dead, and using their knives to dispatch any who were not yet dead.

Some twenty nearest the bridge ran forward, angry battle cries on their lips. They had only reached half way across when the Niscerians ran back through the gates, arms full of arrows, as another volley of sixty scythed into the angry tribesmen, killing over half. They stopped and fell back, but now their blood was really up, they would take them next time.

As they reached the far bank the gates opened again and the Niscerians emerged once more. Bocknostri jumped down from the log on which he had climbed to see better across the river, and shouted an order for Chieftains to gather in his tent. This day had not got off to a good start.

The sun had not moved much farther across the morning sky when his Sergeant called Gerlaff to the gate wall overlooking the bridge. Grenfeld and his Sergeant joined them shortly after he arrived. His Sergeant spoke to them.

"They are thinking about it this time Sir. Be very careful how you look."

Gerlaff and Grenfeld both raised their heads above the wall to see. An arrow flew close over them and they both ducked back behind the wall. They raised their heads again so their eyes were only just above the edge. Another arrow arced over them, but it would be an impossibly lucky shot that hit one of them now. The Sergeant explained the situation.

"They are coming across in nines and tens, crouching low and using the bridge walls for cover from one side and shields the other. We are hitting a few but it is a waste of arrows to volley fire at them. The few archers they have came over first. Once over they spread along the river using the bank for cover. As we rise to shoot at those crossing their archers are loosing at us. We have taken five casualties so far.

"They are building numbers under the shelter of the bank. When they have enough they will charge the wall. They have no ladders so will use the same tactic of lifting I assume, but they will have far more men at the wall this time."

As he spoke, they watched ten Whorleans crossing the bridge, five in single file each side, running in a crouch tight against the low walls, their shields outwards, protecting most of their bodies most of the time. A few arrows flew at them as they ran, one finding a mark in a man's leg just below his knee. He fell and rolled away from the wall. Four arrows killed him where he fell. Another ten men were following about a third of the bridge's length behind.

"I think they will build up to a couple of hundred before they come. We will down a fair number before they reach the walls but they have a good chance of gaining the wall somewhere. If they do, we must kill them on the rampart faster than they come over to keep them from taking the wall. Can I suggest Sir, that we take twenty archers from the south side where we have twice that many, and station them with you? If they get on the wall, the archers can take them down as they come over it, while your men reinforce mine on each side of the fight. Between us we should squeeze them back off the wall."

"That sounds excellent to me. Agreed Grenfeld?"

"Aye, it seems good sense. What happens if they really get a foothold?"

"We retreat Sir, off the walls and back to the buildings. Then we all fight, women, children, everybody, and then we all die. We have to keep them off the walls."

"Bluntly put Sergeant, but we take the point. Wey protect us gentlemen. Ready yourselves."

They moved to their positions, Gerlaff and Grenfeld at the head of twenty men each now. A few of them were too young to be there really, but they weren't going to send them away at that moment, despite their mothers' cries and shouts.

Between the two groups stood twenty archers, centred on the gates. Wherever the enemy got over the wall first, the archers would move below them and the two groups led by the Hunderts would climb the walls by the nearest ladders on either side. Gerlaff suddenly felt very afraid and it was all he could do to stand at the head of his men. Every fibre of his body screamed at him to run.

It seemed an eternity until a huge roar went up as three Tribes rose from the bank and rushed the walls. Almost forty archers volleyed into them, a couple falling to answering shots. They each got a couple more arrows away before the fighting changed to hacking at the Whorleans as they appeared at the wall.

They seemed to be holding well for a while, until one of those weird little quirks that can sometimes turn a battle, nearly turned this one. A large tribesman wielding a huge battleaxe was lifted to the wall on a shield. As he rose he swung the axe around his head. A defender arced his two handed sword at his neck and normally would have killed him before he reached wall height, but this tribesman was left handed, his axe swung from the wrong side and almost cut the defender in two. The tribesman roared and leapt onto the wall, continuing to swing his axe wildly around him.

No defender could duck under the blade nor had the speed to get inside its arc. Two more tribesmen leapt onto the wall. The axe man ceased his wild swings so as not to hit his friends and a tight hand to hand fight began. Once even a small section of wall was undefended it allowed many Whorleans to gain a foothold on its ramparts.

The first volley of arrows scythed into the tribesmen, killing many including the axe man, but more poured over the wall, which was not as high as the Niscerians' tactics needed. Gerlaff went to lead his men to his right to join those on the wall, but many of the tribesmen jumped to the ground inside the village. They had quickly realised that to stay on the wall would mean death from the volleys of arrows.

Grenfell's ladder to the wall was nearer to his left and he was already on the wall with most of his men. Gerlaff held up a hand and shouted a series of commands. His twenty men turned and charged the Whorleans who were rising from their jumps to move on the archers.

A fierce fight developed on the ground. Gerlaff found himself in a completely instinctive action. He parried blows and swung at whoever seemed nearest in the blur of steel and bodies. His sword cut deeply into at least three bodies, all of which he thought were enemy. A sword swung at his head. He raised his round shield and caught the blow but it skidded across the shield and the side of the blade cracked him across the temple. His head spun and he went down, his skin split rather than cut, from his ear to the middle of his forehead.

He couldn't clear his head. He tried to stand and found himself falling sideways and backwards. He lay still, the fight around him diminishing. The archers inside the village had cleared the wall, volley after volley of arrows decimating those that continued to come over it, and those who fought on it, allowing the defenders to close from both sides and again defend the wall completely.

The archers dropped their bows, drew their swords and rushed to help Gerlaff's old and young. Their extra numbers helped win that fight, the tribesmen being overwhelmed and finally all brought down. The Whorleans began to fall back across the bridge.

"Let them go, save your arrows," screamed Gerlaff's Sergeant, as he looked around him to assess their losses. At least forty Whorleans lay dead within the walls and as many defenders too. He saw Gerlaff struggling to stand and ran from the wall.

"Sir, you are hurt."

"A sound observation for a soldier." Gerlaff was trying to sound brave. "Did we drive them off?"

"For now Sir. If they do that again and commit all their forces, crossing the bridge while they are attacking the wall, they will get over, and they will kill us all, but they seem reluctant to attack on mass. I cannot imagine why."

"Because they have a battle to fight against our whole army, or so General Rebgroth would tell you. If he is right, they will come again, but only to cover a crossing. This was supposed to be a sideshow. They cannot fight a major action here with our army just down the road, ready to hit them immediately after. Get everyone back on the walls, I must wash this wound and try to get rid of this headache." The Sergeant looked straight into his eyes.

"Yes Sir," he said simply and smiled, before turning back for the wall, shouting to those on the ground to follow him.

Bocknostri was furious. They had lost nearly one hundred and sixty men so far, two tribes, and they hadn't even taken Gloff. He put the survivors of the three tribes under the one surviving Chieftain. Drew what a mess!

"We will have to bypass them, My King," said Drokhart. "We cannot lose more men to take a village that will fall anyway once their army is defeated."

"I know, I know," snapped Bocknostri, "It's just that I cannot believe these Drew-damned villagers could defend themselves like this."

"There are many trained soldiers amongst them Sire, that is why, which just means their main force will be all the weaker. They cannot leave the village to threaten us, so let's just get past them and prepare for tomorrow, and a real victory."

"Alright Drokhart, see to it." Bocknostri tried to think what Cregenda would have done. He smiled to himself. He probably would have bypassed Gloff completely in the first place.

Almost exactly at midday, the army of Whorle advanced across the bridge. As many archers as they could raise had crossed first, in small groups again, and positioned themselves along the bank. Their whole purpose was to keep the defending archers from inflicting too many casualties on the main army as it passed along the track between river and walls.

It was an interesting stand off, the defenders made only a token effort to pump arrows into the Whorleans, and they did not turn on the walls. They trotted over the bridge and split left and right, those turning left running right around the village walls and meeting the rest south of the village. They formed up in battle order facing the distant Niscerien camp, which had been almost completely struck by then.

There was a lot of movement from the Nisceriens. Two hundred cavalry suddenly broke away to the Whorleans left, looping well clear of them and heading north at speed. Off to recapture the ford at Teekford thought Bocknostri.

The other five hundred or so seemed to be moving away from them, retreating farther south. Bocknostri tried to think things through like Cregenda would. He was tempted to race after them before more numbers might arrive. He was still over sixteen hundred strong, and there couldn't be more than five hundred Niscerians facing them.

No, if he moved too soon those cavalry might just come back. He had to give them time to get further north, but besides all that, he had to keep all of Nisceriel looking north for one more night. Tomorrow was the day for battle. A thought did enter his head for a moment, but only a moment, were they drawing him south? Did they have another army in the south? Where would that leave Cregenda?

No, the same still applied, keep them looking north. Even a second army added to this one would not outnumber him; they didn't have enough people. Tomorrow they would have a lot less and he would rule Nisceriel too. He looked up at the sun. It was well after noon.

Just before noon, Moreton had been sitting in a small clearing, leaning against a tree, just inside the Elven Forest, and almost due east of Castle Nisceriel. The Elves had welcomed them and gladly agreed to their request to move bumbleberries to the Castle as required, rather than have the bushes there.

From the nuances of some of their conversations with the Elves, he tended to feel they were expecting the request, and that granting it was not a problem as they didn't actually expect to have to do it.

He had been restless ever since they had arrived though. He knew the future, or its most likely outcome, yet his vows forbade him from doing anything about it. In this case the long-term future was probably a good one, although the road to it was not so, and there were some huge gaps in his knowledge of how some of the most unlikely events could actually come about.

He was desperate to help, but his vows!

He looked upwards, his eyes closed, the back of his head against the tree, silently asking Wey for help. He opened his eyes to see Retalla standing in front of him. He struggled to his feet, his legs stiff from sitting too long.

"Retalla, it is rare to see you so close to the forest edge."

"I came to see you Elf-friend, and you are here."

"Indeed I am my friend." He paused for a moment but Retalla said nothing. "Why is it you sought me?"

"You are troubled and I would like to help you, perhaps to offer a little Elven logic to your thoughts."

"Ah, I see. I don't think you can help me, I only wish you could. I am desperate to do something, yet the vows of my order preclude it, as you well know."

"I know that your Order studies prophecy and the future, I know that your vows stop you doing anything to change the future you know of, but maybe I see something so simple that you will laugh at me, something so blindingly obvious it has been discounted for generations by your Order, but just perhaps, it is the sight of an outsider that can still see the wood for the trees."

Moreton looked at him quizzically then smiled.

"Please tell me my friend. I certainly will not laugh at your thoughts, I respect them too much."

Retalla turned away and took a couple of steps, half turned, paused as if gathering his thoughts. Choosing his words carefully he spoke.

"You have been of the past Elf-friend, you are of today, and both of these will have had an effect on the future. The words of your vow, as I understand them, solemnly prohibit any action that might change the predicted future, but where do they prohibit you from being a part of it, of helping it to happen. You may have knowledge of those who are to die, and must not interfere to save them, but what stops you helping those that are to live to do so. Perhaps parts of the future cannot happen unless you help them to."

Moreton stared at him in a sort of wonderment. No, it couldn't be that simple. His mentor had told him that one day a friend would help him understand a simple truth, and from that day, his training as a Weymonk would be at an end. This was that moment. He had been so caught up in what he couldn't do, he had lost sight of what he could. He was stunned for a moment, this was his true purpose in life, but suddenly his brain began to flood with thoughts of what he must do, surely he was too late now.

"Retalla, I don't know what to say. I know what I must do now, but without horses, I don't see I can reach the Castle Nisceriel in time."

"There are five fine horses within twenty paces of us Elf-friend. You see we have prophecies too, and perhaps when all this is over you may wish to come and study some of them. They have never been told to men before, but they would be safe with you." He smiled at Moreton's bewildered face. "One tells of the ride of a man priest, an Elf-friend, a ride to save four lives that shapes the future of man. I thought perhaps this might be that time."

Moreton stepped forward and hugged him. It was a completely spontaneous moment. He jumped back apologetically.

"Oh Retalla, I'm so sorry, I just can't believe I have been so blind. Please, I must leave Patrikal in your care."

"Of course, and you must go, but our prophesies also tell of four Elves who help this man priest because he is an Elf-friend, who also help to shape man's future. Ranamo and Ranor are destined to help you, as is Melarne, father of the child Patrikal saved, and Melmern, his brother. They will run with you. Go now, and your God guide you."

"I cannot thank you enough, Retalla."

"Then don't, just go." Moreton smiled at him and went. He rode each horse in turn, leading the others, to make the best time possible. The four Elves ran beside him, due west for Castle Nisceriel. They should get there some time after midnight, and Wey willing, in time.

They made steady progress all afternoon, an afternoon that dragged for Eilana. She was so tense and inwardly excited about the coming night, going over and over all eventualities with Harlmon, to the point where his temper almost flared. He had never been so ready for anything in his life.

That afternoon also saw Cregenda pacing the village of Shepst. They would not sail until early evening, as soon as the tide rose enough. His men sat around preparing their weapons and talking to villagers. A few did more than talk with a couple of the village women, who for their own pleasure, were still keen to see their duties towards these warriors thoroughly done.

Cregenda walked from the bustle of the village to a nearby wood, undoing his codpiece as he walked into the edge of the trees to relieve himself. As he stood urinating over some stinging nettles, he hated the things, a movement to his right caught his eye. A young soldier with no leggings knelt up from between the legs of a naked girl beneath him, his erection standing proudly before him. Cregenda faltered in midstream, and then continued with a laugh. It was one of his men.

"I'm sorry my boy, I didn't mean to disturb you." As he shook off the last few drips The girl raised herself onto her elbows, her breasts were magnificent.

"No my Lord, I'm sorry, I didn't hear you approaching."

"Nor I you!" he laughed again, "Do carry on." He turned out of the wood, fastening his codpiece. He decided he was getting old, in the mind if not in the body, a year ago he would have just joined in; it must be weight of command. With a big grin on his face he walked back into the village.

Bocknostri too was frustrated that afternoon. He moved his army steadily and slowly south, just keeping the Niscerians in sight. They seemed to stop, but then he saw they were moving east, towards the hills.

When they reached the spot where the Niscerians had turned inland he saw the small river Stroue. The Niscerians had moved upstream, although they could have crossed here. He called his Chieftains to him.

He ordered them to make camp there for the night. They would move inland in the morning and force a battle, but it was essential they sent out fighting patrols that night. Only a small number, but they must be seen to be active in the early watch. The men were to be told he wanted prisoners to question.

His Chieftains had learnt not to question their King, so each tribe prepared to send a patrol of six men out after midnight, but long before they set out, a column of men were spotted in the fading light, moving south from Gloff. For a while Bocknostri was concerned it was the defenders from the village on a suicide attack, he had heard of stranger things, but it turned out to be the two Tribes he had sent to Teekford. They had crossed unopposed so felt they would be of more use back with the main force. Bocknostri was delighted to have them back, they made up in numbers for those lost at Gloff, but he was disturbed that they had not met the cavalry that had disappeared northwards just after noon.

The Chieftain that had led the force told him they had seen no cavalry. They had hugged the riverbank all the way down, so it was just possible that if the cavalry were moving north at speed, inland and close to the forest edge, they could have missed each other. It seemed the only explanation, but of course, it wasn't.

Chapter 34

Whilst Bocknostri was laying out his camp, Cregenda was giving his men a final briefing. It was essential everyone knew exactly what was expected of them. He had described their boat journey, landing, advance to the Castle and entrance, in detail.

"When we are inside, Fenlon will lead us to the Royal quarters. Kill every man you see, soldier or servant, and when you have time, have your will with every and any woman you find; such was our oath to those that died on our last visit to Nisceriel. Remember though, whatever sort of animals they think we are, we are soldiers of Whorle. If I see any woman or child wounded or killed, I will personally execute any one of you that does so."

He walked towards the boat then turned to face them once more.

"Whatever happens over there, I need every one of you to give his all. We just have to be tougher than them, and as men of Whorle we are all that. They will tell our tale in meeting halls for years to come. Do you follow me to glory then?"

They cheered him, all thirty-six. Even Fenlon was swept along with the emotion, although he had not understood what was said. He had learnt a few words of Whorlean, but not nearly enough to follow Cregenda's speech.

They boarded the boat, spreading themselves around it. As pre-arranged, six sturdy tribesmen placed themselves on the central cross benches and took up an oar each. The bow of the boat rested on the mud flat beside the jetty, not quite enough water beneath her to float free.

A semi-circle of villagers stood around the jetty to wave them away, a few of the women more than sorry to see them go. Three of the old men moved forward and pushed the bow off, sending them backwards out into the river. Fenlon ordered those to his right to row and she turned to face downstream, stopping her backward movement.

At his orders they all rowed in relative unison, moving their craft towards the Drei's mouth and out into the Number. The Drei's deep flow, combined with the rock headland to their left, pushed the Number's own current diagonally across the estuary, to where the Ffon's waters opposite eventually turned the current tight along the shore from Ffonhaven.

All this flow now fought the incoming tide, making it a very uncomfortable crossing. The boat was deep in the water and the waves sprayed inboard, keeping them wet and cold in the breeze. They rowed across, Fenlon being afraid to risk his limited skills on sails with such a heavy and important load.

The current wanted to push them down the estuary, and they rowed diagonally upstream to move directly across. The tide was beginning to flood hard, but the cooler and heavier salt water was pushing its way in deep, the warmer fresh water seemingly running over it in the opposite direction. It all led to small but fierce maelstroms in places, the surface seeming to boil.

Fenlon wound his way around them until he felt the tide pushing them up the estuary. They were in much shallower water now, over the sandbanks that were exposed when the tide was out. There was no current to fight here and the tide helped them back upstream towards the lights of the jetties and the craft tied up there.

Cregenda thought it odd that there should be so many lights in a small area in time of war. He voiced his thoughts to Gragonor who translated them to Fenlon. He laughed and replied that the Niscerians knew only too well how poor Whorleans were on water and would never expect an attack from the river. The truth was Harlmon wanted to be sure Fenlon had his bearings to guide them in successfully. Cregenda was right to worry, but then he usually was.

It was getting very dark now. The clear skies of the day were clouding over. Cregenda quietly asked Drew to keep the rain away. It did not matter to him, in fact it might even help them, keeping evening walkers that might spot them indoors. He was thinking of the battle the next day. There was nothing worse than fighting in the rain, thousands of feet in muddy ground, mud caking into wounds, blood and gore in every puddle. If it did rain later tonight or tomorrow he would regret missing the battle a little less.

Fenlon steered them just south of the lights. They should come ashore a couple of fields below the jetties. If he judged it right, there was a small stream that flowed weakly out into the Number that meant there was slightly deeper water, which in turn meant they would ground the boat a bit further in.

By pure luck, Fenlon brought them in so that they actually entered the mouth of the stream, grounding and wading ashore on a stoney bottom rather than the mudflats they expected. It left them wet but much more comfortable than with a coating of mud.

Once ashore, Fenlon led them inland along the edge of the stream before turning north. He paused at the edge of the main track from the jetties to the Castle, hidden in the thorn bushes. He waited for the raiding party to close up. Not a word had been spoken since they stepped ashore, and none were now.

Cregenda nodded in the darkness, they were all there. It would be all too easy to lose a few. All it needed was a lapse in concentration for the man in front to disappear in the darkness and they could lose any number of men. The road seemed clear. There were certainly no lights on it in either direction. Fenlon moved across with the five men nearest him and dissolved into a thorn thicket on the other side. In their prearranged groups, they all crossed, looking both ways constantly.

Once over, Fenlon led them north again for no more than fifty paces until he came to the larger stream that flowed from the Castle moat to the jetties. He couldn't quite believe he had got them this far with such relative ease. Perhaps all would be well, provided Harlmon was ready.

He need not have worried. Harlmon knew by now they were ashore and all was ready within the Castle. The servants and Castle folk knew nothing of his plans of course, but at the right moment, Cregenda's raiders would be shocked to meet a Hundert of Bluecoats, ready to greet them.

Eilana had summoned Serculas to her rooms and they had taken the young Prince Gudfel and Rebetha to the observation room at the top of the east tower, ostensibly to look at the stars, but it was so cloudy it was a waste of time. She persuaded Serculas to stay there to give the children a change of scene for the night. It would seem such a lucky break in the morning. Her sister Eival and her other handmaiden, Ereyna, were with them too.

Prince Gudrick was in his room with Harlada in the central Keep. She was sure Harlada would be alright. There was a risk, but she had been assured Whorleans did not kill children. He was her eldest son and would understand it all when she explained afterwards. She would make him a Prince, let him run the Council with her, but for now she had to be sure Serculas was deceived convincingly. It was her that Rebgroth would believe afterwards. She had sent Bradett on a fool's errand to Ffonhaven to get him out of the way. He would accept anything she said.

Moreton was bone weary, his legs almost numb in the saddle. How his Elven companions kept the pace for so long he would never understand, but they were there, running beside him still. It had to be midnight or more, not far now.

Fenlon stopped at the moat. They would all get very wet now, soaked in fact, but it was the only way in. The raiders gathered behind him. He looked up at the windows in the west tower and walls. There was light at a few windows. He hoped no one was watching him that shouldn't be. No one was, but Harlmon grinned silently to himself as he watched Fenlon wade into the moat, followed by the rest of the raiders.

As they approached the wall, Cregenda realised that what he had thought a shadow was the top of an arch that raised itself no more than a forearm above the water. Fenlon turned his head towards him and grimaced. He nodded and Fenlon walked into the hidden opening, just his head in the air at the top of the arch. The others followed in single file.

The floor began to rise under their feet, making them walk in a steadily more crouched stance until the top of the arch started to rise too. By the time they were only waist deep in water they had reached a large iron grille. It seemed rusty yet solid, but only to look at. Fenlon took the right hand end with two Tribesmen. They lifted with him and pushed. The whole thing swung forward, leaving just enough room to squeeze through.

Knee deep in water, they were inside. Cregenda put a hand on Fenlon's shoulder and squeezed a well done, remaining silent. Growing steadily in confidence, Fenlon smiled and led them dripping into the wine cellars he knew so well. He heard the scrape of steel on steel as the raiders drew their swords from their scabbards. They had nothing dry to wipe them on.

Fenlon was delighted they had drawn them, for as they rounded a corner his old wine master stood before him.

"You!" was all he had time to say before a tribesman stepped past Fenlon and drove his sword right through the man. Blood welled out of his mouth and nose, making him cough as he died. A foot in the belly and a shove drew the sword out of him as he crumpled to the ground. Fenlon felt himself smile. He should have felt sick but he hated the man. Perhaps this Whorlean culture was catching. He stepped over him and led them on.

They met two more of Fenlon's fellow workers, who died just as quickly, before they reached the kitchens, but here there was mayhem. Two footmen died before they realised what was happening. Women screamed; cooks. Fenlon and Gragonor shouted for silence or death. They lined the three women up by the central table, two captured footmen with swords to their throats beside them. Cregenda ordered a third Whorlean forward.

"Find somewhere to lock the women up when you're finished with them then follow us on." He turned away after Fenlon. The women let out stifled screams as the two footmen died, swords plunged into their throats.

Turning towards the three cooks the Whorleans fumbled at their codpieces, their swords held towards the women. The women's reactions were mixed. The one in the middle just screamed silently to herself, convinced she was going to die whatever happened next. The other two felt a sense of relief that they might at least survive rape, although both were terrified.

The tribesmen threw them back across the huge central table, tearing their skirts and underskirts away. As they entered them roughly and laughing, they failed to hear the key turn on the inside of a larder room across the kitchen. An Eleven of Bluecoats fell on them from behind. One tribesman managed to turn and parry a blow before he was almost decapitated, his genitals grotesquely hanging from his codpiece.

The others died first whilst still inside their cooks, cut down from behind. The women began to raise themselves from the table, their tears of fear turning to tears of relief, but before they could say thank you, the Bluecoats nearest to them drove their swords into their chests, killing them instantly. They had their orders.

Now they were to guard this passageway in case any Whorleans tried to fight their way out this way. The story was that they had found these tribesmen slaughtering the cooks after raping them and dispatched them after a brief fight. They scattered some furniture and a few more pots and pans around to add to the effect, then settled down to wait for any further action.

From the kitchens, the raiders moved up through the servants' quarters, above the kitchens and below the west tower at the back of the Keep. They came across a number of men and women, who panicked and ran in all directions. They killed most of the men and rounded up many of the women, but some got away. A single bell began to ring out loudly, soon to be joined by another further away. Cregenda spoke.

"They know we are here now so we can expect company. Lock those women in a room; we'll be back for them." He called to Gragonor. "Tell Fenlon to head straight for the Royal Quarters, the shortest route."

Gragonor repeated the order to Fenlon and he led them into the main entrance hallway of the Keep. A dozen Bluecoats stood at the foot of the large curving staircase that led up to the Royal rooms. As one, the tribesmen charged at the Bluecoats, who fought a rearguard action, backing up the stairs. Two of them died carrying out Harlmon's orders, letting themselves be driven back up the stairs, past the Queen's quarters in the west tower, past Serculas' and Rebgroth's rooms, and past the doors to Prince Gudrick's and Harlada's room.

The tribesmen fought their way steadily upward, losing only one man. At the door to the Queen's rooms Cregenda waved three men to the doors. They burst through the anteroom and into the central living room. They didn't know whose rooms they were, but it was obvious they belonged to someone of Royal standing.

Queen Bertal was saved by her weak bladder. She had just stood up from the commode behind a large embroidered tapestry screen that ran across the rear corner of the room, when the tribesmen burst in. She almost stormed out from behind it to demand to know who dared violate her privacy, when she heard the alarm bell ringing through the open door and froze, looking through the tiny gap between tapestry and its upright frame.

She saw the three Whorleans, clad mainly in wet leather, swords and shields at the ready. They saw Allaner rising from the chair where she had been sitting, fear on her face. It turned to terror as the tribesmen grinned at each other and grabbed her, throwing her backwards onto the table. Two held her arms as the third threw her skirts up over her body and ripped the underskirts away from her kicking legs. He forced his way between them and raped her as his comrades held her and laughed.

She fought and struggled until he had finished, she would not stop resisting, much to his delight. He jumped back from her kicks, laughing and tying his codpiece before retrieving his sword and shield and calling his comrades out, telling them the next women were theirs.

Bertal had watched in horror, but she had done nothing. Her mind reeled with guilt. She should have done something, but had she, she would have suffered the same as Allaner.

The tribesmen caught up with Cregenda and the others at the top of the stairs. Some thirty Bluecoats appeared in the hallway below. They came up the stairs behind them them, passing the doors to Queen Bertal's rooms. Harlmon led four Bluecoats through them. Bertal had not moved in her shame. Allaner still lying back on the table, trying to push herself up on her elbows, her skirts still up around her waist, naked and exposed from her hips down.

Harlmon rushed forward his sword raised over his right shoulder. He brought it down on Allaner's head, splitting her skull almost in half. He ripped the sword from her and she fell backwards. His men looked on as he laid the flat of his sword on her stomach, wiping off blood and gore across the hairs at its base. He was suddenly very obviously aroused, but he turned and led his men back to the stairs. Perhaps he would come back later while she was still warm.

Bertal was now in shock. She couldn't believe what she had just seen. She quietly opened the door onto the rear servants' stairs. She heard Niscerien voices below and moved in the opposite direction, ducking into an alcove opposite as she thought she heard someone approaching. She still couldn't comprehend what was happening.

The next rooms, Rebgroth's, were empty when the tribesmen broke in.

The sound of the bell had woken Badraman. Being Prince Gudrick's and Harlada's tutor and mentor in all things, he had been left behind, much against his will, as the Prince's official bodyguard. He jumped up, grabbed his sword and shield, and ran to the boys' room, arriving as the retreating Bluecoats backed towards him. He shut the door behind him, turning to see the boys dressed and armed. He smiled grimly.

"Well my boys, now we will see how well I've taught you." He faced the door and waited for it to burst open. It did, and five tribesmen pushed in.

The first died instantly, a cut from Badraman opening his throat, before the real fight started. Badraman fought with all his skills and downed a second before a thrust slid under his shield and cut through his ribs. He tried to ignore the pain, hacking at a tribesman. He couldn't face them all.

The tribesmen fended off the attacks from Gudrick and Harlada. These were still children, just, and Cregenda's orders were explicit, not to wound or kill women or children. Not even animals would do that.

Two more tribesmen, one of them Cregenda, entered at the sounds of swordplay, and soon a second sword hacked downwards through Badraman's right collarbone. He couldn't raise his sword to parry the blow that killed him. He sank to his knees and collapsed backwards. Gudrick dropped beside him, kneeling over him, sobbing. Harlada jumped astride his body, sword and shield raised to the tribesmen. Cregenda spoke to the others.

"This boy acts like a man, he deserves to live. Honour to you my brave."

"Honour!" the others echoed and they all returned to the fight outside. The tribesmen were being pushed back along the hallway, not far short of the King's rooms, and then Eilana's, but both were empty.

The numbers of Bluecoats had now increased at both ends of the balcony that formed the hallway along the Royal Quarters. Cregenda realised they were trapped and beginning to get squeezed. He counted roughly. There must be at least thirty at each end, to his twenty or so still alive in the middle. There shouldn't have been that many guards in the Castle, let alone Bluecoats. He looked for Fenlon.

Fenlon had seen Harlmon come out of the Queen's rooms and rejoin the push past Rebgroth's doors towards Gudrick's. He ran towards Harlmon shouting, thanking Wey he was there to save him. Harlmon saw him coming and at the last moment lifted the point of his sword to chest height. It took little pressure from him as Fenlon's own momentum impaled him on Harlmon's blade. It penetrated between his ribs, killing him almost instantly. He lived just long enough to die with a look of utter bewilderment on his face.

Harlmon spat on his body and led five men into the boys' room. Harlada still stood protectively before Badraman's body and the now sobbing Gudrick. Harlmon took in the two tribesmen's bodies and Badraman. Blood seemed to have spread everywhere.

"Perfect," he said, "now move aside Harlada." He pushed him out of his way and suddenly swung his sword at waist height. It sliced through Gudrick's neck before he saw it coming. His head span across the room, his body kneeling upright for a moment pumping blood into the air before it crumpled on top of Badraman's. The sword cut through a woven necklace too, and a brightly polished and intricately carved wooden medallion looped across the room and hit Harlada in the chest, dropping into his hand. It felt hot in his palm.

"What have you done," he screamed, hurling himself at Harlmon.

Harlmon parried his thrust with his sword and caught Harlada's wrist with his other hand. Another Bluecoat ripped the boy's sword away.

"Calm down you little fool, by tonight your brother will be King, and you and I, Princes."

"You killed Gudrick you bastard, I'll kill you for that, mother will help me."

"Your mother ordered it you idiot." Harlada froze for a moment, his childhood and naivety melting into the past, the reality of what had happened becoming dreadfully clear to him. He wriggled out of Harlmon's grasp and moved across the room to where Gudrick's head lay, its sightless eyes staring at him. The wooden medallion in his hand grew so hot it was painful to hold, but he gripped it firmly. Only then did he feel the silver coin on the chain around his neck burning his chest.

343

He knelt on one knee and gripped Gudrick's head by the hair, closing the vacant eyes gently. A distant memory came back to him, a voice saying 'This will tell the Water Gods that you are a friend of the Marsh People. They will treat you as such and you will live with our heros. He pushed the medallion into Gudrick's mouth and stood up, turning to face Harlmon. He stared coldly into his eyes.

"I will kill you for what you have done this day Harlmon. As Wey is my judge I will avenge my friend. So kill me now Uncle, or let me live knowing I will bring you death. I will hold your head in my hand and see the rest of your body lying at my feet." The coin went cold against his skin.

Harlmon laughed at him, looking around at the other Bluecoats who joined him, but for once in his life a strange fear made his stomach flutter before his confidence returned.

Harlada moved calmly towards the door to the rear stairs. He opened it and stepped through. Young man or not, tears streamed down his cheeks.

"Let him go till he sees some sense," ordered Harlmon, "he can't go far that way." They returned to the hallway where the fight had intensified.

Cregenda's men had been boxed. They were killing Bluecoats but were dying themselves, and at too fast a rate to win. Their defence centred on the entrance to the King's rooms. The doors were locked. His sword tore through pale blue cloth and on through its wearer's chest. He ripped it away, deflecting a thrust with his shield and stepping back.

Gragonor stood between the fighting lines; he was never any good in a fight. He was great with words but not with a sword. Cregenda looked past him, seven alive on that side, eight on this including himself. When they were down to four each side they would not be able to hold a line across the balcony hallway.

"Get that door open you hopeless cretin." Gragonor looked at him with terrified eyes. "Do it man!" It was as if Gragonor suddenly woke from a dream. He turned his shoulder against the doors to the King's antechamber. He picked up a sword from a dead hand and forced it between them, just above the lock. He pushed sideways. The blade bent but didn't break. He did it again and again until wood began to split, a little at first until it split away from one door. They burst apart.

Cregenda shouted orders and his men quickly broke away back to the door and into the anteroom. The twelve of them were only defending one line now, and only five could fight at a time, filling the width of the room. Cregenda's second in command stood beside him, behind the fighting line.

"Try and get out my Lord," he panted, blood running down his face from a wound on his forehead. "Take that hopeless sod with you and get out. Someone needs to tell our story my Lord. We can hold them here for a while I think."

Gragonor was working on the doors behind. They opened far more easily, swinging into the large King's living room and bedroom beyond.

"Go my Lord, please, for all of us." Cregenda clapped a hand on the man's shoulder and stepped into the King's rooms, shutting the doors behind him. He couldn't believe he had done it. His every fibre told him to fight and die with his men, but something made him go, he wasn't destined to die there, he felt it somehow.

Gragonor jammed a chair back under the handles of the doors. They hadn't long. Just as Cregenda spotted the single door on the other side of the room, it opened inwards.

Harlada slammed the door to his room shut behind him, and stood in the dim light of the service corridor. He leant against the wall for a moment or two. He heard voices down the stairs away to his left and without thinking moved slowly and quietly away from them. He was trying to think where to go, where to hide, or where to run. A shadow jumped out and grabbed him, pulling him into an alcove and beating him with weak fists.

"You little bastard." It was a woman's voice. "That evil scum of an uncle of yours killed Allaner." It was Bertal! The fists thumped down on him but they were not effective. He spun away.

"For Wey's sake stop it, the Bluecoats will hear you," he hissed.

"And why would that worry you, you little rat?"

"Because Harlmon has just killed Gudrick too. Hacked his head clean off!" Bertal gasped, and sank slowly to her knees staring at him. Her head fell forward and she began to shake with sobs. He hadn't thought that he was telling a mother of her son's death.

"I'm sorry. He was my best friend. My uncle killed him and my mother ordered it done. I hate them both for it. They will kill you too if they find you, we have to get out of here." He realised he gripped her shoulders as he whispered at her.

"Why should you help me? You're her child."

"No longer. I swear on Gudrick's soul I will avenge him. I swear on my life, I will kill Harlmon for murdering him, but I can only do that if we get out of here alive now. There are Bluecoats everywhere. They were ready for the Whorleans, they must have been."

Bertal was staring at him. She seemed almost in a trance for a moment. It felt as if she was looking through him. She wasn't, but she saw something, a vision of him, a dream she had not understood at the time now rushed back into her mind.

"Wey help me, it was you!" He stood before her, puzzled by her words. "I will help you, for you will more than avenge my Gudrick. We will get out of here. Come, there is a way."

She led him along the passage to the rear door of the King's rooms. He followed her through it, shutting it behind him. Bertal screamed and he spun around to see Cregenda and Gragonor on the other side of the room, blood dripping from the sword Cregenda held. Harlada recognised him as one of those who had killed Badraman. He had no sword himself now, but he stood in front of Bertal.

"Honour to you my brave." Gragonor translated Cregenda's words without thinking. "Have no fear; we do not harm children nor kill women. Where is your friend?"

"Killed by the Bluecoats, who seek us now," replied Harlada. "They murdered Queen Bertal's Lady in Waiting too." It was a strange conversation, delayed by Gragonor's interjections between each sentence.

"We seem strange allies then, having a common enemy," Cregenda laughed. "Such irony, the civilised nation that kills women and children, but I fear we will not live to take revenge on them."

"We will live. There is a way out, from this room." Bertal had spoken this time. "Only the King and I know of it. I would have told Gudrick when he reached his Sire's day." Tears welled in her eyes. She visibly drew herself up. "Over here."

She walked to the huge fireplace, looked round at them, then stepped into it and pushed the wall on its left side. The stone swung back easily, a counter-weighted door. She smiled and stepped through.

"Bring a torch," she ordered. Harlada took one from the wall and lit it with the flint on the mantelpiece. They all stepped through and Cregenda pushed the stone door shut. To those searching later, they had just disappeared.

Moments after, twenty-two Bluecoats burst through the rear door and ran across the room. They pulled the chair away and opened the doors to the anteroom, attacking the seven tribesmen still fighting for their lives from behind. They died quickly, but they died knowing Cregenda was not in the King's room.

Harlmon stood in the hallway looking at the bodies strewn across the anteroom floor. Some seemed unmarked, clothing stained with blood perhaps, but others were horribly mutilated, in bits even. Many had grotesque head or neck wounds. There was no doubt swords were unsubtle weapons. Far too many wore light blue coats.

"Find Queen Bertal and bring her here," he ordered, "alive or dead, and Harlada too, but do not harm him." He looked up and down the balcony hallway. Bodies were scattered along it too, in both directions. Fenlon had led thirty-six Whorlean tribesmen into the Castle. Three were dead in the kitchens he had been told, that meant thirty-three had reached here. Harlmon shook his head slowly, there had to be nearly fifty Bluecoat dead along the landing and in the anteroom, half his highly trained Hundert. They were tough these tribesmen. Rebgroth was right to fight them with guile; they would lose a straight fight he felt sure.

Bertal came back into his mind, he was so angry she was not yet dead. Why hadn't she been in her rooms with Allaner? Allaner, he had forgotten about her.

"I am going to search the Queen's rooms again. Call me there when you find her." He walked down the hallway, rather awkwardly stepping over bodies. "And start clearing these bodies, I want a count of our losses too, Bluecoats and servants. If the Lady Eilana asks I will be with her in half a quarter or so." Allaner came back into his mind and he hurried towards the Queen's rooms.

Chapter 35

Moreton tied the last set of reins to a bush in a heavy thicket, half a field from the gates of Castle Nisceriel. Four Elves were crouched by the road, watching the arched entrance. Its large studded gates were opened inwards across the drawbridge, which was still down. If under siege it would be raised, the gates closed and barred behind it, and an iron portcullis lowered inside that, but thankfully all seemed normal.

It was quiet now, but when they had arrived they could hear a considerable fight raging inside the Castle; inside the Keep in fact.

"I had better go in and see who I can find. If you can move up unseen nearer the gates, I may well need your help if I get back out."

"If it helps you Elf-friend, our prophecy tells of men rising from the ground surrounded by horses. It may mean something to you." Moreton smiled at Ranor.

"It does indeed; at least I know where I should go first." He walked stiffly up the road towards the gates thinking back many years when Gudmon had taken him through a secret tunnel that led from the King's rooms to the Royal stables. It had been built into the Castle when it was first erected and was known only to the immediate Royal family. Bertal and Gudmon knew of it, Gudrick should not yet but might, otherwise only he did. Gudmon and he had played a trick on Greardel once, pretending at magic, a stupid adolescent trick that needed the tunnel. It was one of Gudmon's better ones, but it entailed letting Moreton in on the secret, with vows of silence of course.

Moreton crossed the drawbridge and was challenged by one of four Bluecoat guards at the gates.

"Do you not recognise me, fool? I am Moreton and should be known to you." The Bluecoat looked at Moreton's maroon habit in the flickering torchlight.

"You had better wait here whilst I report your arrival; there is trouble in the Keep; raiders."

"Go and do as you like, but I have walked all day and half the night. I will not stand around waiting. I will be in the Ale House on the square." He stormed off confidently, up the street towards the square. A moment later a Bluecoat ran past him.

The streets were full of people, even though it was half way between midnight and dawn. The sounds of battle from within the Keep had woken them from their sleep and brought them out.

Stories were spreading from servants, footmen and chambermaids, cooks and others, who had run from the fighting. They told of rape and murder, and now of a fight won. The Prince was dead, the Queen too. The Whorlean animals had raped then killed many women, including the Queen and her Lady in Waiting. They had murdered Prince Gudrick in cold blood, cut off his head, they said. Luckily the Lady Eilana and Prince Gudfel were safe. That did not surprise Moreton in the least.

He pushed his way through the crowds, towards the Royal Stables. They were dark and deserted except for a dozen or so horses. He would need to make sure they were not here when they left. If he got out of the Castle, the only mounted pursuit could come from the Third of Bluecoat cavalry based at their quarters near Castlebury. He could do without them being reached by horse. If they had to be raised by foot it would give them more time.

He walked amongst them, untying any that were tethered and unlocking stable doors of others. He would drive them out when he was ready. If he got them to turn left out of the stables side door, it was a straight run to the gates.

The Bluecoat guard from the gates ran into the Keep, crossing the hallway and asking for Officer Harlmon. He was sent up the staircase to where a Sergeant was supervising the clear up.

"What is it man?" he asked curtly. His pale blue uniform was spattered with blood and gore. He wasn't enjoying his work.

"I have come to report Sergeant; the Weymonk Moreton has just entered the Castle. He would wait in the Ale House he said."

"And you let him?"

"Standing orders are he speaks for the King, Sergeant. I thought Officer Harlmon should know immediately."

"So he should my boy, you are quite right, but I don't think this is the exact moment to disturb him. He is with the Lady Allaner I think." The guard looked puzzled for a moment.

"But I thought she w......"

"Don't ask boy, go back to the gates, I will tell him the moment he comes out." The guard turned and trotted back down the stairs, convinced they were all mad in there. He had only been in the Bluecoats for a season and still felt new to their culture. They all worshipped Officer Harlmon. He just thought he was sick.

In the stables there was a scraping noise from the floor, near the wall beyond the well where Gratax had died. It turned into a grind of stone on stone. A large flagstone was moving a little, being pushed up from below, but dirt and gravel had filled the cracks around it and made it very tight.

Moreton looked around him. His eye caught a large hay rake leaning against the wall. He grabbed it and ran to the flagstone. It was moving still, raising a finger or so then dropping back into place. The next time it rose he jammed the prongs of the fork into the widest crack along the edge of the flag. It didn't drop back. It moved up a little and again he pushed the prongs down, but this time he pulled back on the handle, not quite enough. He pushed down again.

The tips of the fork prongs were now past the bottom of the flagstone. When he leant back this time they levered the stone up on one side, a large black crack open along its side. The stone pivotted back suddenly and a large Whorlean climbed out nimbly, his sword in hand. Moreton held a hand up to him.

"Who ever you are fellow, we are not enemies." Cregenda moved sideways away from the hole, sword still pointing at him. Harlada climbed out next.

"Moreton!" he cried, "What are you... You're not something to do with all this are you?"

"I am here to help you boy, but I am not sure your friend here appreciates that."

A noise made him spin round and a Bluecoat launched himself at him, charging across the stable, sword above his head. It was the guard from the gate. Hurrying back he passed the stable and had caught a movement inside. He looked in to see Moreton and the Whorlean and luckily for them, had reacted before he thought. His inexperience cost him his life.

Moreton swung the rake up and lunged at him. He hadn't realised Moreton was armed at all. The long handle of the fork meant Moreton drove its prongs deep into the Bluecoat's belly before he was near enough to strike at him. He screamed in agony as Moreton fended him off, swinging him round by bracing against the handle and using the guard's own momentum to take him past. The guard's screams were cut short by Cregenda's sword in his throat. He lay dead at his feet. Cregenda seemed much more comfortable about Moreton now. Any Bluecoat enemy was his friend.

Harlada turned and helped Bertal from the hole. He pulled her up as Gragonor pushed. She stood and straightened her skirts unconsciously.

"I heard you say you are here to help us Moreton. Is that true?"

"It is My Lady. A very unlikely four I must say, but I am delighted the rumours of your death are untrue, Ma'am"

"They would not be untrue, were it up to Harlmon. He has murdered Gudrick and Allaner. What is this about, Moreton?"

"I believe it is a plot Ma'am, planned by Eilana. They lured the Whorleans here so they could murder Gudrick and yourself and blame it on them. They will be searching for you now. They must find you and kill you soon if they are to blame it on the Whorleans, that is why they are already saying you are dead. By noon they will be proclaiming Gudfel as King of Nisceriel."

"But Gudmon?"

"Will be dead by now or tonight some time soon."

"Can we do nothing to warn him?"

"It is far too late I'm afraid, and just now we must concentrate on getting away from here alive ourselves. You are the interpreter aren't you?" He said, turning towards Gragonor, who nodded vigorously. "I knew you weren't dead. Did Fenlon lead you here?" He nodded again.

He issued a string of instructions. Gragonor translated. Cregenda put the flagstone back in place and spread straw over it again. Harlada opened the side doors and went out to the right, to turn the horses left. He had asked why they didn't ride out. All Moreton had said was that he would see.

Cregenda, Gragonor, Bertal and Moreton, all began to drive the horses out of the stables, Cregenda and Moreton waving burning torches behind them. They lobbed the torches into the piles of straw on each side of the stables and hurried down the street, as fast as Bertal could manage. Their way was clear as people had jumped aside to avoid the stampeding horses.

The horses reached the gates just as three guards rushed out of the

351

guardroom on hearing galloping hooves approaching. They jumped back out of the road, knowing they had no hope of turning a dozen or so horses. After they had passed, the three guards ran out after them, over the drawbridge, trying to catch any that slowed once out of the Castle.

The five fugitives reached the unguarded gates just in time to see three shadows rise up behind the guards and open their throats. A fourth shadow was leading five saddled horses up the road.

"Elves!" said Harlada, awe in his voice.

"Elves indeed my boy, and sworn to help us. Now you see why we didn't ride out." They moved on across the drawbridge, the street behind them starting to fill with people again. A few came to the gates and watched a strange group on the road outside. It was hard to see in the darkness, but they looked an odd bunch.

Moreton helped Bertal into her saddle. The two tribesmen stood on the roadside and stared at the horses. Neither of them had ever ridden a horse before, and they just didn't know where to start.

"Just climb on the damn things," shouted Moreton, "we don't have time for this." He helped push them up and on. He gave Gragonor's reins to Harlada and took Cregenda's himself. They rode quickly away, due south to start with, Moreton and Harlada leading the Whorleans' mounts. They would have to skirt Castlebury, but then they could stay on the road to the Bridgebury fork, which they would take. The tribesmen hung on grimly, astonished by the Elves running alongside.

Far to the north, the Niscerien army was camped not far from the Stroue Valley, on the banks of its river. The camp itself was relatively quiet. There were always those moving about the night before a battle. Some men could sleep, but many could not, on what they felt could be their last night in this world. They tended to wander about, or gather around fires with others who felt the same, anything to make the time pass more quickly.

All was not quiet around the outside of the camp though. Tamorther had carefully placed an outer ring of picket guards, and they had seen a lot of action that night, all after midnight. They were plagued with small aggressive Whorlean patrols. They had probed and skirmished with the Nisceriens half the night, but only one group penetrated as far as the inner guards at the camp perimeter, and were swiftly dealt with.

Rebgroth found Tamorther on the north side of the camp, with the perimeter guards.

"Are they still coming?" he asked. Tamorther shook his head.

"I think they have had enough. They seemed intent on snatching a prisoner or two. I am pretty sure they failed, but we can't be sure yet. One group got through to here." He pointed at two bodies lying a few paces beyond the edge of the camp, "but I don't think any others did."

"Well done, Tam. Try and get some rest before dawn, set an Officer of the Watch."

"Already done, Sir, I just needed to satisfy myself all was quiet now."

"Good man." Rebgroth walked back into the camp. He needed some rest himself. King Gudmon had wanted to go over the battle plans in detail, 'in case anything happens to you, General'. A lot of good he would be, Tamorther would take over seamlessly if something did.

The King had retired and Rebgroth set out for a final tour of the camp. It was mainly for morale purposes, his soldiers' and his own, but now rest was needed.

Gudmon had fallen into a deep sleep very quickly. All the fresh air and riding about all day had worn him out. Greardel had seen him settled before leaving the relatively small, but comfortable, Royal tent.

Now, however, Greardel crept back in, a long Whorlean blade in his hand. It had been taken from the body of a tribesman outside Castle Nisceriel by a Bluecoat after Bocknostri's first experience of cavalry. It was almost a forearm long, but it was thin, almost like a wool needle. It had a small crossed finger guard below a bound wooden handle, again thin but strong.

He trod carefully and lightly across the grass floor of the tent. He had to stoop a little under its edge as he neared the pallet bed where Gudmon slept. He lay on his back, a light linen bed shirt visible above the edge of a wool blanket, which ended across his stomach.

Greardel had waited for this moment for years, never having had the opportunity to do what he dreamt of and be able to get away with it. Eilana had given him that opportunity, and the promise of a position of power thereafter.

He held the point of the knife just below Gudmon's breastbone and smiled at his sleeping face.

"I'm sorry you won't know who did this," he hissed between his teeth, then he drove the blade deep through Gudmon's chest. Blood pumped around the blade for a moment only.

Gudmon's eyes shot open, as did his mouth, but they were instantly glazed. Greardel hoped there might have been the shortest moment of recognition. Air sighed from Gudmon's dead mouth as his lungs emptied, and an increasing smell told Greardel his bowels had too. He crept quietly and elated from the tent, leaving behind the Whorlean blade, its handle in the centre of Gudmon's chest, its point just protruding from his back and piercing the mattress on which he lay. There was surprisingly little blood.

Harlmon was beside himself with fury. His Second Sergeant trembled with fear as much as Harlmon did with anger.

"Moreton was in the Castle and nobody told me! Tell me you weren't that stupid."

"Sir, you were uh, searching Queen Bertal's rooms Sir, and I thought it best not to disturb you."

Harlmon glared at him for what seemed an age, in total silence. His instinct was to cut this imbecile's throat, but then if he had interrupted him, he probably would have killed him for doing so. He was doubly angry. He was angry with the situation, but he was angrier with himself. His desires grew more extreme, yet he was still not satisfied, not happy, frustrated that he could not find comfort. His perversion with Allaner had left his body spent but his mind even more frustrated. The thought had been exciting, the deed not so, and he felt sure this Sergeant knew what he had been doing. He didn't blame him for not interrupting.

"So where is he now?"

"We don't know Sir. He was supposed to be in the Ale House but he wasn't when we checked........There is worse Sir."

"You may not live long if it gets much worse."

"Sir, please, I did not tell you sooner because I thought you would not wish to be interrupted in your.....search, but none of the rest was within my control Sir, not even men of my Third's."

"Alright Sergeant tell me, but someone may not live through this night!"

"Somebody drove the horses from the stables and set it alight. It is still burning. The fire has been contained within the stable buildings, but parts of the blacksmith's and cooper's workshops are burning too."

"And?"

"And the four Bluecoat guards stationed at the main gate are dead or missing Sir. Three of them were found dead near the road outside the gates. The one who came to report here is missing still. According to the gate log he did not return from here. A party of people were seen mounting horses outside the gate. Only five were on horseback, the rest on foot. Sir, I only tell you what the witnesses say, but they say that those on foot were dressed as Elves."

To the Sergeant's astonishment Harlmon started to laugh. He turned and started down the stairs before shouting an order over his shoulder.

"If it involved Moreton you may assume they were Elves, now get me a body count and question every guard on every door of this Keep, I want to know how they got out."

"Who got out Sir?"

"Whoever was on those horses with Moreton you idiot."

He stormed out into the courtyard, shouting for his First Sergeant, who came running across the cobbles towards him.

"Sir?"

"Have you recovered any of the horses?"

"Yes Sir, about five so far, but there is no tack for them."

"Then find someone who can ride bareback and send them to rouse the Horse Third from Castlebury. Get them back here for orders."

"Sir." The Sergeant went to carry out his orders while Harlmon went to look at the fire. It had a good hold but wouldn't spread if they kept a watch on any surrounding roofs. There was no thatch in the Castle, all tiles. There was no use giving an attacker the opportunity to burn you out.

He re-entered the Keep and walked into the Great Hall. To his surprise Eilana was there. She stood looking at the rows of bodies laid out along each side. She had a morbid fascination for those which had a dismembered limb thrown carelessly across the body from which it came. It really was not a pleasant sight.

"How many?" he asked the Sergeant.

"Forty-eight of our lads Sir, thirty-four of them."

"Thirty-four! And Fenlon?"

"Laid out downstairs Sir, with the Castle staff."

"Get him up here straight away and cut off his face, I want him unrecognisable, Whorlean, understood?"

"Straight away Sir." Before he could move Harlmon spoke again.

"How many Keep staff?"

"Fifty-four men Sir, fifteen women." He hesitated, glancing at Eilana. Harlmon nodded. "All the women had been raped but otherwise unharmed. We killed them as you ordered Sir, along with eight young'uns who saw it all"

"Good, all right Sergeant, get on with it." Eilana turned to him. He knew the question on her lips before she asked it. "Gudrick is dead, and Allaner. I killed them myself. Bertal was not in her room, she disappeared, as did Harlada. He saw me kill Gudrick. I tried to talk sense into him but he ran, disappeared too. Two Whorleans are unaccounted for too." She could see the anger in his eyes, and intuitively knew there was worse news.

"So what's the real problem?" He smiled resignedly at her.

"The real problem is," he paused, "Moreton arrived out of nowhere." Her eyes closed for a moment. "He was seen outside the gates in the company of four Elves. He rode off with four others. Wey alone knows how they got out of the Keep, but it has to be Bertal, Harlada and the two Whorleans; a strange alliance. They seem to have just walked out of the Castle. They drove the horses out of the stables and set fire to the place. The guards on the gate seem to have run out after the horses and been killed by the Elves. They had mounts ready outside. As soon as the Horse Third arrives, I will follow them."

"You will stay here with me. They will have gone south. Elves would never let Whorleans enter their forests, so they have not gone east, and with the army to the north they will not go that way. They will not run to Ffonhaven, for if the tide were wrong when they got there, even if they found a boat to take them, they could be delayed long enough for pursuers to catch them. They will head for Bridgebury and run south to Deswrain, the long way round. Send your First Sergeant with the Horse Third to catch them. He is perfectly capable, and I need you here."

"As you wish, pretty one." There was a definite air of annoyance in his voice.

"Where is Allaner?" She noticed a sheepish look in his eyes, but only for a moment. "Harlmon, what have you done to her?"

"Just had a little fun my sister, nothing that shows now she's dressed, and nothing we can't blame on the Whorleans anyway." She shook her head slowly.

"Right, well when you get some horses sorted, send a couple of men to Castlebury. They must know of an oldish woman of about Bertal's build. Kill her and bring her back here but for Wey's sake don't let them be seen. Dress her in some of Bertal's clothes and cut her about a bit. Ruin her face and do whatever you did to Allaner."

"Clever girl. I'll arrange it now. We tell everybody she's dead. When we catch her, we kill her and bury her, and if we don't and she turns up later, she's an impostor." He grinned then looked straight at her. "What about Harlada?"

"If he won't see sense and come back quietly….," She turned away and stared at a window, just for something to focus on, "have him killed and buried with Bertal." She looked back towards him. He nodded and started to move towards the door. "And Brother, what did you do to Allaner, other than the obvious?"

"I just took a few souvenirs, that's all." He grinned and walked away. She stared after him. One day he would go too far.

Chapter 36

In the Niscerien army, a day is divided into six equal watches, the first starting at dawn and the others evenly spread through daylight and darkness. The length of the darkness on a spring night led Rebgroth to order the camp roused half way through the sixth watch. He wanted the light camp struck before dawn and the four Hunderts of the south, armed with their short swords, long shields and short spears, deployed in the valley mouth before the Whorleans could see the movement.

He ordered that he should be raised before the half watch; he wanted to be there for his men, visible and active. Tamorther joined him as soon as he left his tent, which was struck and packed almost before they spoke.

"I ordered the King roused at the third quarter Sir. I thought you would prefer him out of the way for a bit." Rebgroth smiled at him. Tamorther could have read his thoughts.

"Thank you, Tam. I could do without his advice for a while. You can only be polite for so long on a day like today, King or not." Tamorther grinned broadly, but some raised voices towards the west end of the camp drew their attention. Rebgroth nodded slightly and they strode through the busy camp.

It was the Castle First. As they rose they were given the light blue coats of Harlmon's men, and a few had started to complain, demanding to know what was going on. Cat calls began from the Bluecoat Third camped next to them and an incident was close.

Rebgroth strolled confidently amongst them.

"Attention to the General," bawled their first Sergeant as he realised who had just marched into their midst. The Hundert turned to face him, pulling themselves upright.

"Thank you the Castle First. Is there a problem Sergeant?"

"I am sure there's not Sir. I was just ordering the men into their blue coats Sir. I am not sure they all have ones to fit Sir." Rebgroth smiled wryly.

"I see; that could be a problem." His voice slowly raised in volume, "particularly as the Castle First has such a vital role to play today. You know what that is Sergeant?" The Sergeant had been briefed thoroughly by his Officer who was just walking from his tent. He saw Tamorther's hand raise slightly, its palm towards the Officer, making him slow and stand behind him. His old soldier's brain engaged and he took his cue.

"Well Sir, I think I grasped it, and I was about to tell the boys, but now you're here, I'm sure they would love to hear it from you."

Rebgroth turned to their red faced Officer.

"May I?"

"Please do General, the men would be honoured I know."

"Thank you." He stepped onto a small water barrel and looked around him. It seemed to every soldier that he had looked directly at him.

"Well boys, most of you know me well, and I know you well, which is why I have chosen you for this task. We will win this battle today with the bravery of men like yourselves, but we are outnumbered and must use cunning too. It is essential that we draw the enemy into the valley. That is your job, to offer him a fight and back into the valley without engaging. Once there you will filter through the lines and take up position at the holding line, supporting the main line. There you will have the responsibility to hold that position come what may. I need the best there, and that's you boys."

A rumble of approval almost broke into a cheer.

"Steady lads, we don't want to wake them too early!" Another laugh rose quietly. "There is one thing those Whorleans hate more than anything else I can think of, and that's those blue coats, Wey I can't stand them myself." Now they were laughing. "I need you to wear them to bring them on to us. When you reach the holding line you can throw them off and fight as the Castle First, as you should. Are we all understood?" A ragged aye sounded. "Then let's see you in those damned coats."

He jumped down from the barrel.

"Thank you Sir, I was about to brief them." Rebgroth looked the speaker in the eyes.

"If there is a next time Officer, I suggest you get your Sergeant to rouse you first then you will be ready to stop a problem before it starts."

"Yes General."

"Good man. You've got a job to do today. Do it well." He whirled away before he could answer and stormed over to the Bluecoat Sergeant thirty paces away. He stood with his face almost touching the Sergeant's and hissed angrily.

"If I hear any more of that from your men I will personally put my sword through your throat. You need to work with those men over there today or die for lack of it. Do you understand me Sergeant?" The Sergeant nodded.

"I do Sir."

"Excellent; see to it."

Rebgroth walked back towards the middle of the camp. Tamorther caught him.

"I think you caught their mood perfectly, Sir."

"Our boys' Tam, or the Bluecoats'?"

"Both Sir." He laughed, "The Bluecoat Sergeant certainly got the message too."

A quartermaster Levener moved quickly towards them as soon as he saw them.

"Excuse me General; you are needed urgently at the King's tent."

"Oh Wey! Is he awake already?"

"Not exactly Sir." Rebgroth caught the gravity in the tone of the remark and moved quickly away towards the small but ornate tent. Greardel stood at the entrance. He looked very nervous.

"I came to lay out his robes before I roused him and found him like this." Rebgroth pushed past him with Tamorther behind him.

"Wey!" It seemed all he could think of to say. The King lay staring at the roof of the tent with glazed eyes. Rebgroth leant over him and closed them. It wasn't easy. The body was quite cold. He gripped the hilt of the knife sticking from his chest and wrenched it clear. That wasn't easy either. It was clearly a Whorlean weapon.

"It seems at least one got through last night Tam."

"It does indeed Sir. Greardel, does anyone else know?"

"Only the Levener who found you Sir. I told him to tell no-one"

"Get him in here with you now." It was Rebgroth this time. Greardel called the Levener in and Rebgroth issued his orders.

"Get the King's wagon here now. Get him dressed in his fighting leathers then wrap him in blankets and lay him in it. Keep him covered with the tent and everything that usually goes in there. If anyone is asking about him he is in another part of the battle. Afterwards he will have been killed fighting bravely somewhere early on, bravely trying to halt the first Whorlean charge. It will all be pretty confused.

"Greardel, once the fighting starts, move south through the trees then get back to the Castle and tell them of his death. You didn't see it but you have seen the body and I sent you back. Now let's make it happen. We cannot demoralise the army with the King's death." They all stood looking at him for a moment.

"Go!"

Everybody moved at once through the tent door, dislodging the central upright pole and making the tent sag. Tamorther swore and placed it upright again. He raised his eyebrows at Rebgroth in a humourless grin.

"A good start to the day, General."

"Well Tam, let's just hope it doesn't get any worse." He shook his head and moved away.

Bocknostri too was walking his camp with Drokhart beside him. He looked up at the cloud-covered sky. Drew don't let it rain.

"What report from the scouts?" Bocknostri asked.

"The main body retreated before dawn Sire, into the valley hidden from view from here but beyond that hill. They have formed a defensive line across it. There are a little over a hundred Bluecoats between them and us."

"Bluecoats eh! What's this valley like?"

"They have a shield wall some thirty men wide each side of the river Sire, six or so deep, from tree line to tree line, but they are very close together Sire, too close to fight, I don't understand it."

"Are they fools? How can they stand for long without fighting us? We will just whittle them down."

"I can only assume some ill thought plan Sire. These Bluecoats ahead are no more than a skirmish line. They will give at our first assault, unless they are there to draw us into the valley."

"But to what? Surely they don't see the valley as some ill-conceived trap. I can only think that if they draw us in they believe they will win a pushing match, not a fight. That has to be it. They are not fighters, except those Bluecoats, and there are not enough of them. Form them up Uncle, we go to victory."

The twenty-three Tribes of Whorle formed up, eighteen hundred men in all. It had been twenty-five but three tribes had been decimated by the attacks on Gloff and now formed up as one. None of them carried Cregenda's long spears for use against cavalry. The Niscerien Royal Guard Cavalry had gone north and they were too cumbersome in this sort of fight.

They moved forward three tribes wide towards the line of Bluecoats ahead of them. They were at a brisk walk to start with then began a steady trot.

The blue-coated Castle First Hundert stood their ground until the Tribesmen were fifty paces from them before turning and running in apparent disarray. Their First Sergeant shouted to his Officer as he ran.

"In Wey's name I hope we get to fight them later, I would hate my kids to ask me what I did in the battle at Stroue, just to tell them we ran."

"For good reason Sergeant, but I'm sure we'll get to do our bit."

They rounded the base of the hill to see four Hunderts arrayed across the valley one hundred paces away. They raced towards them seeing gaps in their ranks. They funnelled through them and the line closed behind them. Tamorther shouted to them.

"Keep moving the Castle First, down the valley to the holding line." They had heard the roar of the Tribesmen as they rounded the hill behind them and stopped in a line across the valley. Three Tribes were trying to fit into its width and could not. They jostled and pushed as the Bluecoats melted through the line ahead.

There were indeed some four hundred men facing them, two hundred on each side of the river, about thirty men wide and six deep. They held almost man height oblong shields in front of the first row, a solid wall of metal.

The Castle First ran on to the holding line. They formed a line on the northern bank and stripped off their blue coats, hurling them to the ground behind them.

"At least we ran in blue coats lads, now we fight as the Castle First."

The Third of real Bluecoats had formed up on the south bank with the Eastern First's infantry, their archers in a crescent behind them.

Drokhart forced his way to the front of the tribesmen and roared the battle cry of his home Tribe. It was answered by a commanding shout from Bocknostri in the centre of his men, and the Whorlean Army broke into a run from the front. Only as the front ranks charged at the Niscerien line, did the ranks behind gain the chance to run themselves. It was the first signs of the fatal congestion that would follow.

The front ranks were thirty paces from the Niscerians when at a single shout, four hundred short spears arced towards them, taking many of them in the head or chest. The charge faltered and the ranks behind ran into the back of the shattered vanguard.

They looked ahead to see the Niscerians running back down the valley, reforming another hundred paces ahead. Again the concertina charge began, stretching the Whorleans down the valley until a second volley of spears struck them. Many more were down, dead or wounded, and those following trampled over them to follow the Niscerians who were again running, but they did not seem to be stopping this time. They charged on.

The Niscerians did stop. Drokhart had survived both showers of spears, though many around him had fallen, but now the Niscerians had formed up again, and he could see a second line including Bluecoats behind them. Now they would fight. With a tribal cry he led his men forward again. He was on the south side of the river but the wave of Whorleans crowded both sides.

As he passed a protruding clump of trees to his right he saw another line of Niscerians thirty paces up a side valley. For a moment the crush eased as some of the tribesmen ran ahead and others to their right, but then a third volley of four hundred spears rained down from their front, and two hundred from the right.

Their losses were high, even more so as two more volleys of spears struck from the right. Tribesmen rushed at the fighting lines. At least the Niscerians were taking some casualties now, but only about twenty Tribesmen could fight on either side of the river without striking each other, and thirty or so on the right. The Niscerians had only short swords and could not easily reach them, until the concertina began to close. They had lost nearly two hundred tribesmen to spears, but there were still sixteen hundred Whorleans in the valley, all eager to fight.

The Tribesmen behind pushed up behind the front ranks, forcing them up against the Niscerien line. They had no room to swing their weapons, their arms trapped above their heads or at their sides. The Niscerians however made devastating use of their short swords, thrusting between their shields and stabbing into defenceless Tribesmen.

Bocknostri looked around him, now what in Drew's name was happening? He was crushed in the centre of his men when the wooded sides of the valley came alive with soldiers, Niscerien soldiers, and just when his men were trying to spread into the trees.

The fight raged now on three sides, but so many of his men could not fight, boxed in the centre of the valley.

Rebgroth stood just behind the fighting line in the centre, near the river.

"Now Tam my boy, now." Tamorther gestured to a Hornsman behind him and a clear call rang out above the noise of battle. A Hundert of archers in the trees on each side of the valley loosed two hundred shafts into the mass of Whorleans in the centre of the crush, joined by a volley from the forty behind the holding line.

Rebgroth had made one miscalculation. He hadn't realised quite what a crush it would become. The Whorlean army took up less of the valley than he had expected, and this made the archers' job harder in that they had to be even more careful not to target their own men, but it made their vollies all the more devastating.

Drokhart and his men were engaged in a pushing match now, and the only advantage the crush behind him meant was they might win it. He saw an opportunity to turn the battle and screamed orders to the men around him. They waded into the river, waist deep, and moved between the Niscerien lines on each side. He was sure if enough could make it through the gap they could turn one side at least, and if they could do that then the other side would have to give.

The Castle First saw the move first and their Officer led his men into the water without hesitation. The fight was bloody. Sluggish movements in the water gave the Whorleans' brute strength an advantage, and they were soon pressing the Castle First back with many men down.

The Bluecoats on the south side leapt off the bank along the Whorleans right flank, squeezing them sideways until they too were pushed back. It was the forty archers of the Eastern First who stopped them, lining the south bank and coolly picking off Whorleans as they fought, including Drokhart. The gap was plugged.

Bocknostri had just about managed to turn most of his men back up the valley, but it was carnage. Hundreds had fallen to arrows without being near the fight, it was slaughter, it couldn't be happening. They had begun to fall back when a voice in Bocknostri's ear made him look up.

Two hundred Royal Guard Cavalry were at full gallop down the valley towards them. It didn't worry Bocknostri though, because an arrow entered his throat, slicing through his windpipe and jugular. He was dead before his body hit the ground, and heartbeats later two hundred lances crashed into the unprotected Whorlean rear, as more arrows filled the air.

Rebgroth looked on with little satisfaction. His plan had worked horrifically well.

"Let them go, Tam."

"Sir?"

"Let them go, we've killed enough. Give them a way out."

Tamorther hesitated a moment then gave an order to the Hornsman. Another signal blast rung out, that was repeated by other horns around the field. The Cavalry disengaged and rode back out of the valley, swinging south and forming up on a ridge south of its mouth.

The surviving Whorleans turned and ran back down the riverbanks, most of their weapons cast aside. Just over four hundred reached their camp on the flats below the wooded hills. Over thirteen hundred lay dead or dying in the killing ground of the valley floor.

The cheers of a thousand Niscerians rang through the hills, for over three hundred had died to defeat the Tribes of Whorle. It was no more than half way to midday and yet so many men were dead. In Whorle, some tribes would have lost all their menfolk, others just most of them.

Tamorther gave his General an embarrassed smile, before a tear ran down his cheek.

"I'm sorry Sir. It's a little difficult to take in. I should be so happy we have won but Wey, we killed so many."

"Don't be sorry Tam. I am responsible for this, I am the Death Bringer, and I fear this may only be the start of it all." Tam didn't understand what Rebgroth meant exactly, so he nodded quietly and walked to a fallen tree and sat on it. Almost immediately he stood and walked into the open shouting.

"Officers and Sergeants to me, sound the call Hornsman." The horn rang out over the strangely quiet battlefield, and Rebgroth watched as in twos and threes, surviving Officers and Sergeants gathered around his second in command. Many of the Officers were Hunderts themselves, some were appointed by their Hundert, but none looked very grand that morning and most were subdued. The Sergeants were tougher full-time soldiers and more prepared for what was to come.

"We rest until midday, then we start the clear up. Heap the Whorlean dead for pyres, kill any badly wounded. They won't live anyway so it's better to kill them now. We'll see how many live ones we've got. If they can walk, patch them and send them home. Pile all the weapons and sound clothing, leathers in particular, we'll move them back to the Castle tomorrow. Place our dead in the side valley and bury them there. Name the graves where you can. I leave it to the friends of the worst wounded to decide their immediate fate."

He paused and looked slowly around at the Officers and Sergeants. Rebgroth would have done that.

"Well done everyone. The only problem with winning is we're alive to sort out the mess afterwards." There was a ripple of laughter. "Be about it."

Rebgroth walked up behind him.

"Thank you Tam, I would have found that difficult right now."

"I know Sir, take a rest, I'll sort things here." Rebgroth slapped him on the shoulder. He said nothing. He didn't need to.

He walked to the river, a little upstream from where the fight had centred, and knelt down to take a drink, cupping his right hand and scooping up the water. He felt his knife hilt stick into his stomach as he bent and put his left hand to it to ease it over. The carved wooded handle was so hot he jumped back involuntarily as it burnt his hand.

The swinging two-handed blade brushed his hair as he jumped back. It should have killed him, and would have but for his sudden movement. The wounded Whorlean had seen a chance to revenge himself for the death of so many friends. The sword's weight took his arms way round to his left leaving his right side open to Rebgroth, who whipped his knife from his belt with his right hand and stabbed it between the Tribesman's ribs. The body fell from the knife into the river.

The whole incident had gone unseen, and suddenly Rebgroth realised the knife handle was cold in his hand. He looked at his left palm. It didn't seem burnt, nor did it hurt any more. He sat on the grass bank and wiped the blood from the blade with the leaf of a large weed. Looking at the carved handle a memory entered his head; 'it will protect you from hidden enemies.'

He lay back and stared at the grey clouds above. There was no doubt in his mind; the Death Bringer would have to go through all this again, more than once, perhaps. He shuddered and closed his eyes.

Chapter 37

Before the work of clearing the dead began, almost at midday, a rider arrived with an urgent dispatch for the General. He was sent along the southern riverbank. Rebgroth stood as he saw the Bluecoat approach.

"Well my man?" invited Rebgroth.

"Sir, I bring news from the Castle. It was raided last night by a force of Whorleans. They came across the Number by boat and entered the Castle, murdering many, including Queen Bertal, Prince Gudrick and Allaner. Harlada is still missing. Nearly fifty Bluecoats died defending the Castle and the Royal Household. The raiders were all killed, or so most believe, but some say a few escaped. The Lady Serculas is well, Sir. She was with the Lady Eilana, Prince Gudfel and your daughter."

Rebgroth stared at him sightlessly, his mind racing.

"You must return immediately. Greardel will have crossed your path, hopefully, but in case not, take this news to Chancellor Bradett and The Lady Eilana and Lord Harlmon. I will follow shortly. King Gudmon died this day, giving his life for Nisceriel, fighting in the front line. The Council should be summoned to confirm decendancy and name the King."

Rebgroth realised the man was shocked at the King's death.

"You carried weighty news here, now you must carry weightier back, do it well." His words woke the man from his dreamlike state.

"I will Sir, depend on me."

"I do, be gone."

The Bluecoat wheeled his mount and cantered away. Rebgroth sighed and headed off to find Tamorther, he was going to have to leave straight away to be back by nightfall. Wey, would it never end.

The Whorleans had regrouped at their campsite. Three tribal leaders lived, but Perdredd, the oldest of them, issued orders which the others obeyed without argument. They broke camp, collecting all they could easily carry that was essential; food and water mainly, and blankets.

Just after midday they started their journey home. They would run the wall at Gloff. They would take casualties, but with two of their number having gone the long way round with Bocknostri the last time Whorleans retreated from Nisceriel, they feared being pursued by cavalry and thought they would lose fewer this way and at least be back in Whorle by nightfall.

As it was, the defenders in Gloff only paid their retreat token heed. The archers that lined the walls loosed a few shafts each, but they had all seen too much killing already. The fires in the town from the day before were still smouldering, having burnt themselves out. One still burned fiercely though. They too were a stark reminder of the events the day before, as was the pall of smoke that hung over the town, drifting slowly across the Number and into Whorle.

Moreton held up a hand to slow the group to a stop as they came to a small stream that flowed across their path. They had ridden south steadily and it was now gone midday. They had ridden for long periods then dismounted and walked. It rested the horses and their backsides, especially the Whorleans who had never sat astride a horse before.

They would remount after a while and ride on, but now they were all tired. Apart from the travelling, they had all been up all night. They had covered most of the distance to Bridgebury, but Moreton seemed unhappy to continue, exhausted or not.

Cregenda had learnt to ride the hard way, and was now enjoying it, controlling his mount himself. He could see how Niscerians and others found a horse so useful, they were powerful and strong. Gragonor had not fared so well however, and Harlada still held his reigns and led his mount beside his own.

"Not far to the east is a small clearing," Moreton told the group, Gragonor translating. "We can hide and rest there for a while, and continue after dark."

"Will pursuit not overtake us?" Cregenda asked through Gragonor.

"It will certainly overtake us if we stay on the road," Moreton replied. "We will stand a better chance of getting right away if we move after dark. They will have overtaken us but not be sure if they have. They will wait in Bridgebury to see if we have been seen, there or around about. If we approach the village by night I believe we can get through, and I believe we will find help after dark."

No-one was sure what he meant, but Harlada suddenly spoke commandingly.

"I think we should move off the road quickly. The Bluecoats are coming." Moreton looked at him, noticing him fingering the coin he wore around his neck on a thin silver chain.

He said nothing but kicked his horse and the others followed. They rode up the stream from the road so as to leave no tracks and disappeared into the tree line. Once out of sight from the road they left the stream and followed a rarely used path that led deep into the woods. It was overgrown but wound clearly through the trees, running parallel to the stream. The Elves just disappeared, melting into the trees.

The woodland became denser and they had to duck under the odd branch, much to Gragonor's discomfort and the others' amusement. Just as Queen Bertal felt the need for a break and was about to ask how much longer they would be riding for, they rode out of the trees and into a clearing.

It wasn't a true clearing as it surrounded a deep and still lake, some thirty or more paces across. The trees stopped some ten paces back from the water's edge.

Harlada looked at it, wide-eyed. It was so tranquil and truly beautiful. He assumed the ground was too wet for the tree roots closer to the lake, but the soft grass was lush and green all around it, except where a stream flowed gently into it on the far side and out again where their mounts stood; the stream they had followed from the road.

"We'll rest here for a while and share watches until dusk." It was Moreton who spoke. "Gragonor, you take the first watch. Walk back fifty paces down the stream and listen hard. Run back if you hear anything." He hesitated, said something to Cregenda who nodded, then jumped awkwardly down from his horse and walked back into the trees and down the stream.

Moreton rode a little further around the lake before looping a leg over his saddle and sliding down himself. The others followed, dismounted and began to unsaddle the horses. Once done, they left them to graze and drink.

Moving around a bit further, they all sat on the grass. They were all hungry, but there was nothing to eat in their saddlebags, they had left in too big a hurry. Harlada knelt by the lake and drank from his hand. The water was cool and clear except for tiny eddies of mud that stirred from the bottom as his hand disturbed the surface.

He looked up and smiled to himself. Cregenda was almost undressed, removing his clothes rapidly. Bertal stared dumbstruck until he was stark naked. His large frame had hardly any fat on it, and his pale torso bore a number of scars, some quite small, but two long and white. He walked slowly to the water, his left hand carelessly loosening his genitals as he moved. He was totally unaware of the horror on Bertal's face, not thinking for a moment that his nakedness could be an embarrassment.

As he reached the water's edge he threw himself forward in a flat dive, smacking the surface and swimming into the lake. Whorleans were not boat people, but they were brought up along the Drei and most could swim like fish as boys. Harlada laughed out loud and jumped up, dropping his garments around him. Removing his coin and slipping it into a pocket, he rushed to join Cregenda.

He splashed into the lake, not caring if Bertal saw his maturing body. He was just fourteen and a young man now, and although he had become increasingly aware of himself, Bertal was almost his Grandmother, or so he thought of her. Just after his thirteenth Bornbless, he and Gudrick had lain in bed, trying to prove they were men. The secrets of sex were learnt young in the Castle, and although they knew all about them, performance was a different matter.

That night however, a tension built in him as he fondled himself, and before he was sure what was happening, his seed spurted over his stomach. He was so proud. He and Gudrick examined it closely, its texture, smell, and taste, laughing and spattering it on each other.

Harlada practised his new found skill regularly, sometimes alone, and sometimes beside Gudrick. There was nothing sexual between them, just shared experiences, but no matter how he tried, Gudrick was far less physically mature than Harlada, and had died never having seen his own seed. He had never slept with a woman, only ever having shared a bed with a man, Harlada.

As he splashed into the water the memory of her visions, her insights of Gudrick and Harlada, were in the front of Bertal's mind and that very phrase meant more to her now. Her eyes were on the edge of tears as Harlada doggy paddled into the centre of the lake. He had only learnt to stay afloat in the moat

370

around the Castle, and although he could get around in the water, was not a strong swimmer.

She couldn't see Cregenda, but then suddenly Harlada disappeared with a splash as Cregenda grabbed his legs and pulled him under with him. A moment later Harlada burst up into the air before crashing back with a huge splash into the water. Cregenda surfaced laughing beside him. Harlada shrieked and splashed at him. Cregenda seemed so young, but then he was only about six or seven years older than Harlada, if that.

She looked sideways at Moreton, who was looking at her. They both smiled.

"Go on then, you old fool. I won't look." Moreton laughed at her words.

"Only if you join me my Queen, surely we are both too old to be embarrassed? After all, we are unlikely to live through this night, so who is going to know."

"Don't try that one on me you damn trickster, you know who will live through this night. We both know Harlada will, and I believe Cregenda will, but then perhaps we will not. You are right, curse you, get that blessed habit off."

They stripped and ran for the water. Bertal was fit at thirty-five, her figure relatively trim. Her ample breasts hung lower than they used to but were still a magnificent sight, as none of them could miss. In the middle of all the killing and mayhem, they all found a short time of laughter and fun. They splashed and laughed, as if they were all Harlada's age, until they grew tired.

Bertal splashed towards the lake's edge and climbed out, turning to face the water. Moreton was crawling out a few paces away, still laughing, and Cregenda swam towards them, climbing out too and walking to his clothes. Harlada doggy paddled slowly back, looking across at Bertal, and suddenly aware of her femininity. Cold water or not, he hardened and grew till he throbbed as he looked at her. She was rubbing herself dry with an underskirt and he thought he would burst. He couldn't get out now; his clothes were five or six paces from the edge.

He swam around. If he could have touched himself he was sure he would have seeded in moments and solved his problem, but he needed both hands to keep himself afloat. Moreton waved him over, but he ignored him. Moreton pulled his old maroon habit over his head, and as he did so, Harlada's problem dawned on him. He smiled to himself and walked to Harlada's scattered clothes.

"You always were such a messy individual," he declared, gathering them up and piling them neatly at the water's edge. He walked back to Bertal who was all but dressed now.

Cregenda was dressed. He tapped Moreton on the shoulder and pointed to the trees where the stream flowed out of the clearing and where Gragonor had gone. He just said the name and walked off.

Moreton looked over his shoulder and smiled. Harlada was close against the bank putting his shirt on over his wet body before climbing from the water, trying to hide his condition.

Moreton looked at Bertal and grinning at her, half nodded his head in Harlada's direction. She looked sideways without turning her head to see him pulling his leggings up over a large bulge in their front. She grinned back at Moreton, walked to him and kissed his cheek before sitting down in the grass.

His back to them, Harlada was almost crabbing towards the trees. He entered them and disappeared.

"You seem to have had an effect on him," said Moreton. Bertal giggled softly.

"Time was I had that effect on most men, particularly Gudmon, and Gratax." Tears ran down her cheeks. "I have known such happiness and such awful hurt, my dear Moreton, but then I suppose they say you have to know one to feel the other."

"They do, my Queen, and they are probably right."

"And what of you, have you never wanted the love of a woman?"

"None who would ever love a monk, no. You still have that effect on me though, you always have had, but you were always untouchable, and in love with other men."

She looked at him in shocked silence for a moment.

"It was you who were untouchable you dear fool. A Weymonk and my husband's best friend, the idea only ever crossed my mind in some of my innermost naughtiest thoughts." She chuckled quietly and smiled warmly at him. "Who knows, if we live through all this perhaps we should both taste forbidden love, in fact I can definitely say I will if you will."

"Oh I will my Queen. Mine is not a celibate order, but enough now or I will develop a bulge like Harlada's."

"At your age?!"

"Yes at my age, you horrid woman." He leant forward and kissed her cheek, as with perfect timing Harlada walked from the woods, his bulge gone and his codpiece fastened. He was only slightly breathless.

Within a blink Gragonor walked into the clearing, and waving, walked towards them. He suddenly jumped sideways in momentary fright. Four Elves walked from the trees carrying nuts and berries of various kinds.

"You could have managed a rabbit or two," Gragonor moaned.

"Only if you eat it raw," replied Ranamo, shaking his head slightly. "You wouldn't wish the smoke from a cooking fire to bring your Bluecoat friends, would you?" Gragonor realised he had made a stupid comment.

"I'm sorry; I never was a very good woodsman."

"Well now you mix with the very best my friend," consoled Moreton. "People of the Forest in fact, so learn from them, there is very much to learn."

Gragonor appreciated the gesture from Moreton. He had grown to like him, in fact all of them. They had not laughed at him or teased him over his poor horsemanship, and they had a caring feel. It was nothing like the feel of a Whorlean camp. Even Cregenda seemed in good spirits when he had arrived to relieve him.

"I will take some food to Cregenda," he said, and took a selection of the food laid on a cloth on the grass. "I will eat with him." No-one said anything, acknowledging his good thought. He set off to find Cregenda.

Ranamo signalled and the Elves all stood.

"I will send the Tribesmen to you. You must all sleep till dusk. We have a long night ahead of us."

"But what about you?" asked Harlada. The Elf smiled at him.

"We People of the Forest sleep very lightly. The slightest threatening sound will awake us. We will screen the road side of the clearing and give ample warning of any hostile approach."

The Elves left and shortly after the Whorleans returned. Bertal was almost asleep, Harlada sound after his exertions. Moreton raised an arm in greeting as they walked in and settled down comfortably.

"Till dusk, monk." Cregenda spoke without looking at him, Gragonor translating.

"Till dusk, Tribesman."

Greardel stood outside the rear door to Eilana's rooms, and knocked confidently. He had ridden from the Niscerien camp into the mouth of the valley where the fighting line was just moving into position. He rode into the edge of the woods on the south side and turned his horse, looking into the plain beyond.

The dawn was almost breaking; the sky was light but the sun not yet risen.

He was supposed to wait until the battle started so that his arrival at the Castle would be properly timed to report the King's death at its start. Given that he would be reporting to Eilana who already knew the truth, he could not see the point, especially if he entered the Castle unobtrusively.

He turned his mount and wound his way south, through the trees along the base of the hills. He was afraid if he moved too far into the forest he might lose his sense of direction and get lost, so within a half watch he rode out of the trees. In front of him was the single hill where Gudmon and Eilana had first made love, not that he knew that, he just knew he must ride around it and a watch or so would see him to the Castle.

As he rode from behind the hill he was quite a height above the Number. He looked across its waters to Whorle, before he turned his head and gazed towards the distant Castle of Nisceriel. It was marked by a column of smoke rising from it. He wondered what had been going on there and was intrigued to know.

He had ridden steadily, a little faster than was wise, so frustratingly, he had to walk the last section leading his exhausted horse. With the Castle a couple of fields away his vanity got to him and he mounted and rode to the gates. A Bluecoat guard checked him in. He recognised him at once and waved him through but noted his entry.

Greardel rode towards the Keep but quickly saw the stables were burning, the source of the smoke he had seen so far off. He rode to the other side of the square and dismounted. He tethered his mount near the alehouse and walked to the Keep's main gate. The Bluecoat guard was arguing with a man a little outside to the right, Greardel walked confidently in from the left. He smiled to think how angry Harlmon would be when he told him how easily he had just walked in.

He went to the rear servants' stairs, climbing the spirals until he reached the corridor along the back of the Royal quarters, and walked to Eilana's door. As he knocked he promised himself he would never use the servants' entrances again. It was a promise he was to keep.

Eilana did not call "enter", instead for no reason she could recall afterwards, she moved to the door and opened it. She was taken aback to see Greardel standing there. She had planned with Harlmon exactly what they would do on Greardel's return, but her brother was not there.

She ushered Greardel in, asking him what news he had. He grinned broadly at her as he walked to the middle of the room.

"Gudmon is dead, My Lady, killed by a Whorlean in the night to those who think they know. Killed in the first Whorlean charge by those that believe what they are told after the battle. Killed by me to you and I, and your brother."

"Good man Greardel. There was a raid here in the night, as you know. Fenlon was killed, although as he was already dead to most, he is among the Whorlean dead. The Queen, Prince Gudrick and Allaner were all killed too; altogether an excellent night's work."

"Thank you My Lady. Rebgroth sent me to tell you of Gudmon's death, but I was supposed to wait until the battle started, but as you knew already I came straight away. There is just the matter of my reward, My Lady."

"Yes indeed," she said, turning and walking towards her dressing table. She fumbled in the drawer whilst talking, removing a brush and hidden with it a long thin bladed knife. She tossed the brush onto the dresser top as she hid the knife in her other sleeve. "I have given much thought to what would be most appropriate. By midnight Gudrick will be King, and I, King Mother, a position from which I may grant many things."

She moved back towards him, looking at his eyes and talking all the while.

"You shall become Lord of a Counting and sit on the council, that is the least I can do for one to whom I owe so much, but there should be more, something more intimate between us to show my gratitude."

Greardel could not believe it was happening as she moved tight against him, this was beyond his dreams. His hands moved to her shoulders, pulling her against him. She pushed him away slightly as her left hand slid to his codpiece, feeling him instantly aroused.

He shut his eyes and his chin went up as she rubbed him, but then her right hand drove the knife into his stomach. It penetrated deep, but she wasn't an assassin and it wasn't a killing thrust. He gasped and jumped back from her, pushing her away, not understanding what had happened for a moment, blood spraying from him as the knife wrenched free, splashing down the front of Eilana's dress. He saw the dripping knife in her hand and understood.

"Damned bitch!" he screamed as both his hands clutched his stomach. It felt like his insides were on fire and about to fall out. He staggered a step towards her, as if to attack her, but he knew he couldn't take his hands from his stomach. Wey the blood!

He turned and stumbled towards the door. Eilana rushed forward and stabbed the knife into his lower back, crashing him against the door. She had been frightened he was going to fight back for a moment; had she acted too hastily in carrying out their plan? The crash on the door sent Ereyna rushing to find Harlmon; it also stopped Greardel moving further away.

Eilana ripped the knife free and plunged it again and again into Greardel's back. He just wouldn't seem to die, but he was already dead. He slid down the door as Eilana struck at him, over and over. She knelt astride his body as it lay on the floor, driving the knife into his back in a frenzy, blood all over her hands and arms, her dress soaked in it. The door opened and Harlmon squeezed in, seeing what was happening and shutting out the three Bluecoats who were with him.

"I think you'll find he's dead now sister," he said quietly. She leant on the hilt. Both her hands gripped it as it protruded from Greardel's mutilated back. She sat panting and looked slowly at her brother. Her eyes stared wildly at him before they seemed to come back into focus.

"Wey brother," she panted, "I have never killed anyone before, but I see why you enjoy it so."

"I don't usually make such mess, sister dear. I suppose you were just jumped by a surviving Whorlean. I will put out a warning to be on the alert for any more, and I'll make sure his arrival is removed from the gate record. I suggest you get into the bedroom and get out of those clothes. I will order a bath and get him put with the Whorlean bodies for burning tomorrow, whilst they are filling it." He disappeared back out of the door and she rose to her feet, moving away then turning to the bloody pile of flesh that had been Greardel.

"Great Wey, I am as crazy as him!" She left the room for her bedroom.

Chapter 38

Eilana dressed slowly in her robe room. She had sent her Ladies away. They had been fussing around her since Harlmon had left. They were so concerned that she had been attacked by one of the two missing Whorleans and had killed him with a knife.

Harlmon had done that job well, as usual. The whole Castle was talking about it, how the Lady Eilana had killed one with a knife after he attacked her, and how they should keep watch for the second, as it seemed that the riders seen leaving were probably just frightened Castle folk running from danger.

Harlmon had Greardel's body removed by Bluecoats before footmen began to fill Eilana's bath and mop the blood-drenched floor. The stone flags just looked like they had dark worn patches rather than stains on them, and the rugs that had been stained were rolled up and replaced. After a surprisingly short time all looked normal.

The servants left and Harlmon called Eilana in for her bath. She entered from her robe room, naked and still visibly shaken. She looked at Harlmon and immediately thought that she just could not put up with his usual antics now, but he had no such intentions; he merely took her hand to steady her as she stepped into the tub.

She sank into the scented water which slowly turned pink as Greardel's dried blood dissolved into it from her caked limbs. Harlmon gazed at her body but did not have his usual look in his eye at such times.

"That should make you feel better, pretty one," he ventured.

"Almost heaven," she smiled. It was much better. The trouble was every time she relaxed and shut her eyes Greardel's body was there, and she was driving the knife into his flesh. It was a real comfort to have Harlmon there. It always was. Left alone she would never have got her mind off what she had just done.

"What next sister? I suppose we just wait."

"Indeed we do. If we have lost at Stroue, the Whorleans will be at our gates by dark I would think. We will hold out for some time, but eventually we will all die, some of us more easily than others I imagine. I am sure the General's hard work and preparation will have prevailed though, in which case we should get news a watch or so after noon, a watch and a half if it was close, and Rebgroth will probably arrive half a watch after that; certainly before dark."

"What about Bradett?"

"Anytime shortly, within half a watch anyway. He will have left Ffonhaven just after dawn. Are the Ministers all here?"

"They are, and all alive. They stayed well out of the action last night. It was the best news they ever received when they were ordered to stay in the Castle throughout the hostilities. 'To protect the future government of our realm' you said, brilliant."

"Well it does mean they will all be here to confirm the lineage of the throne. I just hope to Wey Moreton and Bertal are caught and killed. Who leads the Third you sent after them?"

"Drodfar, the best First Sergeant I have, although Harlfel is the Officer leading. He knows to do as his Sergeant suggests, and it means with our brother in charge, and him reporting back to us, we can be assured of even more than maximum effort."

"Good, let's hope he can talk some sense into Harlada."

"I'm sure he will. Listen; do you still not feel we should have this decendancy meeting as soon as Bradett arrives? It would all be done before Rebgroth gets here, he would have to accept it."

"Not with the army at his back, he wouldn't. We assume he has just won a major victory at which the King has died. The army may even name him King before he leaves to return, except that Rebgroth would never accept it, unless for some good reason it was forced on him. No, he will return, and he will accept Gudfel as the rightful Heir. He is the only male relative of Royal blood, and Rebgroth is a traditionalist, Patrikal will not be in his mind, but if we assume too much, anger him or rouse his suspicions, he could take the throne himself and be cheered all around the Kingdom."

"As you say sister, but may I suggest one thing?"

"Of course, what?"

"The bodies in the Great Hall; Fenlon and now Greardel are among the Whorlean dead, and the Queen's coffin does not contain the Queen. I suggest we have the Whorleans burnt now, whilst my Bluecoats can move them. It will save any nosy Royal Guardsman noticing anything. The Queen's coffin we should bury too, and Gudrick. We can argue that they were too mutilated to lie in state, that they were better buried in the Royal Burial Mound now, and memorial ceremonies held later."

"I think you are right my brother, that is sound thinking. Can we get them all out of the Castle and pyres built before Rebgroth returns?"

"Not if we do it outside the Castle, but we should burn them in the ruins of the stables. The fire is almost out and leaves an already scorched area, protected by the ruined stonewalls. We can add wood to the bodies and have a confined and controlled fire just across the square."

"That's very good, yes, very good. Will the Great Hall be available for the Decendancy Meeting? What about your Bluecoat dead, and the servants?"

"My lads have been moved to the barracks, the servants bodies are back with their families."

"You're ahead of me Brother, as usual. Burn those bodies."

"I will order it done." He went to leave and Eilana shut her eyes then called after him.

"No, stay with me a while, I need company. Let me relax a bit and gather myself, then I will get out of this tub and you can call my Ladies."

Harlmon turned quickly and came back to his chair.

"The vividness fades pretty one, but you never forget, and then slowly the desire grows to do it again. You will learn to live with it."

She looked at him in horror and began to cry quietly. This was no good. She had stood quickly and demanded a towel, which he had passed her, and now he was seeing to the pyre and Eival and Ereyna were gone too. She was alone with her thoughts.

She closed her eyes. Greardel was there, but she could look at him now. Wey, all the slaughter at Stroue that morning, whoever won, would mean hundreds of men had killed hundreds of others that day. She had never heard of soldiers haunted by those they had killed in battle, and all she had done was kill for Nisceriel's good too, although to others she had bravely defended herself against a savage. The soldiers would get drunk and boast of their exploits; she must do the same

She took a deep breath and realised she wasn't really upset that she had killed a man; in fact she was proud. She would boast about it but she wouldn't get drunk, not till much later. She was full of excitement again, trembling almost at the thought of the challenges the rest of the day would bring, in finally bringing Gudfel to the throne.

She felt a stirring in her thighs, a tremble in her stomach. Bradett would be back soon, it was him she needed, as soon as he got back. She convinced herself it was necessary to ensure his support at the meeting. It probably was, but it would be a pleasure securing it.

A real pleasure it proved to be, and she dressed again, quickly this time, as did Bradett, in response to a knocking at her doors.

When they were ready, with her sitting at a card table, Bradett opened the doors. Harlmon stood with a dust covered Bluecoat dispatch rider beside him, the one they had carefully briefed in the dawn watch that morning. Many courtiers had gathered behind them.

Eilana stood and formally waved them in.

"News from the General, My Lady."

"Good news I hope soldier." He stood rigidly to attention, staring unseeing to his front as he replied.

"The General Rebgroth reports, My Lady, a great victory with minimal losses. The remaining Whorleans are in full flight. I must report the gravest of news though, My Lady, and that is the tragic death of King Gudmon, struck down fighting bravely in the front line during the first Whorlean charge."

"How in Wey's name was he allowed to be in the front line?" exclaimed Bradett. Eilana was doing her best to looked as shocked; Harlmon too.

"I was told he insisted against all advice, My Lady, and in fact did so secretly, so as to fight beside ordinary soldiers. His bravery and leadership lost him his life, but his death was glorious." Eilana almost believed it herself, and wondered if Rebgroth would ever tell the truth. He would of course, because he had sent Greardel back to tell those that should know, but then Greardel had never arrived.

"That is terrible news indeed," said Eilana. "Is Rebgroth coming here himself soon?"

"He was intending to leave as soon after my departure as possible My Lady. He bid me inform yourself, Lord Bradett and Lord Harlmon, and to request all be ready for a Decendancy Council meeting on his arrival. My dispatches are delivered My Lords, My Lady." Harlmon dismissed and thanked him.

"I will summon the Ministers and arrange refreshment in the Great Hall whilst we await the General, if all approve," he said. All nodded and he turned to leave the room. Eilana called him back.

"Harlmon, gentlemen, I think we should send urgent news to Princess Patrikal and Moreton. Both her parents have died this day and she knows nothing of it. I imagine both may wish to return for the interment and remembrance ceremony." There were nods and sounds of approval.

"I will send a rider."

"And Harlmon."

"Yes, My Lady?"

"Try to pick someone who will remember he brings a young maiden news of her parents' death, not a battle dispatch." There were more nods and grunts.

"Yes, My Lady." This time he left the room. The others slowly followed, heading for the Great Hall and beginning to discuss the situation amongst themselves. As they reached the bottom of the stairs, the last footmen were just leaving the Hall with buckets and mops having cleaned the floors; a decidedly unpleasant job.

Rebgroth had watched the rider move back down the valley and sighed deeply. He tried to concentrate his mind, but it was so difficult. He dared not think how little sleep he had managed in the last couple of days, but he felt very tired now. The excitement of battle had faded, and once he had relaxed the tiredness washed over him.

He walked briskly down stream towards where only a quarter watch ago, his men had held their line across the valley. As he came into their sight they heard him shout for Tamorther, and almost as one they stood and cheered him, chanting his name. The other Hunderts in the side valley and along the forest edges stood and moved into the open where they could see his figure, to some quite small in the distance, but to a man they cheered.

He stopped, amazed, and waved an embarrassed hand in acknowledgement. Tamorther approached him and said something. He cupped his hand to his ear, he hadn't heard his words. Tamorther shouted close to his ear.

"I don't think you'll get away with a wave, the word has gone around that the King is dead. They all fought for you anyway, and you have given them a great victory at comparatively little cost. Only Wey himself now stands above you in their eyes."

Rebgroth laughed and clapped a hand on his shoulder. He walked towards the centre of the valley where the smaller one joined. There he stopped, turning and waving to his men all around him. Still they cheered, clapping rhythmically now and chanting his name.

The cart Tamorther had ordered pushed its way through the crowd, the heavy horse that pulled it was beginning a busy day moving the dead, but first it pulled a mobile dais for his General.

Rebgroth climbed up onto it, standing on the driver's seat with Tamorther beside and below him on the back. He gestured for quiet. The cheering faded quickly at his signal. It was suddenly very silent. He looked slowly around him so that every man felt he was speaking to him. His voice rang out.

"Soldiers of Nisceriel, you have fought bravely this day to defeat your enemy and protect your homes from an invader. But we have lost our King, and a short while ago I received news that in a raid on Castle Nisceriel, the Queen and Prince Gudrick have died also."

A murmur of surprise arose, followed by the sound of the news he had just given being passed on to those who could not hear him directly. He raised his hands again for quiet.

"This army will remain together until we are sure the Whorleans have left our lands. I will leave you now for the Castle Nisceriel with the Royal Guard for a Council of Decendancy to name King Gudmon's Heir. I will return to you when it is done, until then, tend to our wounded, bury our dead, burn the enemy's bodies. I am proud to have led you this day. HONOUR TO YOU ALL!" He slapped his right arm across his chest as he spoke.

A roar of approval grew around him and a low rumble as over a thousand arms crashed against over a thousand chests. A chant of 'Honour To Rebgroth' began raggedly then built until he thought they would hear it at the Castle, but it began to change. He tried to make out their words, then it was clear, 'Honour to King Rebgroth'.

"Not a bad idea that, My General." Tamorther was grinning at him.

"Don't even think of it Tam, I'm not even of Royal blood."

"You have more right in these men's eyes than that bastard child of his. You need only proclaim it and this army will march home with its King at its head."

Rebgroth waved at the crowd around him and jumped to the ground. Tamorther followed as the Royal Guard cavalry pushed their way along the riverside in a column of fours. Cranalie rode at their head leading Rebgroth's black stallion, saddled and ready for him.

"It cannot be Tam, it is not right. I will be back as soon as I can. Send two Hunderts to help clear up in Gloff and wait here."

"It is done My General."

Rebgroth nodded and mounted his horse which Cranalie had led forward to him. He led the column in a tight wheel and moved down the valley as quickly as they could forge their way through the still cheering soldiers who thronged towards him. It was half a watch later that he led them onto the plain and away from Stroue.

It took a watch and a quarter to reach the Castle Nisceriel, and Rebgroth reigned in some thousand paces from the gates. He waved Cranalie alongside him.

"Yes Sir?"

"Bring the men to good order Officer. We enter as victorious soldiers of Nisceriel. I want them dressed properly, if a little dusty." He smiled at the young man. "And Cranalie."

"Sir?"

"A column of four calls for a pair at its head. Return and ride with me."

"Yes Sir." He could not contain a huge grin as he replied to his General. He spun his mount and rode back down the column, shouting his orders.

Rebgroth rode on and was shortly joined by the most proud young Officer in the entire army.

In the high east tower, high above the Castle itself, a Bluecoat lookout blew a long blast on his horn. He could see a column of soldiers he assumed, moving steadily towards the Castle. It was not until they came to a halt some thousand paces or so from the Castle and the dust settled that he could make them out as Royal Guard cavalry.

He had been joined by the Officer of the Watch, a Sergeant that evening, and two runners. The column moved steadily towards them now and the Sergeant barked an order to one of the runners, who descended the tower as rapidly as he could and reported to Harlmon in the Great Hall.

"A column of Royal Guard approaches Sir. The entire Guard I believe Sir, led by General Rebgroth. They are column of four Sir, in six Thirds."

"Thank you soldier, return to the tower." The runner saluted and left the hall. Harlmon looked at his sister.

"Sounds all very formal to me," she laughed, "but if they are in six full Thirds, they didn't lose many men this morning." Harlmon smiled to himself. His sister had gone straight to the point.

"Pour another drink Gentlemen, I have a feeling it may take a while for the General to reach us."

And indeed it did just that, for news of the victory had leaked out. The messenger's words had been overheard and the news spread faster than fire, news too that General Rebgroth was returning.

Castlebury had almost emptied as its remaining occupants, those not with the army, rushed to the Castle gates to wait outside for their hero's return. Inside, all the Castle folk were in the streets too. When the horn sounded all the eyes of those outside turned to the north, and it was not too long before the column was visible and their excitement grew.

Many spread along the roadside towards the column, so that Rebgroth and Cranalie reached them some two fields from the Castle and the cheering began. The column rode steadily on, squeezing their way through the ever harder pressing crowd. It took almost a quarter watch to reach the gates, and then they had to force a passage up the crowded streets to the Keep. The whole time the crowd just kept cheering their General and he tried hard to keep looking pleased and waving. He was so tired he could have done without it all.

Finally, as he reached the square, the first Third of cavalry moved out around him, pushing the crowd back, and being joined by the second Third, forming a hollow into which the rest of the column entered and formed ranks.

The horses all stood uneasily in the noise of so many voices in a small area. Rebgroth slid off his horse and passed the reins to the Sergeant behind him. Cranalie did the same and followed him inside. Harlmon stood in the hallway and greeted them.

"Welcome back General, my congratulations on your victory. The Council is gathered in the Great Hall and awaits you."

"Then they can wait a little longer, I wish to see my wife and daughter."

"Yes of course, General. The Lady Serculas is in the nursery with your daughter and Prince Gudfel."

Rebgroth said nothing and walked straight to the staircase that had been the heart of the previous night's fighting. He ran up two at a time, along the balcony hall and into the nursery. Serculas leapt from the chair and rushed to him, throwing her arms around him, kissing him through her tears of joy. Rebgroth bent and scooped his daughter up into his arms, crushing them both to him.

"Now I know you are both safe I have to go to the Council. It should not take too long, but what happened here my love?"

"I don't really know. Luckily, Rebetha and I were with Eilana and Prince Gudfel to look at the stars and not in our rooms or we might well have been killed too. It was all so terrible, all those deaths. They raped and mutilated women, killed children, I don't understand them."

Rebgroth looked into her eyes. He put Rebetha into her arms and kissed them both before turning and leaving the room. The huge relief at seeing them both well somehow added to his exhaustion, but he walked determinedly back down the stairs and into the Great Hall.

As he entered spontaneous clapping broke out from a crowded gallery. Every dignitary that had not been in the fighting was crammed somewhere around the balcony and galleries. He smiled to himself at the numbers that seemed to have avoided the fight.

The Council rose as he entered. As custom, Eilana sat at the head to chair the meeting, as she had chaired in the King's absence whilst he was alive. Tamorther's chair was empty and a chair was set at the opposite end of the table to Eilana for him, in honour of his victory. Bradett sat next to Eilana, remarkably close he noticed.

Some things suddenly made sense that had puzzled him over the last moon or so. It was funny how people who were intimate often stood or sat nearer to one another than normal relations allowed; only a little but uncomfortably close otherwise.

The door behind him opened and in a blur of red and black, with swords drawn, sixty Royal Guards rushed in, circling the Hall and securing all the entrances. Harlmon was very agitated, they must have subdued the few Bluecoats he had on guard outside, but then with the losses the night before, there was no way he could have matched two hundred Guardsmen. He had instructed his men to give only token resistance to any threat. Eilana still trusted Rebgroth's character. Well now they would see.

Many of the Council began to rise and speak. Rebgroth held up a hand and sat down, Cranalie standing at his shoulder. He looked around at the indignant faces. The galleries were silent, trapped above, Guards on the stairs down and no doors at their level.

"No 'what is the meaning of this' or such My Lady? Nor from you Chancellor Bradett? Officer Harlmon? Your sense of drama disappoints me."

"The words I had prepared were of thanks and congratulation, General." It was Eilana speaking. "I am not sure why you are doing this but I'm sure you are about to tell us."

"Indeed, My Lady, I am. You see the Army of Nisceriel, which means the people of Nisceriel, is crying for me to be their King, but I have even less desire to be a King than I do now to be a General, except that I am a General and I believe there may be more work ahead for me to protect my homeland. The loyalty of all at this table to this realm, however, I am not so sure of."

"How can you question our loyalty?" exclaimed Bradett, "I personally have worked tirelessly for this realm for years."

"So you have dear Bradett, and for the Lady Eilana more recently I would guess."

"Who I bed is my business alone," hissed Eilana, "and has no bearing on the business of this meeting. If you intend to usurp this throne by force then do so, we cannot stop you, but I still believe you more honourable than that General."

Bradett looked at her stunned, who she chose to bed!

"It is Honour that drives me My Lady, you see I need to understand how some forty Tribesmen got into the heart of the Keep and caused such slaughter, unchallenged, without treachery playing a part; how conveniently you were away from the danger, although I thank Wey my wife and child were with you; how Chancellor Bradett was not here. You see even these few of my questions are pressing enough to need answering before we can come to the main question of the day."

"All of these things I can tell you General, but I risk embarrassing you in public. I would prefer you trusted me now and let me explain all later."

Rebgroth found himself laughing, and he leant back in his chair and rubbed his tired eyes with a hand.

"My Lady, I don't think anything in this land could embarrass me now. This morning the army of Nisceriel took the lives of over a thousand Whorleans, that was real embarrassment. I walked amongst the dead, that was real embarrassment, but it was all necessary; I simply need to know that this was."

He looked up slowly at Eilana. She looked back coldly, no emotion at all on her face. He decided she really was an astonishing woman.

"Well in that case General, I will tell you of what we have learned so far." She sat upright and leaned forward a little over the table, her hands clasped in front of her, her elbows just off the table's edge.

"The Tribesmen entered by the stream culvert into the wine cellars. The iron grille there has rusted through and is movable. This is reported in a Royal Guard security sweep some eight summers ago and nothing was done about it, so the opportunity to enter the Castle was brought about by the negligence of the Royal Guard, albeit before you became General."

Rebgroth sat expressionless while she continued. He had to admire her, but he was fighting off his tiredness that hit him now with waves of nausea between waves of exhaustion. All he really wanted to do was wash and then lie quietly in Serculas' arms and sleep. His mind registered her voice again.

"Amongst the Whorlean dead was the interpreter Gragonor. He was reported dead from his wounds over a moon ago. He was under Royal Guard jurisdiction." She was taking a risk here. He had been in the Bluecoat wing but she was sure Rebgroth would not have been aware of detail. He was not.

"Apparently he did not die but escaped. We found this map on him, with instructions of how to escape from the Castle; through the wine cellars and out of the stream culvert. Having got out that way, it was not a big step for him to lead a raiding party back in that way."

Everyone was staring at her, mesmerised, none more so than Harlmon.

"The map and instructions are in a hand I know well, that of Greardel. It is my belief he bribed the Guard or some such with a raid very much in mind. He always hated Gudmon, the Queen and me. I believe he saw an opportunity with the impending war to gain revenge for a lifetime of servitude."

Glances shot around the table. Looks of disbelief on faces slowly changed as the Councillors began to understand.

"One thing surprised me though General. The death of the King I was expecting as I began to uncover the truth of the raid here, but his death in battle was a surprise."

Rebgroth was looking straight into her eyes, his own black ringed and cold. He spoke as coldly.

"The King was murdered in his bed half a watch before the battle; a long bladed Whorlean knife through his chest. We could not tell the army of this on the dawn of battle, so we hid his body and invented his death in the front line to maintain some morale."

"It would appear lies and subterfuge have their uses for you on occasion then General, for the right reasons!" He ignored the comment.

"Are you suggesting, My Lady, that Greardel murdered the King?"

"I am General, right under your nose, with the King asleep under your protection."

"So I assume you are holding him under arrest then."

"We have not seen him since he left with the King and yourself," she lied, so easily, "Should we have?"

"He left at dawn under my instruction to bring you news of the King's death, are you telling me he never arrived."

"I am indeed, General. I think that is proof enough of the truth, do you not?"

Rebgroth sat with his hands over his face, his chin resting on the heels of his palms and his fingers on his forehead. He was shaking; they all assumed in rage, until he removed his hands and looked up. He was laughing softly. Shaking his head he stood up, Cranalie pulling the chair back as he stood.

"A fascinating tale, My Lady, but I am tired and have had enough for one day. Whatever the truth, there is only one possible heir to the throne, one male descendant of Royal blood. The army and people of Nisceriel recognise Prince Gudfel as the rightful heir. Long Live King Gudfel!"

The Council jumped to their feet and echoed him, along with every other voice in the Great Hall.

"LONG LIVE KING GUDFEL!"

Chapter 39

It was a quarter watch before dusk in the forest clearing when Harlada awoke and jumped up with a start. He tore at his soft leather shirt, pulling it over his head. As he did so, a large stag beetle fell from it onto the soft grass at his feet. He flicked it away with the toe of his boot and it flew for a few paces through the air, into the edge of the trees.

"Wey, I hate those damned things," he growled. Soft laughter sounded to his right and he looked to see Moreton, Cregenda and Bertal looking at him. Gragonor was just stirring and the Elves were still in the woods.

"Well I do," he said and walked to the lakeside. His hand was unconsciously holding his coin medallion. He hated crawly things. As a boy, changing his clothes and finding the odd flea, having his hair combed for nits and lice, both gave him the shivers. Gudrick didn't mind crawlies; he hated rats and mice, which Harlada had no fear of at all.

The thought of Gudrick struck him like a blow. He saw Gudrick's head lift from his body as Harlmon's sword sliced through the young neck, the eyes frozen by death in a startled stare. His medallion was ice cold against him and he shivered. He should have cried but equally cold anger surged through him and overwhelmed the grief.

The others all rose slowly, stretching and loosening stiff limbs. Cregenda picked up the cloth that the Elves had wrapped the remaining nuts and berries in and spread it on the ground. He pointed to it and said a few words in Whorlean. The others grasped the meaning and moved towards him. They were all hungry.

Harlada walked from the lakeside, drying his face and body on his shirt.

Holding it in his left hand he knelt and reached for some nuts. Cregenda suddenly stepped forward and grabbed his shoulder, lifting Harlada to his feet and spinning him to face him. Harlada felt his coin vibrating softly against his chest. Cregenda was staring at it, his eyes wide. He spoke quietly, awe in his voice.

"Er rel Crakulta!" He dropped to one knee. "Gragonor, er rel Crakulta." Gragonor almost ran to his shoulder and seeing the coin, knelt too, staring at Harlada's chest.

"What is it you see?" asked Harlada calmly. Gragonor and Cregenda exchanged words before Gragonor spoke in Niscerien.

"Do you not know what you wear on that chain?"

"It was given to me by the Lord Priest Cralch of the Marsh People, so that all Marsh Dwellers will know me and help me when needed. They called me Boy Warlord. He said it had been gifted by the first Lord Priest Cralch thirty-four generations ago."

Gragonor spoke reverently, as if explaining something delicate to a superior.

"It, Sire, is the only surviving coin of Crakulta, lost to the Whorleans about that many generations ago. All Whorlean children are shown pictures of this coin and told that throughout life, they must always be alert for it."

Moreton was listening to every word, trying to see the coin more clearly, he had heard of it before. If it was indeed the coin!

"So who is this Crakulta, and why is it so important?" Harlada questioned. Gragonor again exchanged words with Cregenda before continuing.

"Crakulta was a Whorlean holy man and a magical man, as one with Drew himself. He began the line of Drewbards that exist to this day. He minted a hundred silver coins, blessed by Drew, and possession of any one of which showed you to be favoured by him. He kept them in a wooden box chest, bound with metal braces, but he died tragically in a fire that spread from the forest, destroying his temple home. The box was found. The wood had burnt away and the coins had melted into a single ingot of silver.

"Two moons later, at a ceremony to commemorate his life, the newly elected chief Drewbard held the shapeless lump of silver above his head in praise. It seemed to jump from his hand and crashed to the stone floor, splitting in two. At the centre of the ingot was one undamaged coin, the only surviving coin. It is said that the blessing and power Drew placed in all the coins was concentrated into the one.

"Many years later, in a raid on our coastline, the coin was stolen and lost to our people, but it is said that it will be found, and if it is worn by a man who knows not what he wears, that man will lead Whorle back to greatness. You wear it Sire, and you knew not what you wore. We are yours to command. We are avowed as Whorleans to protect you and to bring you to Whorle when you are ready to go there."

The coin was almost buzzing against Harlada's skin. He placed a hand over it and spoke.

"It would appear the first Lord Priest Cralch may not have been such an honest man, but if this is the coin of Crakulta...."

"It is Sire." Harlada glared at Gragonor in rebuke. Moreton smiled to himself as Gragonor cringed at the look.

"If this is the coin of Crakulta, then it is also now blessed by the Water Gods of the Marsh Dwellers and doubly revered. It seems fate has chosen me for something."

"We must first escape from Nisceriel if any of this is to mean anything." It was Moreton that brought them back to reality as the sky began to get noticeably darker.

As if by arrangement their four Elven friends appeared at the edge of the clearing and beckoned them. Moreton waved back.

"Let us get mounted then," he said, "and see what this night brings, we may need all the blessings that coin has to offer if we are all to survive it."

They walked to their horses, Cregenda lifting Gragonor up into his saddle. They all smiled but nobody said anything. Cregenda mounted easily, with a little more thought than the rest. Together they rode towards the Elves and followed them into the woods, falling into single file behind Ranamo. Ranor was some twenty paces ahead and Melarne and Melmern drifted out to either side. They moved easily and quietly through the undergrowth whilst Ranor followed a game path.

They came to a fork and Ranamo moved right towards the edge of the woodland forest and the road. Harlada was suddenly very aware of a hot pain on his chest. He called softly to Ranor.

"Stop my friend; I think we should take the other path." Ranor looked back at him and then to Moreton.

"If Harlada says the other path then that's the way we should go," confirmed Moreton. Harlada looked at him and Moreton added, "Harlada is doubly blessed by Drew and the Water Gods. I can tell you that to have come this far in his life, indeed to be alive still and free; he is blessed by Wey also. His words are more authoritive than mine my friends. Do not look to me for guidance; Harlada's words are more than mine. I follow his lead." Gragonor was whispering to Cregenda who nodded in agreement.

Ranor returned to the fork and started to the left, then looked back at those following.

"This path follows the edge of the trees but at least fifty paces inside the forest. It will take us close to Bridgebury, but when the trees end to the south, we will be some five hundred paces from the walls with open grassland between. Stay close to Ranamo, he will be able to follow my lead, but it is going to get very dark, so stay very close to the one in front of you. Melarne will drop behind in case anyone should lose the one in front of him, but we will need to move at a good pace to reach there before midnight."

"Lead on then good Elf," said Harlada, "we are with you." Ranor nodded and moved off, Ranamo in his footsteps, the rest close behind.

They travelled this way in the woods for a little over a whole watch before they suddenly bunched up as Ranor stopped and every one almost collided with the horse in front before they realised what was happening.

Harlada felt a warmth on his chest, but not heat. He was beginning to understand his coin's signals. He pushed his mount past the others to the edge of the trees but still inside their line, and looked across at the low walls of Bridgebury.

The town wall had been constructed as part of Rebgroth's defence plans two summers before, but it was soon felt the main threat was from the north, so when the wall reached a man high, resources were felt better used elsewhere. The wall was rough along the top, uncapped, with a half height fighting step on the inside.

They were indeed some five hundred paces from the wall, and two hundred to the right was the north gate. Three mounted Bluecoats were visible in the moonlight, their horses standing on the road just outside. As they watched, two more rode from the west beyond them and stopped to talk briefly before riding on around the wall, across in front of them and on towards the eastern gate, where the road left Bridgebury that ran along the Ffon's north bank.

Moreton's mount stood to the right of Harlada's, Cregenda's to his left, with Gragonor next to him.

"What do we think gentlemen?" Harlada asked. Gragonor spoke softly, Cregenda at some length, and then Gragonor spoke for him.

"Sire, there will be about thirty or so Bluecoats, that would seem to be the limit of their horsemen. They have three on this north gate, and so one can assume three on each of the east and west gates. There are at least two patrolling the wall, but probably only two. If there were four, each pair would cover from the river to this gate, and this pair crossed the gate, so only two. That's eleven of them. I would guess patrols of two on each road, making seventeen; two on patrol inside the wall makes nineteen. That leaves eleven at the bridge in reserve, a third of their number."

"That makes a great deal of sense. Moreton?"

"I'm sure he's right my boy. I think Rebgroth is lucky Cregenda is here with us this day." Cregenda tensed at Gragonor's translation, but looking hard at Moreton he relaxed back on his saddle. It was meant as a compliment, but it touched a nerve. He regretted not being with Bocknostri and feared the worst. He had also felt terribly guilty about leaving his men to die covering his escape, but finding the coin had eased that. It was clear to him that the coin had called him to guard it and its wearer.

"So," continued Harlada, "we need to get into the village, we need to draw off the Bluecoats from the bridge, cross it, then make it to the cover of the trees the other side and lose our pursuit. Should be easy really." The sarcasm was strong in his voice, but it was said with clear humour, not defeatism.

"Can I suggest we make use of the special talents of our Elvish friends?" said Moreton. Ranamo spoke.

"We must leave the horses here. They will return to Retalla. We must get close to the wall and let the Bluecoat patrol pass us on its way back. You must get across the wall and we will follow the patrol around. Once it has passed the north gate we will attack the guards and draw them off. The noise should bring the reserves from the bridge. We will lead them up the road a little then double back and join you at the bridge. From there we must make it up depending on circumstances, but we will be across."

Harlada's coin vibrated gently. He paused a moment before speaking.

"I am sure Ranamo is right. I can't say why but I am sure we will be alright once we are across the bridge, but it leaves you Elves with a dangerous task."

"Not so dangerous for us Elf-friend, and I can see no other way. It is simple, that is its strength."

"Then let's do it," he said, dismounting as he did so. He took Bertal's hand.

"Can you cope with this?" he asked. He wasn't being rude, just practical.

"I am not that old young man. Look to Moreton, he's older than me by a good few summers." They all laughed, except Cregenda.

Melmern spoke softly.

"There is a small stream forty paces this way." He led them towards it. Harlada looked along its course. It could not have been better. It crossed the open ground between banks almost a man high. It had a bed of small stones with water a forearm deep. It ran almost straight to the walls before cutting left and around to the Ffon. It would give them cover almost to the wall.

"The Gods are all with us my friends," he said, "lead on Melmern."

The four Elves led the three Niscerians and two Whorleans in a slight crouch, down the stream until in turned sharply. They lay flat against its bank within twenty paces of the wall as the two man Bluecoat patrol crossed in front of them. Ranor whispered urgently into Ranamo's ear. He had had a better thought. Ranamo nodded, and they ran lightly after the Bluecoats, drawing their elvish blades and jumping lightly onto the horses' backs. They stood on their hindquarters, grabbing the unfortunate Bluecoats by the chin, pulling their heads back and slicing their blades across their throats.

Elves very rarely killed men; in fact it was a hundred summers and more since they had, and twice that long since an Elf had killed an Elf, but when they had to, they were very good at it. Melarne and Melmern were already running lightly and incredibly fast across the open land, diagonally towards where the trees almost met the road north of the gate.

Ranamo and Ranor threw the bodies of the Bluecoats out of their saddles to the ground and something equally rare; they rode the horses at a gallop towards the gate. As they neared it they cut the corner and swung north.

Harlada led the others to the wall. Cregenda lifted him easily up onto it. He looked left and right but could see nothing. All the houses were in darkness. The villagers who remained in the village were staying well out of the Bluecoats' way. He waved them up.

Cregenda was invaluable. He lifted Bertal, giving her backside a none too soft but effective hoosh upwards. He linked his hands into a step for Gragonor, then for Moreton, who he subtlely helped with an extra bit of lift. Moreton knew what he had done and appreciated it, respected it. Cregenda then pulled himself up surprisingly easily, before helping each one of them down the other side and jumping down beside them. They melted into the darkness and shadows around the small houses.

As they crossed the wall they heard a horn blowing loudly from the gate. Two Bluecoats raced along the inside of the wall from the east gate, their horses blowing loudly, and as they crept through the village towards the river, they heard the Eleven from the bridge riding at full gallop towards the north gate.

It seemed Cregenda was exactly right in his assessment. Bocknostri would have told them he would be.

When Ranamo and Ranor reached the point of the road nearest the woods they jumped from their mounts which galloped on up the road. Melarne and Melmern were already there. They turned to meet the three charging Bluecoats from the gate, whose lances were levelled as they approached at speed.

The Elves avoided the lances with ease and seemed to catch the front legs of the horses as they passed. Only an Elf had the speed to do so, and the horses rolled forwards, throwing their riders heavily before them.

The Elves left them in the road and broke left and right, looping around the Eleven that was charging up the road towards their fallen comrades. Elves could run in a crouch, their brown and green clothes making them almost invisible in daylight, and at night they were, completely so. They met at the gate to hear sounds of a fight at the bridge.

Cregenda and Moreton were exchanging blows with two Bluecoats. Three had been left to guard it; three Cregenda had not counted on. When they had to leave the shelter of the houses, some fifteen paces from the bridge, Moreton and Cregenda had charged them immediately, hoping to surprise them. They did, but they were alert enough that although Cregenda killed one with his first blow, the others were up and fighting.

Gragonor pushed Harlada and Bertal towards the bridge. Harlada had no sword, which was just as well, and Gragonor guided them around the fighting men and onto the bridge. They turned to watch. Moreton was only just holding his own, but Cregenda was on top and the Bluecoat knew it. He parried desperately, the force of Cregenda's blows more than he could cope with. He twice tried to disengage and run for his horse but Cregenda was too fast for him. Harlada shouted.

"Let him go, help Moreton." The Bluecoat leapt back and Cregenda jumped after him. Gragonor shouted Harlada's command in Whorlean. Harlada cursed himself. This language thing was getting ridiculous.

The lucky Bluecoat fled for his horse as Cregenda ran to Moreton's aid. He was not as young as he needed to be and was close to defeat at the hands of this young and aggressive Bluecoat. Cregenda was merciless, running up from behind and cleaving the Bluecoat's head almost in half from crown to neck. He wrenched his two-handed sword free and gripped Moreton's arm, dragging him onto the bridge.

The Elves seemed to appear from nowhere beside them.

"We are all here, over the bridge," ordered Harlada. As they reached its middle, on the brow of its slight rise above the arch below, the Elves stopped.

"Run on Elf-friends, we will hold them here awhile."

Harlada was going to argue but didn't. They ran as fast as Bertal could across the rest of the bridge, and reaching the far side, Harlada looked up the slope. It was about three hundred paces uphill to the tree line. If mounted Bluecoats got over the bridge, he could not see how they would get away from them, even if they reached the trees, but his coin hummed and he knew they must run that way.

The Bluecoat Cregenda had let go was blowing a horn repeatedly in triplet blasts, and soon all the surviving Bluecoats stood mounted at the edge of the houses facing the bridge. There were twenty-five of them. If Harlada could have seen in the darkness, he would have recognised Harlfel, his uncle, at their centre.

"Over the bridge Sergeant?" he suggested.

"Yes Sir, but cautiously. Second Eleven," he cried, "lead over."

A young Levener led the Second at a full gallop across the gap to the bridge and onto it, the rest following slower in reserve. The Sergeant was not sure what had happened when he told the tale later, but the Elves did not seem to have any weapon in their hands, they just held their right arms horizontally out in front of them; their wrists bent upwards; their palms facing the charging Bluecoats. Their fingers were outstretched but they seemed to bend their middle two downwards, leaving their thumb, first and little fingers outstretched. As the horses charged onto the bridge, their hooves clattering on the stone road, the Elves began a low whistle it seemed, and the horses stopped in their tracks, skidding to a halt and rearing. The Levener and two others were thrown forward, one off the bridge and down into the river, others were thrown backwards as their mounts reared away. Some stayed in their saddles and fought to control the panicking animals, which were trampling on some of their fallen comrades in their fright.

The Elves turned as one and ran after Harlada and the others, who were almost halfway up the slope. By the time they were two thirds of the way up, they had caught them, but so to, almost, had the Bluecoats.

It took a few moments to clear the mayhem on the bridge. A few of the Second Eleven remounted, but only a few. Harlfel led the rest of the Bluecoats across the bridge after their quarry, the survivors of the Second Eleven spurring their mounts after him.

They spread into line abreast as they galloped up the slope. They would catch them before the trees and they lowered their lances.

Harlada's coin grew hot and he looked around. He cried out and they turned to face their attackers, fifty paces behind them and closing at a gallop, if hindered a little by the slope. Moreton and Cregenda stood either side of Harlada in front of Gragonor and Bertal, two Elves on either side.

Harlada should have been frightened but he knew he was safe, if not why.

The multiple cracks of longbow strings sounded from the tree line and there was the hiss of a flight of forty arrows as they flashed close over their heads. They slashed into the Bluecoat riders and horses alike. Harlfel took one in the stomach. He doubled forward in pain and a second entered the top of his shoulder penetrating his lung from above. As he swayed back upright a third took him in the chest killing him instantly.

It was the same around him. His Sergeant took an arrow high in the right shoulder, spinning him and his horse. He rode back down the hill. At the bottom he was joined by three other survivors of the three volleys of arrows that had hit them. All were wounded to varying degrees and the Sergeant led them back across the bridge.

"Where in Wey's name did they come from?" said Moreton. He turned as Harlada spoke pointing at the trees.

"From our friends in the woods," and as they looked, Klarss, War Chief of the Western Marsh, appeared from the tree line with his company of Marsh Fighters, their longbows as tall as them.

He called down the hill but Harlada couldn't understand him. Another damned language he thought. They walked up the hill, and as they went Harlada explained to the others who their rescuers were.

"You knew they would be here," said Moreton. It was a statement not a question.

"In a sense," answered Harlada, "Help, yes, but not who or what exactly."

As they reached the trees Klarss walked forward and slapped his forearm across his chest as he had learnt from Rebgroth.

Harlada tried to introduce everyone but it was impossible. Instead he pulled the coin out of his shirt and held it up as far as its chain would allow.

"Know me, Marsh Dwellers," he called. To a man they dropped to one knee. Klarss knelt before him and spoke something Harlada did not understand. He pushed the coin back into his shirt. It hummed against his chest.

Cregenda moved in front of him and knelt beside Klarss and spoke in Whorlean. The coin was vibrating wildly. Harlada was totally aware of it as he put his left hand on Klarss' shoulder, and his right on Cregenda's.

"There's no doubt," he said, "That if we are going to take Nisceriel back from my mother, you two are going to have to speak my language." A warm surge of energy flowed from his hands.

"Indeed we will, Sire," said Klarss and Cregenda in unison, and in perfect accentless Niscerien. For the first time, the coin had let Harlada use its power.

The story continues in the second of The Niscerien Chronicles

The King Mother

The King's Mistress
Glossary

People

Gudmon — King of Nisceriel

Gudrick — Deceased King of Nisceriel. Gudmon's Father

Berissa — Eldest Princess of Deswrain, deceased First wife and Queen of Gudmon

Bertal — Youngest (3rd) Princess of Deswrain, second wife and Queen of Gudmon

Duke of Merlbray — Ruler of Merlbray

Patrikal — Princess of Nisceriel. Daughter of King Gudmon and Queen Bertal

Patrika — Half Elven grandmother of Bertal, long deceased Queen of Deswrain

Moreton — Weymonk and childhood friend of King Gudmon. Tutor to Princess Patrikal

Serculas — Royal Nanny to Princess Patrikal. Later wife of Rebgroth

Rebgroth	Second Officer of the Royal Guard. Later General
Greardel	Body servant to King Gudmon
Rowl & Rawl	Queen Bertal's wolfhounds
Allaner	Lady in Waiting to Queen Bertal
Reassel	Lady in Waiting to Queen Bertal
Gratax	General of the Royal Guard
Ferlmun	Personal Healer to the King
Harlada	The ostler in the castle's Royal Stables
Eilenn	Harlada's wife
Harlmon	Harlada and Eilenns' oldest son
Eilana	Harlada and Eilenns' oldest daughter, wet nurse to Prince Gudrick
Little Harlada	The ostler's grandson, Eilana's child
Little Gudrick	Prince of Niscerial. Son of King Gudmon and Queen Bertal
Keffnon	An itinerant tumbler. Father of little Harlada
Eival	Harlada and Eilenns' third living child
Harlfel	Harlada and Eilenns' fourth living child
Ereyna	Eilana's best friend
Grendal	A village girl from Castlebury

Fenlon	Apprentice winemaker in Royal cellars
Bradett	Chancellor of Nisceriel
Mendel	Envoy of Deswrain
Gabral	King of Deswrain
Kadrol	Prince of Deswarain, then King
Nordrall	Captain of the Lone Hart, legendary adventurer
Bertralac	Queen of Deswrain, then dowager King-Mother mother of King Kadrol and mother of Queen Bertal
Dombard	Captain of the Lady Wrain and ex crewman of the Lone Hart on the long voyage
Glurk	A Marsh Dweller scout
Klarss	Marsh Dweller War Chief
Cralch	Lord Priest of the Marsh Dwellers. The first a seer, followed by thirty four named after him
Gudfel	Prince of Nisceriel. Son of King Gudrick and Eilana
Badraman	A Sergeant of the Royal Guard promoted to Officer. Arms Tutor and Mentor to Prince Gudrick and Harlada
Tamorther	Second Officer of the Royal Guard
Rebetha	Daughter of Rebgroth and Serculas
Nedlowe	Personal Healer to the King
Brenham	Servant then Personal Servant to Rebgroth and Serculas

Bocknostri	Tribal Prince, then King, of Whorle
Draknast	Tribal King of Whorle, father of Bocknostri
Drokhart	Brother of Draknast, uncle to Bocknostri
Cregenda	2nd in command to Prince Bocknostri
Crondak	Advisor and friend of King Draknast
Gerlaff	Hundert of Gloff
Laranna	Wife of Gerlaff
Gragonor	Whorlean interpreter to Prince Bocknostri
Drenton	Sergeant in the Bluecoat Special Third
Dramburld	Minister of the South Counting
Cranalie	A young officer of the Royal Guard
Grenfeld	Hundert of the Northern Third
Balkmern	Tribal Chieftain of Breecombe
Perdredd	Tribal Chieftain of Lerbalck
Drodfar	Sergeant in the Bluecoat Cavalry Third

Elves

Retalla	Chief of the Western Elves
Ranamo	Forest warden. Nephew of Retalla. Brother of Ranor

Ranor	Forest warden. Nephew of Retalla. Brother of Ranamo
Ralima	Scout
Balida	Scout
Meyala	Baby saved by Patrikal and dogs
Meyas	Mother of Meyala
Melarne	Father of Meyala
Melmern	Uncle of Meyala

Places

Nisceriel	The Kingdom
Castle Nisceriel	Castle Royal of the Kingdom
River of Number	A large tidal river running south-westerly and forming western border
Gloff	Fortified village on the River of Number at the far north-west corner of the kingdom, guarding the lowest crossing point of the river
Whorle	Tribal Kingdom to the West of the river of number
Moonmarl	Tribal capital of the King of Whorle
Deswrain	A Kingdom to the far south of Nisceriel
Castle Deswrain	Castle Royal of Deswrain, on the north coast
Merlbray	A Dukedom to the East of Nisceriel

River Ffon	River that forms Nisceriel's southern border
Brocklow	Village to the north of Castle Nisceriel
Castlebury	Village just outside and to the south of Castle Nisceriel
Ffonhaven	Fishing and trading port at the mouth of the Ffon on the River of Number
Dorthaff	Main port on the south coast of Deswrain
Wrainhaff	Main port on the north coast of Deswrain, at the foot of Castle Deswrain
Bridgebury	Village in the south-east corner of Nisceriel. Lowest crossing of the Ffon
Drean	Large forested area in the east of Whorle, on the north bank of the River of Number
Teakford Vale	River ford to the north of Nisceriel, just beyond its borders. The lowest natural crossing point of the River of Number
River Drei	Flows through Moonmarl through the beautiful Drei valley in Whorle to the River of Number
Shepst	Whorlean village close to the mouth of the Drei
Breecombe	Whorlean tribal area
Lerbalck	Whorlean tribal area